PACK RAGE

PACK RAGE
THE SPLINTERED BOND

MERRI BRIGHT

For Tami

CONTENTS

AUTHOR'S NOTE AND CONTENT ADVISORIES

Thank you so much for reading Pack Rage. This story includes death of a parent, murder, abuse, references to off-page sexual assault, feelings of guilt and unworthiness due to repeated forced intimacy (MMC), extreme violence/battle, decapitation, dismemberment, intimacy in a group, offering a "brotherly helping hand," and other notable content. Please go to www.merribright.com for the full list of advisories.

THE SPLINTERED BOND
SERIES RECAP

Welcome back to The Splintered Bond!

When we last saw Flor and her guys, she and Glen were recovering from the brutal battle at Southern, Brand had just flown from Mountain to get to her, and Luke and Grigor were being carted away by Elina McDonnell to Eastern for her own nefarious purposes.

If you've slept since you finished Pack Ruin, you may have forgotten a few key details. This section is intended to get you up to speed so you can dive right into Flor's final book.

Pack Reject

Flor is the "prey" in her pack's Hunt, a nightly event where Southern's unmated males attempt to trap and claim her. Some want a mate, some want the glory of capturing the most elusive target in years, but for many, the real prize is the extra food rations awarded to the winner in the dirt-poor pack. After she mouths off to an Enforcer in the dining hall, Flor is forced to flee into the woods, waiting until the Enforcer Games begin at the upcoming North American

Conclave, her only chance to escape and be adopted into a better pack.

Disguised as a boy, Flor hides in the woods, but tragedy strikes back in the compound. Del, the only person who had protected her since her mama was thrown to the rogues to die, is murdered by Alpha Callaway and his Head Enforcer, Van Blackside. When a group of extremely hot visiting Alpha Heirs discovers her, they suspect she's not just a rogue and Del's accused killer, but something far more dangerous: a true mate, and possibly to more than one of them. Flor wants nothing to do with the guys, though; she just wants to get the heck out of Southern. The four Alpha Heirs and a mysterious stranger, Joaquin, help her to sneak into the Games to give her the chance.

At the Games, she fights and wins against Finnick, the Eastern Heir. She barely survives her second fight and is promised sanctuary in Northern by Margarette Hillier, Glen's mom. Southern Heir Luke challenges his father and wins, but ends up leaving Callaway alive and both their positions in question.

The Council Head, Bradley Hillier, plans to put things right in a meeting, but Southern's leadership has no honor, and they attack their visitors, setting Callaway free. Battle erupts, and Southern comes to the fight with silver weapons.

During the battle, Flor goes into a rage, decapitating Van Blackside with her trusty steak knife, and saving everyone. Afterward, she takes Margarette up on her offer to hit the road. Luke lets her go, knowing it might cost him his life. Finnick attempts to reject her for reasons of his own, but stops short. Flor leaves for Northern with Brand, Glen, and the Hilliers, while Finnick's chickenshit father assumes the role of Interim Alpha of the Council.

Pack Refuge

Northern isn't the refuge Flor had hoped. Upon arrival, Glen's snake of a cousin Vanessa escorts her to the servants' quarters and sets the ranked males on her. Despite its claims of equality, Northern's unranked members live in fear. Margarette swiftly punishes Vanessa and the offenders, while Brand vows to take Flor to his own pack if she says the word (lake). She chooses to stay, for now, though her hostess is annoyingly obsessed with Flor being her son Glen's true mate.

Under the watchful eye of Sergeant, an older, scarred shifter who seems oddly familiar, Flor trains with the lowest ranks, not revealing her years of experience fighting with Del. She's willing to earn her place, with her ranking fight only weeks away. When the day arrives, Sergeant angrily realizes he's underestimated her and assigns her to spar with Brand. Distracted, Brand inadvertently stabs her. The wound refuses to heal, which makes it obvious he is her true mate. Near death, she survives when Brand asks her to accept their bond.

But guilt consumes Brand. Unable to forgive himself for the circumstances of their claiming, he distances himself, determined to earn her love. Before he can, Flor is abducted by Vanessa and delivered to Russian rogues. She escapes, only to be hunted by the silver-toothed General Ivan until an unknown dark presence slaughters his shifters. The stranger is Joaquin from the Games, but he tells Flor his true identity. He's Grigor Dimitrivich, an ancient, evil, super sexy, magic-wielding shifter. When the others arrive, Grigor vanishes to hunt Ivan.

Back at Northern, the revelation that Flor was in the presence of one of the most infamous serial killers of the shifter world horrifies her allies. Meanwhile, Finnick announces his departure for Eastern, but Flor's wolf takes control, marking him on his tongue before he can leave.

Flor confronts Margarette and Bradley, who was secretly healed by Grigor as a courting gift to her, about the injustices in their pack. They are appalled; even if they had good intentions, their "protection" led to great harm done to their vulnerable unranked, even the children. As the Hilliers quickly attempt to put reforms in place, some of their own powerful Enforcers attack. The Hilliers win the battle, but lose an Heir. Disgusted with his parents' past actions, and unwilling to be parted from his future mate, Glen renounces his pack and leaves with Brand and Flor for Mountain.

But trouble is brewing back at Southern. Luke is being tortured... by a witch.

Pack Ruin

At the Mountain pack's border, Flor is struggling with her first independent shift when she senses Luke's impending death through their incomplete bond. Desperate to keep him and Flor alive, Brand channels energy through their mate bond, aided by Grigor, who left a link to Flor's soul during their earlier meetings. The process of saving Luke and Flor permanently alters Brand, changing his eyes.

Grigor immediately heads to Southern to keep an eye on Luke, and to indulge in his favorite pastime: turning the entrails of those who harmed Flor into grotesque "flower arrangements." To raise the odds of Luke's survival, he magically binds their souls, and is left weakened.

Meanwhile, Glen is imprisoned at Mountain on orders from Interim Council Alpha Aidan McDonnell. Flor, learning about shifter history as well as her own family's past from Brand's grandmothers, finally reveals her true name, but the author was a total asshole and didn't share that with the readers.

When Glen is released, he bonds with Flor at Brand's lake—only for her to sense Finnick's intimacy with another woman. After enduring torture, Finnick has been coerced into sleeping with a woman under the threat that his underage sister will be given to the same shifter who tortured him. Sacrificing his own future with Flor, he agrees, then devises a plan to send his sister far away before financially destroying his family. In the lower levels, he helps the Hilliers and discovers the missing Alpha Callaway living in comfort. Finnick manipulates him into revealing Flor's true story.

Samuel struggles to resist the Council's orders to turn Flor and Glen in for execution. To free him from his oath, Brand challenges and defeats his father, but with Flor and Grigor's help, leaves him alive. With his new Alpha status only partly secured, Brand remains behind to grow stronger to face Aidan himself, while Flor and Glen leave to rescue Luke.

There, Flor and Glen discover a pack of rogues calling themselves Tenebris, led by Sergeant and Flor's long-lost mama. With their help, Flor sneaks into Southern, but is immediately captured and placed in the shifter girls' dorms. Glen finds Luke and is caught by a dying Grigor, who can only survive if Glen bonds with him. Glen agrees as long as he can think of him as Joaquin, not Grigor, because who wants to be brother mates with the boogeyman?

Flor faces her old nemesis, Holly, who is killed in a very satisfying scene by the abused residents of the dorm. Flor discovers that these women secretly supported her for years during the Hunt, and she helps them flee to Tenebris. Reunited with Luke and Grigor that night, she plans their escape, but when Grigor is captured by Finnick's mother Elina, running is no longer an option. It's time to fight.

In the battle, Flor and her allies take on Eastern troops armed with silver and guns, led by Torran, the Eastern executioner. Nearly overwhelmed, they are saved by the Tenebris pack, Flor's mama, and the remaining Southern shifters. But victory comes at a cost, when Luke and Grigor are both taken back to Eastern.

Brand, having channeled the power of his half-pledged pack into Flor and the others from afar, arrives too late to help fight. Their reunion is overshadowed by the grim reality: both Grigor and Luke are up shit creek, and with the full moon and Council meeting looming, the real fight is just beginning.

CHAPTER 1

ANGUISH AND ALLIES

FLOR

There were some kinds of pain you could avoid, and others you could ignore. But the kind of pain I carried in me now, since Grigor's tenuous connection to me had snapped, was the sort I'd only felt once before, when I'd found out Del had been murdered.

The kind that would never fade.

"No, wildflower," Brand said quietly. "You also felt this way when Luke was suffering."

"When he was dying, you mean," I gasped, as I hunted around on the cave floor for some clothing. The shorts and shirt that came to hand first was stuff I'd been given by Iris. She was an unranked Southern badass who'd helped all the other women escape from the compound, only to lead them all right back in, to fight the Eastern Enforcers with mops, brooms, steak knives, and sticks.

Fucking crazy women, all of them. I'd fallen in love with every wild-eyed, revenge-obsessed one of them, even before they'd executed Holly in the bathroom of my old dorm. Fucking Holly deserved it.

But remembering her brought it all back, and when I

glanced down at the shirt, I noticed blood. Then, when I took a breath, I smelled a hint of the gasoline the Enforcers had used to try and burn me and Glen.

Shitfire, I'd come damned close to being burned alive. I shivered and dropped those clothes like I'd grabbed a handful of copperheads. I had brought a bag from Mountain... *There!* I found the small pack that held my sword, a few books, and a change of clothing that smelled like Mountain.

Like home. Well, Brand's home, anyway, and the only place I'd ever felt safe. Where I'd felt loved.

My fingers trembled on the button of my jeans shorts as I thought of the others I was in love with... or at least halfway there, even against my better judgment. Luke had been stolen away, taken back to Eastern. Finnick was trapped there already. And Grigor...

I swallowed a sob, then cursed, giving up on the button. Brand's massive hands were there almost instantly, taking over. Taking care of me. My Mountain mate was always doing that, even if it meant sacrificing everyone else. Giving up on gathering power, leaving his pack in the middle of his Alpha ascension rituals...

Two fingers traced a path from my temple, down one cheek, then tucked under my chin, lifting my face to his. I always felt small standing beside my Bearman, my five-foot-one next to his seven-foot-plus height probably making us look like the oddest couple.

The truth was that our real mismatch was on the inside. Brand was everything good, strong, powerful, and kind in our world. I was a mess. A scrappy fighter, sure, and I knew right from wrong. But I'd been raised at Southern and, to paraphrase the saying, you could take the wolf girl out of Southern, but you could never get the stink off.

I was just glad Brand didn't seem to notice how far beneath him I was. I sure as hell wasn't gonna be the one to clue him in.

An odd surge of emotion hummed in the bond that connected us, and I pressed one hand to the place on my shoulder where Brand's mating claim lay. "You are the best of us all, little one. And Luke didn't die. You can't lose hope."

I forced a grin. "Can't lose something you never had." I had a hate-hate relationship with hoping. It had never gotten me in anything but trouble.

Brand's words interrupted me. "Well, I have hope enough for both of us. Right now, we don't know"—he hesitated, and I peeked up to see his jaw working under his dark beard, his nose wrinkling like he'd smelled a skunk— "that Grigor is dead. You can't feel him in the... nonconsensual bond he made with you. That doesn't mean he's dead."

"I can't feel him in the fully consensual bond we have together either, Dream Girl, but I'm almost certain he's not dead," Glen said softly from the fire he'd been banking in the center of the cavern floor. We'd made love all night, ever since Brand arrived, then slept. At some point, Glen had woken up and cooked us a meal. It had felt for a few hours like we'd slipped into another world. A private hideaway, where we could take a moment to grieve our losses, take a well-deserved nap, and make love. At Mountain, new couples got two months alone to do nothing but fuck.

But all three of us had known it was time to get back to the compound, and make a plan.

Within the next two days, Brand had to report to the Council headquarters, the Eastern pack's Mansion outside New York City. He was required to vow his allegiance to the

Council, and then he would be permitted to take part in the Council vote on whether Glen's father, Bradley Hillier, would be allowed to reclaim his seat as the Council Head, or if that position would be permanently filled by another.

Namely, Finnick's father, Aidan McDonnell.

To make things more worrying, Glen's parents were also facing trumped-up charges that they'd unjustly killed their own Enforcers—even though they'd only done so when the unranked women of Northern bravely shared that those Enforcers had been systematically harassing, even brutalizing, the women for years.

I crossed the floor to Glen's side and ran my fingers through his shaggy blond hair. He had a new scar on his collarbone from a machete that had almost taken his head, and had taken a chunk of his curls. Trying not to think of how close I'd come to losing him, I pressed a kiss to his head before he stood and returned the gesture. "You really think Grigor's alive. Why?"

"Well, the way I see it, you may have an incomplete mate bond with *Joaquin.*" He stressed the name, which made me smile. For some reason, Glen couldn't wrap his head around the idea that Grigor Dimitrivich, the legendary serial killer and magical boogeyman of all wolf shifters, was the same guy who he'd bonded with only a few days before. "I have a deeper bond, at least right now. His soul... it's numb. But it's not dead. It can't be." His gaze rose to Brand's face, Glen's blue eyes flashing white for an instant, reminding me of Brand's moonblessed ones. "Because if Joaquin had died, I'd be dead, too."

Brand let out a soft curse. "He bound you—"

"Our souls, yeah," Glen said, rubbing the back of his neck almost sheepishly. "Um, when we were... making love to Flor, just now. Didn't you feel it?"

Brand's cheeks flushed as he pulled his clothing on as well, or tried to. He'd shifted into wolf form when he found me that morning, and had torn his clothing to shreds.

Speaking of which... "Brand, when you shifted. Your wolf form was, ah, different."

"Bigger, yeah. Dad said that might happen," he muttered, poking around in the deerskins. The rogue shifters who'd occupied this place wore a combination of old clothing and tanned hides and furs from game they'd hunted. While I was almost certain there was something Brand could wear in one of the chests, it wasn't ours to take. I leaned down and picked up a particularly long deer hide, then cut a hole in two places, and pulled it around his waist. He stood still while I fashioned a crude button with a gnawed piece of antler, slid it through the holes, and grinned up at him.

"Nice. Very Tarzan," I complimented him, pulling my backpack over my shoulders, the hilt of my sword sticking out the top.

"Come on then, Jane," he teased, picking me up and wrapping my legs around his waist. "We have to go."

My heart sank, but I knew we had to face the world again. And I did want to find out how everyone was. The last time I'd seen my mama, she'd been stabbed by Torran with a silver blade. "Back into the compound?"

"Yes. We don't have long." His strides ate up the cavern floor, and we were stepping into dappled sunlight in less than a minute, Glen right behind us. He held a curtain of kudzu out of the way for Brand and me to walk though.

"Until what?" I asked.

I grabbed tighter to Brand when a low, masculine voice I wasn't expecting answered. "Yeah, until what, Alpha?"

Brand stopped, an embarrassed grin covering his face as

he faced his friend, Dean, who was being held at knife-point by Bo and Leroy.

Well, sort of at knife-point. Bo had one hand on Dean's wrist, and a knife aimed at his belly button. Leroy, on the other hand, held a sharp stick, his weapon poking pretty close to Dean's crotch.

Dean didn't look amused, but he wasn't scared, either. "Alpha Mate," he said with a short nod. "Are these your..."

Leroy cut him off. "We're her guards. Her protectors. Don't be lookin' at her, ya hear me? Don't be talkin' to her."

Dean bit his lip, while Glen made a choking sound behind us.

"What do you want with this 'un, Miss Florida?" Bo snarled. "Want another arrangement? I ain't afraid to pull out his guts if he's one of them Council fucks."

"Yeah, me neither," Leroy added. "I can turn his tally-whacker into a right nice daisy stem."

Bo's shoulders slumped when we all burst into laughter, including Dean. "I told you to stop callin' it that, Leroy. Call it a dick, or somethin'. Crap on a cracker, you're dumb."

"Thank you, boys. I appreciate the offer. But this one's an ally." I nodded at Dean, all my humor fleeing. "And we're going to need as many of those as we can get."

CHAPTER 2

PACK PROTECTOR
FLOR

Sometime earlier that day, in between bouts of lovemaking, Brand had mentioned he'd left his pack halfway through their vows of allegiance, unable to stay any longer when he felt me panicking here at Southern. He'd said there was a spike that drove him to start the trip. So much had happened, I wasn't even sure which spike of panic he'd responded to.

After landing, Dean had spent the past few hours tracking Brand through the forest, though he'd sensed in the pack bond that his new Alpha was all right, and waited for us to come out rather than barging in.

I, for one, was glad. We'd needed that time in the cave. Dean was just as glad to hear that Southern was under our command, more or less, and that we could go back and get food, showers, sleep, and set up a place for the rest of the Mountain fighters to join us when they arrived.

On the walk back to the compound, Dean filled me in on exactly what Brand had done to get here, and my heart started racing almost as fast as it had during the battle.

"So I was flying him here, right? And he starts to shift.

But he's gotten bigger, and you'll have to ask the moon how it works, but he's heavier, too. I thought the plane was gonna go down. Then, a couple of hours later, you must've been going through something pretty dicey, because he started pulling on the pack bonds he did hold. But he forgot that his pilot was one of the first to pledge to the new Alpha, and I almost passed out."

Brand grumbled, "She doesn't need to hear everything. We got here, didn't we?"

"We?" Dean's lips went tight. "Flor, I haven't even gotten to the good part."

I swallowed hard. Brand was still carrying me, but I pushed his arms off me and scrambled down. "Go on."

"So we get to the dirt road where you and Glen left the truck, right? Of course, I can't land in the middle of the forest. My flight plan was shot to hell anyway when Brand started having what I thought was a seizure on the plane, flopping all around, fur and teeth sprouting everywhere—"

Brand grunted. "You try siphoning thousands of pack members' energy through a metaphysical bond into a mate miles away."

Dean raised his voice. "And I tell him to hold tight, that I'm gonna circle, look for a field or a deserted road big enough to touch down. Hard as hell to do, as it's the middle of the damned night, and there's nothing but a bonfire coming from the center of the compound, which is enemy territory. I'm pretty low, maybe a hundred feet over the canopy, maybe less, with a crazed Alpha next to me, and not nearly enough flight hours under my belt for this shit. So I turn back toward the road into town, looking for lights. And guess what? He didn't wait."

For a moment, nobody said anything. Leroy and Bo

were ahead of us, Glen behind, but everyone went still when I let out a screech. "Brand Becker, you *didn't*."

He refused to look down at me. I kicked him in the shin. "Ow!"

Dean let out a laugh. "Good. I was gonna have to kick his ass if you didn't."

"I didn't kick his *ass*."

Glen snorted. "You would have if your leg went that high," he teased, then ducked out of the way as I aimed a donkey kick at his balls. I didn't need to be tall to take down a male.

"He needs his ass kicked if he did what I think Dean's saying." I turned my attention back to Dean. "Please tell me he had a parachute."

He shrugged. "You'd smell the lie."

I rubbed my forehead, a headache coming on fast. "How many bones did you break when you jumped out of a moving airplane, Bearman? How are you even alive?"

"I had to get to you, my love. I couldn't wait." His reply was immediate and raw. Filled with stark emotions that took me back to where I'd been the day before. Terrified that I would never see him again. Wishing I'd been able to tell him, one more time, what he meant to me.

I sighed, and finally said, "You healed up pretty fast." I took his hand in mine and squeezed once, sending my love through the bond.

He squeezed back, gently. "I'm the Alpha."

"A hell of an Alpha," Dean said as we approached the fence. "Even his dad would have taken at least a week to hea... What in the *hell?*" He stopped, staring in disgust at the pink piles of guts and body parts on the ground just inside the fence. Bo and Leroy held the hole in the fence open, and Glen, Brand, and I stepped through. Dean followed hesitantly behind, tiptoeing around the piles of magically preserved entrails. "What are they?" he muttered, as he took in the scene.

"Ah, they're my courting gifts," I began, but Bo and Leroy cut me off, practically falling over themselves to explain.

"It's the work of the Flower Arranger, see? He took all of Miss Florida's enemies—"

"Not us, we was kids when we hunted her, right? We never meant her no harm, we weren't even gonna mate her, all we wanted was the prize, the food rations for bein' a mated pair—"

Leroy shoved his friend over. "Shut up, Bo! Like I was saying, the Flower Arranger hunted down ever' one of her enemies, and made flowers out of their guts, and even fingers, see?" He'd fallen over the pile that had Lyndal's fingers spelling my name. The fingers hadn't moved, and Leroy ran his own hand over them, sounding it out. "Flor, right? That's the kind of courtin' a woman like her needs."

"That better have been a compliment," I snarled, my face burning as Dean stared at me like I was some sort of space alien.

"Oh, it was. Any female like you, a bona fide homicidal ninja, who can get shot a thousand times and walk away—"

Bo gasped. "Who's fireproof! And faster than lightning. I heard from the girls that Miss Florida can move faster than any shifter born—"

Leroy cut him off. "*And* she's an Alpha Mate seven times over."

"Seven times? Something you want to tell us?" Glen managed to ask through a clenched jaw. Shooting him a death glare, I swiped out at him with a fist. He tripped over one of the arrangements and fell on his ass in the middle of what used to be Lyndal Fentress.

"You idiots better shut them up before I do. Permanently," I growled at the three fully-grown shifters, two of whom were red-faced and wheezing with laughter. Only Brand had managed not to lose it completely, but I could feel his humor in the bond.

None of them said a word. Well, Leroy and Bo did, but in whispers. They went on and on, making up wild stories about me under their breath, and the others kept on listening, breaking out into quiet chuckles.

"I give up. I'll see you fuckers at the dining hall." I broke into a jog and went in the back door to the kitchens, steeling myself for the flood of memories I thought might overwhelm me. But the kitchen was buzzing, filled with men and women, working together to cook what looked like a massive dinner. The scent of garlic, simmering meat, and melted cheese filled the air.

One of the women I'd helped escape the dorms, Deb, stood in the middle of it all with her back to me, wearing a white apron and holding a wooden spoon that was as much a threat as any knife. "Stop tasting the sauce, William Robert Spinnaker. None of the rest of us want your spit in our dinner."

"Yes, Chef. Sorry, Chef," a narrow-shouldered man called back, his cheese-sauce-splattered face turning even redder when he saw me. "Chef. Chef, it's her."

Deb turned. "Flor!"

The kitchen went silent, except for the bubble of cooking sauce, the sound of a mixer running on a counter, and the breathing of a half-dozen shifters. Well, a couple of them were holding their breath. Rogue males, looking like they might freak out and shift. Or... holy shit, *surround* me. Were they going to attack?

Deb moved up alongside one and laid her hand on the back of his arm. "It's okay, Caleb. She's a friend." She offered me a half smile, which I returned shakily. "She's pack. She's our pack protector."

Before she finished speaking, the rogues all dropped to one knee around me. "Pack protector," Caleb repeated, in a voice that sounded rough, like he hadn't spoken words in a long time. The others echoed him. I blinked, unsure what was happening.

Sergeant came to my rescue. "That she is," he said from the door to the dining hall. His eyes met mine, and I saw relief in them. I wondered what he saw in mine. Whatever it was, it made him frown, before he cleared his throat and went on. "But if any of us want to have a pack left to protect, you'd better let her through."

As soon as we all found seats in the dining hall, it was time to eat, and food was arriving on the long tables. Somehow, they'd found or hunted enough supplies to pull together a decent meal, with steaming bowls filled with venison stew, baskets of warm cornbread, and even peach cobbler in the long metal pans that were a bitch to get clean. Not that doing the pack's dishes was my job anymore.

That felt weird. It felt weird enough just to eat at one of these tables myself, and not the scraps that had fallen underneath, or the leftovers that made it back to the kitchen. Not that there would be leftovers tonight; we were all eating like the plates might grow legs and run off.

I was impressed at how well the mealtime ran. Half the shifters in the compound ate in the first shift, while the others stood guard and did work to clean up after the battle, or care for our wounded.

Then the other half came in and repeated the process. We'd shown up near the end of the first dinner round, and witnessed the calm transition from one group to the next. The first group was almost half female, with seventy-some women, both ranked and unranked, sitting side by side. For the most part, the ranked females weren't acting like they had any right to more food or drink than the others, and the few I saw trying to pull rank had a wild-eyed rogue snarling at their throats within seconds.

That settled them down real quick.

The second group was mostly the remaining male Southern shifters. More than one of those rat's asses sneered at me when they entered, though I had a feeling it was meant to hide their fear of me or my mates. The rest of the group were male rogues, though most of them were wearing real clothes now, instead of animal skins. The rogues still smelled sour, and acted wilder than the others, except for one pair of males who sat close together. Those two exchanged subtle, affectionate touches more than once during the meal. One was a rogue, and the other an older, ranked male who I'd seen at Southern, but never spoken with. When the older male turned his head to press a gentle kiss to the young rogue's shoulder, I noticed a mating mark on his neck, and realized they were a mated pair. True mates? It seemed possible.

Had this young male been drawn to Southern some-how, seeking his true mate? I tucked that thought away to ponder later, and tore into the stew that Caleb set in front of me.

When we'd finished our meal and a group of the males got up to clear the dishes without being asked, Glen let out a low whistle. "Sergeant's only been inside the compound for twenty-four hours, right? Can you imagine what it'll be like in a month?"

"Possibly a pile of rubble. We're sitting ducks inside this fence. They can come back and pick us off at their leisure," Sergeant said, sitting next to Brand.

Sergeant gave a quick whistle, and in twenty seconds, every other shifter had left the dining hall. Only Sergeant, Brand, Glen, Dean, and I were left. When the door shut behind the last shifter, Sergeant pulled out a pad of paper. I peered down at his notes. He'd been making lists: numbers of Enforcers in each main pack as well as some smaller packs, numbers and types of weapons, and vehicles with locations marked beside them.

"Nobody here had a laptop for you to use?" Glen asked.

"Welcome back to Southern," I muttered.

Sergeant sighed heavily. "We have to assume the laptops and phones left behind are Eastern's. So we aren't using them. But it means we're cut off from our allies. Until we can get our hands on some... What did the girls call them? Burner phones."

I almost smiled. "The closest town is a couple dozen miles down the main road. Are we at a point where we can send someone out?"

"Not yet. We know Torran and a few of his Enforcers left, but we don't know how far they went."

"I have the sat phone from the plane," Dean offered. "Samuel has another one back at Mountain."

Across the table, Glen perked up at that. "Patrick has one, too. We can call them both and coordinate an attack on Eastern. We have cars and trucks, enough to bring a good number of fighters to their doorstep within days."

Brand shook his head. "They'll see us coming and be ready."

"Not if we move fast—"

"They have drones, and maybe even satellite surveillance. They knew Dad was still alive, that I was Alpha, and that the pack was making their way to the Den to give their pledges to me. They've been watching us. Hell, they knew when you crossed into Mountain, Glen. They had Dad on the phone within an hour, commanding him to lock you up."

"From the trees," I mumbled. "I bet they had cameras installed."

"Cameras. Like trail cameras?" Glen asked. I nodded. "What if they have those here at Southern?"

Before he could finish speaking, Sergeant had whistled and two rogues came running through the door, dropping to one knee beside him. "Yes, Alpha?"

"You've got a job. Get help from the women." He sketched out what they were to look for, then sent them away. "I should have thought of that last night. Northern didn't use that kind of tech, or not much anyway." He faced Glen. "Your brother was always asking to bring some in, to train our Enforcers, and to have extra eyes, but your dad believed in tradition..." We all went quiet, remembering just how wrong that had made things go at Northern.

Sergeant broke the tense silence. "Brand tells me he's been called to an emergency Council meeting. If he attends with an army at his back, Aidan McDonnell won't hesitate to use everything at his disposal to stop him, and make him out to be an Alpha gone rogue." I frowned. It was kind of the truth. Brand wasn't planning to join the Council. "Brand will be thrown out of the Council, and his vote removed from the emergency meetings."

Brand grunted. "That leaves only Aidan and Luke as voting members. He can ram through anything he likes, except for major changes of pack law."

Like rescinding the law that stated Alpha's children couldn't leave their own packlands without permission. But wouldn't there have to be a majority vote?

That wouldn't matter. "Luke would never vote with that possumfucker."

Sergeant shrugged. "He wouldn't need to. As Acting Council Head, Aidan can break a tie. And Luke is only Acting Alpha of Southern."

"Shit. We don't even know where Callaway is," Glen murmured. "If they have him, Aidan will find some way to use him."

"If they do have him, I wouldn't be surprised if that's what they planned all along," Sergeant said. "There is no other Heir to Southern, so far as they know. If they..." He hesitated, his eyes falling on the mate mark on my neck. "If they remove Luke from the equation and put Callaway back in, then Aidan will have all the votes he'll ever need."

"But Callaway lost to Luke."

"They'll find some way to stage another fight. Make sure Luke's too weak to win, juice the old Alpha up somehow. There are plenty of ways to cheat the moon. I would know." His tone was filled with shame, but I didn't have time to think about what he'd done at Northern, under Bradley Hillier's command. How he'd cheated so many of the unranked there, mostly females.

I cradled my head in my hands, my mind whirring, trying to see the way through this mess. "Can this situation get any more fucked?"

"I'm afraid so," Sergeant said, speaking so softly it was

hard to hear him, even from this close. "Bradley's still Northern's Alpha, but the moon's full in four days."

I blinked up at him, unsure why that mattered, but Glen gasped. "No."

Brand cursed. "Yes. Bradley's being held for the crime of killing his own Enforcers without cause. If he's found guilty and executed on the full moon, and no one's there to stop him, Aidan could take over Northern. The moon and the power of Bradley's death would be enough..."

He didn't have to go on.

"Fuck," I whispered.

CHAPTER 3
RUNNING OUT OF TIME
FLOR

My bond with Glen buzzed like a plucked guitar string as Brand's meaning sunk in. Glen ran a hand through his mussed blond hair, pushing the loose strands away from his face. "Killing an Alpha outside of a challenge would be against Council law. Pack law. Aidan is bound by that, by his own oath."

"That Alpha has never been bound by a law he couldn't find a loophole in," Sergeant replied calmly. "He could have Bradley executed by order of the emergency Council tomorrow night, or have him killed beforehand in the lower levels by one of his minions. But I think he'll wait. If Bradley dies on the full moon, with no Heir in attendance, there's a strong chance Aidan could receive the Alpha power over Northern. It's not how the Council normally does things, but it's legal, as you know." He nodded when Brand sat up in his chair.

Shit. "Brand was Samuel's Heir. That was different."

"Shifters without an Alpha will turn rogue," Sergeant said, playing devil's advocate. "I'm sure he would claim he was doing it for the good of the pack."

"He's right," Brand whispered. "In the absence of an Heir, the power can be given to another Alpha. Glen was still the official Heir when the Hilliers were taken, but he was declared rogue. As good as dead, according to pack law."

"What about Patrick?" I asked. Glen's brother was ready and waiting to be named the Northern Heir. He was young, but would make a fantastic Alpha someday.

"Declaring a new Heir has to be done before the full Council. The last one to do that was Callaway, with Luke," Sergeant replied. Luke had been adopted into the pack when he was a child, when Bradley was the Council Alpha. Back when no one knew Callaway had a mate who could even bear him an Heir.

"Fuck a damned duck."

Sergeant's lips twitched. "Exactly. We have to assume the worst. Not only that Aidan might take Bradley's Alpha role after the meeting, but that he in fact is planning to. That he may even use Margarette's safety to force Bradley to step neatly into his trap."

I didn't know how to react. I wanted to scream, rage, shout every cuss word I'd ever learned, and cry all at the same time. Brand's hand closed around my wrist, and I realized at some point, I'd taken my steak knife out of my belt and was gripping it, ready to use.

Glen let out a shaky breath, and I grabbed his hand. Both of us were shaking as Brand spoke. "We'll assume Aidan has held onto Callaway as insurance, as Sergeant suggested. That if Luke refuses to go along with Aidan, he'll be killed and the Alpha power will remain with Callaway. Aidan might even find some way to force Luke back into the role of Heir and use Callaway's Alpha power over the remaining Southern shifters to assign his own handpicked leader. The older McDonnell males were all cut from the same cloth. They wrote many of our laws, and Aidan will have every loophole and technicality ready to use."

We all went quiet. It was becoming clearer by the second to me that the Council needed to be destroyed entirely. And maybe not rebuilt.

"Can we just... act like the Council doesn't exist? That we're just fighting Finnick's asshole parents and their pack? There's more of us than them, right? Mountain and Northern won't go along with them. Even Southern— what's left of us—won't support Aidan." Saying Finnick's name aloud made the claiming mark he'd left on my neck ache slightly, but I ignored it.

I zoned out of the conversation for a moment, thinking of my Eastern mate. Wondering what had made our bond feel so painful, and now fragile, almost as if it was fading. I pressed my hand to his mark and sent a thought to him, or tried to. *We need you. I need you. Hold on.*

I might have been imagining it, but I thought I felt something bounce back, like an echo. *Yes.* He would help us from the inside, if he could. At least I hoped so.

Brand murmured, "Hope is good. Finnick is as well. Don't doubt him."

"Stop reading my mind," I whispered back.

Glen and Sergeant were arguing about the political ramifications of attacking Eastern and taking over the Council. Glen got up and started pacing. "Aidan was the one assigned to liaise with the Alphas from the other countries. He's the one with the connections. If Brand goes in there with an army, with the biggest pack in the world, and with those silver eyes, you know what they'll say. They'll say he's the next Alpha of Alphas, and they'll all come for him. For us."

The Alpha of Alphas had been Grigor's father, centuries ago. He'd been a true monster and a despot, forcing all the packs on that side of the world to bow to his perverted rule. Grigor had killed him and gone on to become even more of a legend, though I was certain he didn't deserve a reputation as blackened as his was. For the few months I'd known him, he'd only killed shifters who more than deserved to die.

Sergeant nodded in agreement. "Six thousand shifters, you said? That's almost a quarter of all the wolves left in the entire world. I wouldn't be shocked if Eastern has allies on their side, lined up and ready to move against us."

I thought of Ivan. "Allies like the Russians? Ones with magic? Witches, even?"

Brand shrugged. "I would put nothing past him."

Glen paced faster, cursing under his breath.

"If it wasn't us about to get buried under a whole ocean's worth of shit, I'd be impressed with his planning," I said. "This kind of hunt for power? He's been planning it for a long time. It's evil, but it's clever."

"Too clever," Glen muttered. "Aidan isn't the genius in that family."

"No," Brand said. "That would most likely be Elina, Finn's mother."

"Elina?" My mind started to spin. The woman who'd been here, who'd showed up during the battle. Torran had called her Mistress. She was his boss.

Elina was Finnick's mother. I let myself remember her high-heeled shoes, and her icy voice, calm even as she stood in the middle of a bloodsoaked field.

"Yes," Brand said, seeing her in my mind. "That's her."

"Sergeant, have you ever met her? Did you see her at the battle?"

He frowned slightly, probably wondering why I was asking. "No. She was gone by the time the Tenebris pack arrived. To my knowledge, she never came to any Conclaves at Northern. And I never traveled to one after Bradley's father gave me sanctuary." I wanted to ask a whole lot of questions about that, but now was not the time. "All I know of her is that she mated Aidan at the Conclave Eastern hosted eight years after the Betrayal."

The Betrayal. He had been there, had witnessed everything. "The Southern Conclave, where all the shit hit the fan and Western was thrown under the bus? You wrote about it, but the details of exactly who did what to cause the fight were sketchy."

Sergeant let out a long, slow breath. "I've never spoken about it. I couldn't, not when almost every shifter in the pack had been commanded not to speak of Western, or magic. But I didn't *want* to speak about it either. No one knew I was from there. Your parents hid me, in exchange for my help with... many things." He and Glen exchanged a solemn look. "Some of which I should not have done. I gave up honor for safety and solitude."

"You'll have a chance to regain it," Glen replied.

I tapped the table, something bothering me. We were missing a clue, and I had a feeling it was all tied into that old Conclave. If Aidan wasn't the smart one, Elina was. And if she was as good at strategy and planning as Finnick was supposed to be...

"How old is Elina?" I wondered aloud.

Brand answered. "Older than my parents. Older than Aidan as well. She must be close to sixty."

"Sergeant, you wrote about the fight. You said your father was killed with silver. By treachery. That your mother went mad with grief and..."

"And led the rest of our pack to our doom. Yes."

Brand's voice was quiet. "Can you tell us the story?"

Sergeant's brow furrowed, and his voice was gruff. "Someday. But now isn't the time for stories. We have to act."

Glen ran his hands through his hair in frustration, pulling my attention back to the here and now. "We need more time to plan. We can't go racing in there with Enforcers, and get slaughtered. Maybe end up facing guns again. They'll have traps ready for us. We'll lose every advantage. But if we wait, my parents will be..."

"They'll be fine. I'll start out for Eastern today," Brand said, his moon-bright eyes on mine. "And I'll go alone."

"You said—" I began, then bit my tongue to keep from sounding like some whiny brat. I knew he had to go. We couldn't let the Hilliers die.

"Flor. Wildflower." Brand's voice was raw as the others stepped away, giving us a moment. "If there was another way..."

"I know." He'd promised he would stay with me from now on, and I could see in the lines of strain on his face what this was costing him.

I also knew it was necessary, but I couldn't get the words out. Then I remembered I didn't have to. *I get it, Bearman,* I thought to him, as the others quietly spoke about the logistics of feeding and housing the Mountain troops once they arrived. *I'll be okay. Save Luke. Save Margarette and Bradley. Get Finnick to help. And... you know. If you can.*

His eyes gleamed with love and resolve. "I'll have to start out as soon as possible, and drive through the night. The rest of you can plan. I'll find a way to delay the vote. I'll buy your parents some more time, Glen." He sighed. "And yes, my love, I'll try to find where they're keeping your psychotic little stalker."

"How will you delay it?" Glen asked.

"I can pretend that I'm considering putting my pack under Council rule again, but insist on a revision of some of the wording of the vow." Brand smiled. Well, he bared his teeth, anyway. It was a terrifying expression.

I loved it.

"If that won't work," he went on, not smiling now, "I can tell them the truth. That my pack doesn't support the new ways, and that the North American packs stand to lose three thousand Mountain shifters if they won't work with me."

"Three thousand?" I asked. Mountain had six thousand or so shifters. "What about the rest?"

Brand's smile turned to a full-blown snarl. "They seem to have forgotten, when they insisted I come now, that only half the pack calls me Alpha. They'll be greedy for the whole pack."

"Half the pack is on its way here, Alpha," Dean said. "What do we do with them when they arrive?"

"Whatever Flor says. She's their Alpha Mate." I sputtered, until he stopped me with a kiss. Then he stood, with a nod to Dean. "Call Dad and Patrick on the sat phone and tell them what I'm doing. See if they have any good ideas." Dean nodded and jogged off. "Sergeant, I'll stall for as long as I can. I'm going to need you to plan some sort of attack, or rescue mission, if I get stuck inside. Work with Flor. Listen to her if she has one of her wild ideas. She's sneaky."

I grabbed his arm as he tried to step away. "Brand. What if we can't come up with a way to get you out? To get all of you out? What if they lock you up, like the Hilliers?"

He hesitated, his eyes gleaming a tiny bit brighter for a second. "I don't think Finn will let that happen."

"That piece of shit," Glen snarled.

Brand kissed the top of my head. "Finn is a lot of things, brother, but—"

"A cheating asshole for one," Glen interrupted. "We can't trust him. Flor, you don't trust him, do you?"

"I do," I said, surprising myself as well as Glen. "I know he hurt me. But I could tell... I think *he* was being hurt. Hurting himself worse. Whatever he did wasn't his choice." I wrapped my arms around Brand for one last kiss, then whispered, "Tell him that for me, when you see him. Make sure he knows I get it."

"How can you be so forgiving?" Glen asked as Brand pulled away.

"I lived a long time in a pack where people had to do terrible things to protect the ones they loved. Where pride and dignity were as out of reach as... I don't know, filet mignon. Don't get me wrong—if it turns out he *chose* to do that, without being coerced? I'll snip his balls off, dry them into raisins, and wear them as earrings for the next few decades."

I forced myself to turn away as Brand left the dining hall, not sure I could watch him walk away. Not sure I could bear not being with him.

But I would have to.

I felt a surge of love in our bond as the door shut behind him, and then Glen's arms around me. I pulled away after a moment, knowing I needed to keep busy, or I'd collapse. I'd slept the night before, but was still exhausted. Fear had a way of sapping energy, and I had been afraid for my mates and myself for a long time now.

"Break it down for me, Sergeant. What resources do we have, if it comes to a battle?"

"Half of Mountain will be here in the next few days. We could divert them to Eastern, but it will still be after the full moon. Our own troops are nowhere near ready. We have thirty-two starved Southern males, seventy-six untrained Southern females. The Tenebris pack has twenty-four left alive after the battle."

At least six of their small group had died. "I'm sorry for your losses."

"They died with honor, serving their Alpha," Glen said quietly. "The moon will sing them home."

Sergeant nodded. "We still have three gravely wounded. Flor, that number includes your mother."

"Mama?" I remembered Torran stabbing her with a silver blade. I'd assumed it was a superficial cut, since she'd kept on fighting like she was fine. When I said as much to Sergeant, his eyes gleamed with pride and sorrow.

"Lily's pain tolerance is higher than any shifter I've ever seen. She was tortured for years by your father."

"Don't call him that." Callaway had never done anything to deserve that title.

"By her mate, then. Torran sliced across her midsection with silver. Her liver is compromised. Flor, she may not live through the week." His expression was haunted. My mother was his niece, and he'd only just found her again.

I'd only just found her again. "I need to see her."

"Of course." Sergeant didn't meet my eyes.

Glen took me by the hand as Sergeant led us down a hallway to a room that I'd been in before, after my first battle at Southern. There were two rogues standing outside, both armed with swords. They nodded at me and Glen, murmured, "Alpha," to Sergeant, then let us in.

26

"Mama?" I asked quietly, uncertain what kind of reception I'd get. Sometimes I was a stranger to her now, sometimes an enemy. Once or twice, she'd seen me as her daughter. Of course it had always been hard, with Mama. Even when I was a little girl, she'd looked right through me more often than not, her mind broken by her mate's infidelities.

She lay on the bed, white bandages wrapped around her abdomen, and a sheet up to her hips. Her hair, almost as white as the sheets, wreathed her face on the pillow as she gazed out the window.

But when I spoke, her golden eyes swung to me. Taking me in.

I held my breath, until she asked, her voice shaking, "Is that you, my baby girl?" Her lined face creased into a smile as she recognized me. "I'd know those eyes anywhere. I've missed you so much, sweetheart. So much."

CHAPTER 4
GUESTS AND PRISONERS
FINNICK

I'd had years to learn precisely how to hide my pain. Both the physical pain inflicted on me from child-hood, as a method of toughening me up, and the deeper pain of knowing my parents didn't love me. Or at least, not as much as they loved the power or influence I could help them amass.

I'd gotten good at hiding my reactions, until the pain coloring my connection with Flor threatened to make me forget all my hard-won lessons, and bawl like a baby in the lower levels of the Eastern pack Mansion. I wasn't certain what was happening to her, but it felt like she was dying. My own vision went black as energy rushed out of me like it was dropping down into a bottomless well.

To my relief, I passed out briefly, coming to before the guards who watched those halls even realized what had happened. I made my way up to my room, and slept that night like a dead man.

When I woke, I still felt half-dead, but I had work to do. I spent the next few hours learning all I could from the house staff about what had happened, though it was difficult to gather intel when every move was being recorded and watched by the men in the tech room below.

I did find out a few things, though. Mother had gone to Southern, met with Torran, and was on her way back, with prisoners. "And a guest," the soft-spoken maid whispered, her lips hardly moving. Both of our faces were turned away from the camera in the corner of the parlor, where she was serving me tea. "We're to make up the best guest room, for one." She placed a few sandwiches on a plate and passed it over. "For one of the Heirs."

"Brand Becker?" The others had all been given rooms in my wing when they'd fostered here. Brand's was across from mine.

"No, he'll stay in his old room. The other one."

I blinked. If Brand wasn't the Heir who was coming... "Luke?"

Her eyes dropped once, a silent yes, and she gave a little curtsey before leaving the room.

The Mansion was silent, the staff staying out of sight more than normal, a calm before a storm. Unusually, Father hadn't come home the evening before. It was possible that he'd stayed in the city at the penthouse apartment he kept for late meetings and socializing.

It was also possible he was with another woman. My gut twisted as I remembered the agony of being unfaithful to Flor, even with an incomplete bond. My parents were true mates; Father had shared the story of their meeting once, at a Conclave here at Eastern, thirty-two years ago. He'd spoken about how impossible it was to refuse that metaphysical connection. Apparently, both my parents had figured out how to work around it, in order to have their many affairs.

Calvin Callaway had claimed my mother was a witch,

that she wasn't from a small pack on the Georgia side of the border, but from the Florida side. From a coven, one that was known to harbor dark witches.

The same coven that Callaway had secretly contracted to kill his own true mate, Lily.

I'd never considered that my own mother might have magic. Might be guilty of an unforgivable crime, which she had somehow hidden for my whole life. Now that Callaway had said it out loud, though, so much I'd wondered about began to make sense.

I had no knowledge of magic. Almost no shifters did, since it was forbidden to speak about it. But if witches could manipulate bonds... Maybe she'd been able to do something to her own mating bond to make infidelity painless, for both mates.

What else could she do? What else had she done? I'd known she, Niall, and Torran had murdered more than one visiting shifter, one of them an Heir to a small but influential Italian pack. A pack that should be abducting Tana from the sidewalk outside her school any minute now, I thought, checking my phone.

My sister walked to a nearby dance studio seven blocks from the pack schoolhouse in the city. It was a safe walk, with cameras always on, and guards in place.

Cameras and guards that I'd made certain the Italians knew about. I had to trust they would honor our contract and take her out of the packlands, and the country, and keep her hidden for as long as she needed.

For as long as my parents were alive.

The ornate clock on the mantel chimed once, and my phone buzzed in my hand at the same time, with what appeared to be a spam text about a local human politician. My heart raced, knowing what it meant, that she was safely away. I had given them the private code words she and I had used since we were children that meant everything was okay. She would know exactly who had sent these unfamiliar shifters.

It was the only contact we would have, unless I traveled to Italy to retrieve her myself.

It was done. I stared at the food and tea that sat untouched on the table, and waited for the next call. It came an hour later.

"Alpha Heir. Your sister didn't make it to her dance class. The cameras were out. We don't know where she went."

"What about her guards?"

"They were... slacking."

Perfect. I wasn't sure what the team assigned to evacuate Tana had done to distract the guards, but it had obviously worked. "That's the last mistake they'll make. Bring them to the lower levels of the Mansion for questioning."

"Yes, sir. Any other orders?"

"Search the school again. Maybe she never left campus. The other girls may be up to some mischief. Look in the closets, restrooms, everywhere."

Tana didn't have friends at school. She'd confided that the others either saw her as a way to increase their status in the pack, or stayed away from her out of fear of drawing the Alpha's eye.

"I'll let my parents know. Follow the protocols." I hung up and went down to the lower levels, calling Mother and Father on the way. Neither one answered.

Odd.

I let myself into the main tech hub of the pack in the lower levels, making sure the Enforcers on duty were doing everything they could think of to locate Tana, and that they witnessed my supposed anger and frustration at their failure.

By the end of the first hour, they were every bit as frustrated. I'd hacked into traffic cameras and sent our own drones in every direction except the one I believed her abductors would have taken. Giving them the time they needed to get her out of the city.

I'd just picked up my phone to call Mother, when it rang in my hand. It was her, and she was pissed. "Finnick, come to the back. We have a special delivery."

I ran to the secret rear entrance to the lower levels, opening the door just in time for Mother to stride through, followed by two Enforcers carrying a body bag, and then... "Luke?"

"Hey, Finn," he said, his lips tight, but his tone casual. "I didn't know your pack had a dungeon."

"We like to call them containment cells," I said, stunned when Mother ignored me entirely, following the Enforcers down the hall to the cell next to where the Hilliers were being kept. The males carried the body bag into the room, dumping it in the center.

Mother began barking orders. "Get every scrap of silver chain you can find. Silver nails and the nail gun as well. The entire cart, and—"

"Mother?" I interrupted. "Thank the moon you're here."

Her eyes were wild when they met mine, though I couldn't tell if the mania in them was from excitement, or fear. "Finnick, escort Luke to the guest room that's been prepared. The emergency Council meeting's in two days. We'll have a family meal tonight where we can discuss the week ahead. He'll be staying until—"

"Mother, you haven't checked your phone." Sparks

flashed in her eyes when I interrupted her again. I bowed my head slightly. "It's an emergency. It's Tana."

"What has that useless little bitch done now?" My gaze flicked to Luke, then back to her. "*Speak!*" she demanded, a whip of her dominance in the word.

"Vanished on the way to her dance lesson," I said. "We can't find any trace of her. She may have been taken. If she was, it was a professional job."

A wave of power—the dominance she'd honed and used as a weapon—rushed out of her along with a scream of fury. The Enforcers fell to the ground, writhing in pain. Luke staggered slightly under it, but I grabbed his arm and pulled him down with me as I pretended not to be able to stand under it.

"Where is your father?"

"In the city," I told her. "I couldn't reach him."

"What? What is he..." She closed her eyes, her nostrils flaring slightly, one hand moving to her neck and the old, silver mating claim mark there. A flicker of what might have been pain crossed her features before her expression went cold again. "Of course. Of fucking course." She didn't explain, but stalked toward the exit. "Take Luke to his room; assign Niall to keep him *safe*. Lock down the Mansion, then get back in here and make sure none of our... guests... vanish."

I understood. Luke was as much a prisoner as the Hilliers, or the poor soul in the body bag, whoever he was. As the door closed behind her, I stood and held a hand out to Luke, taking in his altered state. He was skinny, dirty, and with odd specks of blood dotting him from head to toe... but he had a small set of teeth marks low on his neck, and a faint hint of cinnamon in his scent.

"We have some catching up to do," I murmured.

"You have no idea," he replied as we went to follow Mother's orders.

"There are cameras in every room of the Mansion." I breathed the words as we made our way to the guest room that had been prepared for him. He nodded, his lips tightening almost imperceptibly. While we walked, I messaged Niall, then sent another notification to the house staff and Enforcers to lock down the Mansion.

The maid I'd spoken to before was waiting in the hall, and opened the door to the guest room my parents reserved for their most important visitors. You could almost hear the hum of all the cameras and microphones inside. Even the closets and bathrooms of this room were constantly monitored from the tech hub.

Usually, it was human guests who stayed here. Chief executives, politicians, every kind of white-collar criminal who wanted to work with, invest in, or beg money from my family's businesses. There were no guests in the Mansion now, though I knew Father had invited some of the smaller packs for the Council meeting under the full moon this week. With Tana missing, I knew he'd send them to some of the hotels in the city. He would never allow anyone to witness this family scandal.

"I'll need some new clothing," Luke said, hesitating at the open door. He was noting the cameras inside the room. In the distance, a buzzing alarm announced the lockdown.

I paused, knowing I only had a few minutes to speak with Luke at all before Niall would join us. "We're close to the same size. Come to my room, and I'll find you something to wear. Then you should rest in your room until dinner."

Our eyes met, and we both turned together toward my

wing. In less than a minute, we were almost at my door. Luke murmured, "I'm sorry to hear about Tana."

"She'll be fine," I said, letting some of my relief color my tone. "She's too important to let anything happen to her." Luke's hand on my arm had me glancing at his startled expression. I let even more of my relief show, then opened the door to my room, dropped my phone on my bed, and escorted him into my closet.

"I was always jealous of your closet. It's every bit as big as most of the rooms back at Southern," Luke said, pointing to the corners of the room.

I shook my head and mouthed, *No cameras.*

"Let me find you some things." I pulled clothing down and placed the stack on a table, then pulled him close, my mouth nearly touching his ear. Her scent was even stronger now, the cinnamon and jasmine making it hard to contain my wolf. "Tana's safe. I made sure of that."

It may have cost me my future with Flor, but at least I had saved my sister.

He gripped my arm. "Thank the moon." I breathed deeply, allowing myself to scent my lost mate, while Luke spoke. "Your mother is a witch, Finn." I nodded, and he went on. "She forced me to tell her about Flor. Who she is to me."

"Does she know who she is to me? The others?"

"No. She commanded me to tell her *everything*." He huffed a quiet laugh. "I've been obsessed with Flor since I was a little boy. I gave your mother so many trivial details, she almost fell asleep listening." He paused. "Although, I think that may have been exhaustion."

My mother, exhausted? I couldn't imagine it. "Who was in the bag?"

"The reason she's tired. Somehow, she captured Grigor Dimitrivich," he whispered. "He's alive."

"Why?" I knew Flor had claimed Grigor saved her when she was abducted from Northern, but I'd been relieved not to hear anything about him since. Though I'd spent most of the time in the weeks since I'd left Northern either being tortured by Niall, or suffering from mate sickness.

"I don't know. But it's a good thing." When I reared back to see if he was joking, he blinked before breathing the words, "He's hers as well. *One* of hers."

I gasped. "Oh shit." Flor was mated to that monster? He'd slaughtered tens of thousands of our kind. "Does Mother know?"

"No. And they aren't bonded yet, though he has some kind of connection. But the thing is, he's bonded to Glen... and me."

My mind spun as I registered the honesty in his words. Some kind of connection? It had to be a magical one. My thoughts about Mother's ability to manipulate bonds were answered.

"Tell me everything, fast."

He spoke until his voice was raw, and my heart was racing. I'd suspected some of what he shared, but nowhere near all of it.

"Grigor Dimitrivich. You're sure?" I was dizzy from the implications of everything Luke had just told me. My mind, trained to strategize from the time I was small, was whirling with possibilities.

And impossibilities.

Magic. Mother had it, Grigor had it, and Flor... Flor was his mate, or would be.

"Yes. You have to get him out," Luke whispered, his voice raspy. "He's alive, but he's done something to keep me from feeling the pain he's in through the bond. If he dies, I'm pretty sure Glen and I will, too."

"And Flor is mated to you both."

"Yes."

I knew what that meant. Once a mating bond had been completed, there was no backing out. All of us were tied together now, unless... unless the Russian had magic to cut us all free.

"Luke, your father is here," I began. "Callaway." He sucked in a breath, but I could hear my phone buzzing on the bed outside, and knew our time was up. "He's in the lower levels, along with the Hilliers. He spilled a lot of dangerous secrets. Flor's his daughter. Her mother is from —" My mouth worked, but I couldn't speak the name of her pack.

"I know. He's insurance. If I don't vote the way your parents want, they'll kill me and reinstall him somehow." Luke swallowed. "Your mother made it clear on the trip here. I'm to pledge myself to the Council, after which Aidan will reinstate me as Acting Alpha. Then I'm to pledge my pack to the Council, and vote to give permanent power to your father as Council Head, and to execute Bradley and Margarette for crimes against their pack. I'm assuming they'll execute Callaway at some point, so that the Alpha power really moves to me."

"Luke, if you do all that..." There weren't that many shifters left at Southern, but his vote would still count, and his power... I didn't even know how the bonds he had would work. But if he was mated to Flor, and connected to Brand, it was possible the Council would have access to that power through him.

"I know. They'll have every scrap of power they'll ever need, with no way to stop them short of war."

I thought of all the weapons my parents had amassed. The poisons that worked on shifters. The silver-coated bullets and the thousands of forbidden blades that lined the walls of more than one "storm cellar" on our property. They'd been preparing for this for years. "War may not save us either. We need a miracle."

A pounding on the door to my bedroom brought us back to the moment. Niall's voice had us rushing out of the closet. I quickly grabbed some clothing and slung an arm around Luke's waist.

When I opened the door, Niall was red-faced. "We're meant to be on lockdown, Finnick. Where's the... Alpha Heir Callaway." He nodded to Luke. "There you are."

"*Alpha* Callaway," I corrected. "He's here for the emergency Council meeting." Luke slumped against me. I hoped he was pretending to be this weak, but I wasn't sure. "Help him."

Niall hesitated. "What's wrong with him?"

"Weak," Luke panted out. "Need... to rest."

Niall took him from me, the shy maid behind him rushing forward to grab the clothing from my other arm. I waited a moment, then grabbed my phone and headed back to the lower levels.

From my parents' messages, I had an hour before they would be back. Just enough time to find out if Mother had brought a prisoner home.

Or a Trojan horse.

CHAPTER 5
LILY'S STORY
FLOR

The light that streamed through the window into the room where they'd brought Mama lit up her white hair for a moment, making her look almost angelic as she smiled at me. Her eyes were clear, the gold irises sparkling with what I wanted to think was love. The scars on her face might have been laugh lines, if I hadn't known how she'd gotten them. If there hadn't been so many.

I cleared my throat, my eyes darting to Sergeant, who circled her bed and perched on the far side, taking one of her hands.

"Who's that?" Mama asked when she caught sight of Glen entering the room. Her voice had gone slightly brittle. Maybe it was because he was an Alpha. Maybe just because she didn't know him.

I wasn't about to tell her he was my mate. She'd warned me for years not to let a true mate near me, and I had a feeling it would set her off. I mouthed the word *Go?* at my Northern mate. He blew me a kiss and slid back out of the room, understanding flooding our bond.

39

Sergeant answered for me. "No one to worry about, Lily. A goodhearted rogue."

Mama tasted the air for a lie, her nostrils flaring, and relaxed. "I like those rogues. Such nice boys."

"They are, aren't they? Really shaping up."

I stood with my back to the side wall of the room, not certain if I should approach her, but Sergeant nodded to me to step closer. I took a seat on the mattress opposite him, fearful that I could set her off again. That something I said or did would pop the bubble of peace, like I'd always done in the past.

But she reached out with her hand, took mine, and squeezed it, her smile widening. "I missed you."

"I missed you, too, Mama," I managed to say at last. "How are you feeling?"

She winced. "Stomach hurts." I refused to let my gaze drop from her face to her abdomen, where the fatal wound was hidden under bandages. I could smell it, though. Her blood, tainted with the acrid stench of silver.

If I ever saw Torran again, I would return the favor. Though not with silver. I would make his death long and slow, and let him appreciate all the skills Del had taught me.

"If you rest, maybe you'll feel better soon." I had to work to keep from lying.

"I'm dying, baby," Mama said after her next labored breath. "It's okay. I've been dying ever since... since Calvin..."

Her eyes clouded for a moment, and it seemed like she was slipping away, but Sergeant placed both hands over her small one and spoke quietly, his voice thrumming with power. "Stay with us, Lily."

I wasn't sure what he'd done, but her eyes fluttered

open again and fixed on my face. She stared for a long moment, then said, "You were supposed to be Violet."

What? "Violet?"

"Your name. I was going to name you Violet, in the tradition of our family. All the girls are named for flowers."

My heart felt like someone was squeezing it. "What about the boys?"

She grinned slyly at Sergeant. "They got the normal names. I was so jealous, I gave the boys ridiculous nicknames to get revenge. Uncle Jonquil. That's what I used to call Julian."

"Uncle Jonquil?" I wiggled my eyebrows at his scowl. "I'll have to remember that."

The room went quiet, until she whispered, "I remember. I remember everything, like I'm waking up from a dream."

Sergeant murmured, "Our connection, our family bond, makes us stronger."

I closed my eyes and concentrated on the warmth in the room that wasn't just sunlight. Magic. It moved in the air around us. "Wolfcraft," I breathed. "Your Alpha power... it's healing her?"

"As much as it can. Her own power is helping. Her *other* power." He didn't say witchcraft, but I understood.

I opened my eyes and smiled at Mama's hand, running a thumb over the scars that crisscrossed her skin. "Violet. I like that name."

"My mother did, too. If I had a sister, she said, she would have called her that. But I was the only child. Not many were being born, even then. The children of the moon were already lost, long before the war. Long before the Betrayal." She took a breath and began telling a story. Her story, of a life I'd never imagined she'd lived. And with every sentence, every word, a piece fell into place that showed the deeper truth of what had happened, and when.

"I was a young girl at the Betrayal. So I didn't see it. All I knew was that half my family didn't come home. And the ones who did were broken inside. We were shunned, cut off from meeting with the other packs, even speaking to them. Those who'd mated outside our pack began to show up at our borders. Mates rejected from their new packs, tainted by association. More of them were killed before they ever reached the foothills of the Blue Mountains. Within a decade, we lost so many... And the ones who were left lost sight of what it had meant to have honor." Her face turned toward Sergeant. "Julian. You sent me and Mama away."

"It was so hard to let you go. You hadn't even shifted yet." He sighed, and her eyes returned to me.

"He gave us directions to a pack on the border of Texas. We were set upon by some rogues on the way. Mama didn't make it. I shifted for the first time, and ran, following my wolf's instincts. Her guidance. She seemed to know where we were going, and wasn't about to give me control when she was so damned certain. But she was on the hunt for her mate, not safety. She led us here, to the borders of Southern. We hid in a cave we found, at first, grieving our mother. We used a little spell to hide, one Mama had taught me on the run. It worked, too, until she smelled him, her mate, and lost her mind. And found him."

Tears flowed unchecked down her face. "He didn't want me. Didn't let me mark him, said it was too dangerous."

My gut churned. Too dangerous for him, he'd meant. I wanted more than ever to find him, to make him suffer. Maybe saw his head off like I'd done Van Blackside's.

Mama's voice was growing raspy. "He hid me in a shed, telling me he was coming up with a plan. A plan for us to be together, I thought. He was Alpha now. I'd thought he would speak for me and my pack, help the rest to understand that we were all the moon's children. To forgive us. Instead, he brought in a witch. A strong one. She was meant to kill me. She's the one... the one who took your name."

"Took it?"

"Bought it. She'd almost died, trying to break our mate bond. To kill me. She didn't know you were already on the way. You were so strong, even before you were born." Her narrow fingers tightened in mine. "He didn't know about you, baby girl. He didn't know he'd already given me..." Her breathing rattled, and she began to cough. I sprang to the small table and poured a glass of water, bringing it to her lips when her coughing had stopped.

She drank, then lay back on the pillow, her eyes closed. "She forced him to promise... not to kill you. He had to swear to give you her name, so she could force a connection." She smiled hazily, or sneered; I wasn't sure which. "Stupidest shifter I ever met. Florida... Witch..."

CHAPTER 6
HUNTING FOR MAGIC
FLOR

My mama's words echoed in my mind. *Florida Witch.* My stupid name was my father's fault, of course. A name I'd never understood. I'd hated it before, but to know it had been his attempt to sell me, to bind me to a witch or save his life or hers, or both, was the shit cherry on top of the sewage sundae of his failure as a parent.

"I could have been Violet," I whispered. It was so unfair. I fucking *loved* flowers. Even ones made out of intestines. For an instant, I felt a surge of amusement in my bond with Brand, but it faded as fast as it appeared.

Sergeant's eyes met mine, as he whispered back, "It could have been worse. Flor means flower, you know. And no one's ever called you by your given name, have they?"

I blinked. He was right. Practically nobody knew I even *had* a middle name. "No."

He shrugged. "The moon has her ways."

Mom's hand tightened in mine once more before she slid into sleep. Then Sergeant and I slipped out the door. Glen was waiting right outside, next to the guards who nodded respectfully. I grabbed Glen's hand as we left the Pack House, Sergeant on my other side.

"Do you need some privacy?" Sergeant asked gruffly. "Time to... What do they say these days? Process?"

I almost smiled, but then thought about it. I needed to get outside, out to the trees. But for once, I didn't need to be alone. "No. I'd rather walk with you. I have so many questions."

"I have a few myself. Let's walk and talk."

We were silent for the first few minutes, though I was taking in everything. The work crews were cleaning up the battle, and pitching tents close to the training field for the Mountain troops that would start arriving the next day. But there was an almost palpable tension when Sergeant, Glen, and I got closer to the groups that were made up mostly of Southern shifters. As if they were afraid of one of us, though I wasn't sure which one. The women and rogues, on the other hand, seemed to relax. Like they wanted us close for some reason.

They didn't feel safe here. I didn't blame them.

Even without an attack from outside its borders, Southern wouldn't feel safe to anyone as it was. There were too many bad memories here for some, and no Alpha to guide the rest.

They needed Luke... or someone.

I stared at Sergeant's profile in the light, then his scars. The patterns were almost hypnotic, and I knew some of them told a story. "Tell me about your tattoos?"

"My scars, you mean?" He held up an arm, and we slowed. "My camouflage. My sister—your grandmother— did most of them before she left our pack's borders. She was always a great artist, and had a firm grasp on her magic and her wolf's power, until her mate died. She helped me hide my... well, my magical signature, if that makes sense, from shifters and witches alike."

"Why?"

"The pack had dwindled to a few dozen males, maybe sixty women, and only a handful of younger ones. There was no future Alpha besides me, and I wouldn't lead them in the way they decided to go." He let out a long, shuddering breath. "I couldn't. Our Alpha had been killed at the Betrayal, along with many of the other males in his line. The surviving Alpha Mothers were the ones who decided to ally with the Russians, and go to war. When I wouldn't join them, they declared me an enemy of the pack and gave an order to hunt me."

I gasped. I knew what it was to be hunted by my own pack. But to be hunted by a pack who had magic was even more terrifying. "How did you escape? Do you... did you use magic?"

He ran his fingers absently over one forearm. "I couldn't. The markings I bear stifle my magic almost completely. But they also make it nearly impossible to track me using spells. I only had to make certain no one got close enough to sniff me or see me, and recognize who I was. Brand's grandmother found me sneaking across the border of Mountain." He grinned. "I thought for sure I was dead. She was terrifying."

I laughed. "Grandma Ida?"

He shivered. "That woman may be small, but it's dangerous to underestimate the small ones. And her wolf is the size of a fucking pony."

I snorted, but Glen was nodding. "It's true. *Huge* wolf. I almost pissed myself the one time I saw her shift."

When I got hold of myself, Sergeant went on. "The powerful women of that pack were the ones who allowed me to cross through their lands, keeping it secret from the males. They gave me a letter to take to Northern and, well, you know the rest."

Glen whistled low. "You were in hiding from your old pack, all that time. I used to wonder why you never came to Conclaves, why no one seemed to know much about you. Hell, no one even knew your name."

Sergeant chuckled. "For the longest time, other than your grandfather, no one thought to ask." He lifted his left sleeve, revealing a swirling pattern that looked like a labyrinth, with a scar running through it. "That particular spell of my sister's was handy, though it stopped working when it got cut with a silver Russian blade near the end of the war."

I wasn't sure how to ask the question that was bugging me. "You never saw anyone you knew... across the battlefield?"

"I did, Flor." He swallowed and stared out into the forest, his expression haunted. "I just made sure that if they saw me, I killed them. Even the males I'd grown up with."

"Your friends?"

"They were trying to kill me as well. I'd given my allegiance to Northern, and I was a traitor to my own pack." He put a hand over his heart, like it ached. "I gave up my magic and my family. All I had left was my honor... until you walked into the training yard, and I saw my little Lily's eyes in your face."

We stopped, all of us lost in our own thoughts, staring into the forest, in the direction of the cave. I wasn't sure what they were thinking about, but my mind was whirling. Planning what came next.

I had a bad feeling about Brand going into Eastern. But something told me the only way out of this mess was by striking at the heart of the evil. That meant going to the Council, to Finnick's parents, along with all of my mates. I wasn't sure what we could do once we were there, but the first problem was getting in.

Going with an army meant almost certain death for Brand. But sneaking into a well-defended pack, one that used technology as well as magic?

It would be so much easier if we had magic of our own. I didn't have any, from what I could tell. My wolfcraft and witchcraft powers were both on the blink.

I turned my head to the side and stared at Sergeant's arms, thinking about the books I'd read, about his journal. "I'm not sure I could give up magic, if I had it."

"You never showed any signs?" Sergeant asked. I shook my head, and he grunted. "Well, you're still an incredible fighter. You don't need it."

I wasn't sure about that. "Del taught me all about weapons. How to protect myself. I used to stash a knife made out of pipe and duct tape under my mattress. I had that kind of stuff hidden all over Southern. Del made it a part of my training—to find or make weapons, to know how to get my hands on them, and to never forget they were there."

"How many do you have stashed in the compound?" Glen asked.

I thought for a moment. "Nine blades tied to tree branches, unless some of them came down in a storm or somethin' after I left. Four... no, five spools of wire and three jars of my ghost pepper-cinnamon blend."

Sergeant cleared his throat. "Would you be willing to share where those things are? So the unranked women could have a few more weapons they can handle," he explained when I hesitated. There weren't many I would tell about my secret caches of weapons, but Iris and her crew had helped me more than once. They could have any weapon they wanted. Except maybe my steak knife.

"Sure." I listed out all the places, and when I was done, Glen was wide-eyed and Sergeant was almost smiling.

"I'm impressed."

"That was all Del. He taught me everything I know." Something had been bothering me, and I gestured to the markings on his skin. Sergeant had said he'd given up his magic, but I'd smelled an almost unnoticeable hint of a lie. "He made sure I knew that the best weapons we have are the ones we're born with. Our minds, our feet, and in your case, magic. You still have that weapon, don't you? It's just hidden."

His bushy eyebrows furrowed. "What are you getting at?"

"It's where we need to get into that's the issue." I took a deep breath. "We can't storm Eastern with an army, though it might be a good distraction if they think that's our plan. We need to sneak in, me and Glen. But to do that, we need magic. We need *you*, Uncle."

For a moment, seeing the pain flicker across Sergeant's face, I felt bad calling him out. "I wasn't lying, Flor. I don't have access to my magic. Not the witchcraft side, anyway."

I softened my tone. "But you still have it?"

He hesitated, running a hand over his marked arm before answering, "Yes. Magic is in the blood. You would have it, too."

"My scar." I pressed a hand to my chest, and he looked at the star curiously. "Do you think it's blocking whatever magic I might have? Maybe that's the reason I can't shift, or not like I should."

He hummed thoughtfully, his eyes on the end of the

scar that poked up over my neckline. "You could be right; getting that scar before you were even born could be the reason for a lot of things. Whatever spell the witch from Florida cast might have affected both branches of your magical heritage."

"Both?" Glen asked.

He nodded. "Witchcraft and wolfcraft are sides of the same coin, phases of the moon's power. Their separation is what's killing our kind. Or so I believe."

Glen was the one to hum this time, thinking about what that might mean, I supposed.

Sergeant sighed heavily. "If I could use magic to save your mates, and our people, I would. These scars are spells, though, ones I chose. I'd have to carve them out of my skin to use my witch magic again. It would most likely kill me. Though if it would save my pack, my family, I would make the attempt."

Now I did feel bad. I wanted a way into Eastern that wouldn't get anyone killed. Okay, not anyone on our side. "Well, shit. I'm sorry," I muttered. "We can't lose you. *I* can't. You're my favorite great-uncle." I forced a smile that became real as he grumbled about smart aleck nieces.

Glen and Sergeant discussed options for ways past technological defenses as we made our way back to the center of the compound. Glen knew a lot about the cameras and other tech equipment they'd used, though as far as he knew, the only way to disable them was from inside the Mansion.

My steps slowed as we approached the back of the Pack House, the darkness around us growing lighter and filling with the sounds of dozens of shifters. Someone had strung lights in some of the trees that ringed the flat space behind the dining hall. It was almost cheerful.

Of course, the music probably helped. Someone had turned on a radio, and a country song was playing, with guitars and fiddles and a deep-voiced singer going on about his aching heart.

Dean and a bunch of the rogue males had gathered in the center of the dirt ring that had been one of Callaway's favorite places to deliver public punishments or announcements. For some reason, Dean had chosen this spot to... teach them steps to something?

"Are they *dancing?*"

"Yeah, it's a line dance! I know this one," Glen said aloud, pulling me toward the ring. I shook my head and let him go, pushing him on when he tried to stay with me. I could tell he wanted to dance. When he started, the rest of the rogues did, too, as well as a few of the unranked women.

The dust flew up around their feet as they repeated the steps, turning in each direction. I wanted to join in, but I couldn't. This place might still feel weirdly like home, but it had never been a happy one.

The ground where they danced was the same spot Callaway had announced me as the prey for the Hunt. I almost smiled, thinking about the arrangements that dotted the packlands now, the remains of those who hunted me serving as a grisly reminder that power could change hands. And abusing the weak could cause you to lose yours —your hands, or heads, or any other part—when the wheel turned.

I glanced around in the shadows of the trees, noting the sour looks on the faces of the previously ranked Southern members. I wasn't sure if they disapproved of the dancing, or if they wanted to join in and felt like they couldn't.

When that song ended, a new one began, and Glen

came back to my side, smiling. "Why aren't you dancing, princess?"

"This place holds a lot of bad memories," I said after a moment. "This exact spot. I don't know if this place will ever feel like the kind of pack I should dance in."

He wrapped an arm around me, his body warm on mine in the cool night air. "What about dancing on?"

I peered up at him. "What does that mean?"

Glen shrugged. "Think of this place as a graveyard. Heck, most of the pack that was here is dead now. Not all the ones who hurt you have graves you can dance on. But you can dance on the memories of pain, and show the remnants of this broken pack how to move on." He held out his hand. "And show the rest of them that they don't matter enough to keep you from living. Dance with me."

The song changed to a slow song at that very moment, and I slid into his arms. The moon had risen high enough to fly over the pines, and the area practically glowed. When that song ended, Sergeant grabbed me for some sort of polka, whirling me around. Then Bo and Leroy begged me to join them for a line dance so easy, even I could do it without practicing. Most of the Southern shifters were still hanging back, dozens of eyes gleaming in the shadows, but all the girls and rogues joined in, and Iris made her way to my side.

"Thank you," she said, as we moved side by side.

"For what?" I flapped my hands, then my arms, then wiggled along with everyone else. Laughter rang across the improvised dance floor, all of us looking ridiculous. Even Sergeant had joined in, and the Tenebris pack shifters were mobbing him.

She nodded to the Southerners watching, though some of them might have wanted to dance, from the way their hands and feet were twitching. "For showing those assholes whose side you're on."

I had no idea what she meant. I wrinkled my nose and clapped four times, then turned to the right. "Whose side?"

"The side of the dancing chickens." She squatted, flapping her arms like a chicken and wiggling her butt, then waved a wing at the Southerners. "Or the constipated chickenshits."

CHAPTER 7
LOOK AWAY
FLOR

"The chickens or the chickenshits, Flor?" Iris repeated her question, and for some reason, it tickled my funny bone harder than anything had in a while.

I let out a hoot of laughter, but lost my step, which caused Iris to trip me. Our legs tangled, and I fell down on my butt in the dirt, coughing on the cloud of dust that rose up. For a split second, I was thrown into a memory. I was a child, being beaten in this very spot, screaming. Luke was there, too, though, throwing himself over me.

Protecting me.

A chorus of growls pulled me from the flashback, and I gazed around in amazement.

Seeing me down, some of the Southerners had moved out of the shadows toward me. I wasn't sure if they meant to help me up, or take advantage of my fall. But the Tenebris boys were there instantly, their backs to me, guarding me in a circle, snarling at the perceived threat.

My heart burned with gratitude and pride. These boys were starved, still exhausted from months or years of living wild, and from the past few days of battle and rebuilding. They were still willing to face down the more well-trained Southern shifters, for me.

There was no way I would take these boys to Eastern and get them killed.

Iris helped me up, and I thanked her and the boys for having my back. Glen began to follow me into the kitchen, but I waved him off. "Grab a drink for me? I'll be right out."

The toilet off the kitchen was full, so I wandered down a hallway and slipped into one I'd never been allowed to use before, since it was inside the Alpha's private wing. As I came out, I heard something—a floorboard creaking, an indrawn breath?—and went still. No one would have business in this wing, not at this time of the evening. I padded silently down the hall, listening, my steak knife in one hand.

Halfway down the corridor, a strange sensation, like ants swarming over my skin, started up at my feet, and I went still. Cautiously, I took another step, and the feeling intensified. It was deeply unpleasant, my gut churning and my head fuzzy as I kept on, forcing my feet toward the open door at the end of the hall.

I did not want to go down there. The only thing that kept me moving was the knowledge that someone was already inside the room, someone who shouldn't be. I gritted my teeth and continued, one hand on the wall as dizziness hit me in a wave... then vanished as my fingers touched the doorframe. The feeling of dread vanished as quickly as it had appeared.

I inhaled, and a familiar, unpleasant smell wafted around my face. I knew whose room this was. The Alpha's.

I peered inside. The moonlight that sifted through the

drapes on the wall opposite the door was all that lit the otherwise dark room.

A soft sigh in the darkness had me holding my breath to hear. "He never loved me, you know. Not for an hour. Not for a moment. His wolf, yes. His wolf recognized mine. Wanted her. But Calvin never once looked at me with love."

"Mama?" I stepped closer. She was sitting on the edge of the bed, a pillow in her hands. She lifted it to her nose, and sniffed. The moonlight showed a flicker of something. Disgust? Longing? It was too dim to tell.

She put down the pillow. "You walked right through my spell." She hummed in approval. "Good girl. Strong."

"You... you did a look-away spell in the hall," I said, putting it together. "Just now?"

"My mama taught me that when I was little. Our pack was already in disarray, males going rogue. We had to use every weapon we could. I never had a lot of magic. But I could do the easy things better than anyone else in my pack. Except Mama."

I eased to a seat next to her, hoping she was lucid, ready to move away if I set her off. She sounded fine, but I knew how quickly that could change. This close, I could tell she wasn't fine at all. The stink of silver-tainted blood rose from her abdomen, apparent even over the Alpha's residual funk.

"That's how you hid yourself, and the boys—the Tenebris pack—in the woods."

She nodded. "A simple spell that grew stronger over the years. Mama had only taught me how to hide myself, but I must have worked out how to make it bigger, over time. I don't recall... much of the years after he threw me out." Her eyes glinted bright gold as she turned to me, and the moonlight played on her silver hair. "I'm dying, baby. My wolf... I can feel her slipping."

"No—" I began to protest, but she held up a hand.

"I am. If my wolf was closer to her mate, it might buy me a little time. But now..." She shook her head, an odd smile twisting her lips. "The silver that's killing me, it keeps my head clear. I don't know why, but it's true. I can *think*, for the first time in so long. My wolf... I'm pretty sure the silver is what's stopped her howling for him. I can hear something else now. The moon."

"You can hear the moon?" That sounded like the crazy stuff she used to say.

But her face when she met my gaze was peaceful. "It's calling me home, baby."

I fought not to cry, but this was one battle I was doomed to lose. Instead, I hid my tears, hanging my head and allowing them to fall on my lap. It wasn't fair. The silver in her veins had brought her back just to kill her.

"I don't want to lose you," I admitted. "I just found you again." Her arms wrapped around me, and she tucked my head to her chest like she'd done a few times, long ago. I let go, allowing her to see the weakness I couldn't show anyone else, while she hummed what might have been a lullaby into my hair, though I'd never heard it before.

"I was never there for you, baby, not like I should have been. I wasn't able to keep you safe, not from the very start. When they hunted you... It broke me. I wish I could have stopped the Hunt. I tried—" Her voice cracked, and then it was me comforting her, my arms completing the circle.

"I'm done running, Mama," I whispered after a long moment. "I'm not gonna to be the hunted one anymore." I let out a long breath. "I've got to leave, though. I'm going to Eastern. To my mates."

"Mates," she echoed, and we both sat silent for a long moment. I wondered if this was what it would take to send her back into a spiral, into the version of my mother I'd known and almost feared for so long. "They're... good to you?" she finally asked in a whisper.

"They are," I replied just as softly. "They love me, and I... I love them, too, Mama. I'm going to Eastern to save them."

"Of course you are." She nodded, and her chin jutted out as she added, "And I'm going with you."

"With me? Mama, you can't. You're..." I couldn't say it. She already knew anyway.

Blue and red flames shone in the backs of her eyes as she straightened, sitting up. "I'm going to see my mate, too."

CHAPTER 8

CONNECTIONS

GRIGOR

"Damn, it stinks in here." A man's voice pushed through the agony that wracked me. "How much silver does she think it takes to hold one shifter?" The unmistakable feeling of a boot hitting my ribs punctuated his question. "How many silver spikes are in this asshole?"

Sixty-four, I thought.

"Huh. One fell out, looks like. Here ya go, fucker. I can't believe you're still alive."

A stabbing sensation, followed by a wash of agony and nausea, almost sent me back into the darkness. *Sixty-five.*

I had no idea where I was, or how long I had been in this state, but I was so close to my final death, I knew that even one more splinter of silver might carry me away.

I'd done all I could to close off the connections I'd forged with my little blade, and her mates, Glen and Luke. They didn't deserve to suffer with me. I deserved it, though.

After all the years of thinking myself stronger than any other, I'd let a moment of surprise and a well-crafted containment spell catch me off guard. Of course, I'd depleted my power almost entirely saving Luke and Glen. Then I'd cast the look-away spell over the house so she could rest and be safe. Like a fool, I'd cast one over myself as well and waltzed right into the Pack House, looking for Torran.

Instead, I'd found a creature-I hadn't seen in centuries. Her spirit was bloated like a tick, filled with stolen energy, pure darkness. Recognizing that might not have been enough to drop my guard, but this one had worn a face that was so like the one I'd bound my soul to long ago, I'd left an opening for her to strike.

My Anya had been born into a coven filled with witches whose line was so pure, and so evil, there was no mistaking them for any other breed. Anya herself had those same sharp features, the same red-gold hair, the eyes... but hers had always been filled with compassion, where Elina's were as cold as deep winter.

Elina McDonnell could pass as a twin of my Anya's coven sisters. The thing that haunted me was this: I had killed every single one of her line. Every last man, woman and child from that line of witches, who fed on misery and drew their power from blood sacrifices, willing or not.

All but one. Our son. Mine and Anya's.

I'd hidden the boy in a village and left his new family with wealth and guards, and him with every form of magical protection I knew how to create. He'd had no magic of his own, from what I could tell, and he'd lived and died in that village. I'd kept track of all of my descendants. Or so I'd believed.

But I'd been mistaken. At some point, somehow, one of mine must have come to this side of the world, where my existence was a legend, and nothing more. And that descendant had retained enough of Anya's magic or mine, to produce the one who now had the entire continent in her grip.

And me in her dungeon. That was where I was. I was wrapped in heavy cloth, and even heavier magic. Blood, that fueled her power. Blood magic, used by a witch who was half wolf as well. A witch who was my many-times-over granddaughter.

I couldn't smell through the cloth bag they'd bound me in, but the heavy fabric was tissue compared to the weight of the power that had soaked into these walls from the blood magic performed here.

I inhaled slightly, my broken ribs screaming in pain as I did so. So much sacrifice. So many had died.

I began to slip away again, into blessed darkness, when another voice, one I knew, roused me. "What are you doing down here?"

"The Alpha Mate messaged on her way out. Said to double check the silver bindings on her latest project." Another kick, and the sound of chains moving. "Some Southern shifter."

The familiar one spat a curse. "This isn't some shifter. And he's not a Southerner. It's Grigor fucking Dimitrivich in that bag. I don't know why Mother brought him home, but he could be burned into a pile of still-smoking ash, and I still wouldn't turn my back on him."

"Grigor... No way, Finnick. There's no—" I faded for a bit, only resurfacing when I felt silver sliding through my body. I mustered the strength to snarl, though the sound was so muffled, I'm not sure he heard it.

"Hold still," the voice—Finnick—whispered. "If you move, they may break off. More of them, anyway." Another slide of silver. It was agony, but he was removing them. I stopped breathing again, as he pulled a long one out of my right shoulder. "I'm going to leave these under the bag for now, and I'll come back as soon as possible. I'll take out as much silver as I can, and bring you some food and water. For some reason, the cameras aren't working in this room." He pulled the next dozen nails out more quickly.

My mind began to clear slightly, and I felt a tiny green thread of energy, almost within reach. His? His connection with Flor. I was desperate to grab hold of it, consume it, but I wasn't certain if it would hurt her.

My magic right now was a ravenous void, and I would most likely kill anything I touched. Like I had the cameras. I assumed that was what had drawn me back from unconsciousness. I could draw power from anything—electricity, blood, or moonlight.

Even unintentionally. Nervous, I checked on the threads of my own magic that had been tied into the others. They were cauterized now. As good as destroyed.

"I hope what Luke said was right. That you're on our side, or hers, at least. If you kill me, you'll hurt her. If you let me help, I can get you... well, I'm not sure about free just yet. But I can help with some of this." As he spoke, he slowly, carefully, pulled out the silver along one side, then rolled me over onto it and began removing the nails from my back. "They brought Luke here. Brand is on his way, at least that's what I've heard from my parents. The emergency Council meeting will take place after Brand vows his allegiance to the Council."

More silver was withdrawn, a spike that had punctured one of my lungs. I inhaled slowly, trying not to weep with relief.

"The Hilliers are in a cell next door, bound with silver. They're alive, but they'll only stay that way as long as they're useful. Patrick is gathering an army at Northern, and may already be on his way. I stopped into the tech room, and they're tracking vans on the way to Southern from Mountain. If they come here... well, they may think their numbers will give them superiority, but they won't be ready for the kind of weapons my parents have in their arsenal."

The last nail slid out, and I let out a long, shuddering breath. I could still feel the silver chains on the outside of the cloth around me, but I heard clicks and knew it was locks being removed, and a zipper opening.

Finnick leaned closer and breathed a question. "I can hear your heartbeat. Are you awake?"

"Yes," I rasped.

"What can I bring you? I can get you food and water, but what will heal you fastest?"

"Blood," I whispered without hesitation.

He stopped breathing. Then he muttered, "Vampires are real, then." If I hadn't been so close to death, I would have laughed. Flor had accused me once of the same thing.

But he did the unexpected. He stuck his hand through the unzipped opening and pressed his wrist to my mouth. "Take what you need."

CHAPTER 9
BLOOD BROTHERS
FINNICK

"I mean it. Take what you need," I repeated, hoping my fear wasn't obvious. Or that this male, the most feared creature in shifter history, wouldn't react to it if he sensed it.

As I pressed my wrist to his mouth, all the stories of him over the years rushed through my thoughts. He was by every account a monster who would kill indiscriminately, and had no regard for life. From what I'd heard of the creative slaughter at Southern, I knew it was true.

But if he was Flor's mate... If he'd protected her, and rescued Luke... If Glen had bonded himself to this male willingly, to save all their lives, then I could do no less.

Desperate need emanated from the wounded shifter inside the bag, though he was obviously so much more than a shifter. More than an Alpha. His dominance was oppressive, almost suffocating. He hadn't felt like this at the Conclave, when he'd called himself Joaquin. The strength it must have taken to hide this much power was shocking. Of course, now he was ridiculously weak. Starved.

Still, his lips against my wrist remained shut. I tried to remember the fairy tales my nanny had read to me as a child, before she'd vanished for being "too lenient" with me. Magic numbers, magic words... Maybe he needed to be asked three times?

"Take my blood, Grigor Dimitrivich."

His lips moved, and I fought not to flinch, but all I felt was an exhalation on my hand. "Noble pup. Thank you for your kind offer, but I will not take your blood. I fear I would take your life, and although I may yet do that, if your answers to my questions are not satisfying, I will wait." I blinked, unsure what that meant. He exhaled again. "Can you release me from this cloth?"

"Ah, yes." I scrambled to unzip him entirely, pulling the silver chains away from him, careful to keep my gloves in place. I'd put on thicker ones than the usual wetwork latex, and was glad for the protection, though the silver burned even through the thick leather of these.

I piled the last of the chains beside Grigor, glancing nervously at the camera, glad to see the red eye still dead. The room lights were dimmer than normal as well, I noted as I pulled the zipper down.

"By the moon," I whispered as the man's face became visible. He'd been beaten until he was almost unrecognizable, only his dark hair and the gleam in the one eye he could still open familiar at all.

"The moon had no part of this," he panted, trying to push himself up. Quickly, I kneeled beside him and helped, carrying him to the wall and resting his back against it before grabbing the bag I'd brought down. It had water and food intended for the Hilliers, but Grigor needed it more. I uncapped the water bottle and held it to his trembling, bloody lips so he could sip.

When he was done, the water bottle was empty, and his face relaxed. I let out a shaky breath. "Do I call you Joaquin, or Grigor?"

He almost smiled. "Glen... calls me Joaquin. He says he cannot be bound... to the boogeyman."

I shook my head. "Sounds just like him. So, you are bonded. Luke told me Glen allowed it to save you. To save Luke, and Flor."

"He is very brave for one so young. Brave and generous." Grigor's eyes narrowed. "You should be stronger than you are. You have almost no magic. Your mother, though... Ah, I see."

"Magic?"

"You are the child of both lines of magic. Yet I watched you in Northern, and never saw the connection. Even now, there is no magic in you."

I leaned back, uncertain what he meant. "You think I should have magic from my mother? I was hoping my lack of it meant I didn't inherit her evil."

"I'm afraid you inherited mine, pup." He placed a shaky hand on the wall. "One moment." While my mind buzzed, trying to decide what he'd meant by me inheriting his magic, he closed his eyes. The light in the room dipped again, and I could smell something like ozone coming from him. He had on black pants, though they were torn in many places, but no shoes and no shirt. As I watched, static lifted the hairs on the few inches of him that weren't covered with blood. What was he doing? When the swelling in his face receded, and his other eye opened, I had my answer.

Witchcraft.

"You can heal yourself with electricity?"

"I can. Power of any sort, though the easiest for me is the darkest kind."

"Blood?"

He grimaced. "Blood magic, yes. I don't drink it, or not anymore. It's addictive." He closed his eyes, smiling like he was remembering an especially pleasant dream.

"You *don't* drink it, then?"

"I have. But I only need to spill it, and absorb the power in the pain and fear, the life force as it moves, as their eyes close..." His voice trailed off again. I held my face still, trying not to show how much his wistful tone disturbed me.

"Maybe this will help take the edge off." I reached back into the bag, unwrapped a protein bar, and handed it to him.

"Apologies, pup. I would never drain your blood. Though your mother's..." He took it and chewed slowly with one hand still on the wall, taking energy from two sources at once. "What was she like when you were younger?"

"As bad as she is now, maybe worse. Every week, she'd bring me outside, or down here, to one of these rooms, if she was worried about the pack witnessing my 'training.' Father said she did it to toughen me up, to make me worthy of the role of Alpha. I needed to learn how to bear pain, and how to give it." I'd spent many of the darkest moments of my life in the lower levels of the Mansion.

"She forced you to kill as well." He stated it in a compassionate voice, like he knew what it had cost me.

"Killing was the least of it. Once I could defend myself, she made me do things, they made me..." I choked back a sob. "I was their torturer for a while. But I made a far better whore. And if I wasn't willing to do it, I had a little sister. So I did what I had to."

The room went silent for a moment, until he took his

empty hand and placed it on my trembling one. My mind spun. Grigor Dimitrivich was... comforting me?

"Your mother consumed your pain," he whispered. "The blood, the sex. All of it fueled her, and drained you."

"What do you mean?" I leaned forward to hear, and when I did, he raised that hand to my face, cupping my cheek almost tenderly.

"She should never have had so much magic. So much power. My blood and my wife Anya's would be so diluted..." I blinked, a chill moving through me as the lights sputtered out. No, that was power. He was feeding electricity into himself, and then to me. "I never knew one of my descendants came to this world. I never imagined a coven existed who would know how to pull the power from the blood..."

I felt something, almost like wet kindling, trying to spark to life inside me, before he let his hand drop.

"What was that?"

"Me being a fool. When I have regained my strength, though, I will give you back your birthright." Our gazes locked, and I knew what he meant.

I wasn't sure whether I wanted to throw up, or weep, or pass out. "She's one of your descendants. My mother."

He nodded slightly. "And you as well."

For what could have been a minute, or an hour, I merely stared at him. "I'm... You're..." I couldn't get the words out. It seemed preposterous, but there was no hint of a lie in the air, and none in his gaze. "We're family."

The shifter who sat with me was infamous for being cruel. But the dark eyes that glinted with flecks of red and blue in their depths wore the kindest expression I'd ever seen directed at me. "I'm afraid so. Don't worry, I won't tell anyone if you choose not to. Unless our little queen asks me directly, I will even keep it from her." One side of his mouth turned up in a rueful smile as my own jaw worked, trying to put my emotions into words. "I can imagine you are feeling horrified right now."

I wasn't horrified. I was *hopeful.*

I reached out and laid my hand over his, looking for some resemblance in the shapes of our fingers. There wasn't any, but the slight zing of energy that arced between us like a strong static charge, felt comforting again, not frightening. Finally, I let out a breath and sat against the wall next to him, not sure if I could stay upright either. It felt as if my whole world had tilted on its axis, and I was relearning the horizon.

"I was a little boy when she first started... draining me, I suppose. They called it lessons, for when I was Alpha some-day. I was to stay still while she or Father... did things. Hurt me, or others in front of me. I was not to react, but keep all my emotions hidden. Never to cry. When they were done torturing me or their victim, Mother would comfort me. Well, she'd lay her hands on me for a few moments. She never helped me up. Never promised to make the pain stop."

He let out a soft growl. "She was feeding on your pain as well as your magic."

I thought for a moment. "That makes sense. She never loved me. Neither did he. They never said it, and they never pretended. I learned to disassociate, to distance myself from what was happening. When I was very small, I would daydream about what it would be like, to have a different mother or father. To have a family who was strong, but good. Who didn't think I needed to learn to hurt others in order to be a strong Alpha."

"Truly strong Alphas only hurt those who would attack

the innocent, the vulnerable. They don't need to prove their power. They *are* power."

"I've seen that with Samuel, and Brand. I used to wish I really was his brother. I wondered what it would be like to be a Becker, or a Hillier." I let out a short laugh. "I was whipped once, when I was twelve, for writing my first name with other last names in the back of a notebook, dreaming of being someone else's child. I thought Finnick Becker had a nice ring to it."

"It does." He went silent, his eyelids closing. I thought he might be sleeping until he said, "I wish I had known of your presence in the world. I wish I could have... been there, for you."

"I wish I could help you now," I replied. "If you won't take my blood, can't we do something else? You have a bond with Glen, and Luke. I'm strong. I can help you heal, help you escape."

"We don't need a bond, pup. We already have one."

"We have... a bond?"

He smiled then, for a moment, his eyes still closed. "Of course we do. You're my blood, my descendant. We have the deepest kind of connection that exists outside of a mate bond. We are already bonded. We're family."

I swallowed to ease the tightening in my throat. "Not that just saying it out loud does us much good."

His eyes opened as he sucked in a sharp breath. "It could do some good, actually."

"How?"

He managed to turn his head toward me. "Words have a magic of their own. You know this?"

I frowned. "Words like—"

"The vows shifters take. Alpha commands. The words uttered when a pack is joined, or left. When a mate is—"

"Rejected," I finished for him. "Words do have power."

He took a moment to breathe, then said, "Take my hand, Finnick, son of my bloodline." I did, turning until I was on my knees, facing him. "I said I would restore your birthright, and I will when I am able. But for now, I can give you one thing. A new name."

"A name?" My heart was in my throat. "What do you mean?"

"You could still be Finnick Becker someday. But I would offer you mine, though I am ashamed to say it might be as bad as your own."

"I could be Finnick Dimitrivich?"

"Or Finnick Grigorovich, if you like," he suggested. "I'm afraid... if you go by Dimitrivich, no one will invite you... to their dinner parties."

I almost laughed, but he was falling down again, so I gathered him up. He felt frail and light in my arms. "No, I like Finnick Dimitrivich."

"Then that is your name. The moon may not be visible in this place, but She sees all. By Her power, I name you Finnick Dimitrivich, child of my line." He repeated it two more times. At first, I didn't feel anything change, though my heart was lighter. But after a few seconds, something did seem... odd. I closed my eyes, focusing on the sensations.

Flor's bond with me was where it had been since she bit me at Northern. But now, there was something else—a misty, elusive connection, like someone was calling my name from very far away. It was a welcoming sensation, a settling in.

It felt like, for the first time, I'd come home.

"I can feel it," I told him. "Our bond."

"Already? That's good. That's a facet of our magic, our

bloodline. We're good with bonds. We can manipulate them, use them. Create them. Draw power from them. Eventually, you will be able to use bonds for healing as well." His voice dropped to no more than a whisper. "She won't be able to draw your power now, Finnick Dimitrivich. She has no hold on you, though your father, as Alpha..."

"Right." Getting rid of his last name was the easy part. Getting rid of *him* would be much more perilous.

CHAPTER 10
SKETCHING OUT THE PLAN
FLOR

Glen and I went back from the Pack House to Del's cabin that night, my head buzzing with plans, but also pain, and more fear than I liked to acknowledge. Fear for Luke, Grigor, Finnick, Glen, and Brand. For my mama. For myself, even.

I wasn't sure if the plan that had started forming in my mind was just crazy enough to work, or crappy enough to get us all killed.

Glen used his hands and lips to convince me to set aside the worry for an hour. It was exactly what I needed. We made love tenderly, both of us ignoring the feeling of doom that stemmed from the odd pangs and cold patches within our bonds.

Afterward, we fell asleep, and the fear returned when I couldn't fight it. I had vivid nightmares starring all my mates tied up in silver wire in wolf form, whimpering in pain, near death. In every dream, I was handed a puzzle with a clicking timer, while Elina McDonnell wrapped more silver around the men who'd somehow worked their way into my heart. I couldn't solve the puzzle in time, and I had to watch them die, again and again.

"You can't really love them, little witchling," Elina hissed as she used the wire as a garrote on Brand's thick neck. "If you did, you'd already be here. They don't have to die."

Sometime around three a.m., I woke, her voice seeming to echo in the bedroom, the word *die* bouncing through the dark. "I don't fucking think so, ya skanky ol' bitch," I muttered through gritted teeth while Glen turned restlessly in his sleep.

I needed to plan better. Faster. I stared at the ceiling, silently asking Del to help me see how to do it all, how to keep the ones I loved safe. Maybe he heard me, maybe it was just being half-asleep and able to see things I couldn't in my waking hours. But the knowledge of what I had to do, and how, began to fall into place like puzzle pieces.

An hour before dawn, Glen's voice drew me from my plans. "You're awake? Did you sleep at all?"

"Nightmares," I explained absently, my mind still whirring. "Brand'll be there this morning. I'm..." I was terrified. "Concerned," I said instead.

"They'll be all right," Glen murmured. He kissed me drowsily, then curled up behind me, tucking my hair behind my ear and toying with the metal tag that hung from the top. "And after Brand's pack gets here, we'll come up with a plan, one that doesn't risk you—"

"We can't wait."

"What do you mean?" He sat up, staring down at me in alarm.

He wasn't going to like this at all. "We don't have time to wait for them to arrive. We gotta go now, and try to sneak in."

Glen took my hands, and our bond started tingling as the nervous energy inside me moved to him. I told him about the nightmares, then swallowed hard. "It wasn't that part that got to me. It was what came after." He waited, and finally I said, "I sorta prayed for help. Del answered. It was like he was right there with me. He was pissed all to hell at Brand for puttin' himself in the enemy's hands. Said he'd handed the most powerful pack on the continent to an evil Eastern witch. And if she's a smart one, she'd waste no time making sure he was leashed." I thought for a moment. "I don't know if it was Del in my dream, or just my memories of him, but it *felt* like him, Glen."

I closed my eyes and repeated what Del had said. "If you can't run, then try to talk your way out. If you can't do that, then fight. But if you know you'll lose—if you aren't as strong or as fast or as smart as your opponent—never forget, you can always be ten times as crazy. Unpredictable shifters are the most dangerous." I opened my eyes. "It worked in the forest with that fucker Ivan. I keep feeling like being away from the others will be why we might lose everything. We need to be together, Glenda. All of us."

Glen half-smiled as our bond zinged again. He agreed with me, I could tell. Or at least he was gonna go along. "How do we get into the Mansion?"

I swallowed hard. "With magic."

He frowned. "Sergeant told you he doesn't have magic to hide us."

"But my mama does. I spoke to her last night. She talked to me for a good while, and she had an idea." I explained what Mama had said about the silver, and her magic. "Then she said she's going to Eastern, to confront Callaway, whether I go or not. That she's dying anyway.

She wasn't lying." My lower lip trembled, but I jutted out my chin to make the tears stop.

"She can do what Grigor did for this house?" Glen whispered. "The look-away spell?"

"She used one on the hallway outside the Alpha's bedroom last night. She used it on herself all these years in the woods. She says she can wrap one around another person, if she needs to. Or two people." I turned in his arms, facing him now. "What I need to make this work is more information. You've stayed at Eastern, right? You know the layout. I heard you tellin' Sergeant about the cameras and security systems and whatnot."

Brow furrowed, he nodded. I jumped out of bed, throwing on one of Del's t-shirts and a pair of sweatpants, plus some clean underwear that one of the girls had snuck under my arm as we left the Pack House the night before. I threw some more clothes at Glen, then jogged into the kitchen and gathered up paper and a stubby pencil from Del's junk drawer, calling for Glen to join me.

"Can you draw it?"

Glen did a quick sketch, then added a few more details. "The Mansion is set on about two hundred acres of land, in New York, northwest of the city. There's a fence that surrounds the Mansion and a few dozen acres, with gates at the front and back. There are three entrances to the Mansion itself—here, here, and here, plus the servant's entrance here." He pointed to the front, both sides, and the rear of the main building, which was a sprawling estate that made the Southern Pack House look like a broom closet. The servant's entrance was through a massive, connected building that he explained was a garage. "They have Enforcers at the gates, but they don't use many guards to monitor the fences, or at least they didn't. They rely on their tech, the cameras, with Enforcers inside watching. If they see anything, they send out guards."

"How many Enforcers do they have?"

"Not entirely sure. Eastern has a thousand or so shifters total, but most of them don't live near the Mansion. They have pack meetings here." He drew a semi-circle on the east side of the main building, a good distance away, with trees between it and the house. "The fights and pack runs start here. Council meetings are held there as well, under the moon." He sketched out the doors to the main house, adding in some guarded outposts.

I squinted at the doorways. "Those are the only ways into the main house?"

"No, there's one more." He drew it in, an entrance surrounded by trees on a winding drive that came up to the western rear quarter of the house. "No one outside the family and senior Enforcers are supposed to know about this entrance, but Finn showed me and Brand some secrets when we fostered there. That was the biggest one." He let out a long breath. "I remember when he took us past the rear entrance to the lower levels, on a morning run around the property. We didn't go in, but Brand went poking around and asked about it. Finn was shocked that he could even mention it to us. He said there was an Alpha command on everyone who knew, even him and his sister, not to tell anyone other than family or their pack's inner circle about it."

"Good thing you're family. He calls you brothers, and he means it," I said, staring at the map. "Do they use keys, or...?"

He shook his head. "That entry's a gate covered with ivy that blends into the back wall. After you drive in, a door inside requires a thumbprint. One of the family."

Finnick. I knew, if I could get close, I could send some thoughts to Brand, and he would get Finnick to let us in. But the cameras there would be hard to take out. "What about the servant's entrance?"

He blinked. "I... don't know. They have a lot of house staff, and I'm pretty sure they wouldn't give them keys." He closed his eyes, thinking. "I passed by that entrance once, and saw a woman bringing in crates of meat for the kitchens. She pushed a button and called out her name, Susan. That was it. And then someone buzzed her in."

I almost grinned. Del had taught me that if I couldn't hide, a disguise was a good second option. "Perception is every bit as important as reality. People see what they expect. What did Susan wear?"

"The same thing all the staff wore. Black shoes and skirts. White shirts."

"Skirts. They're all women?"

He shrugged. "All the staff I've seen in those uniforms. The males are guards or Enforcers."

I sneered. Of course the women did all the real work. "Do they wear something like an ear tag? Or a leather choker?"

"No," he said, rubbing the stubble on his chin. "They're quiet, though. Just like the Southern Pack House staff was under Callaway, only the clothing is nicer at Eastern."

"That's it. That's how I'll get in. With a little magic, a little disguise, and some luck." I tried to think of what I'd missed. "Where exactly are the cameras in the back of the property?"

He added them to the map. "Two years ago, they were here. They could have added more since."

"Why would they? That's a shit ton of technology already."

I stared at the dozen cameras he'd indicated. "Nice of them to hide those on the trees for me," I muttered. "Hope they left some good low branches to get up to 'em. Hmm. Drones, too. Maybe... Maybe we'll need one of those guns after all."

"Guns?" Glen echoed me, his voice faint.

Our bond flared with alarm, and I grabbed his hands. To my shock, they were trembling slightly. "Not for the guards. For the cameras we need to take down, and the drones. We could even use a slingshot."

He pulled his hands away, folding his arms to hide the shaking. "No, you're right. A gun will be faster, and more effective on the tech. All right. I'm not any good with a slingshot, but I do know how to shoot."

I knew he was remembering the feeling of the bullets tearing through him; I could sense it in our bond. "We can find another way. It's not our only option." He took a breath to say something, when a knock interrupted him.

"Flor?" Dean called from outside. Glen jumped up and opened the door. It was raining slightly, but Dean didn't step inside. He had the sat phone in his hand and gave it to me. "Brand's just pulled up at the Mansion. He says something big has happened at Eastern." When I gestured him in, he shook his head. "Also, vans are arriving at the main gate here. Ten of them so far."

Shit.

"Council troops?" Glen demanded.

"Mountain, I think," Dean replied. "They made good time."

"Flor?" I heard Brand's voice on the phone in my hand, and I pressed it to my ear, my heart in my throat.

"Bearman. Are you all right?"

His deep voice rumbled in my ear. "I'm fine. From the

feeling in the bond, Luke is fine, too. But Finn, I can't feel him. Is he..."

I knew what he was asking. I closed my eyes, reaching for Finnick. "Huh. He's happy, almost. Nervous, but whatever you're noticing, it's something good. Or at least he thinks it is." I couldn't imagine what good could be found in this mess, but my connection to Finnick was lighter. I tried not to think about him and our bond, and how much it had hurt the last few times I'd felt it more strongly. He and I were gonna have us a talk soon. If we lived long enough.

"Good for us, then. That's what I needed to hear. All right. I'm driving through the gates at the Mansion now. Dean says the first of the Mountain troops are arriving there?"

"They're coming down the road now."

"Good. The rest should be there before the full moon. When they arrive, make your plans. Let Sergeant guide you."

It would be too late then. I had to act immediately.

"Once I'm inside the Mansion, I'm sure they won't allow me to call you," Brand said, but I cut him off.

"You won't need to. I've already got a plan, though. Glen and I are—"

"Flor, stop. Don't tell me."

"What? Why not?"

His reply was blunt, and more than a little terrifying. "I'm about to walk into the home of a witch who wants to kill you and everyone else who can stand against her, and take over the North American packs. I'm not sure if she can read minds, or force me to tell her secrets. I'm far enough from you that I can't follow your thoughts precisely. If I don't know exactly what you're doing, if you don't tell me, then she can't find out either."

I felt a surge of love in our bond, and I sent one back, hoping he didn't notice my fear.

"I'll do what I can, Flor. I'll find Luke and Finnick, and speak to them first. Then I'll see if I can get into the lower levels, to talk to the Hilliers and discover where your little psycho is."

"Thank you, Bearman." I thought for a moment. "Just don't get locked up with anyone. I may need you to cause a distraction."

"What?" I heard someone on the other end of the line, shouting. But Brand was growling, "Flor, don't tell me *you're* going to be anywhere near this—" The shouting got louder.

"Okay, I won't," I said. I didn't share that I was promising not to *tell* him. I was absolutely going. "Love you." I hung up before he could ask me anything else.

Dean had jogged off, but Glen was staring at me as I pressed the button on the phone, his eyebrows raised so high that they vanished under his blond curls. "You hung up on him? He's going to spank you for that, if I don't beat him to it. This isn't a plan, Dream Girl, or if it is, it's the worst plan in—"

"The history of plans?" I almost laughed. "Nah, this is only the second worst. Get dressed. We've got to go meet the Mountain shifters, then find a car to take to the big shitty, as Grandma Ida would say." As we quickly straightened up Del's house, I sketched out the final details of the plan, if it could be called one.

Glen was paler than the paint on the walls when I finished. "This really is crazy. There's no hope that it'll work."

"Southern shifters are all about the crazy, Glenda." I passed him, slapping him on the butt before I stepped into the drizzly morning. "And up to now, I would have agreed with you on the *no hope* thing. But look at this place." I gestured to the pack, to the shifters who I never once thought would work together, doing just that. Unranked females, ranked males, and even rogues, working to clean up my shithole of a home pack before Mountain arrived, and doing it cheerfully. "I never would've dreamed this could happen. I kinda hate to admit it, but there's hope here."

He still looked skeptical. "Is hope enough to save us all from the Council?"

I pondered that as he followed me out the door. "Maybe not," I admitted. "We'll probably need some duct tape, too."

Use every weapon, girlie. Every last one. Del's voice echoed in my mind as Glen's rang out, attracting the attention of the cobbled-together pack that was hard at work, rebuilding.

Or building something new.

CHAPTER II

IN THE WOLF'S DEN

I t was all I could do not to flinch when Aidan McDonnell's oily voice slid over me as I stood, my hands on my head and my legs apart, in the front foyer of the Mansion. "Young Brand Becker, welcome back to my home. I'm glad you decided to join us for the emergency meeting."

His words were welcoming. But the rough hands of the two burly Enforcers searching me—one of them holding a wand of some kind that clicked at the metal buckles on my clothing and bag—made it clear I was not a trusted guest.

Not that anyone was right now. I'd never seen as many Enforcers inside the Mansion as I did today. One stood at each door, eyes tracking me as if I might attack. I grunted as one of them took my bag and opened it, dumping the contents out on a small table and inspecting each item.

"Really, Aidan? Is this necessary? I'm well-versed in protocol. I entered your home unarmed and on your invitation."

The Alpha stiffened at the lack of a formal title. But he'd chosen not to use mine, so he couldn't protest. I had on a pair of sunglasses and left them on, even inside. I didn't want him to see my eyes, not yet. He may have heard about the change already, but I wasn't certain.

"It is, I'm afraid," he replied. "You can't know this, of course, but someone has taken our daughter. We don't know where she is, and until we do, our security will be increased."

Tana, missing? I felt a surge of relief that I was forced to hide. Finn must have gotten her out. Some part of me relaxed, knowing there was one less innocent who might be harmed in the coming days. "That's shocking to learn. Who would take her?"

"All leaders have enemies. It's a wise Alpha who takes precautions to protect his pack," he replied, flicking his fingers for the guards to retreat.

I picked up my bag, the sparse clothing I'd neatly packed now rumpled. "A shame when even an Alpha who takes precautions can have the things he values stolen from him. I hope Tana is safe and well, and where she should be within the day. I understand your reaction now. Fear drives your actions, not a desire to insult."

His lips tightened at my carefully worded caution and criticism. "Of course not. Though I did think you might not answer my summons at all."

"Why would you think that?" I knew what he would say, but wanted to see what he would admit to. Find out what he knew, if I could.

He ushered me into the sitting room, snapping for a young maid to fetch refreshments. "More often than not, as you know, your father chose not to attend to Council matters. I had wondered if you might do the same once you took his place." He settled back in his chair, pretending nonchalance. "Though I'm extremely curious as to how you managed to become Alpha while leaving him alive."

"The old ways, of course. You know my pack has always followed them. In the few instances that we did not, we regretted it. It's a good thing that with my rise to Alpha, we can begin to set things right again," I replied, as the maid delivered a tray with steaming tea, along with a plate piled with warm scones, jam, and clotted cream.

Aidan stared at me in silence as I ate a few bites. Perhaps in shock, that I even knew the law. Unless and until the Council had me under its rule, I had the power here.

My father had rarely cared enough about Council politics to play these sorts of games. I had a feeling the Eastern Alpha had forgotten that we weren't just brawn at Mountain. We were strategists as well. Of course, he'd never spoken more than a few moments with me. In his eyes, I was still a dumb pup, one he could take advantage of.

I sipped my tea while Aidan stewed. "My father taught me a lot about how shifters were meant to live, and govern. I may be a new Alpha, but I will follow the old ways. I believe the Council might do well to also return to them."

"The old ways?" He almost barked the words. "The old ways would have his blood feeding Mountain soil."

Usually, Aidan was calm, even cold. I'd unsettled him. *Good.* I breathed calmly, controlling my own wolf's response to hearing this weak Alpha speak of my father so disrespectfully. It was time to unsettle him a bit more.

"Now, Aidan, you know as well as I do that the Moon Goddess cannot be tricked. We fought under the moon, in the presence of the pack. The power flowed from my father to me. We followed the old ways, and were rewarded." I chose that moment to look down and take off the sunglasses. "His survival was not the only surprise. I was also gifted with Her favor."

When I set them on the table and looked up, his face turned almost as white as my gaze. He began to sputter, finally getting words out. "What... *How?*"

So he hadn't known. I relaxed slightly. I didn't need to tell him when my eyes had changed. If he thought it was a result of the fight for leadership, he would be hard pressed to find a valid reason to claim I had been affected by magic.

"My grandmother did some research. Moonblessed eyes have only been seen once before, hundreds of years ago. It could be a sign that our pack's adherence to the old ways, that my own leadership, has the moon's blessing." I let my gaze harden. "My pack sees it as such."

"They would," he muttered, standing in a move intended to show his dominance. He even sent a push of power at me, which should have felt intimidating with the strength of the Council in his hands. But the Council's authority no longer encompassed the Mountain pack.

It felt like a toddler punching my chest, if that.

I smiled gently, as I would at a misbehaving child. "As Mountain's leader, I am certain I'll be combining a few new things with the old. I'm not my father, and I have no intention of retreating to Mountain and leaving the governance of all the packs to others, when it will be my responsibility to be deeply involved." I stayed seated, but allowed some of my new power to emerge, filling the room with an almost oppressive electricity until the pictures on the walls began to shake, then pulled it back until it was completely hidden away. Before Aidan could call me on my disrespect, I went on. "I think I could use my power to help the Council. So of course I came when you called." I wasn't lying. I fully intended to help the

Council. I'd help it by restoring its rightful leader, for one thing.

"You've already taken the vows of your entire pack?" he asked cautiously, blinking at me. "Your father took far longer." He pulled his glasses out of his pocket, toying with the handle.

I smiled, remembering how Flor had accused him of lying, by wearing them to appear more human before his business associates. No shifter needed glasses, but he thought his were a tool.

They were more of a *tell*. He was nervous. Nervous and greedy.

I sipped my tea. "Unfortunately, your summons prevented me from establishing connections with my entire pack. The power I hold is only half of what I will someday soon. The other half are waiting at home, or traveling to the Alpha's Den, to pledge themselves to me."

"So they have no Alpha until you go back," he said, tapping his chin in thought. "We'll need to make sure you return quickly, so they don't feel the effects of being without your guidance." The threat was so subtle, I was almost impressed.

"I can't see why I should be delayed. The full moon is in two days. The Council meeting then is to decide on Margarette and Bradley's fate, as well as your own election as Head Alpha, isn't that right?" I knew he also wanted me to pledge to the Council, but that was the only thing I could delay.

And I would.

"Don't be obtuse. You can't take part in any Council activities unless you and your pack are pledged to us," he snapped.

"My half pack, you mean."

He flinched. "You'll have plenty of time to build up your power after we take care of our emergency business. After you make your vow." His face grew hard. "In fact, you should do that now."

Of course he wanted me to pledge now, before I'd even caught my breath, or finished my fucking tea.

I knew I might be forced to do just that, even if I had promised my father I wouldn't repeat his mistake. But I would delay as long as possible, to give the others time to gather their forces.

"I find myself concerned, Aidan, at what might happen to me and my pack, if I make that pledge now." I gestured to the floor, knowing he would follow my train of thought. At that very moment, Margarette and Bradley were imprisoned beneath our feet. "I find myself curious as to who will even be at this emergency Council meeting. Southern's pack's leadership is still in question. One of the other Alphas and his mate are imprisoned, his pack given no voice."

Aidan and I were the only legitimate votes remaining, the only two Alphas with power left standing. Although I supposed Luke might be allowed to attend an emergency meeting, even vote, if Aidan and I both concurred. I was certain he would be given permission, if Aidan was sure Luke would side with him.

But when it came to power—the kind that came from the moon, the kind that the wolves of all our packs would respect—there was no question that Aidan needed me as well. So he needed leverage over me, and fast. And I needed to keep him from gaining it.

"I find I have deep reservations about the charges against Bradley. Why would I give the current Council power over me and mine, when I am not yet sure... of who the full Council might be? Or why the rush is necessary."

Emergency meetings could be conducted only with the four main Alphas, if necessary, and didn't have to be held with much notice at all. A full Council meeting, though, the kind that was supposed to be where decisions like the ones Aidan was insisting be made quickly, could only be held on the full moon. I would need to force him to wait.

Of course, I knew Aidan intended that Council to consist of Alphas and Head Enforcers who were under his thumb, or over whom he held power of some kind. Aidan and Elina and their Head Enforcer Torran would be balanced against me and Dean and Luke.

As my mate, or Luke's, Flor would have been allowed to vote in the Council, if I had any intention of allowing her near this place. Which I absolutely did not. She'd be executed for witchcraft almost instantly, if she set one foot on Eastern's land.

But a full Council would also include an Alpha from Northern. That most likely meant Patrick, if the Hilliers were executed, or banished. Patrick and an Enforcer, since as far as I knew, he hadn't yet claimed the woman from Northern, Kristin.

I knew the McDonnells might keep the elder Hilliers alive, to force Patrick and his supporters to bow to him. That would give Aidan all the power he'd need to become a true dictator.

Not a true Alpha. Not there to protect the pack, but himself. My wolf snarled soundlessly.

"The rush is necessary because the entire nation is in disorder, thanks to Bradley and his pack," Aiden said. "And those aren't the only pressing matters. As I told your father, you'll need to pledge to the Council before all of us even meet. We need to face them as a unified group, to keep the smaller packs from growing fearful, among other things."

He rose and retrieved an old book from a shelf—a record of pack law, I assumed. He'd made it clear on the phone that he wanted me to pledge loyalty, and that I'd need to do it immediately. Dad had warned me about what that would entail.

"You can put the law book away, Aidan. Until I know who makes up the Council, I cannot in good conscience give the authority the moon blessed me with, over to them."

"I'm the Council!" he spat out, slamming the book down on a side table.

"No, you are the Interim," I said calmly. "Bradley's fate has not been decided. Or Margarette's, for that matter. She's imprisoned for what reason? Supporting her Alpha, her mate? I find myself wondering if you're the one who needs to read over that law book again. You've overstepped. Who's to say you will not attempt to overstep again, in my direction?" I allowed my wolf to peek through my eyes at him, daring him to argue.

His face turned red, and he took a breath to speak, but the door opened again, and another voice interrupted him.

"Oh, Aidan. No one told me Brand had arrived." Elina McDonnell glided into the room, her black pantsuit and heels the same as always, though her hair was slightly windswept, and her expression more brittle than normal. She perched on the arm of the chair next to Aidan and tilted her head to look at me. Her eyes widened. "Your eyes."

"Moonblessed." One word was all I would give her.

Her face had shifted now, filled with a lust that disturbed me. It wasn't for my body; I could sense that immediately. She wanted my power.

"Such a powerful Alpha," she half-purred, moving to sit in the chair next to mine, her hands clenched as if she were in danger of reaching out to touch me.

"I'm surprised you didn't know about my eyes," I said, leaning away from her. "I thought your spies would have kept you informed." When Aidan began to stammer about unfounded accusations, I turned back to him. "What did you learn, then?"

Elina slid to the edge of her chair. "We learned how you became so strong."

I clenched my jaw. "You know I took a mate."

Aidan chuckled. "I do know. You didn't bring her with you?"

"Of course he didn't," Elina said dismissively. "She's a rogue. Trash."

My wolf began to emerge, fur prickling the backs of my hands. It was considered extremely poor manners to shift inside the Mansion. It was a punishable offense to attack either one of these two, outside a formal challenge. I took a deep breath, forcing calm. "She is not. She's the Alpha Mate of Mountain, my true mate."

Elina's smile was a terrible thing. "Now, Brand. She isn't *true*."

My teeth grew sharp. "Your meaning?"

But it was Aidan who answered. "Your mate's a whore."

CHAPTER 12
INSULT AND INJURY
BRAND

I took every ounce of control I'd learned over the years not to shift and tear out Aidan's throat. To hear these dishonorable fucks speak of my little mate in that way was almost more than I could stand. My wolf was clawing to emerge and rip them to pieces, so they would never make the mistake again.

But for now, he was not only the Council Alpha, he was my host. I had to resist.

Though it may have been foolish to take my attention off the monsters in the room, I closed my eyes, allowing my wolf to reach down the bond to Flor. I felt her concern, and a wave of support from her... and then, through her, from Glen. He felt warm, reassuring, his energy flowing freely to her. Keeping her safe, even when I was too far to do so.

It would have been enough, should have brought me back, but something fell on my arm.

My eyes shot open. Elina had her hand on my forearm, her fingers resting lightly on my skin. My arm felt like thousands of spiders were crawling on it, racing to the rest of my body, each prickle a pin, holding me in place.

I couldn't move.

"So much anger. So much power," she murmured, licking her lips.

I shot a look at Aidan, but he was staring down at his glasses, toying with the frames, as if he was totally unaware of what his mate was doing.

Elina dug her fingers in. "Just be still, Alpha. Just let me in."

Something that felt like sand blasting at my mind started up inside my head, infinite tiny claws scraping their way into my mind. I couldn't speak, and I was suddenly glad, so grateful, that Flor was not here. If this witch could do this with a touch, there was no way I could have protected her.

I had to move. I had to... I managed to open my mouth to speak, and uttered one word. "Witch."

"What a terrible accusation." Her red lips twitched. "You're one to speak, baby Alpha. Those eyes of yours have magic that hasn't been seen in centuries. Just imagine what a witch could do with them, plucked out of your thick head."

I had no doubt that was exactly what she had planned, but I couldn't tear away from her. Though I knew she could probably feel something happening to me, I refused to reach for Flor again; I wouldn't drag her into this. My whole body felt cold, almost icy, as Elina's fingernails dug into my flesh, drawing blood. The room grew silent, or perhaps my ears had stopped working. I couldn't even hear my own heartbeat.

Perhaps it had stopped altogether.

But then the lights dimmed, the power in the house interrupted by something. There was no storm outside, though, and if the main power went down, the Mansion had generators.

They didn't kick on.

Elina bared her teeth, still focused on me, but I could feel her control slipping. The lights grew even darker, and stayed that way for a long moment. Somewhere in the Mansion, guards shouted. A woman shrieked.

Then the lights came back, and something inside me... warmed. I let the feeling grow, not sure what it was. It became more intense, almost as if whatever thawed the center of the ice was approaching.

The door slammed open, and Elina's hand dropped from my arm as a rush of energy and sound chased away the odd, deadly silence. "I didn't think I'd see you again so soon, brother."

Luke. Thank the moon, he was here, and alive. He looked far gaunter and paler than he had been the last time I'd seen him, but he hummed with energy.

He strode to my side and half-lifted me from the chair. I felt a surge of energy coming from his hands as he gripped my forearms, smiling into my face, though his eyes were shadowed. "I'm glad you're here. I thought it might just be me and Alpha McDonnell for the meeting tonight."

The collar of his shirt was open wide enough to see the bite mark on his neck. "Nice bite," I whispered.

Aidan interrupted. "Yes. He's mated, though it shouldn't be a surprise. He's mated to your mate, after all. The whore." Luke's nostrils flared, but I squeezed his forearms in warning as Aidan went on. "And she needs to appear before the full Council for questioning."

As he was speaking, Niall entered the room, panting. He'd obviously been chasing Luke, and the look Elina shot him promised he would be punished for not keeping the Southerner away.

Behind him, another half-dozen Enforcers pushed through the entry, the one at the front moving to face Aidan, and bowing his head. "Alpha—" Aidan held up a hand.

Luke's grip still firm on my arms, giving me strength, I turned to the McDonnells. "Why would I bring my mate before the full Council for questioning? Whoever that full Council may consist of. From what I can tell, her fate would be determined before she opened her mouth to explain our situation."

"You dare to question the Council?" Aidan protested. "We've done nothing but uphold the law." He wasn't lying; there was no scent of deception. That was his way, finding loopholes and technicalities, to make sure he was seen to be following the law. Though he tore at the spirit of what pack was meant to be with every law he twisted to his own ends.

I snarled my reply. "You've imprisoned the Hilliers, called for the execution of their son, and your mate just tried to break into my mind and—" When I mentioned his mate, Aidan's eyes narrowed, his wolf peeking out.

The strength I'd always thought lacking in Aidan showed in his wolf's eyes as he challenged me to continue. I almost respected it. The wolf. Not the man.

"I think we all need to calm down, Brand," Luke said. "You've been traveling and you're tired. Tana has been taken. If we want to be able to work together as a Council when all this is over, and keep the North American packs whole under new leadership, we need to be clear-headed about many things." He pulled me away. "Come on, I'm sure there's a room ready for you."

Aidan and Elina allowed him to pull me to the door. I glared back inside, ignoring the gasps from the Enforcers who noted my eyes. Elina called out before we exited,

"We'll see you at dinner," like nothing had happened. Three of the guards followed us, though Aidan commanded Niall to stay.

"Is there any sign of her?" Aidan's murmur from the sitting room was more enraged than concerned.

"None, Alpha. It's like she vanished. There was one flight going to Rome that we suspected, but there was no scent or trail of her. We need you in the city."

"I can't hold an emergency meeting over the fucking phone," Aidan spat.

The door shut, but not before Elina snapped out, "The full Council meeting is all that matters. Call our Italian connections and get them to meet—" Her voice was muffled but agitated as we crossed the entry and walked quickly down a hall.

"You look like shit," I muttered to Luke.

"You look like you're two seconds away from going feral," he replied. "Nice eyes." I took a breath to explain, but he nodded to the corner of the room. "Eyes everywhere."

I noted the cameras with a nod. "Where are you taking me?"

"I have a room. We can be alone there."

Alone. As long as it was away from the McDonnells, that was fine. "Where's Finn?"

"I haven't seen him all day," Luke told me, his tone filled with concern. "Not since he went to the lower levels."

"The lower levels?"

"His mother took Grigor Dimitrivich prisoner." As if the name itself was a curse or a spell, the lights dimmed once more, casting the hall into darkness. Even the small red camera lights went dark. The only illumination was what sunlight could make it past the blinds.

"I know," I admitted. "*She* wants me to check on him." I

wasn't going to speak Flor's name out loud in this house. I was already panicking, just thinking about her coming here.

Elina had almost had me under her power. How could she be that strong? I hadn't even been able to break away from her grip. What if she got her hands on Flor, and I couldn't save her?

"Finnick went to do just that. I was worried the old guy might be dead, but I felt something just after you must have arrived. I reached out to him through our connection, and he... slapped me away, shutting it down. He's alive, but he's feral, starved for power, it feels like. If Finnick gets too close, I'm not sure what'll happen."

Shit.

CHAPTER 13
POWERLESS
LUKE

The power stayed off for almost a full minute, and I stood with Brand outside my door, listening to the distant curses and screams.

"Do you think it's Gri—" Brand's whispered question was cut off when the lights flared, brightening the hall.

I shook my head, reaching for the door to my room, but something stopped me. A feeling that I shouldn't go inside. Instead, I grasped Brand's arm and pulled him down the hall, toward Finnick's wing. Some of the red eyes of the cameras were lit on the way, but some flickered, and one was out completely.

Good.

When we reached Finnick's room, the door wasn't locked, which worried me slightly. The faint scent of other shifters drifted from inside as I cracked it open, and I knew either maids or guards had been here. I held a finger to my lips as Brand staggered to a halt behind me.

"Hang on," I whispered, pulling a stone out of my pocket. I'd gathered a few from the parking lot of the gas station that had been our only stop between Southern and the Mansion, some with sharp edges. I'd remembered Flor talking about Del's lessons, about using any weapon you could get. About anything being a weapon, if you thought about it.

This stone was heavy and round, and after I lined up my shot, I threw it along with a prayer to the moon.

Maybe the moon was listening. The camera's eye shattered, and the red light began blinking. I wasn't sure if someone would come to investigate, but I hoped the guards might think it was just another malfunction.

"I need water." Brand's voice was strained, and fear shot through me when he leaned heavily on my arm as I led him into the room. He had always been bigger than me, taller and more well-muscled. Especially now, after months of being comatose, I should be the weaker one.

Had Elina had enough time with him to do something to him? Or was he staggering for some other reason? I helped him sit on a wide bench that sat along one wall of the bathroom, and grabbed him water, leaving the tap running, then turning on the taps to the showers and tub as well. I locked the door and flipped the fan on, then sat down next to him.

"I'm glad you're alive," Brand said after a long, uncomfortable moment, his eyes shut. He and I had never been close. The moment we'd shared at Southern when he'd stapled my gut wound closed was the most we'd spoken alone. But now....

"How is she?" I asked, rubbing my abdomen over the scar. "I can feel that she's alive. But was she hurt?"

"She was. Glen almost died."

"But they healed? They got away? Escaped into the woods—"

"No. They didn't escape." The words were slow to come, as if he didn't want to say them aloud. "They triumphed."

"How?" My heart began to race.

"The rogues came in, led by Sergeant. Her mother, as well. They had weapons in the woods, and Sergeant to lead them. Oh, and all of the remaining women of your pack, armed with sticks and kitchen knives."

Dread filled my belly. "How many of them died?" I wouldn't have been surprised if they all had. I knew how skilled Torran's men were, and how weak we'd made our women and girls. None of them would have been able to use a real weapon, not with the Alpha command still on them.

"Not as many as you'd think. The Southern shifters who were left rose up when she called them." His lips twitched. "She called upon them as future Alpha Mate. Your mate. And they obeyed." His eyes snapped open and landed on the bite mark on my neck.

"They... They won?" My mind spun. I hadn't let myself dream of that, though some of the phone conversations I'd overheard on the ride to Eastern had led me to believe things hadn't gone according to Elina's plan.

I'd seen Glen peppered by bullets. Flor fallen, her back broken. I'd clung to the knowledge that they had lived, the sensation of our bond, with only the dull, numb place where Grigor's thread had been, now lifeless.

No. Not lifeless. I took a shallow breath and realized there was a faint humming there, and a taste in the back of my mouth, like aluminum. A scent of ozone.

"Grigor's alive, too." I pressed a fist to my mouth, a surge of relief rushing through me.

"Not for long, if he's a danger to my flower." Brand's pale eyes fixed on me. "I know you sacrificed for her, even if you let her suffer for far too long. I know your life was as much a hell as hers, Luke. I'll learn to share her love with you as I have Glen. When I finish beating the shit out of him, I might even let Finn sit in the same room with my mate. But that psychotic killer? There's nothing redeemable about him."

His gaze had grown brighter as he spoke, and his face paler. A shudder ran through him, and the veins on his neck stood out for a moment. What was happening?

"What's wrong?" I grunted as he slumped against me, trying to keep him from falling to the marble floor.

"Something... arm..." he groaned. I looked down. There were three half-moon cuts on his arm, with small traces of blood there. Blood and... I leaned down and sniffed. An aroma, incredibly faint, that I didn't recognize, but which threw me back into my memories. When I'd fallen unconscious, after Flor left. When the woman—Elina—had come and tried to pry open my mind, tear loose information about my mate.

Her hand had been on his arm when I'd interrupted them in the parlor. Had she poisoned him? Or cursed him somehow? I had no idea how magic worked, but as Brand's eyes rolled back in his head, I realized I needed to find someone who did, fast.

The scent of ozone grew stronger as the bathroom door handle suddenly jiggled. "Luke?" Finnick's voice was soft, guarded. I managed to help Brand lie on the floor and opened the door.

Finnick's eyes were bloodshot, and his face almost as pale as Brand's, though he seemed steady on his feet. "What happened?" we both whispered at the same time.

"I'm not sure. Your mother cut him with her nails, I think."

"Fuck. Blood magic. It's just like he said." He rushed into the room and placed his hands on the sides of Brand's face, staring into his bleary, silver eyes. We both peered down at his arm, where the blood that kept welling in the cuts vanished before it trickled down his arm, evaporating almost. "Brand, I think my mother is siphoning energy from you somehow."

Brand mumbled an affirmative sound.

I cursed softly. "What can we do?"

"We?" Finnick cursed softly. "Nothing, most likely. But Grigor would know exactly what to do."

"Is he alive?" The thread he'd added to mine to save my life still felt... off, somehow. Like he was keeping it closed off.

When I mentioned it, Finnick almost smiled. "Yeah. He's protective of us, it turns out. He's trying not to drain us all." There was an odd note in his voice, something like wonder. He respected the wizard.

I focused on what he'd said. "Drain us. That's what your mother's doing to Brand, with his blood somehow, isn't it?"

"Grigor told me about this. He can do the same thing. He told me..." His eyes slid to mine. "He told me I should be able to do magic someday. That my mother must have been draining me from the time I was a baby, to keep me from having power. Me and Tana, too."

"Grigor gave you power?"

"A little. As much as he could, for now." There was something else he wasn't saying, something significant. Just then, his phone went off. "Yes, Mother?" Finnick snapped out the words, his whole demeanor growing icy in an instant. "Yes, he's secure. I came up to see what was going on with the electricity. The cameras... None of them are working? Ah, I see." He muttered a few more things, then hung up, agitated. "She's leaving the Mansion, going into the city. Supposedly, Tana's been spotted." I laid my hand on his back, and he let out a shuddering breath, then focused on Brand again, whispering to himself, "She'll be fine. She *has* to be. If they couldn't get her away, no one could."

I didn't ask who he meant. "Do you have any ideas for how to help Brand? After your mother leaves, can we get Grigor to help us? Or go to him?"

"No. I had to leave him down there, in the damned body bag. The cameras are out, so Mother's assigned triple guards for the entire lower levels."

"He's trapped?"

Finnick shrugged. "For now, maybe. He's gathering strength; you must have noticed. I'm supposed to come up with a plan. But I need Brand for any plan that might work."

Brand let out a low, pained groan. Finnick grabbed a towel and folded it, placing it like a cushion under his head.

"We have to stop the drain she's put on him."

"Slow it," he suggested. "If it stops, she'll know something's happened. If it slows, maybe she'll think he's just weakened."

"How—" I began, then thought. "Grigor bound us together, me and Glen and himself. He gave us access to his power, or some of it. Then Brand funneled power to Flor in the fight, and to Glen. It's what saved us all. We need someone who can do magic."

For some reason, Finnick dropped his gaze. "Maybe Brand can do something. He could have some kind of magic. His eyes..."

"Not magic. Moonblessed," Brand managed to grumble.

I bit back a curse. Brand would need to get over his aversion to magic. He was going to be co-mates with Finnick and Grigor, for fuck's sake. I sighed, trying for patience. "With the moon's blessing, then. Can you interrupt Elina's access to your power, or slow it down?"

"She did something. I can't—she's pulling as fast as I can draw from my pack." Each word was drawn forth slowly, painfully. "Don't want... Flor to be affected."

The thought of Finnick's mother growing as strong as Brand had been, of her somehow tainting Flor in the process, filled me with dread. I'd sworn to protect her, and I would. I just needed to see the way through this mess.

Closing my eyes, I focused on the bonds inside me. The triple-braided one that I could almost feel. The bright, bold connection to Flor that hummed with purpose. I could even sense the places where she was connected to the others, through the mating bites they shared.

Mating bites were blessings from the moon. I remembered the sharp taste of her blood, the salty-sweet flavor of her racing along my tongue as her soul and mine slid closer together. My wolf raced in my mind, as if guiding my human mind on a hunt for the answer.

Our blood had been mingled. Mingled for years. From the moment I threw my body over hers when she was a toddler, and I was the only one in my pack who wasn't frozen, watching our Head Enforcer try to beat her to death.

Blood, mingled blood. Maybe Elina had cut Brand, and left some of her own... I leaned down and sniffed at the cut again. It smelled of magic.

"Blood is the answer," I said, suddenly understanding. Magic. Moonblessed. They weren't the same thing, but...

maybe close enough? My wolf howled his assent. "Brand. Can I try something?" Brand didn't speak, though Finnick's focus sharpened on me. "I'm not certain this will work, but…" I explained what I suspected, told them both what I'd smelled.

Finnick leaned close and sniffed as well, his eyes going wide in shock.

"I think, if I connect with you, it will help." I swallowed, hard. "If I, uh, bite you."

"Bite me?" Brand's eyes snapped open and bored into mine. It felt like I was being judged by some wolf god. I hid my trembling hands, but returned his stare until he narrowed his gaze.

Then he shook his head as he struggled to answer. "Never."

CHAPTER 14
BROTHERLY LOVE
BRAND

Luke flinched as he hovered over me, waiting, but I'd begun to cough and couldn't finish my reply. As I struggled for breath, Finn leaned close to me as well, the two of them working to lift my head and torso off the cold marble of the bathroom floor. Luke was full of nerves. Finn was laughing his ass off.

"Give him a set of mate marks on the other side, Luke. Make it symmetrical."

Finally, I could breathe again, but Luke rushed to explain the idea he'd suggested before I could speak. "I didn't mean on his neck; it's not some kind of mating bite. Stop *laughing*, Finn!" Finn slapped a hand over his mouth, but his green eyes still shone with mirth. I almost had enough energy to give Finn the finger.

Almost.

Ignoring Finn, Luke jutted out his chin and went on. "I think if we establish a bond—a *brotherly* one—between us, it could cut off Elina's access to you. Or slow it somehow."

My voice was raspy as I asked, "How?"

Luke shrugged. "I'm not really sure how, or what'll

happen if we try. But when Flor was little, and she was being beaten, my blood and hers mingled together. I think that's what ignited our bond so early. It tied my strength to hers, and kept her from dying."

"Mates," I grunted.

"No, not back then at least. It wasn't a mate bond when we were children. That happened later."

For some reason, that set Finn off again. "Your love... could grow."

Luke blanched. Nothing about this situation was humorous, but I still found my lips turning up as I mustered the strength to finish my original reply to him, the words slurring as my tongue grew numb. "Never thought I'd take a second mate. What'll Flor think?"

Luke's concerned expression eased slightly, and he shrugged. "There's no way of ever telling what that woman'll think. She's unpredictable."

"To say the least," Finn muttered.

I could feel my strength being siphoned away, though I'd done my best to shut down the pack bonds and even Flor's, though not feeling her in my mind made my wolf rage. Luke and Flor were mates now, already bonded. If she trusted him that much, who was I to argue? Who was I to trust him less? We were mate-brothers, or brother-husbands, whatever expression Glen had come up with.

I refused to think of Grigor, and whether she would want to add him to our ranks. That was not the same. Every shifter had limits, and he was one of mine.

Luke's grip on my shoulders tightened, his hands warm through the cloth of my shirt. If he really thought this would help, I was willing to try, but not if it meant he was putting himself at risk. "Don't want... to hurt you."

His brow furrowed. "I don't think you will. I can't

explain why I think this is right. My wolf is just telling me it's the only way."

For some reason, hearing it was his wolf's idea had me relaxing. Our shifter sides were so much more intuitive, aligned with the moon's power. Smarter than us, in a lot of ways. "Do it," I whispered, turning my neck to one side. I'd hoped to make him laugh. It worked.

He snorted, then lifted my left arm to his mouth, the same one that Elina had marked. His jawline changed slightly as his canines grew, and he set his mouth to my forearm, striking right over the marks she'd left with her nails.

He froze in place, his blazing, silvery-blue eyes locked on mine. Emotions flew across his face. Fear, fury, and resolve. His mouth stained with my blood, he snarled as he bit deeper.

Lightning moved through my veins, and even though Luke had said it wasn't a mate bond, it felt similar as it began to bind us. But rather than filling me with the need to protect and love a mate, I was flooded with a wave of deep brotherhood. I could feel his own bond to Flor that mirrored mine. Could read his thoughts as they flooded my mind, and I knew he read mine as he swallowed a mouthful of my blood.

We were united in our need to protect our mate. Our packs. Our kind.

I read his soul, as the connection formed. Luke felt the responsibility to care for shifters in his marrow, and had since before he protected Flor as a child. He was strong, but not in the same way I was, or the other Heirs. His strength lay in his resilience.

He may have come from a smaller pack in Europe; he may not have been destined to stand shoulder to shoulder with the strongest shifters in North America as an Heir. But he had earned that place, by surviving the tortures at Southern. By living through and overcoming the hundreds of Alpha commands he'd been given, letting every scar become a part of his armor. By sacrificing himself for our mate when she was a tiny child, and doing it again and again ever since. He may have failed to protect Flor from all the injustices in her young life, but he and his wolf would never fail our little one again.

And he didn't fail me now. *Brother*, he breathed into our bond.

Brother, I agreed.

With that thought, I felt whatever channel the witch had opened to my well of strength narrowing, the greasy feel of her magic almost entirely stripped away and replaced with the clean scent of blood, and a sudden sharp odor of ozone.

There was still a disgusting connection there, a residual hint of her evil where she'd touched me. But mostly all I felt now was my bond to Flor, and to... Luke. Though I could also feel Glen through both of them, and Finn through Flor. And one other, coiled like a sleeping asp among them all.

"It worked?" Finn murmured. The lights that had been sputtering went out again, and I answered in the quiet.

My own silver eyes were reflected in the blue ones that stared down at me now, and we both smiled, though my heart was racing. I'd just thought of something. We had a magical bond, not a natural mating one—not in the way of wolf shifters. I had been able to speak to Flor, and her to me. I was almost afraid to try, but I knew I might need this. We might need this.

Can you hear me? I thought.

Holy shit, he replied. *I can.*

109

While Luke kneeled with his face growing paler and his jaw hanging wide, I nodded to Finn, then pushed myself away from the floor. The magical drain on my power was mostly cut off, and the outward flow grew slower by the minute. If I focused on it, I could probably close it completely, but it wasn't worth Elina discovering what we'd done. For now, I hoped she would just think she'd drained me more or less fully.

"It worked." I stood, my legs unsteady. *Shit.* Maybe she'd taken more than I'd realized.

When I staggered, and would have fallen back down if Finn hadn't caught me, I realized I may have overestimated my strength. "Come sit on my bed," he said. "The camera in my room might still have audio, but not while the power's off. You can rest there while we figure out what to do next."

He helped me through to the darkened bedroom, but I nodded toward the sofa by the far wall. "I don't need to sleep in your bed, Finn. I can lie there."

Finn's reply was bleak. "You can have my bed. I can't sleep in it anymore. Haven't since..."

I knew what he meant immediately, and knew I wouldn't touch that bed either. "Since you were unfaithful. You hurt her, Finn. How could you?"

"I had no choi—" he began, but cut himself off. "No. That's not true. I chose my sister. I chose to keep her safe, just like I'd done a hundred times before."

"Except this time, it wasn't only you that got hurt. Do you regret your choice?"

His shoulders slumped after he helped me sit on the sofa. "I regret my life, Brand. I told you before, back at Northern, that I didn't want to be tied to Flor. Hell, I told Flor twice that she wasn't my true mate, to her face. I was going to reject the bond, to save her."

Luke and I both stopped breathing at that. I hadn't known he'd gone that far.

"I couldn't go through with it, couldn't force myself to say it a third time. I was too much of a coward." He let out a shaky breath. "I knew being connected to me wouldn't be safe for her. Mother held my leash then, and still does. I'll never be free of her until she's dead."

"Well, that's not the worst way to start our plan," Luke said softly as he sat beside me. Finn found a candle and a lighter, and in a moment, the small flame was flickering, casting light on our faces. He carried it to the far wall, turned the gas fireplace on, and lit it as Luke continued. "Your mother needs to die. There's no way to keep our mate safe with her alive." Finn merely nodded. "She's obsessed with Flor. She was there, when I was suffering from mate sickness at Southern, months ago. Asking me questions, trying to force answers out of me. She did it again, on the trip here. Used her magic to force me to tell her all about Flor."

My wolf bristled inside, and only the knowledge that Flor was far away from Eastern, surrounded by friends and some of my pack, eased the upwelling of fear and rage. "What did you tell that bitch?"

Finn answered for him, but his tone was almost amused. "Everything, apparently. Starting from the first day they met. Luke here went into excruciating detail."

"I have plenty of practice keeping secrets, even when I'm being questioned under Alpha command. Her magic was even more painful, like scissors cutting at my mind. But I didn't give up anything that would help that witch get her hands on Flor."

"I believe you," I said, when he hesitated.

Luke ducked his head. "I had a lot to say about Flor's

work in the kitchens, and, ah... the way her red hair shines in the sunlight. Her eyes and her gracefulness, that sort of thing. The bitch actually nodded off at one point." He laughed quietly, remembering. "She already knew who Flor's father was, though I tried to keep that from her. She asked a few questions about Flor's mother, but I was able to change the subject and tell her about how hurt Flor was when Lily was dumped outside the gates. She doesn't know Lily's still alive."

Finn murmured, "Calvin Callaway is alive as well. They're keeping him in the lower levels, in a nice room." It was exactly as Sergeant had thought.

Luke seemed to know about his father already, since he didn't react. "I have to kill him, if Grigor hasn't already," he said softly, as if to himself. "I need to get to him somehow."

Finn sat beside him. "No one besides me will be allowed in or out of the lower levels, not while we're on lockdown. Even if we could disable the locks somehow, there are guards armed with silver blades and bullets down there."

Luke cursed. Finnick, though... Why was he smiling?

I asked, and he shrugged. "They're trapped down there with the boogeyman. He may be weak, but he's getting stronger by the hour."

"Is he strong enough to kill the guards?"

Finn shrugged again. "Maybe."

"Is he strong enough to take out your mother? Will he be?" Luke asked. Finn didn't answer.

I thought for a moment about the ancient shifter in the lower levels. Though I hated to admit it, he might be the key to taking care of Callaway, and possibly even releasing the Hilliers. We'd definitely need him on our side when it came time to face Elina. Still, I wrestled with the idea of trusting him.

If he truly was on Flor's side, on our side, he would want to keep her safe. And he'd shown exactly how far he'd go to get revenge on her enemies. I wouldn't mind seeing Callaway's entrails twisted up like roses.

But it felt beyond foolish to have faith in such a creature. He was just as dangerous as Elina, or more so.

Luke spoke quietly to Finn. "If we can't sneak the Hilliers out, and I can't get down there to kill Callaway, what do we do?"

"We wait."

"Until when?"

Finn's eyes met mine, and I could see my silver-white orbs reflected in his green ones. He straightened, whispering, "The full moon. That's all we need, all of us."

My wolf lifted its ears, curious. Finn was an exceptional strategist. "What do you mean?"

"Father wants to force you to pledge to him, then have an emergency Council meeting to take down Bradley before there are witnesses to his political maneuvers. So I'll make sure those things can't happen."

"How?"

Finn arched an eyebrow at me, then went to his bedside table and withdrew something small from a narrow, almost hidden drawer. Plugging it into the bottom of his phone, he began typing. "I'll use the technology your pack dislikes so much to give Father a financial crisis that will take his mind off what's going on inside his own house." He mumbled about backdoors and weak SEC regulations, his fingers never stopping for a long moment. Finally, he stopped and smiled grimly at the device. "That should keep any emergency meetings off the table. Father will start calling within the next few minutes, once our stock starts crashing. Or the bank calls him, whichever comes first. You two will stay here, and gather your strength. I'll need both of you to be able to fight at my side when the moon is full."

"At the Council meeting?" His eyes flashed as he nodded, and I could tell he had a plan. "Fight who?"

His smile was sharp. "Anyone can challenge under the full moon. Luke will fight Callaway. I'll fight Bradley."

Bradley? "You're going to fight another fake challenge?" I asked, remembering his epic blunder when he'd ended up fighting and losing to our little mate in the ring at Southern. "You'd have to kill Bradley to get him to give up his pack to you."

Finn narrowed his eyes. "Not necessarily. You didn't kill your dad."

I hummed. Maybe he was right. But pulling that same trick again seemed unlikely, especially surrounded by enemies. It had taken power from all of us—even the serial killer—to accomplish it at Mountain. "What about Aidan?"

"Once Luke and I are Alphas, any one of us can challenge him as Council Head."

"That's not legal—" Luke began.

I let out a low whistle. "It is, though. The old ways allow for any Alpha to be challenged, and the power he holds transferred, under the moon, before witnesses. Just because the Council always transferred power by vote doesn't mean it's the only way it can be done. Or should be done."

Finn explained, "The Council Head position is a manufactured title, but by law it's an Alpha position, one that can only be held by strength or consensus. Aidan challenged Bradley once for the spot before, years ago, and was voted down. If he had challenged under a full moon, by strength—"

"The way any shifter should gain power," I interrupted.

"—then Bradley would have killed your father, and

none of this would be happening," Luke finished softly. "The new ways really have gotten us into a shitload of trouble."

"We'll fix that," I promised.

Finn nodded. "The only caveat is that only a reigning Alpha can put himself forward to take the Council Head. One of us will need to challenge my father as soon as we become Alpha."

"Or I could challenge him before either of you step into the ring," I reminded them.

"You could, but..." Finn's gaze dropped to my hand, to the fingers trembling on the arm of the sofa.

Shit. "Right." There were a lot of things that could go wrong, but it was a decent plan. With the smaller packs assembled, Aidan would be forced to abide by the law. He would have to fight. "If I'm strong enough, I'll fight Aidan," I murmured.

Finn sighed. "You'll have a bigger battle on your hands first." I blinked, not understanding. "You're going to need to fight your instincts, in the lower levels."

I knew I wasn't going to like this.

Finn turned away. "Luke, you'll stay here. Brand, I'm going to lock you in a cell when Father calls me into the city to help—" As he spoke, a light on his phone started blinking. "That was fast."

Luke and I blinked at each other as Finn took the call, his father's voice strident on the other end. For some reason, Finn headed to the bathroom and returned with a roll of some sort of silver tape, pressing it into my shaky grip. It smelled odd, but not like real silver.

"I'll make sure he's taken care of. Where's Mother... Really? All right, I'll be there in twenty," he said to his father, then put his phone in his pocket. "Perfect. Mother is on her way upstate to meet with what's left of Ivan's 'rogues.' I have to take a car to meet Father."

"You'll be okay?" I asked as Luke helped me stand. I didn't need the help, but having him beside me made me feel so much stronger, like our bond amplified my strength with every small contact.

"Absolutely. I'll keep him busy for the next couple of days. Then, the moon will be on our side."

"What if your mother returns, and tries to reestablish her hold on me?" I didn't want to admit how much that thought frightened me. "Or Luke?"

Finn sighed. "Luke isn't a threat to her. He's worth more as an Alpha she thinks she'll control. He'll be safe."

Luke cursed. "But Brand won't be, if he's trapped in a cell!"

Finn grimaced slightly. "I'm pretty sure the cell I'm going to put him in is the safest place in the Mansion."

Aw, hell. "Don't tell me—"

Finn cut me off. "We don't have time for this, Brand. The only one who can fight my mother and win is Grigor Dimitrivich. And it's time you two met, for Flor's sake. He is hers as much as I am. There's no other way." His voice rang with truth.

There was no way around it. I was going to have to meet the asshole.

CHAPTER 15
CLOSE CALLS
FLOR

The air was colder in New York, and I could see the puffs of my breath as I stared through a pair of borrowed binoculars across a heavily wooded valley. A few housetops poked out of the fall foliage, chimneys releasing their smoke into the early morning light to the north, but I had my eyes trained on the gleaming silver roofline in the distance. It was still ten miles away, down one hillside, and on the far side of the wide valley, or so the maps indicated. We'd hopped out of the Mountain pack van a few miles back and jogged just inside the tree line up a narrow, winding road until the Mansion had come into view.

"I can feel him," Mama said, her voice cracking as she stared ahead. "He's there." She stood beside me, glaring toward the east. She had one hand pressed over her wounded abdomen, and the other clutched around an old short sword she'd brought from the cave at Southern. Sergeant's face had gone pale when he'd seen it, and I had a feeling it was significant—maybe to our family—but hadn't asked. I'd been too busy trying to convince half of the Mountain pack, all of Southern, and the Tenebris boys from jumping in their own trucks, cars, and vans and coming to Eastern as well. I'd only been partly successful.

I peered over my shoulder at Sergeant, who sat with the entire Tenebris pack, all of them in wolf form now, except for Leroy and Bo, who couldn't shift yet. Leroy waved when he noticed me looking at him. Bo just blushed.

"Bringing them was a mistake," I muttered. Sergeant had insisted on coming with me and Mama, and the Tenebris pack was too new to be without their Alpha—and loved my mama too much to let her go without them.

"I'm not about to watch my last living family walk into the jaws of death without me there," Sergeant had stated the afternoon before, when I'd argued we needed a faster, smaller, quieter group, since we didn't know if they had drones or cameras that watched this far out.

My "plan," if you could call it one, had required Mama to be there. I'd welcomed Sergeant as backup, once he'd scolded me that magical traps existed. "Elina is a witch, and while she's kept it under wraps for decades, she may use that power a little more overtly at home. I can still sense magic, even if I can't use much. Lily can keep you hidden. My Tenebris boys will stay back and wait. You may end up going in alone, but all you have to do is howl and we'll come running."

I wasn't confident that they could stay hidden. A pack of two dozen wolves would be impossible to miss. In the van, Bo and Leroy alone had made more noise than a flock of turkeys until Glen took steps.

"At least they're quiet now," Glen whispered from behind my other shoulder. "I wasn't sure what you wanted the duct tape for, but you're right. It did come in handy."

He'd slapped a long piece over Leroy's mouth in the van

an hour before. He'd finally snapped when Leroy had asked for the fiftieth time if we were there yet. Bo had asked for his own piece of tape, "Just in case I start asking stupid questions, too." It had made everyone else in the van—even Mama—smile.

It had been the last time any of us smiled. My bond with Brand had gone flat on that ride, as if it were being pinched off. There had been a moment of pain and sheer panic, before it had cut off. It was a familiar sensation, one of my mates clamping down on the bond to keep me safe. I hated it. Grigor's bond was still numb, Finnick's was frail, and now Brand... I could feel him growing weaker, fast. I wasn't sure what was going on, but at least I knew he was still alive.

And he was with Finnick, Luke, and maybe even Grigor. It would have to be enough until I could get there.

Shifting the backpack with my supplies on my shoulder, I turned to Sergeant. He was a massive, grizzled wolf, with silvered markings on his dark gray fur, but his eyes were the same, sharp and watchful. I nodded at him, then took off at a slow jog, Mama and Glen right behind me. The three of us were dressed in brown camouflage clothing the Mountain crew had arrived with, and we'd already rubbed leaves and pine needles all over our bodies and clothes to hide our scents as much as we could. Mama had done some small thing with her magic as well, or at least she'd tried. She had gone around and touched all of the boys on the face, going pale by the time she got to Sergeant. He'd refused to let her touch him, and muttered something about her giving too much, too soon.

We heard the drone before we saw it, the tinny buzzing alerting us to its presence, though we were staying under the canopy. Mama crept away, or at least I thought she did.

She'd obviously used a look-away spell, since only I was aware of her silver hair vanishing behind a patch of thick-leaved bushes.

Glen and I waited until the drone was gone, walked until we could see the fence in the distance, then climbed a maple to get a better look. The fence was tall, a black-painted steel barrier of two-inch-wide bars, topped with gleaming silver razor wire that stretched out on both sides as far as we could see.

The camera on this side of the compound was supposed to be in a massive pine, and Glen pointed it out silently. It was only seventy-five feet or so ahead of us, and to the right. We climbed down and made our way silently to another tree, going up to get a better vantage point. I pulled a slingshot out of my backpack, tucked a stone into the pouch, and aimed at the camera. The sound of the rock hitting the metal casing was louder than I liked, and it didn't do any good.

Sturdy fucker.

I motioned for Glen to stay put, then slipped down our tree and made my way to the back side of the huge pine and shimmied up, my nails extending slightly as I had to dig them into the trunk for a grip. I almost grinned. My wolf was so close to the surface, now that I was mated to four of my five guys. Well, mostly mated. I pushed the thought of the conversation I would need to have with Finnick to the back of my mind, focusing on the camera.

A small piece of duct tape over the sensor would be the easiest way to shut it down, but we'd wanted to make it seem like an animal or something natural had caused it to stop working. I laughed when I noticed a large glob of bird shit on a nearby branch. I used a small bunch of pine needles to smear the bird poop over the lens, making sure it covered the whole thing. Glen let out a short chirping sound, and I descended the pine as fast as I could without making noise, then rejoined him in the maple.

I was glad the red leaves matched my hair almost perfectly, as a drone zipped out from the fence line, followed less than a minute later by an Enforcer in a black uniform. He pulled out a phone, snapped a quick picture of the camera, then climbed the tree and cleaned the lens. In less than a minute, both the drone and the Enforcer were gone.

"Shit," I whispered.

Movement below caught my eye. Mama stood there, a scowl on her face, one hand raised. She muttered something and waved one hand at the camera, and instantly, a small plume of black smoke rose from the device. She stared up at me and Glen. "Stop messing around, you two. We need to move."

I cringed, following Glen to the ground. "Why didn't you tell me you could do that?" I whispered when I stood next to her.

"Same reason Del let you fall on your ass a thousand times. How else are you gonna learn?"

Glen was stifling a laugh. I shot him the finger, then followed Mama. She led us straight to the gate, but we only had a few seconds to duck behind a holly bush as another drone shot past, going back to the broken camera.

The gate opened thirty seconds later, and two Enforcers came running back out, sniffing the air.

Now, Mama mouthed. She took my hand, and I took Glen's, and we crept back around the tree and into the open. We were completely exposed, and I had a feeling my hair was a red candle in the morning sunlight. But no one came after us or called out.

I knew she'd done another look-away, a bigger one. Sweat beaded on her upper lip, even in the chilly morning air, and her hand trembled in mine as she muttered soundlessly the whole time we moved. Hand in hand, we walked straight to the open gate, and right through just as it began to automatically close. The two Enforcers who stood on either side of the gate didn't even glance in our direction.

But the scent of blood from Mama's wound got stronger as we moved, and her hand in mine shook like she was holding a live wire. "Help," she whispered to Glen. He scooped her up with his free arm, and I held onto him as we ran across the clearing, toward the Mansion.

Glen knew where to go, and even though we didn't see any more drones inside the fence, the grounds were teeming with Enforcers. Without Mama, we would never have had a chance. Finally, he slid to a stop beside a noisy air conditioning unit on the back side of what I thought was the garage building. I checked for cameras, but there were none. I could hear people in the distance, but there were no windows facing out by the industrial-sized AC boxes, and the closest door was the one that led in through the garage. The servant's entrance, according to Glen.

"Drop the look-away, Mama," I breathed. "Take a break."

I knew when she did, since the sounds around us got a little bit louder, the air colder, and... my mates figured out I was close. My bonds started going wild, filling me with alarm and fear. I couldn't hear their voices, but I could feel Luke, Finnick, and Brand going nuts inside the Mansion.

I reached for Grigor in my mind, but there was... *Wait.* Something twitched, in the place that had gone numb. The final not-quite-a-bond sputtered like a damp branch catching fire at last. Then it went out.

122

My wolf whined. I tried not to do the same thing out loud.

My skin itched, like it wanted nothing more than to turn to fur, attack, and run into the Mansion. My mates were inside, too weak to escape. I was strong, but I couldn't take on a whole pack house, not even if the witch was gone for now.

I was good at waiting. I'd had to sit in treetops until I nearly froze, waiting for hunting males to give up looking for me. I'd had to wait years to escape Southern. But the idea of letting my mates sit in a prison cell for even an hour longer made my stomach churn. Time was running out; I could feel it.

Glen whispered, "What's wrong, Flor?"

"We need to go. Now. Grigor needs me," I replied as he gathered me in his arms. I let myself feel his love for a moment, then turned to Mama. "Mama, will you—," I began, but I was talking to thin air.

She was gone.

CHAPTER 16
CELLMATES
GRIGOR

I lay quiet in the thick cloth bag Finnick had left me in, harvesting power as quickly as I could, and sleeping. The need to sleep surprised me. As I'd grown older, I'd needed less and less rest, drawing power from the night around me. But here, in this room, the only source of power I could access was the current that flowed through the walls. Soon, I hoped, I would be strong enough to reach for my queen and not harm her. I ached for the touch of her mind, for the fresh, clean sensation of her spirit.

I did not let myself think of the touch of her hands, her lips, though my own burned with remembered fire.

Drawing power from the current in the walls alone was time-consuming and tiring, and I'd been forced to use some of my reserves to remove the final slivers of silver from my body. If only a guard would approach the cell, and linger for just one moment too long nearby...

As if I'd summoned him, a guard did just that. *No,* two *guards,* I thought, as the door swung open and I listened to males speaking. Two guards, and two others...

"You should have given my father your pledge when he

gave you the opportunity, Becker," Finnick said, his voice loud enough to hear clearly even through the cloth bag. "Maybe you just needed some time to consider it?"

"Fuck off, Finnick." Brand's reply was a deep growl.

Finnick laughed bitterly. "I'll fuck off then, and leave you to think. When Father gets back, you'll have another chance."

"If he's alive," an unfamiliar voice broke in.

"What do you mean?"

"I'd swear that's not where we left Dimitrivich, Alpha Heir. The bag, I mean. And... there's blood on the floor, and the silver—"

Finnick cut him off. "Then that will be an inducement, won't it? I wonder... who would win in a fight? The Alpha of Mountain, or the broken boogeyman? Maybe we'll find out."

"Alpha Heir, the cameras down here. They're still not working. We won't be able to tell if—" The door shut with a loud bang, and the rest of what the guard was saying was lost. The room was silent except for the sound of my breathing, and Brand's. The silence stretched for a few minutes, until an aggrieved sigh split the quiet.

"Right, get out of that thing then and let's see what state you're in." Rough hands moved the bag, and light entered the opening at my head as he widened the sack with his hands. I slid free and propped myself on the wall, glad to know that I had enough energy to move even that much. Even if this one was on Flor's side, my wolf didn't want to show any more weakness than necessary.

"So, we meet at last—" I began, but when my gaze rose to meet his, I was stunned into silence. Silver orbs shone on me, into me, it seemed. I'd heard of his moonblessed eyes, but seeing them was a different matter. Power practically flowed from them. No, it *did*. A clean trickle of energy lit up my face, sharp and cold as a mountain stream in early spring, and flowed across my skin and into it, giving my magic enough of a boost to heal some small cuts along my cheekbone.

"By the moon, you're a mess," he grunted, lowering himself to sit cross-legged in front of me while I stared. He had silver manacles on his wrists—not handcuffs, but the type of devices I'd seen used on feral Alphas twice before, and on more than one bear shifter when they still existed. His dark eyes were red-rimmed, the skin beneath them almost purple with exhaustion. I knew the silver restraints must be hurting him, but before I could even consider if I had enough power to offer my assistance, he reached into his sleeve and withdrew a small roll of foil. With quick, deft movements, he unrolled it. Carefully, he placed the tape along the inside of the cuffs, until the silver no longer came in contact with his skin.

"What magic is that?"

"The magic of technology," he grunted as he relaxed, those moon-bright eyes spearing me. Judging me. We sat for a long moment like that, the electricity in the wall at my back humming in my mind as I harvested it, his gaze growing brighter and brighter, until the room didn't need any other light.

I was transfixed. But, as the minutes piled up, wisps of an unusual feeling began to dance through my mind. It wasn't shame, not precisely. It reminded me of how I'd felt as a young boy, when my mother had tried to teach me a simple spell, and I'd overshot, destroying a favorite clay pitcher in the kitchen. As if I had disappointed a teacher, and needed a chance to try again. To do better.

The feeling grew until, to my surprise and his, I dropped my gaze.

He breathed what might have been a curse. I swallowed and stared at my filthy, blood-speckled bare feet, shocked at my instinctive response. I'd stared down stronger shifters than this one, but something about meeting his gaze felt like committing some unknown sacrilege.

As if the Moon Goddess was there, just behind his eyes, telling me in my mother's voice to try again. To be careful with my power.

"Tell me why I should let you live," Brand said at last. When I didn't speak, he went on. "Explain to me why I should let you be in Flor's world, in *any* way. Give me a reason to... accept you. Help me understand how a creature like you could deserve her."

"I don't," I said truthfully, my voice raw. "I don't deserve her. None of us do. I cannot undo my past. All I can tell you is that I will never harm her. If she chooses not to accept me, I will never touch her, only watch from the shadows and protect her."

After another long moment, he spoke again. "The histories say you killed your first wife. How can I be certain you've changed?"

Rage was a source of power as well, and for a split second, I met his eyes, my own probably glowing as red as his were silver-white. "I *never* hurt Anya. I could never have. She was the mate to the half of my soul that came from my mother. My witch mate." When he didn't ask what I meant, I wondered if he'd heard of that before.

"When I met Anya, when she marked me, my magic expanded so fast, my soul felt as if it might burst at the seams. Perhaps a crack did form then. My wolf... separated himself from me. He spoke to me, as if we were not one soul." Brand blinked slowly, but stayed silent. "I'm not certain if I was born that way, or if my soul's connection with an incredibly powerful witch caused it. But something inside me broke."

I'd never imagined such a thing was possible, that a hybrid like me might have two mates, one for each half of their magic. It had never happened before, or again, from what I'd learned over the centuries. I wouldn't have believed it was my fate... until I'd lost Anya, and stayed alive. Until my wolf had kept me that way, insisting that his mate would come to us, someday, if we waited.

"My father murdered her to punish me. I slaughtered him, and all the corrupt males of his pack, to avenge her."

Finally, he spoke. "And then killed ten thousand more shifters, for what? More revenge?"

I closed my eyes, taking a shaky, deep breath. "You don't understand. The pack structure there was as rotten as the packs on this continent were fast becoming, before Flor came into the world. Magic was used to kill and maim. Other forms of shifters were driven mad through curses and spells, until they had to be put down. Alphas gained a taste for power instead of protecting their vulnerable, and fancied themselves kings. I reminded them they were only mortal." I pressed a hand to my chest, tempted to open my illicit bond with Flor, just to remind my wolf his mate—*our* mate—was alive and well. "I may not have only killed the wicked... I was too far gone to the madness of grief to be certain every creature I killed was fully corrupt. But I never intentionally killed a child. I never knowingly killed a shifter female."

The silence returned, heavier this time. But not as heavy as the large hand that landed on my arm, his grip firm and unyielding, yet not punishing. Not yet.

"You'll need to help me kill one here," Brand said.

I nodded, gratitude flooding me. "With pleasure."

He moved to the wall, keeping the silver manacles away from my exposed skin. "Reach into my pocket. Finn left some sort of energy bars there." He lifted his arms, and I did as he instructed, then unwrapped the first of three narrow bars. It tasted of chalk, sugar, and chemicals, but I ate it with gratitude. I offered him the next, but he shook his head. "I choked down as many as I could before he brought me here." As I ate, he brought me up to speed on what was happening in the house above, and with Flor.

"She said something about coming here before we got cut off on the phone," he growled. "But my friend Dean is bringing the Mountain troops to Southern, and that should give us at least a couple more days. We need to keep Flor clear of this place, and the witch Elina, until the battle is over."

I almost choked on the energy bar. When I could speak, I had a hard time hiding my amusement. "Have you met our queen? I half-expected her to tear a hole in the wall here, or tunnel through the floor, any second. She is a wonder."

He pushed up his sleeve and rubbed at his arm, and I froze as he went on. "You don't need to tell me that. The only thing keeping me from losing my shit entirely is knowing the witch is away for now. I just need to get a little stronger."

"You won't, though, not with her mark on you. May I see it?" He grumbled, but rolled up his sleeve and let me lift the arm to my nose, though it took all of my strength to do so. "She's still draining you, but Luke did well to offer to mate bond you. I had no idea such a thing would work."

"It's not a fucking mate bond!" he half-roared, then

stopped as he saw my smile. "I didn't expect an ancient, evil serial killer to have a sense of humor," he grumbled as he settled. "You and Glen will get along like a house on fire."

"Glen and I get along very well, though he prefers to think of me as Joaquin. I think it makes him feel safer."

We both chuckled at that, and then we spoke, haltingly at first, of the one we both adored. Flor.

He shared the story of her introduction to the Mountain pack. I shared how I'd been drawn to the continent when she was kindled in her mother's womb. He spoke of his lake, and how she loved it. I shared stories of Anya and our son, finding myself able to speak of them for the first time without pain.

"Finnick is my descendant, you know. Elina is some great-great-granddaughter."

He wasn't surprised. "No one gets to pick their family," he said. We both glanced at each other, knowing that wasn't entirely true. Hours passed, and we grew closer in the way that prisoners must. I slept a bit more, then he did.

"Her scar," Brand said simply when I woke, the electricity humming in my veins now. "What do you know about it?"

"I believe pieces of her soul were set loose the day it was made, marking her for the ones she was destined to find."

"You mean the one. Only one of us was meant to be her mate. Was it you?"

"Does it matter?" I was truly curious. He appeared to be as steadfast and unmoving in his affections as the mountains he called home. Would learning that he wasn't her moon-destined mate alter that love? If it were even true. There was no way to know which of us would have—in another, more peaceful world—been her only bonded mate.

"Not to me. But if knowing would make any difference in protecting her, if it was witchcraft that caused it..."

"It had to be," I mused aloud after a long moment. "I had thought perhaps a moon blessing, like your eyes. But when I saw the scar, after her fight at Southern, I knew it came from a darker root."

He waited patiently, and I considered how much to share about my conjecture. *All of it*, I decided. He might need the whole story, especially if things went the way I feared they might. I would not be here to tell it to her myself.

"I told you that my soul was broken, somehow. Split into two halves." He nodded. "I believe Flor's soul was split as well."

"Her scar has five points."

"Five arrows to find her mates," I agreed. "Five mates to help her change the world. Flor's and her mother's magical legacies were far too powerful for one witch, even a strong one, to overcome." I almost smiled, my next thought amusing me more than it should. "I believe Flor drank down the witch's power, fed on it while she was still unborn, and that it became that part of her that fights so brilliantly. She used it to fight to hold her soul together in the womb. To stay alive in her wretched pack as a child. To bind Luke to her, when she needed her first protector, and the rest of us when she found us. We make her stronger. She makes us whole."

His brows furrowed. "Do you believe she will die if one of us does?"

"As true mates do?" I shrugged. "I should have died when Anya did. Instead, her death gave me the strength to do unspeakable acts. The strength to stay alive, to wait for Flor."

"That doesn't make sense. She wasn't born yet."

"I know. Hybrids like me can live many years past the normal span, though I am the oldest I've heard of." I shifted under his assessing gaze. I had wondered if the sheer number of lives I'd taken, all the blood I'd spilled, had turned the moon against me. Made me unwelcome to ever run with the eternal pack, for my crimes. I hadn't understood exactly why I was so long-lived, but I'd felt certain it was not a gift. "I thought my long life was a curse, until I felt her soul descend to the earth."

The waiting had been a terrible penance, a fitting punishment. Only the moon's monthly promise, as she waned to nothing, like my sanity and my soul, then grew full again, kept any hope alive of finding her.

"I did what I could to make the world safer for her, when she came," I whispered. "Searching for her, I sensed her arrival. And then, days later, I felt her spirit break apart, and go still."

"You thought she was dead?"

"No. I was frantic, hunting for her. I scented her blood on the wind, years later. When our brave young Luke saved her."

"Our Luke?"

"He's as much a part of my soul as Finnick, or Glen. I'm not certain they have any cause to rejoice at the connection with me, but I know precisely how little I deserve to be called their brother. I do not regret giving my power to them." I glanced at him. "Or to you, when you had need." Brand grumbled a thanks, and I went on. "The scar on Flor's chest was formed in the womb; I am certain of that. A witch—perhaps Elina, more likely her coven leader —used a spell to break a mate bond on the mother."

"Lily."

"Yes. And when the witch discovered there were two souls standing against her... I assume she died. But not before Flor was injured."

"She could have died then."

"Could she have?" I met his eyes, and recognized the moon's power in them again. "I believe the moon has Her ways. I believe our little queen was tethered to this world with the five points of that star, with the same magic I see in your face now. And I hope that the moon's guiding all of our steps. Even those of us who live in the darkness." I exhaled slowly. "It doesn't matter who her intended mates were. She may have been destined to have one, or even two. We should just thank the moon that she was born requiring five."

Brand opened his mouth to say something, but a sound in the hallway had us quieting. Boots moved down the hallway, though no one entered.

"The full moon is tomorrow night," I mused quietly. "I don't have enough power yet to face Elina on my own."

Brand hesitated, then offered, "I will fight beside you, if you teach me how to face a witch."

I shook my head immediately. "She has a connection to you through that mark, which exposes our little queen to danger as well. I am the only one unbound. The only one who can be sacrificed if need be."

"She won't like that," he muttered. "For some reason, Flor wants you to be... hers." He wrinkled his nose and for a moment, looked like a small boy taking a bite of some bitter vegetable. I stifled yet another smile. What was it about my queen's mates that made my pitch-black spirit feel so much brighter?

"I cannot teach you how to face a witch. But I can face her for you, for Flor. For my little brothers." I sighed. "If I had the strength. I can hardly sit upright."

"Blood, Finn said. You can feed from the moon, pain, and blood."

"And electricity, among other things. There isn't enough power in these walls, I'm afraid, and pulling it out is tiring." Before he could offer, I hurried on. "And I won't take your blood, Brand. You'll need your strength as well."

He took a breath as if he was going to speak, then let it out and looked to one side, rubbing his brow. "I can't," he murmured. "I can't do it." He slumped down on the floor, and I let my own weight fall on the wall, both of us lost in our thoughts. Not a moment later, though, we both sat up straight, as if we'd been shocked, or stabbed.

His white eyes met mine in horror. "She's here."

CHAPTER 17
AN UNEXPECTED BOND
BRAND

The quiet hours of the long day I'd spent learning about Grigor vanished in a second of panic. She was *here*, the last place I ever wanted my wildflower to be discovered.

And she would be, I had no doubt. The Eastern Mansion was still on lockdown, and that meant dozens of armed Enforcers on alert both inside and out. Aidan might be an evil Alpha, but he was a thorough, paranoid one, and his shifters were well trained.

I'd been keeping my bond with Flor closed down to make certain Elina's slight drain didn't affect her, so I hadn't dared to reach for her with my mind and read her thoughts. The only way I would be able to sense her would be if she were so close...

"She's touching an exterior wall. Sleeping, I think. Her mind is quiet." Grigor had risen to standing and had a hand pressed as close to the air circulation holes as he could reach. He had his eyes closed and moved his fingers in a small circle on the concrete, like he was picking a lock. "She's no more than a few hundred feet away."

"Why the hell is she *here?*" My wolf was enraged that we couldn't get out of the cell to rush to Flor's side. I was horrified. But as he lowered himself calmly to the floor again, Grigor didn't appear concerned.

When he lifted his head, I realized I'd been wrong. He was shaken to the core, his eyes filled with fiery sparks. "She's here to save us. We don't have time to gather our strength. When she wakes, she'll come inside. She may be waiting for nighttime." He glanced at the door as if considering going to open it, then raised his hands, which were trembling with weakness.

"Pain," I gritted out. "You can feed on pain. How?"

He blinked at me, his jaw dropping open. "If you think for one second that I'll harm you," he began, but I'd already let a claw shift, and ran it down my right arm, holding it up.

"How much pain do you need?" I demanded. I had silver on, and I twisted so it burned my wrists. The silver hissed and spat as my blood dripped down onto it. "We have to get out, *now.*"

"Stop!" He cursed in some languages I didn't know, including one that made the hairs on the back of my neck stand up, then held out his hand. I gave him my arm, but instead of licking the blood—or however something like him fed—he pressed his fingers over the wound. A warm flush permeated the skin, and when he dropped his hand, I was healed. And he was even weaker.

Well, shit. "Don't you want to go to her? Do you even love her?"

"Do you? I would burn the earth to a cinder for her."

"I would light the match," I agreed. "So, how much pain?"

He grumbled something in Russian that had to be an

insult from the tone. "There's a better way to gain strength. We combine it. The bond creates its own power."

"Bond. Like you did with Luke and Glen?"

"Too weak. Too... indirect," he rasped. His teeth had lengthened slightly as he spoke, the canines extending over his lower lip.

I groaned, understanding instantly. "Promise me two things," I said, holding my arm up to him again. He tilted his head, the dark hair falling over one of his creepy red and black eyes.

"What?"

"Promise me that you'll never kill another innocent. Not one. No going mad and burning down villages."

He gave a quick nod. "I'll allow you to kill me first."

I kneeled at his side and growled my final request. "And swear to the moon you'll never call this thing a mating bite."

When he set his teeth to my arm and bit down, it sounded like he might be choking back laughter. I almost choked from the feeling of power that rushed through me.

The first wave smelled odd, leaving a taste of ozone on my tongue, and the sharp bite of lightning in the air. *The electricity*, he said in my mind. I flinched, not ready for the intrusion.

I was really not ready for what came next. An intense surge of dark power entered my arm and climbed up my chest. It barreled into my own Alpha power and slid around it, wrapping itself like a steel vine around the nearly empty well of my own power, then squeezing. Luke's bond within me flared to life, alarm racing from where he'd bitten me. Flor's bond sparked next, and I felt Glen and Finn as well, in the distance. Worried, fearful. I had no time to send reassurance back.

Grigor's grasp on my arm tightened to the point of pain as he dug his sharp teeth deeper. I could feel some of my strength moving into him, and his sliding into the spaces left behind. The two energies were as different as night and day, and the places where they met felt uncomfortable, as if small thorns were embedding themselves into my soul. Thorns that bore traces of her. My wildflower.

His magic leaned on mine, asking for entrance, showing the only key that could ever convince me to bind myself to him.

For her, it whispered in an icy voice.

For her alone, my wolf agreed.

There was a distant sound in my thoughts, like ice breaking, a soft, ominous crackling, and the resistance I had to him dissolved.

When I'd bonded with Luke, I'd felt the others there, though Grigor's power had been negligible. I knew now he'd been allowing only the barest thread of his connection to remain, to protect the others. For a terrifying moment, his hunger, a ravenous beast of its own, reached into my soul, swallowing everything—the pack bonds, the Heirs' braided connections—before it came to the place where Flor's spirit was entwined with mine, the base of our love.

I smelled her in the cell, her jasmine and cinnamon filling the space. I felt her small hands on my arm for a moment. I heard her call out. *Bearman?*

Grigor tore his mouth away from my arm. "My queen," he rasped. And the vortex reversed, his power rushing back into me, mingling with mine. There was more, far more of it than there should be, considering how weak we had both been.

I held him up now, feeling a blaze of heat, as if I stood

too close to the white-hot center of a constellation. Behind my eyelids, I could see it: her scar, with its five arms, but each one ended in a star. Three of the five points glowed hotter than the rest. Mine, Glen's, and Luke's. Finnick's was frail, and Grigor's was a strange texture—a shadowed tendril connecting him, rather than the bright mating bond the others shared.

Then there was our center: Flor. As I thought of her, her power met mine, and flowed into me, filling me with her feminine, wild energy. The combined power from all six of us swelled even higher, as if it were trying to reach some unknowable peak.

Grigor grunted with exhaustion in my arms. I took almost all of his weight, as my arm burned where Elina had marked me. "Let it," he rasped.

"I can't." I had to disconnect myself from the others. I didn't know how.

But Grigor did. Twisting in my grip, he mustered the energy to fling himself away from me. The instant he did, the connection with Elina sputtered to life, a splinter of her power present in my veins. A pulse of energy shot down my arm and shut her off completely. From my wolf, or Flor, or the remaining connection with Luke? I didn't know.

My arm flared with heat, all my limbs humming like I was on some strange drug. "Fuck," I muttered. "Too much power." I'd only meant to shut it back most of the way, but I'd inadvertently done far more than that. I felt invigorated.

Grigor, on the other hand, had fallen into a heap. He was trying to rise, but couldn't.

"What's wrong?" I asked, approaching him. He held up one shaking hand, warning me away, as he tried to catch his breath. *Is he...* "Are you *laughing?*"

"Yes, though there is nothing amusing about this," he eventually said, as he rolled over onto his back, staring up at the ceiling. "Except one thing, I suppose. My father dreamed of this sort of power."

"You're too weak to stand," I said slowly, wondering if he'd fried his brain.

"Yes, for now. But I can feel the potential. Once I've bonded with our queen, with all the bonds between us complete... it shouldn't be possible. It's dangerous." He went quiet. "No one can know. Together, if we make it—"

I shushed him. "She's waking up." I listened to her thoughts, the fear of her being discovered warring with the thrill of hearing her in my head. I was glad she didn't seem to mind my presence there, and sent a small surge of worry and love down the bond.

Don't distract me, she thought. *I'm in the kitchen. Mama's here. We're coming to get you—oh, shit.*

Her thoughts became a jumble. She was carrying something; there was a strong scent of blood that was disturbing her wolf. Her *wolf*. For the first time since I'd taken on my position as Alpha, I could sense her wolf side clearly. My little flower was growing much stronger.

Her wolf was more cautious than Flor, and even more vicious. I approved of her quiet, cunning thoughts, keeping footsteps quiet, staying close to shadows.

"She's coming down with her mother, and someone else. A maid," I said out loud. "Someone is bleeding... or there's bloody food? I don't know."

Grigor managed to stand and move to the door, placing his hand on it. "There are guards in the hall."

I joined him. "Are you strong enough to help me break out now?"

"Give me a few minutes, and I'll see if I can get through

the lock." One dark eyebrow rose as he looked up at me. "The guards aren't innocents, right?"

Blood, pain, and fear. I assumed two Eastern Enforcers would provide enough of all three to help the little psycho power up. "Right."

CHAPTER 18
GONE ROGUE
FLOR

Glen's fear and worry prickled in our bond, and I tried to control my own. This was bad, but not a disaster. Mama had gotten impatient and gone rogue, slipping away using her magic. She knew exactly where to go to get inside, and had helped me with the plan.

"She's gone to the garage," I breathed to Glen. "I have to follow her."

His eyes went wide, and he grabbed my arm. "It's not safe. You don't have magic to cover you."

"I know. But I'm sneaky." I pressed a kiss to his hand, then broke away, adjusted my backpack, and checked that my steak knife was secure on my belt. "You coming with me, or...?"

A voice that was definitely not Glen's answered from a distance. "Hey, look over there!"

"Shit," I whispered. "They've spotted us."

Glen's features hardened as he made a decision. "I'll lead them away. You get inside." Glen pressed a quick, desperate kiss to my hairline and stood. Then he sprinted away, ducking around the corner in a second.

I didn't hesitate, knowing the guards would come to inspect the area for others. Staying as low as I could, I snuck along the last few feet of the pale gray stone garage extension, then slipped around the corner and through the door that Mama must have left slightly open. Closing it, I silently slid the old-fashioned deadbolt lock just in time for someone to jiggle the handle from outside.

My breathing was loud in the cold space. I'd never seen a garage like this one, not even at Northern. It was a long room, with gleaming concrete floors, but instead of furniture, it had cars that all had mirror polishes, and shiny tires that must never have gone down a dirt road.

There was no one inside, as far as I could tell, only my breath making a sound as I tiptoed past a silver sports car. The air warmed slightly as I moved toward the far end, where a half-open door let a faint cloud of steam escape. The familiar rumble of washing machines and dryers dampened the sound of my footsteps.

I was terrified for Glen, but I could feel that he was still running. If he could get out of the fence line, he'd be fine. Sergeant and the Tenebris boys would help him out, and he was fast and strong.

But I couldn't focus on him, so I pushed the bond down, concentrating on my own hunt. I crossed behind the rest of the cars, doing my best to stay low, my head covered with my backpack. There were two cameras in here, though I wasn't sure if they were working, since there was no telltale red light. But just in case, I kept silent and as hidden as possible while crossing the floor.

When I reached the door, I saw Mama was doing the same, crouching low inside a laundry room. The washers and dryers rumbled on the opposite wall, next to an ironing board that jutted out into the small room. In the corner squatted a very young woman in a maid's outfit, a white top with a short black skirt. Her face was marked by tears, and her arms by what looked like claws, or maybe just fingernails. Her expression held fear but also defeat, like she'd given up, though she couldn't have been much more than eighteen.

"What do you want?" she whispered. She had a slight accent, not an Eastern one. More like Grigor's, or that bastard general Ivan.

"Not to hurt you," I said softly. "I promise that." Mama just tilted her head and sniffed.

The girl's eyes moved over me listlessly. "You're not from here, not with that accent and those clothes. You here to what? Kill somebody? Steal stuff?" She didn't look or sound like she gave a rat's ass if I did.

"Not exactly." I wasn't sure how much to share, but when I pushed my hair back, tucking it behind my ear, I didn't have to.

"You really aren't from here." Her eyes were fixed on the metal tag at the top of my ear. "Why are you... *How?*"

"You smell that?" Mama whispered, interrupting us. She slid across the floor toward the girl, who went very still as Mama held out a hand. She offered her own after a second, and Mama gently lifted the blood-streaked arm to her nose, sniffing. "It's him." I moved a step closer and sniffed, too, his familiar sour odor with hints of tobacco and menthol wafting up not only from the girl, but also the laundry piled on the floor by my feet. I glanced at Mama, hoping she wasn't losing grip on her lucidity with the stench of her mate so close.

"That asshole Callaway? You know him?" The girl let out a soft sob, and I padded across the room to sit beside her. This close, I could smell more than blood and laundry detergent. I could smell other things. Sex and sweat. Her thighs were marked, too, with blood and semen.

"Yeah, he's my father, unfortunately." When she flinched, I went on. "I might not have been honest about not killing people. If I see that fucker, I'm going to make the time to end him. What's your name?"

"Vanya," she whispered, her lips tightening as she shifted position and straightened her back. "I'm Vanya Volkovskaia. I was given to this corrupt pack four years ago. My father was told I would be a foster daughter here. But they only wanted me as a hostage, and a slave. I haven't been outside this house since I was left here."

"You work in the lower levels?" I asked quietly.

"I do. There and the kitchen. I take meals to the prisoners, and to the 'guests.' Your father—"

"Call him Callaway, or the Rat Bastard. That's what I did."

She didn't smile. "He's the worst guest we've ever had. He sent two girls to the hospital. Two *shifters*. I'd be down there now, if I hadn't gotten locked out taking his laundry."

"The doors automatically lock?" She nodded. "When they open, will you help us get inside? I need to rescue my mates from the lower levels. And my mama here—"

Vanya's eyes went wide. "He's her mate?" Any normal wolf would want to rip out the throat of a woman her true mate had touched. Would demand revenge for the pain it would have caused. She must've known that, since she tried to scramble away.

I raced to reply. "He is, but you see her scars? All of those? He gave them to her. She knows what he is. Her wolf knows. You don't need to worry; she won't hurt you. We just need a way in, and when we leave, you can come with us."

"I don't have anywhere to go," she whispered. "But if you promise to kill him... Him and as many of the others you can—Enforcers, all of them. Not the Alpha Heir, if you can help it, though. He's the only one who's ever kind." Her nose wrinkled. "I'm not sure how those two evil ones had a son like that, or a daughter that's even kinder. She got out, though. That's why we're locked down. She escaped, and her parents went to find her. I bet her brother helped her run."

"Tana, right?" When she nodded, I grinned. Tana being safe made our own escape a little bit easier. "I wish I'd met her. I know her brother pretty well. He's kind of stuck up, but he grows on you after a while, right?"

She gave a tired smile, as she slumped back down. "Sorry, I'm tired. I have to rest to heal."

"You've never shifted?" Mama asked quietly, moving even closer. She raised an eyebrow, and when Vanya nodded curiously, she placed a hand on the center of the girl's chest. "You have a very strong wolf. Very powerful."

Vanya did smile then. "My mother came from a royal line, she used to tell me. Kings and Queens, in the time before Alphas."

"Alphas and Alpha Mothers," Mama whispered. For a moment, I thought she was going to do something else. She pressed her other hand to her own chest and inhaled, but then her eyes got hazy, and she shook her head like she was clearing away cobwebs. "We'll kill them all, princess." Lifting one finger to the girl's face, Mama traced the path of a tear down her cheek. "We'll do the moon's justice for you and all the others."

She tucked Vanya under one arm, the rumbling dryer behind her back as we spoke softly about what we needed, and made a far better plan than the one I'd come up with.

There were maid's uniforms in the room, real ones with the Eastern crest, though there were black trousers as well as skirts. Small favors.

Vanya would be sent back to the lower levels with food as soon as the locks opened. "I can't get you in," she admitted. "They only let one in at a time, and only a few of us have clearance. The guards have silver, by the way. There's a lot of silver down there; some of the rooms stink of it. Anyway, once you get inside, even if you *can* get past the guards, there's no hope that you can get back out, not alive."

"No hope, huh?" I murmured absently, closing my eyes and thinking of my mates as the rumbling of the dryers and the warmth of the room began to lull me to sleep.

"Hope is a trick," she replied, her voice sharp. "Hope is the thing that traps girls like us. Makes us think there's something better around the corner. That someone will save us."

My eyes snapped open, and I turned my head to her. She sounded so much like me, only a few months ago. Certain that the only thing that lay ahead was more of the same torture I'd known up to then. Sure that I had no friends left in the world, once Del had been killed.

"Hope is the thing that'll save us," I said, tasting the truth in my words for the first time. "We have to hope that the moon is with us, and that we can change this shitty world the older shifters have stuck us with. If we don't have hope, we won't have energy to move the mountains of bullshit out of our way, and start making the packs do what they were always meant to do. What they're fucking for, in the first place. To *protect*."

"The pack protects," Mama agreed, moving between me and Vanya. "And a pack can be small. Two wolves, even. Or three. Come on, now. We'll need our rest for the fight ahead." She held out her free arm to me, and I inched closer, moving carefully to keep from jostling her wound. Then I rested my head on Mama's shoulder, and Vanya half-crumbled against her chest as she began to hum the lullaby she'd sung to me.

We woke a few hours later, though we'd taken turns getting up to switch the dryers back on when they finished their cycles. The noise and smell of them protected us as much as anything. Most of the day had gone, and we took turns in the small toilet, then put on the maid uniforms, waiting for the lockdown to end. I had to help Mama into the black trousers and shirt, since she was weak, and her wound had bled an alarming amount. She swatted my hands away when I went to check it, though.

"Mind yourself. We don't have time to fuss." I liked her scolding me. It felt like the kind of thing a normal mother would say, a thing she'd never really said before. "Now help me stick this to my back," she told me, picking up her sword from the floor. I'd almost forgotten she had it; I'd left my own with Sergeant.

She turned around, lifting her white maid's shirt. The scars went all the way around her ribcage and up and down her back. A brand-new surge of hatred for the Alpha who'd done this to her—beginning when she wasn't even as old as I was now—had me tasting bile. I pushed the rage down, storing it with all the rest of my hatred for him, as I made sure my own steak knife was hidden under my clothing. He'd answer for his crimes soon enough.

I shoved my backpack under some dirty clothes, and had no sooner buttoned up the too-loose white shirt than a bell in the house rang, and a voice from inside shouted, "Back to work."

"Gotta hurry or they'll come looking." Vanya quickly sprayed some fabric softener on Mama's clothes to obscure the scent of blood, then splashed some on me. It smelled awful, and far too strong. "So no one wants to get close, if they see a new girl," she explained. "That's it. We can go in now."

"Look-away," Mama panted as she walked stiffly to the door.

"No, Mama. We have disguises; we don't need that. Save your strength." Vanya gave us an odd look, but passed me a basket of clean kitchen linens, before taking one herself and handing Mama a light stack of folded towels.

We followed her inside, surrounded by the chilly air of the house and the scent of something I didn't recognize but never wanted to smell again. Mama sniffed and whispered, "So much pain," then fell silent as Enforcers confronted Vanya, demanding to know where we'd been.

She answered, but not fast enough obviously, since one of the men slapped her across the face. "Get to your station."

Mama and I scurried behind her, though we knew better than to help her up. But when our eyes met behind the girl's slumped shoulders, I could practically hear Mama's words. They would all need to die.

I nodded slightly. *Absofuckinglutely.*

CHAPTER 19

Hiding in Plain Sight
FLOR

The kitchen at Eastern was a sterile, too-quiet space, white tile from floor to ceiling. Four women moved around inside, wearing uniforms identical to ours, but with aprons. At least the room smelled good. There was a huge spread of food on the white ceramic table in the center, and three pots bubbling at the stove. No one hummed, whistled, or spoke, and when we entered, no one even looked up.

When I finally dared to, though, I noted the camera in this room was also dead, or at least I hoped it was. I whispered the question to Vanya.

"I think so," she said aloud. "They all have a light, and none of them so far have been on. Something's messing with the power." The others in the room froze at her words, though no one spoke. It was creepy. In the kitchen at Southern, even though it had been an awful pack, Del and I had been able to talk to each other. No one had wanted to watch what we did in there, or cared what we said as long as they got their food on time. "Becca, is the camera here still out?"

The oldest woman at the stove stopped stirring and turned to face us, her eyes wide. She was as old as Brand's grandmothers, at least seventy-five, and had a long, deep scar that ran in a jagged arc from her hairline, where her silver-brown hair was caught up in a tight bun, to the corner of her mouth. That one had been made with silver, for sure. "Who'd you bring in, you stupid girl? You're going to get us all killed."

I opened my mouth to reply, but Vanya beat me to it. "Which would be better than this. These shifters are here to kill Alpha Callaway, and I'm going to take them down there to do it."

The woman's dark brown eyes stopped on me for just long enough for her to curl her lip, and then landed on Mama. "Who are—" she began, then went silent. For a moment, her lip trembled as she took in Mama's scars. She sniffed, and her brow furrowed. "You're dying already. Who are you?"

"I'm the Alpha Mate of Southern," Mama replied, and I had to swallow hard to contain a gasp of surprise. She'd never called herself that before.

"You here to take him away?"

Mama let out a soft short laugh that only sounded a little bit crazy. "I'm here to serve him the moon's justice."

"The old ways," Becca murmured. "You need a sword?"

Wait, what?

"I have one." When Mama didn't say anything else, I gave her a look—I needed to know what they meant by the old ways when it came to swords and cheating true mates —then sketched out the details of what we were up to, as many as I figured they needed, anyway.

It wasn't enough. Becca sat us down and fed us, pulling

the entire story out of me, one detail at a time. By the time an hour had passed, they knew a whole hell of a lot more than I would normally have told a group of strangers. I scowled at Becca, wondering if she had some kind of truth-telling magic. When I grumbled the question, her smile wrinkled up the scar. "Used to have a lot more. But it takes it out of a person, feeding a hungry bitch every day for decades."

"Feeding?"

"Elina, the Alpha's mate. This pack used to be halfway honorable until she showed up."

"Tell my girl about her, about the witch," Mama asked quietly. "She'll need to know."

Becca shared a few details about Elina and Aidan's odd relationship, and how important it was never to let her touch you. How Tana and Finnick had seemed far stronger when they were young, but had grown weaker over time.

"Stronger?"

"Magically. Like you and your mama here. An Alpha Mother, sitting right here with me," Becca muttered. "I never thought I'd live to see another one."

Mama just lowered her head and asked a few questions about the lower levels. I was in awe. She seemed so normal. If it weren't for the smell of her blood and the lines of pain at the corners of her eyes, I would have thought she'd been healed. But I supposed that was partly being closer to her mate.

I closed my eyes for a moment, checking my bonds. Grigor's weird bond was still numb, but Luke's was stronger than ever. It felt good, in my soul, though I could tell he was worried.

He probably sensed me near, and couldn't find me. I

wouldn't let myself worry about him. Finnick was not close at all, Glen was growing more distant, and Brand... I felt an odd twitch in the bond that had been silent since the trip here in the van. I pushed on the quiet place, trying to send a thought through to him. *Bearman?* He didn't answer, but I could feel his fear and anger, and then Grigor's voice echoed in my mind.

Naughty little blade. You should not be here.

"Grigor?" I said out loud, then zipped my lips. *You're alive.*

Of course I am, my queen.

Where are you?

In a cell, for now. His thoughts fluttered through mine, setting tiny fires in my soul. *Where are you? You're very close. Your Mountain mate is raging beside me. He cannot get to you, cannot protect you. I feel the same pain.*

Brand is with you? My gums itched as my teeth tried to lengthen. *They put him in a cell? Can you get out?*

Not yet. Still too weak. Brand says to leave... Wait for the full moon. Council... His thoughts got quieter until they trailed off, no matter how hard I focused.

When I opened my eyes, the younger girls were looking at me like they thought I might sprout horns and a tail and demand a fiddle contest. No one spoke for a long moment, until Becca started barking whispered orders to the others. They all moved quickly, assembling a heavy platter for Vanya and placing it on a cart. Becca lifted the cloth and motioned for me and Mama to crawl under to hide. I didn't love the plan to ride beneath the cart across the Mansion— it felt too exposed—but Mama needed to conserve her energy.

I crawled under, crossing my legs to make myself as

small as possible. Mama climbed on my lap, grunting in pain. Vanya kneeled to pull down the cloth. "Wait, you do know they have silver, right? They know how to use it, too." Her eyes flicked up to Becca and the scar on her face.

"We'll get in, and once we do, we'll have help," I assured her. "Anyone down there you want us to take care of, besides Callaway?"

Her eyes gleamed. "Yeah. If you see a guard with a black goatee who wears a silver claw on a necklace, and he happens to die in some truly horrific way? I wouldn't complain."

Five minutes later, we were moving down the hallway, traveling over hardwood floors and marble, holding our breath half the time and holding onto the legs of the cart to keep from tumbling out from underneath the cloth. Vanya was stopped twice, and when we reached the door to the lower levels, she had to lift the tray to go in. Mama held onto my arm as we slipped out the back. I could feel her magic moving over my skin in a gentle wave as we raced to follow our guide into the dungeon of Eastern, hiding in plain sight.

The lower-level lighting was dim and spooky, as we followed Vanya down the hall. A scowling guard approached, and when he commanded her to stop and be inspected, while she held the heavy platter of meat and potatoes, my fingers itched to take out my steak knife and inspect his spleen up close.

But Mama was already pulling me down the hallway, drawn like a magnet to Callaway. And when the guard unlocked the door and half-shoved Vanya inside, it wasn't my steak knife in his spleen, but Mama's sword.

"Go back into the hall," I whispered to Vanya, as the guard fell into the room, squealing like a dying rabbit. She launched a gob of spit that landed on the guard, then obeyed, stepping out into the hall, but leaving the door partly open.

I was glad. The room stank of old food, piss, spilled liquor, and the Alpha himself. Without thinking, I did what Del had taught me to: I took in everything in the room, assessing how it could all be used as a weapon, or a hiding place. There was a table piled with dishes and cutlery, a big bed with dirty, twisted sheets and pillows, two chairs, some sort of tablet and wired chargers on the arm of a sofa, a stack of folded laundry on the floor by one wall, and more empty bottles of booze than even a wolf shifter should need to get drunk.

It was a freaking buffet of potential weapons. I could work with this, if I needed to.

My father was sitting on a sofa inside the room, wearing dark sweatpants and a stained, white undershirt, his stomach round as a basketball underneath, a tumbler in one hand and a half-empty bottle of bourbon in the other. He wasn't at all surprised to see Mama, and he flat-out ignored me. All he had eyes for was his mate, and the irises were practically glowing a pale blue as he stared at her, drinking her in.

"I knew you'd come." It almost sounded sweet, until his eyes dimmed and he went on. "Scarred-up old bitch. Never did have any damned pride."

Mama's hands—one holding the sword, one pressed against her stomach—trembled as she stared at him. She did have a hungry look in her eyes, though I wasn't sure what it was for. I had a feeling she was trying to decide whether to decapitate or disembowel him. But her lip quivered as she managed to reply, "Calvin. You look terrible."

He stood slowly, moving slowly toward us, his gaze on

the sword. "I'll look better when the witch upstairs finishes the job her boss couldn't manage twenty years back. I'll be Alpha again, but this time, I won't have you in the back of my mind, driving my wolf half crazy." He still didn't look at me. I shuffled one step closer.

"I'm not dying today, Calvin. At least, not until you do," Mama said, lifting the sword slightly. "You mated me, and left me alone. You tried to break our moon-given bond, even if it killed me in the process. You tried to kill my baby girl before she was born. You sicced your dogs on her for years. You tortured me with silver and worse. You're a foul man, Calvin Callaway, and a terrible shifter. I feel sorry for your wolf, and I'm here to deliver the moon's justice to him."

He stiffened, as she went on, stepping closer. "The old ways are clear. When a wolf is shackled to a man who's gone mad, who's turned against nature and the law of the pack? His Alpha, or the one who is closest to him is given the sacred duty to deliver the wolf back to the moon. To put an end to his suffering, with kindness. You don't have an Alpha. All you have is me."

"You think you're going to be able to kill me?" He laughed, his stomach jiggling. His eyes were fully human now, and absolutely batshit insane. "I'm tempted to let you try. I've been gettin' bored." He stepped forward menacingly, sniffing the air. "You're bleeding."

"Gut wound. Silver blade. It's actually been pretty helpful. Cleared my mind, you might say," Mama said calmly, though the air practically hummed with her anger.

I edged around her, trying to give her space to move, my steak knife in my hand, just in case she needed backup. Callaway didn't spare me a glance.

Crap on a cracker! He *couldn't* see me. Mama wasn't

156

touching me, but she had wrapped me in a look-away. I circled until I was to one side, staying out of his reach just in case the spell dropped.

"Cleared that crazy mind? Bet that took some doin'." He took two steps, kicking empty beer cans out of the way, until he stood directly in front of her, the tip of her sword poking into that round belly.

But she didn't move. Didn't stab him. Didn't even blink.

"Don't move," he murmured. It was a soft sound, but filled with Alpha command, and the words hit me like a leaf skittering past. My allegiance was to my mates now, and myself. I didn't have to obey his commands.

But she did.

I lifted my steak knife, waiting for the right moment. *Mama?* I mouthed, but she still wasn't looking at me. "Mama," I whispered. She twitched like a fly had landed on her face, but didn't even glance at me. Callaway's nostrils flared, and he swiveled his head, but his gaze slid over me.

Mama stared up into his face, her features hazy. She looked like she had for most of my life again, and I hated it. Slowly, casually, he reached down and tapped the sword blade. "I smell silver, but this ain't it."

"No silver. We don't believe in it."

"Where'd ya get the blade? Tell me."

"This sword is my pack's," she said, her voice monotone and raspy, like she didn't want to speak. "I found it in the woods. I hid it in a cave. It belonged to the Alpha Mother. It belongs to me now. It's a family heirloom."

"Huh, looks expensive. And here I thought you weren't worth the shit on my shoes." Callaway plucked it from her hands faster than I could reach them, and backhanded her as he took it away. "What's yours is mine, ain't that it,

Lily?" he jeered as she fell on the ground, crying out in pain. "What's yours is—"

He was probably going to repeat himself, like he usually did. That fuckhead always did love to hear his own voice. But before he could finish, I'd lunged at him from the side, and had my steak knife buried up to the handle in his gut.

"Hey, Dad."

CHAPTER 20
THE SOURCE OF STRENGTH
FLOR

Some moments in life were perfect. Not perfect like when Brand showed me his lake, or when Luke told me he loved me. But perfect in a petty, vengeful way.

Seeing the shocked look on my father's face up close as he realized I was there, with my knife in his gut, was that kind of perfect. It was just a shame it couldn't last a little longer.

In his shock, he broke one of Del's cardinal rules: he let Mama's short sword fall. It clanged to the floor, and his empty hands flew up and clawed for mine, his eyes boring into my face. "Back away!" he commanded, the Alpha command in his voice as heavy as a sledgehammer.

I didn't even blink. Instead of moving back, power pinned my feet to the floor, energy that tasted like Brand and Grigor and all the others. I was so much stronger than I had ever been, far stronger than him. Something was happening in the bonds, something that made me think that a vast pool of power was just one thread, one thought, away. It wasn't there yet, but the energy that thrummed through me felt similar to when Brand had taken on the Alpha position.

"I said, back off!" The Alpha's hands, tipped with sharp wolf claws now, landed on my shoulder. He twisted at me, gripping me and trying to force me away, though I'd wrapped one of my legs around his to stay close. His blood spilled over my hand and arm, and mine poured down from cuts that seemed to heal as fast as he made them. The blood made things slippery, but I had a solid grip on the knife, and the Alpha couldn't get a hold on me, no matter how hard he tried.

For a split second, I was a helpless child again, his hands bruising me, his foul breath in my face. The times he'd whipped me, beaten me half to death, flashed through my mind in the space of a heartbeat. Back then, I hadn't been able to defend myself.

Now, it was time for payback. He was still physically strong, but I was already well inside his guard. And I had a hidden pool of strength from my mates, pressing up like a bubble rising to meet my need. So the next time he tried to reach for me, I slipped my hand out, grabbed his arm, and used that power, twisting hard. His arm popped out of the shoulder socket, and he howled loud enough to make my ears ring.

Maybe I was the right mate for a serial killer. The sound of his pain was like sweet music.

But I had a feeling his dying breath would be sweeter still. All I had to do was deliver the final twist of the knife, and it would shred his heart.

But before I could do it, Mama fell to the floor, screaming in agony. I flicked a glance down at her. She was holding her own abdomen, and blood gushed through the bandages.

Shit. Shit! For a moment, I'd forgotten that she would feel this in her bond. "Toadfucking son of a rat bastard," I snarled up into his face.

I wanted nothing more than to finish him off, but I couldn't kill Mama. I knew I would lose her soon, but I couldn't bear for it to be now, at my hands. I couldn't lose her yet.

"Flor, baby, do it," Mama wheezed from the ground. "Finish it."

I didn't answer, my mind scrambling to find another way, searching through all of Del's advice, all of my knowledge. Callaway had to die. He *deserved* to. But maybe there was some other way.

"You don't wanna kill your mama, now, do ya?" he dared to ask. "Let me go, and we can talk about this." He was still trying to use his Alpha voice on me. He twitched again, like he thought it might have worked, and I twisted the knife, snarling as the blade cut into his heart.

"Shut up and lemme think, asshole!"

We all went quiet for a moment, until Mama let out what I thought was a laugh. "See what you did, Calvin? See what you did to our baby?"

"I didn't make her crazy," he muttered.

"No, you made her strong." Mama dragged her hand to her face, wiping away the silver hair that had fallen across her eyes. "You made her stronger than she ever could've been otherwise." She set one bloody hand to the floor and tried to rise, but couldn't. Instead, she speared my father with her gaze—no, her wolf's gaze—and spoke. "You tried to break our bond, and forgot that you were on the other end. You ruined your wolf in the process. Weakened him. When you learned she was in my womb, you tried to sell your own child to the darkness. But you forgot it was your

161

own line she cursed. You didn't want me because I had magic, and you were afraid."

The Alpha was breathing hard, and fur was sprouting and shrinking back into his arms. His scent got stronger, wilder.

"I was raised in a magical pack. If you'd stopped to ask me what using magic against your own mate, your own child, would do, I would've told you. My line, Flor's and mine, is the most powerful one in existence. If you'd stayed true to me, you could've been the strongest Alpha alive." She gasped. "But you're... nothing."

"Fuck you, crazy bitch," he spat. I yanked at his dislocated arm to shut him up.

Mama started dragging herself across the floor, stopping where the sword had fallen. "When you break a bone, it heals stronger. Harder. When you break a bond... you offend the moon." She wrapped her hand around the hilt and opened her mouth to say something else, but shouting in the hall had her pausing to listen.

Someone yelled, "What the *hell* is going on down here?"

Mama nodded to me, her eyes panicked. "Do it now!"

But it was too late. The door slammed open, and an angry Aidan McDonnell stared through his glasses and down his narrow nose at me. In one hand, he held a silver knife. In the other, his son... or what was left of him. Aidan had Finnick's arms behind him, and was holding him up in what had to be an incredibly painful position. Both of Finnick's arms could be broken, or dislocated.

"You." Aidan's smile was the coldest thing I'd ever seen. "Now this is a welcome surprise."

My heart raced, and for a moment, I felt like I might pass out.

Finnick was a mess, and I thought he might be an unconscious one, until I saw his head move, like he was trying to look up at me. He wore the tattered remains of a business suit that might have been dark gray, but was as soaked with blood as the rest of him. There was a long slice along his neck that had to have been made with a silver blade. It wasn't healing, and every time his father shook him—which he did now, like a dog with a rabbit it had caught—blood oozed down onto his collar.

"A *very* welcome surprise. Calvin, looks like you got yourself into trouble again." Aidan lifted an eyebrow, but didn't drop Finnick or the knife. "Let him go, girl, and I'll make your death quick."

I adjusted my grip on the steak knife and shifted my grip to Callaway's thick neck. "Call me girl again, and I'll make his slow," I replied as calmly as I could, trying not to let my eyes fall to the floor, where a pool of red was collecting under Finnick's sagging head.

I wasn't successful. Aidan sneered. "I should let you kill him and save me the trouble. But I have an Heir upstairs who's insisting on facing his father tomorrow night under the full moon." Callaway went very still at that.

Something wasn't making sense. "You want Callaway alive. Why?"

"It's not your problem. But if you don't let him go, I'll give you a real one. I can head down to the cell and kill that Mountain mate of yours." He tilted his head curiously. "I wonder if you'd even die from it. You fuck around, from what I hear. The Northern Heir, the Mountain Alpha..." He kicked Finnick in the side of one leg. "This disappointing piece-of-shit son of mine probably had you. I can't think of any other reason he'd betray his pack. He always did love pussy. Wasn't particularly picky about whose, either. Whores, both of you."

Finnick drew a dangerously liquid-sounding breath, but managed to speak. "Don't... call her... whore." Aidan kicked him again, hard enough that I thought I heard a bone break.

"Stop hurting him!" I demanded. The Eastern Alpha's watery green eyes narrowed, and I knew I'd given too much away. I struggled for calm, tightening my grip on my father. "I'll make you a deal. You put Finnick down and leave, and I'll give you this sack-of-shit Alpha."

"You're not leaving this cell," Aidan said slowly, like he was looking for a loophole. Did he still not know that Finnick was my mate? "I'm locking you in."

I nodded, trying to keep my expression blank. "Take it or leave it."

"Aidan, you oughta kill this little bitch now. You don't know—" my father started, but Aidan cut him off.

"Done." He dropped Finnick and shoved him the rest of the way through the door, glancing at Mama as he did. "We'll never get the smell of Southern out of this room," he snapped, and I let Callaway go, stepping well away from him in case he tried to attack.

I didn't need to worry. He scurried away, his dislocated arm hanging limp at one side, his other hand pressed on his bleeding wound. I guess a savage stab to the heart might make even a stupid ass like that think twice before picking another fight.

Aidan let Callaway past, then shut the door, never dropping his gaze from my face. I made sure to drop mine, though I didn't feel compelled to. I'd already let him see too much of what I was capable of. There was no need for him to know I could stare him down.

And Finnick needed me. As soon as the door closed, I snatched up a clean napkin from the table and rushed to his side, cradling him on my lap as much as I could without making him bleed even more, and pressing the wound closed as much as I could.

"Fuck, Finn, this is bad," I said, my voice too high.

His head lolled to one side, and I thought he was going to speak, but it wasn't his voice whispering. "Let me see him, baby." Mama was at my side, her arm pressed over her abdomen. She was almost as wrecked as he was. I made room for her, though, and she placed a hand on his throat. "Not good," she murmured. "When they're that deep, the silver can get into the blood. Still, maybe..." Closing her eyes, she hummed low.

Her body gave off a surge of heat, like she'd turned into a space heater or something. Static electricity made all of the hairs on her arms stand up, and then she went rigid, falling over on top of Finnick.

"Mama?" She didn't answer, but she was still breathing. I lifted her carefully off him and carried her over to the sofa. She was so light, it was like her bones were hollow, and when I put her down, I noticed how much paler she'd grown in just the past few hours.

"Flor?" I whirled to face Finnick, who was sitting up now as well, one hand on his neck. "Your mother... healed me?" He let his fingers fall, revealing the long silver scar along the base of his neck. It was still red on the edges, but the bleeding had stopped.

For some reason, seeing that scar broke me. I started crying, ugly, wracking sobs, my whole body shaking. So I didn't even see Finnick move, didn't know what was happening when he shifted me onto his lap, cradling me.

"Hush now, Wills. It's going to be all right. I'm alive. You're alive. We're going to get through this."

I couldn't stop crying. Finnick's scent of ginger was almost erased under the blood. There had been so much blood today. But his long fingers on my hair, soothing me, and his murmured words of comfort helped me to get control of myself.

"How, Finn?" I asked, staring up at him. "How are we going to get through this?"

"One breath at a time, I suppose. That's how I've been surviving," he answered. He drank me in with his eyes, and for an instant, his hand dropped to my neck, to the mate mark he'd put there, before he snatched it away. "Sorry."

I stared up at him, aching to touch him, to grab his hand and place it back on my neck. But a deep insecurity filled me, and a deeper ache inside that came from my wolf had me holding still. "You said that before. Right after we bonded. You said it was a mistake, and that we shouldn't have done it."

He kept his eyes on mine, though his were filled with pain. "I've said worse. Hell, I've done worse. I tried to reject the bond entirely at Southern. Flor, I..."

I waited for him to finish, but he'd fallen silent. The space between us was filled with unspoken accusations, and explanations that might never be enough. Memories and fear and anguish. The moment at the lake, when I'd known he was touching another woman, flashed back like it had just happened.

"Tell me. I felt what you did. It hurt me, Finn. It hurt me worse than a beating. I need to understand why you did it."

He closed his eyes for a moment, a single tear tumbling from his pale lashes, then opened them and spoke. "The first time my parents whored me out was when I was fifteen." I gasped, but he went on, staring into the wall like he was watching a movie of his past. "She was the wife of a businessman Father wanted as an investor. I was scared. I'd never had sex before, and she was far older than me."

His lips twisted. "She liked young boys. Father made the deal, but she told him in front of me I wasn't a good lay. When she left, I swore on the moon I wouldn't do it again. He locked me in a cell for a week with no food or water, sending Torran to give me some... encouragement to take back my vow. I did. I went back to my room, and a week later, another woman walked through my door.

"It got easier. I got good at the sex, and at hiding my disgust. I hated them all, and some of them seemed to like that. I was also learning all I could about finance, the markets, how to help the pack succeed. I told myself once I had more to offer, something more valuable, the whoring would stop. It didn't, of course." He sighed. "I was doing what they demanded; I was earning money for the pack. But instead of getting praised for it, Father detested me more every year. When the day came that I would rather be beaten to death than touch one more woman, I confronted them both."

His voice broke. "Father said it was fine. They'd just let Tana take over for me with those duties. They had a deal for Chinese silks, and the man was alone with her in the parlor. When I ran in to see if it was true, the bastard had her on his knee. Tana was twelve. She was terrified."

"Oh, Finn." My heart was shattering for him.

"I cut a deal. Tana would be safe until she was eighteen, as long as I did what they demanded. But that day, I started laying the groundwork to get her out. I had everything in place, but when I stayed in Northern to be near you, and didn't return when Father called, they let me know they were giving her to one of the worst shifters at Eastern. I had to come back, even though I knew what was waiting for me here."

I needed to know one thing, one detail. I didn't want to, but I had to ask. I swallowed hard, forcing the words out. "You were forced to sleep with another woman, to keep Tana safe?"

"I didn't sleep with her. Physically, I *couldn't*." He twisted his head to the side, as if he couldn't look at me. "I did... I was intimate with her. I did my job."

He was shuddering with the effort of holding back his emotions, and I placed my hands on his face, turning him back to me. "You didn't want to do it. You got Tana out. She's *safe*. Finn, look at me." His expression was tortured as he obeyed. "Would you ever do it again? Will you?"

"Even if you never let me be in a room with you again for the rest of my life, I will never touch another woman. Even if you never let me touch you or kiss you again. I'm yours until I die, though I don't deserve you. I'm tainted, Flor. That's why I said what I did. Why I pushed you away. I'm not worthy of you." A tear rolled down his cheek, then fell to the floor.

He fell silent, but I kept my hands on his cheeks, considering. Nothing he'd said was untrue, except maybe that last part. "I'm the one who gets to decide if you're worthy. And you're not tainted." He took a breath to argue, but I placed a finger over his lips. "You were coerced, Finn. I've met so many shifters, in almost every pack now, who were forced to do things they didn't want. Some of them were female, some male. The pack didn't protect them, just like yours didn't, and they had to do a whole lot of things to survive."

"My wolf knows," he rasped. "I can't let him surface. He tried to bite off our tongue. He tore off every inch of skin she touched on my arms, my shoulders. Every time I fell asleep, he rose and made sure I knew I had failed him. Failed you. But he couldn't get us... clean."

I shushed him, worried at the sudden scent that reminded me of the more feral wolves from the Tenebris pack for a moment. He really believed that he was to blame. "Now you listen to me, Cityboy. Nothing you did to survive, to save your sister's life, could touch the core of who you are. Nothing they ever did to you—with words, or actions, or magic, even—could change your heart. You're not their tool anymore. You're not their torturer, or their spy, or their strategist. Finn, you're my mate." And it was time for him to start acting like one.

He trembled under my hands as I traced his plush lips. They were my favorite part of his face, and I'd stared at them far too long at Northern, wondering what it would feel like to have them on me.

"Kiss me, mate."

He pulled back. "No. I can't... I can't touch you with my..." His wolf rose, gold flecks surfacing in deeper green irises. "No," he growled. "Filthy. Dirty."

I let my own wolf rise, as much as she could, and growled back. She glared at his neck, for some reason. "Mate. *Claim.*"

His wolf seemed confused for a moment, though not as confused as I was, but a moment was all it took. My teeth lengthened, and before I knew what was happening, I had my head buried in his neck and his flesh in my mouth. His blood was wild ginger and salt, spicy and clean, as I bit down.

Mate, my wolf snarled as she marked him again, this time where the whole world would see. Finnick's arms came up to hold me close as I licked the fresh wound, tasting his blood. Then he pressed his lips to my neck, to his own mark, murmuring something that I was almost certain was a prayer.

"I don't deserve you, Florida Wills," he said after a long moment.

"I think you do," I replied, my hands on his face again as I pushed back to examine those sexy lips again. "And I deserve a second kiss."

CHAPTER 21

A BETTER MARK

My wolf howled inside as Flor's words sank in, and I closed my eyes, unable to maintain her gaze. Not from shame this time, though. From gratitude.

She'd forgiven me for hurting her; I could feel it inside our new bond.

No, the bond wasn't new. But somehow, it had changed. The fraying thread that I'd tried to keep safe, that my wolf had hidden deep down after I'd chosen to save my sister instead of protecting my mate, was a solid cord of acceptance. Now, a steel cable connected us, one that could never be broken. It glowed like a beacon inside me, leading to her wolf, a shining, reddish-black creature who greeted mine with gentle nips and nuzzles in my mind. I gasped aloud when I realized how much more she had done than accept me.

She'd remade the bond between us somehow, and changed me and my wolf as well. I'd grown stronger when I bonded with Grigor, and I felt him rejoicing in the part of her that was connected to him, though his joy tasted of frustration and anger. But my spirit wolf had been a starved beast since I'd betrayed her.

Now, with this new mark, with Flor's forgiveness, he stood tall, threw back his head, and howled. The sound rang in the cell, and I shook myself. Flor grabbed my snout, running her fingers through my fur, and giggling as she shushed me.

My snout? I wriggled, shucking off the bloodstained suit and nudging the shoes aside with my claws. When had I changed?

Not important, my wolf thought, as he licked her face. *Mate. Mate!*

Flor laughed even louder at his antics. "I didn't mean a kiss from your wolf, Cityboy. Stop licking me!"

With some difficulty, I wrestled control back from my wolf and did as she asked, my tongue lolling out as she scratched my ruff. I wasn't sure how I'd shifted so quickly. It had been as fast as stepping through an open door, and just as easy.

"Hey, lemme see that," Flor muttered, and grabbed my tongue. "Huh. Didn't know two mate marks on one shifter was a thing. You learn somethin' new every damn day." I made a garbled squeaking sound as she inspected the mark on my tongue with her small fingers, and giggled again.

That sound floated deep into my cynical heart, like a windblown seed, and I felt a deep resolve as it cracked open, my soul shifting to make room for a new purpose. Her happiness was everything. I would spend every day of my life from now on—not trying to earn her forgiveness, because I already had that. But trying to bring that smile to her face, that sound to her lips.

I would fill her life with so much joy, it would blot out everything that had come before. She'd changed me, and I would show her how much, and worship her in every way I could, from now on.

"Change back," she whispered from where she sat beside me. "We probably need to talk." I was in human form in less than a second, my head spinning. "Wow! That's faster than Brand. And you made sparkles."

"Sparkles?" I reached for her hand, needing her touch.

Her amber eyes almost glowed. "Like magic, when you shifted. Little sparks came flying off your fur."

"Hmm. Strange," I murmured, not sure if I should be worried about it.

"I thought it was kinda sexy." She wiggled her eyebrows and peeked down at my body, an adorable blush dusting her cheeks.

By the moon, she was perfect. How had I ever thought anything else? Her hair had grown longer, and she'd put on weight, giving her limbs a hint of softness. When she leaned forward, the white maid's shirt she had on gaped open, tempting me to peek down to see if her breasts had changed.

I forced my eyes up like a gentleman, clearing my throat. "So, about that kiss."

"Yeah, we'd better get that out of the way," she teased.

"Brat," I admonished, grabbing her and pulling her back onto my lap. My cock stirred as she threaded her arms around me, closing her eyes halfway and licking her lips. I started with a gentle kiss, exploring her mouth.

At Northern, we'd had an audience to our disastrous first kiss. This time, no one was watching, though her mother was snoring softly on the couch across the room. There was no rush. I ran my hands through her hair, tugging at the ends gently so that she opened her mouth to mine. She moaned slightly as her head fell back, and I circled her throat lightly with my free hand, holding her in place while I delved into her mouth with my tongue, learning her tastes and sounds, paying attention to every movement, every shift. She liked it when I tightened my grip on her throat slightly, and my cock went hard as iron. I dropped my fingers to one breast, pinching her nipple gently through the fabric, but she covered my hand and forced me to pinch harder.

Her own hands explored my naked body, squeezing my biceps, moving down to trace the ridges of my abdomen, and landing on my cock, giving it an experimental squeeze. "Think we have time to see if this thing'll make sparkles, too?"

She really was a brat, and I was going to enjoy using every technique I knew to bring her to climax again and again... if she behaved.

I sighed into her mouth as she writhed on my lap. "Oh, Wills, you're going to be so much fun to play with. But not yet. We need to talk."

"I'd rather kiss. You're really good at it." She groaned as I lifted her up, moving her away from my cock, though it was the last thing I wanted to do. "But questions first."

She hopped up to check on her mom, and I stood as well, feeling strength pour through me. I sniffed the air, then stood and crossed to a stack of folded clothing in the corner, slipping into the first thing I found, a pair of dark gray briefs. Someone was coming.

"How'd you shift so fast?"

"I don't know how." I moved to the door, picking up an unfamiliar, discarded short sword on the way. I had a feeling I wouldn't need it, though. "I mean, I bonded with Grigor—"

"You did?" She spun around, her mouth open, and it was my turn to laugh.

"Not a mate bond," I explained, but she was holding onto the edge of the table, one hand over her mouth to stifle her giggles.

"Yeah, that's what he always says. Just a little bond here, just a connection. It's not a mate bond, we'll talk about that later," she teased when she could talk again. "He's got Luke and Glen and you, too. Brand better watch out."

The energy I'd felt crested, and I jumped back just in time, sword raised. Inches away from me, the door flew open, slamming against the wall and leaving an enormous, dented line.

"Too late for that, wildflower."

CHAPTER 22

FAMILY REUNION
FLOR

"**B**earman!" I ran across the cell, kicking scattered clothing and beer cans out of my way. My Mountain mate was dressed in a dirty collared shirt and a pair of equally filthy jeans, and no shoes. His beard and hair were wild, but not as wild as his eyes as he held up his arms to catch me when I leaped onto him, giving him a kiss almost as hot as the one I'd shared with Finnick a few seconds before.

Finnick muttered something about wanting to be climbed like a tree as well, but we ignored him. Brand held me out, examining me for injuries or something, until I kicked him, forcing him to let me down. "Are you hurt, little flower?"

"I'm fine. Not a mark on me," I said. "Though I can't say the same for you." His sleeves were pushed up, showcasing two very obvious bite marks. "Looks like you're a favorite chew toy, Bearman. Should I be jealous?"

He growled and lifted me back up, giving me a thorough, chastising kiss, and a soft swat on the bottom before he put me down. He nodded at Finnick, taking in the new scar on his neck, his silver eyes widening as they snagged on the bite mark I'd just given. "I could ask the same. Should I be jealous? You've given Finn two marks now."

"Never. You were my first. And you gave me a lake. Hard to top that." I wrapped an arm around his wide waist, or tried to. It almost seemed like Brand had grown bigger in his human form since he'd become Alpha. My own wolf purred in approval. More of him to love.

He leaned down and nuzzled my hair, breathing in my scent. "I wish I could take you there now. But I'm afraid we're stuck down here."

My heart raced. I hated feeling trapped. "Yeah, I heard the guards have silver weapons."

"The lower-level guards aren't a problem currently. But we can't get out. Aidan has dozens of Enforcers at the only exits and, yes, they're all armed with silver." He sighed, then straightened and turned his head to the side. "Hello, Finn. I'm glad to see you're still alive."

"Same here, but sorry our plan didn't work," Finnick replied, standing. "Are you alone?"

Brand rubbed the back of his neck sheepishly. "Ah, no. The little psycho's still not at his best, so he's having a snack in the hallway."

The serial killer in question ambled through the door, licking what looked like blood off one of his thumbs. He shot an amused look at Brand. "Call me Grigor, brother. You can use my name now. After all, we're mates—I mean, *brother* mates. Isn't that what Glen calls us?" He was wearing a guard's uniform that was only a little too big on him, the shirt still unbuttoned.

Brand grumbled something rude and tried to hold my hand to keep me from approaching Grigor, but I pressed a kiss to his wrist and pulled away. I'd been so worried about

Grigor. I had to touch him, though the flickering sparks in his eyes had me wary.

He looked thinner than the last time I'd seen him, and he had marks from what had to be silver, all over him. Some of them were stripes, as if wire had been wrapped around him. Others were small and round, from tiny bullets or... nails? I peered at one in the middle of his cheek that obviously had been a puncture, but was healing quickly, the skin returning almost to normal as I watched.

"Hello, little *behrserk*," Grigor half-purred, obviously not in any pain now, as I reached up to feel the healing skin.

"Hello, boogeyman," I teased. My voice came out breathy as the familiar tingles started up from his touch. I could get addicted to those. "Where'd you get the uniform? Any chance it belonged to a guy with a black goatee?" I asked, slightly disappointed as he buttoned up the shirt, and trying not to blush at the lust in his dark eyes when he noticed.

"Did you know him?" He moved so close, I could feel the heat of his body in the air between us, and stroked my hair with the back of one bloody hand.

"I just knew he was down here." I had to drop my gaze —though it might have been from embarrassment that I was getting turned on so fast—and noticed he'd misbuttoned the shirt. I took the excuse to touch him again, unbuttoning him halfway. The tiny divots in his skin went all the way down, and I touched each one lightly as I uncovered them, making a promise to return the insult to whoever had done this. Though Grigor may have already taken care of them. "Did you kill him?"

"No, I left him for dessert, my queen," he murmured, halfway closing his eyes as my fingers brushed his chest. "He's down the hallway. Tied up, of course. Why?"

Dessert? I wouldn't ask. I finished buttoning him, taking my time, before I pulled away reluctantly. "He needs to die horribly."

Grigor dropped back with one leg extended, doing some old, courtly bow. He murmured, "As my queen commands," planted a soft kiss on my hand that gave me more electric shocks all up my arm, and raced back out the door.

"I'll help him. I'll need some more clothes as well." Finnick followed him, the briefs doing nothing to hide his toned ass, and my blush grew deeper.

"Don't go to any trouble on my account," I muttered, watching his butt cheeks flex hypnotically as he left. I couldn't keep my eyes off him, off any of them. Damnit, I was turning into a pervert.

The sound of muffled screaming started down the hall a few seconds later, bringing me back to the reality of our situation. "Bearman, are we safe here, for the moment? You said we were trapped."

Brand had already moved to my mama on the sofa and was kneeling beside her, examining her almost as closely as he had me. She was still asleep, but the frown line in between her brows made me think her dreams weren't good ones. He pressed a clean cloth over the bloodsoaked one on her stomach, but it didn't wake her. He shook his head. "Safe? Not until we're home on my packlands, little one. But we have some breathing room for a few hours. The witch isn't here, and the moon is full tomorrow."

He came back over to me, sitting cross-legged on the floor and pulling me down onto him. I laid my head against his chest as he spoke, letting the rumble of his voice soothe me. "We had a plan to wait until the Council meeting. Luke would challenge Callaway and put an end to that problem.

Finn would challenge his father right afterward. Grigor and I would take care of Elina."

"You want to tell me how this happened?" I whispered, running my hand over the new mark on his right arm. "Did you bite him, too?"

The shaking in my chest might have been his laughter. "We didn't exchange marks. One bite is all it took. We're not mates."

"I wouldn't be jealous," I teased. "I've got four mates so far. I don't have a leg to stand on."

"You won't have a butt to sit on if you're not careful," Brand mock-threatened.

"Do I need to defend you from my brother mate, little blade?" Grigor called from the doorway. He looked refreshed, somehow. Like he'd just had a long nap, though his stolen uniform was even more rumpled. His hands were bloodier as well, but he picked up a discarded napkin and wiped them clean before approaching.

Not a nap. Dessert. My wolf was preening about her thoughtful mate-to-be.

I wasn't going to ask if he'd really eaten the goatee guard, but my imagination was going wild. "Where's Finn?"

Grigor's attention was on my mother, but he answered while he grabbed a chair from the table and carried it over to the sofa. "He's releasing Glen's parents from their cell."

While my mind spun—how had I forgotten about the Hilliers?—Brand asked, "Breaking the lock?"

"It's electronic," Grigor replied, reaching for one of my mama's hands. "I taught him a little trick. He's a clever pup. Someday he'll be a powerful one, too." He leaned over and pressed his forehead to the hand he'd lifted, so that it looked like she was checking him for fever. What was he up to?

"Pup?" I asked softly, but Mama was already awake.

"*Get away!*" she shrieked, her voice high-pitched and frantic. I jumped up and raced to where she could see me. Brand was behind me in an instant, protecting my back.

"Mama, it's okay! He's with me. He's one of my mates."

Mama's face froze. Brand sighed heavily. I didn't dare look at Grigor, since I'd sort of jumped the gun on that one.

"I should be so honored," Grigor murmured at last.

"Good that you know it," Brand grunted like a possessive cave bear as he sat back down.

Mama wasn't having any of it, as she kept scooching to the end of the sofa. "Baby, you'd better be lyin' right now. That man is filled with evil. I can hardly look at him." She blinked furiously as she hit the opposite sofa arm, obviously seeing something in Grigor that I couldn't.

"Finally, someone with a little sense," Brand grumbled.

I gave him a *shut up* look, and went to join Grigor and Mama. Well, Grigor anyway. Mama looked like she might tumble off the far end of the sofa to keep her distance. When I put an arm around Grigor, though, and pressed a kiss to his shoulder, the only part of her that moved was her mouth flopping open.

I grinned. "You look like a largemouth bass, Mama. Close your mouth and come over and meet my... suitor," I finished, wondering when I'd started blushing every second minute. "This is Grigor Dimitrivich. You've probably heard some things..."

"I don't need to hear a thing," Mama spat out, pushing her wild silver curls away from her scarred face. "I can see it. *Look,* baby. Really look at that creature. He has no business anywhere near you."

"Except that the moon has seen fit to give me a path to redemption, Lily Rain of the Western Pack," Grigor said gently. He squeezed me gently, and that cold, prickly feeling that I'd grown to love returned, like energy moving between us. Maybe that's just what it was; I felt stronger after he touched me. "If your daughter decides to allow me to stand with her, I will do all I can to deserve that honor. I will die for her."

"You almost did," I grouched. He still looked far weaker than when we'd first met. "I don't want any of my mates—or suitors—to die. I want us all to live, which means working together. Even if you think his soul looks like road-kill, Mama. He's my mate, or will be. You're gonna need to get along."

My heart broke a little more, because that might not really be true. Mama was mortally wounded, and the rest of us were up shit creek. None of us were guaranteed to survive. Without reinforcements or divine intervention, we might not make it to the next full moon, and that was only... hours away, I realized. One more night, and then tomorrow, as soon as the moon rose, there would be a Council meeting.

Grigor kneeled before Mama. "Alpha Mother, I know you. I see you as well, your shining spirit wrapped with a tainted bond, an evil you never earned. I will vow on the moon not to hurt her, or any of her kin, if that helps you to see how precious she is to me."

Mama narrowed her eyes, staying silent for a moment. When she did speak, her tone was sharp. "No vows. Some of her kin may need to be hurt."

Grigor understood immediately. "I'll make an exception for him."

"You'll need to get in line," Brand snapped.

Grigor's tone softened even more. "May I help you now, Alpha Mother? You're bleeding too quickly."

"If I die, so will that bastard," she said softly. "Even if I had hoped to deliver the moon's justice firsthand." I felt Brand's eyes on my face as I fought tears, and lost.

Grigor's focus stayed on Mama, though he was still in my mind, soothing me. "We need all the hands we can get, Alpha Mother. Please allow me to do this small thing for the mother of my beloved, my wolf's mate."

She hissed, then slumped back down onto the sofa. "Go on, then. Just... stop calling me that. I didn't earn it."

Grigor moved slowly to sit at her feet and held out a hand, waiting for her to take it. "If we all got what we earned, I would never have the courage to walk under the moon."

She placed her hand on his, and he did that thing again, where he pressed his forehead to it. Her hair moved first, sort of standing up on end, the curls waving in an invisible breeze. Then her eyes began to glow golden, and her lips parted. "Enough!" she said, just before Grigor listed to one side, catching himself on the sofa's edge.

"Grigor?" I kneeled beside him, but he waved me away, pressing a hand to his sternum. Now Mama was the one who looked well rested, and Grigor had a little of that "rode hard and put up wet" aura he'd had before *dessert*. "Are there any more guards?" I asked, worried.

"I'm well. Give me a moment." I frowned, but did as he asked.

"Shit, that's weird," Brand said, rubbing his own chest. "He's really good with the bonds. I could feel him pulling just from his own power, not from mine."

Wearing another guard's uniform, Finnick stepped into the room with Margarette clinging to his arm. "This room reeks, but it's the only food we have down here. Flor, can you—" he began, but I was already on my feet and running to help.

The woman I'd met at Southern was gone. In her place stood a refugee, her hair ragged, her scarred face drawn, and her clothing filthier than Brand's. "Flor," Margarette cried out as I enfolded her in a gentle hug. "I'm so glad to see you. Where's Glen?"

Bradley staggered into the room next, Finnick leaving me to rush to his side. The two chairs were carried to the table, and we sat the Hilliers down to eat. I was glad that the kitchen workers had piled plenty of meat onto the plat-ter, since they both looked like they hadn't eaten a meal—maybe not anything—in weeks.

Bradley made sure Margarette had plenty before he began eating, turning to me as he grabbed a small piece of meat, and took his time with it. I knew why they weren't gobbling it down; I'd been starved enough times to know it would just come back up if you ate too fast.

He finally asked, "Why isn't Glen with you, Flor? Is he safe?"

"I... I don't know." I explained what had happened, how Glen had drawn away the Enforcers outside. "I would've felt something if anything had happened to him, right? In our mate bond?" My mouth dried up as I tried to feel him through our bond now. It was oddly quiet, as if he was sleeping.

Margarette's hand flew to her mouth, the usually perfect nails split and ragged, only a few chips of red polish remaining, and her eyes welled. "You're mated? You and my Glen?"

I blinked, not sure how she was taking this. What kind of tears were those? The "I'm so glad to have a daughter-in-law" ones, or the "I'm so disappointed; my son could have done better than this trash" ones? I jutted my chin out. "We are. I'm mated to Glen... and Brand, as you know. And Luke, who's up in the Mansion, I think. I'm, ah, also mated to Finnick." Her eyes had gone wide, and Bradley had stopped chewing with a mouth full.

Grigor slid up next to me, and the meat fell out of Bradley's mouth as he stared. "Do you want to tell them, or should I, sweetheart?" he murmured.

I elbowed him in the gut. "Not helping, Grigor." He stifled a laugh, and I stepped away.

Finnick moved up beside me, stopping in front of Grigor just in time. Bradley had stood to do something—maybe launch himself at Grigor? Throw something? Finnick's appearance stopped him in his tracks.

Finnick spoke to the newcomers. "I think this might be a good time to do introductions. Bradley, Margarette? This is my great-many-times-over grandfather, Grigor Dimitrivich. Grigor? These are our allies. Please don't kill them."

"Your grandfather?" I managed to squeak out, before all hell broke loose.

CHAPTER 23
A NECESSARY VOW
LUKE

My wolf paced inside my soul while I did the same in the room I'd been assigned, wearing a path in the plush carpet as I tried to process everything that had happened, without truly knowing what was going on. I'd endured torture, abuse, witchcraft, a lethal dose of silver, and managed to survive it all. But staying in my room in the Mansion while my mate and brothers were sealed in the cells below might be what killed me at last.

I'd felt Flor enter the Mansion, or at least come close enough that I could sense her through our mating bond. I'd even scented her in the air in the hallway when I'd opened the door, but the Enforcer stationed there, Niall, had shoved me back inside. "We may not be in lockdown, but until one of the family returns, no visitors are allowed to roam the halls."

I paced a little faster, trying to think of what might be happening. I'd felt strange things in the assortment of bonds I held with Flor, Grigor, and even Glen. Glen seemed to be excited, though worried. Grigor had closed off our connection as much as he could, though I could sense ripples of surprise, shock, and rage as the hours wore on, and then strange mini-surges that felt like my heart was being touched with tiny sparks of static electricity.

Flor, though... She was the one my own soul, my wolf, gravitated toward in the tangle of bonds I held in my heart now. And the one I needed to stay clear of, since I could tell she was doing something that had her on edge. Which meant she needed to focus.

At least all of the McDonnells were gone, and I would know when they returned. I stopped pacing for a moment, praying that the McDonnell who came to release me from this room would be Finnick.

Of course, an hour later, it was Aidan, dressed in a dark suit as usual. But he was also covered in Finn's scent, and some of his blood. And another scent, one I hadn't smelled in months... *Callaway.*

My wolf's hackles were raised as I greeted Aiden with a half-smile, using all the years of practice I'd had at Southern to hide my true feelings. "Aidan. Any sign of Tana?"

"Come to the parlor," he said brusquely, ignoring the question. "You have a decision to make."

I followed him, though the skulking Niall walking too closely at my back made the hairs on my neck prickle. When we reached the parlor—it looked more like a library to me, with all of Aidan's collection of pack histories and law books—the Alpha stopped at the door. His voice was heavy with command as he spoke to me. "Enter and sit on a chair. You will not shift. You may not fight... yet."

His commands hit me with the force of rocks, stinging... and rolling away. *Shit.* Whatever was in that room, whoever was there, Aidan thought I'd shift, or attack immediately. I could have stopped there and refused the command, but I didn't want him to know I'd somehow grown powerful enough to resist a direct Alpha command from the Council Head. Because behind that door sat the one shifter my wolf wanted to kill more than any other in the world. And now we had the power to do it.

We're hunting, I said to my wolf as I stepped through the door, picking up the scent of the one who waited inside. *Be patient. The prey is not in position. Wait for the right moment.* He growled, but agreed to wait, just in time.

Shakily, I moved to a chair, keeping my gaze off Callaway and on Aidan. "I'm disappointed, Aidan," I said, enjoying the flinch at my familiar use of his first name. "This one was reported to have vanished. Fled like the coward he is, from an Alpha challenge. Bradley had Enforcers hunting him on behalf of the Council. Has he been your guest all this time?"

"No," Aidan answered honestly, taking a bottle of whiskey and pouring a large tumbler, not offering any to me or Callaway. "We found him running off like a rat, on a side road fifty miles away from your pack's front gate. We've kept him in the lower levels ever since." Every word he said rang with truth.

"A prisoner? Why would you do that?"

He clearly didn't like being questioned, his fist flexing at his side. "Why indeed? Could it be that we needed to wait for a full moon, when you were recovered from your illness, to finish the challenge you so foolishly left incomplete?" He couched his words in questions now, though I had a feeling none of the things he suggested were anywhere close to the truth. "Can you understand how dangerous it would be to leave an entire pack without an Alpha? Maybe not. Whole packs can go feral, you know.

And have. The Wes—" His face turned red, and he took a large swallow of whiskey.

He meant the Western pack, I was sure. I didn't know if he'd choked because he was trying to speak of them, or tell a lie about what had happened to them; it was hard to tell. There had been a hint of deception in the air that accompanied the choked-off words, but the room was already rank with the scent of my adopted father's decaying soul, the harsh smell of a feral wolf.

I couldn't believe I hadn't put it together long ago. It was unmistakable now, what that odor was. How many others in our pack had known exactly what was wrong with our Alpha? Feral Alphas were especially dangerous. Even if they'd known, there hadn't been anyone in the pack who could've challenged him, except his own Head Enforcer. I let myself remember Flor beheading Van Blackside in front of the gathered Enforcers at the Games, a wild smile on her face, her red hair short around her ears. It was one of my favorite memories.

Huh. Maybe I was more like Grigor than I'd realized.

Callaway interrupted my thoughts, his yellowing teeth bared as he spat out, "I wasn't his prisoner. I was his guest. I had food, drink, women. And as of tomorrow, I'll have you dead at my feet, and no one will question my authority ever again."

"You have no authority," I answered calmly. "I defeated you before, and I will again. I demand the right to challenge him in the ring on the full moon, Aidan. Tomorrow night is the full Council meeting. I am formally challenging the old, once-defeated Alpha of Southern, Calvin Callaway, for his position."

Callaway rose, struggling to stand and attack me. He had blood on the front of his shirt, I noted. His own, judging by the way it began bleeding again as he fought to get to me, and failed. Who had hurt him? Brand? Grigor? Flor? This house was so full of enemies, it could have been anyone.

"Calvin, you were told to remain seated and silent," Aidan barked. "I am Council Head. I am your Alpha. You may not speak another word until I give you my express permission." His Alpha command hit Callaway in the solar plexus, from the look of it, as he wheezed and obeyed.

My gums tingled as my wolf surged to the fore, desperate to answer the aggression from Callaway, and also... *Interesting.* To show dominance. My wolf had never been the most dominant in a room that included either of these two, but now he was. *Patience,* I reminded him. *We're hunting the old Alpha.* I wrenched my gaze away and peered at Aidan, who was retrieving a book from a shelf.

He was hunting *me,* I was certain, and his next words proved it. "Luke, your father pledged on this very law book, vowing to the moon to follow the Council Head."

"Bradley," I murmured. Aidan's watery green eyes met mine, and I had to force myself to look down.

"No, to the Council, and the one who leads it. Which means he has vowed to follow my orders. My leadership. If I allow you to challenge tomorrow night—" He held up one hand when I would have interrupted. "No, it is my right to decide what occurs at a Council meeting at my own home, on my packlands. And there are many more important things to take care of."

I knew what he meant. He was planning to execute Bradley and Margarette, and possibly Brand as well, if he couldn't secure his allegiance. And Flor... *Wait.* Did he even know she was in his home?

"The most important is dealing with the whore who

has somehow bewitched so many of the potential Alphas for the positions that need solid leadership. Mountain, Northern, and—if you were allowed to challenge, and won—even Southern." He nodded to my neck, and the obvious bite mark there.

"The whore? You can't kill her," I said as calmly as I could, raising an eyebrow when he bristled. "You shouldn't, at least."

His slow smile was as evil as any I'd seen. "And why not? I have her in a cell below this very room. I have a perfect execution planned. She's obviously a witch. It's my duty to execute her. After a trial, of course."

Fuck. He did know she was here. I reached along the bond and felt sadness and concern, but not panic. *She's fine,* I assured my wolf. *She's in the lower levels with Brand and Grigor and... the Hilliers.* It was almost too much power in one place. A miscalculation on Aidan's part, though he obviously didn't think so.

I nodded to the book in his hands, almost glad for the years I'd spent learning to hide my emotions from my father while he tortured Flor. My acting skills might be all that could keep her safe, and me outside of the lower levels, where I could do the most good. "A witch? Of course. How else would she have so many of us yoked to her?" I let my lip curl. "Can you imagine how it feels to have the female you're bonded to fucking someone else? Touching other males?"

Aidan's eyes widened, and a hint of his own enraged wolf emerged. He did know, or thought he did. Finnick had told stories about his parents' infidelity. Had Aidan been hurt by his mate's behavior, all these years?

I crossed one leg over the other, almost lazily. "Are you

considering keeping her in your dungeon? Sorry, lower levels."

"Or killing her," he admitted, his gaze taking me apart, looking for the lie in my words or behavior.

I shrugged. "Of course I would be against that, considering I'm stuck with her. And killing her outright will leave you with no leadership of many packs. The smaller packs could get ideas. The larger ones could attempt to become independent. Mountain's power ..." His gaze sharpened with greed as he considered that pack's thousands under his command. *Time to make him see.* "Mountain could fall back into Samuel's hands. He's still alive. If you kill his son by executing his mate, even if she is a witch... well, you know how loyal those Mountain shifters are to their own. I've heard they may have a witch who lives on their packlands."

He snarled. "You're trying to find some way to keep her alive."

"Of course I am. Look at him." I nodded at Callaway. "Look at what happened with too much distance from a true mate." Aidan's glass stopped halfway to his mouth, though I was almost certain he was pretending his shock. "You didn't know? He had a true mate and threw her out of the packlands to die, years ago. That's why he's so weak. Why he smells two seconds away from going feral. You don't want *that* running Southern." I gestured to Callaway, who was practically foaming at the mouth, proving my point.

"Do you know who she is, his true mate?" Aidan demanded. Callaway tried to answer, but he barked a command. "No, you stay silent. Luke, tell me about her."

I had kept this information from Elina, even under magical duress. But now, I was almost certain this would only help Flor to survive. "Lily was her name, wasn't it?" I directed the question at Callaway. "Flor's mother."

Aidan didn't react, and I knew somehow he'd figured this out. "Do you know who she is?" he repeated, and I got it. Aidan knew about Callaway having a mate, probably knew she was still alive, since Callaway was. But he didn't know who Lily was, where she'd come from.

"I know some, though it was a surprise to learn she came from the We—" I pretended to choke on the last word, like Aidan had, though I would have been able to speak of it now. I had no allegiance to this shifter or his packs. My only queen was Flor, and I was going to do whatever it took to keep her alive, no matter what that might be. Even if it meant speaking a promise I had no intention of keeping.

I cleared my throat, ducking my head gratefully when Aidan waved me to silence. "No need to share more now. We'll speak of it after the Council meeting. Everything will change tomorrow." I didn't know what he meant, but he wasn't wrong. Tomorrow would be full of changes for all of us.

A few moments later, with my hand on the law book, and Aidan's greedy eyes on mine, I did just that. I made the vow to follow the Council's rule under Aidan's leadership, then stated, "My vow and full obedience is contingent on this: I demand to formally challenge Calvin Callaway for the leadership of the Southern Pack, tomorrow under the full moon. And that the Alpha challenge portion of the Council gathering will occur before any other decisions are made, so I can cast my vote as the Southern Alpha, at the side of the Council Head." Aidan's eyes narrowed, and I tacked on, "Your side, Alpha Aidan McDonnell."

"It sounds like the perfect way to start a new chapter in

our pack's history," he agreed, as Callaway twisted and fumed on the sofa, snarling, though he was unable to speak. "Your challenge will take place first. Then you and I will clear the way for a new era of leadership at Northern as well." Aidan nodded at Niall, who had just stepped inside the doorway. He tossed back the rest of his drink, then gestured carelessly at Callaway. "Escort the old Alpha to a room and keep him there. Our guest and I will dine."

His hand was heavy on my shoulder as he guided me to the formal dining room, and the atmosphere was tense during the meal, the servant girls obviously terrified of their Alpha. But I made it through dinner without breaking down.

When I reached my room that night, though, I slept, until an energy surge of terrifying proportions woke me in the night. It felt as if I'd been drinking from a garden hose that turned into Niagara Falls, but all I could do was open my mouth wider and try not to drown, until it suddenly eased off.

Hello, little brother, Grigor whispered, his voice in my head as loud as a ringing bell.

Before I could reply, another voice was there. *Hello, mate.*

Was that... *Flor?*

Her laughter rang in my soul. *Well, it ain't the Princess of Peoria.*

CHAPTER 24
NAMES
FLOR

It took a hot minute to get everybody to stop trying to kill everyone else, and I was well past pissed when the cell finally got quiet enough to let them know it. "Honest to goodness, I never seen so many grown-ass adults throwing fits like it's an hour past your damned naptime. Now y'all hush the *hell* up, before I start kickin' your butts and blessin' your hearts the old-fashioned way." I stood on a chair, glaring at every one of the idiots who'd been wrecking the already messy room. At least the food was still mostly on top of the table, and not under it.

In the far corner of the room, Margarette was holding Bradley back from attacking Grigor—again—and agreed. "If you can't calm down, Bradley, I'll help her."

"What does she mean by blessing our hearts?" Grigor asked Finnick, wiping a fleck of blood off his lip. He'd let Bradley get a few punches in, I was pretty sure, but they hadn't fazed him. He was biting the inside of his cheek, trying to keep from laughing.

"You don't wanna find out," I promised, hopping down to check on Mama, who'd gotten agitated and started acting like her old self again, crazy and muttering. My heart sank.

"What's wrong with her?" Margarette asked after a moment. "Silver poisoning?"

"I don't know. She's got silver in her system. But that's what's been keepin' her sane. I thought, anyway. But when she was with my dad, she was clear-headed. Now... Yeah, this is the mate sickness she's had most of her life, and all of mine." I sighed as Mama pressed a hand to her gut, and another to her temple, like she was hurting in both places. She probably was.

"I've never met your mother," Margarette said hesitantly. The last day I was in Northern with her, she'd more or less admitted she knew who I was, in relation to Callaway. "I thought she was..."

"Yeah, so did I." I sighed, but relaxed a little when Mama seemed to settle. "Where are my manners? Margarette, this is my mama, Lily. Lily, this is Margarette Hillier." I didn't add their titles, since I wasn't sure how Mama might react to me saying it out loud to Margarette.

"She's your mother. She's the Alpha Mate of Southern," Margarette breathed, taking in all the silver scars on Mama's arms and legs as she crawled around. "Poor soul."

Mama kept muttering as she looked for something. "Heads and hearts. He's not our Alpha. His wolf is weak." I didn't think she was talking about Callaway, though.

"Maybe something happened to Callaway?" Margarette let Bradley go, though he still looked like he might attack Grigor.

Brand stepped between the two males again, taking Bradley's arm. "We should catch you up on a few things, while you finish eating."

The Northern Alpha moved stiffly back to the table, like

he'd aged a few decades since the last time I'd seen him. Eventually, after he made sure Margarette had eaten all she could, and that Grigor wasn't close to her, he moved over to the corner along with Finnick to listen to what Brand had to say.

Margarette listened to their conversation with half an ear while I tried to get Mama to return to the sofa. Instead, she went to the low bed and scraped around under it with an arm. "Ha!" She pulled out the short sword that must have been kicked there during the fight, and stood, one hand still pressed to her abdomen. "I don't know you," she said to Margarette, her eyes moving over the long scar that stretched across Margarette's face. She traced one of her own scars and sniffed, her eyes glowing gold. "Your wolf is strong."

"Hello, Lily," Margarette replied with a soft smile. "I'm Margarette Hillier, Alpha Mate of the Northern pack. My son Glen Hillier is mated to your daughter, Florida Wills."

"Boreal, a strong pack," Mama said after a few seconds. "I'm Alpha M..." She stopped speaking mid-word, her eyes dimming, her lips getting tight. "Florida? Florida Witch?"

I was surprised no one could hear my heart break as I watched her completely slide back into the mama I'd known for so long. When her eyes went wild and landed on me, clouded with hate, I covered my mouth with a hand to keep from making a sound.

To everyone's surprise, Grigor stepped over to her, holding out an arm, and bowing in that odd courtly way he had done before. We all ignored Bradley's growl in the corner, listening to Grigor's formal words. "You are Lily Rain, Alpha Mother of Occidens. Mother to my wolf's true mate. Heart of the Tenebris pack." She eyed him suspiciously, but didn't seem afraid now. Maybe a little wary, but he was blood-spattered. "The Florida witch is long dead. That witch's daughter is alive, but I vow I will kill her, and keep your child safe."

Mama's brow furrowed. "My... daughter. My..."

"Your Flor," Margarette finished for her, as she reached out a hand. "She is such an exceptional young woman. Can I tell you what she did for my pack? How she saved us?"

"Y-yes." Mama allowed Margarette to lead her to the sofa, and they sat together, talking softly about me. While the other males cleaned up the mess they'd made, I allowed Grigor to wrap his arms around me, his chest to my back. The little shocks that always came from our contact were muted through our clothing.

"It's my name, isn't it?" I asked. "Florida Witch Wills. She hates it. When she hears it, she thinks I'm *her*." I swallowed hard, trying not to let my pain show. "Is it because my father named me?"

Grigor pulled me over to the chair, lifting me to sit on his lap. He was the shortest of my mates, but we fit perfectly, our limbs twining together like we were holding each other up. "Witches can do spells. Both light, bright magic, fueled by the sun or the moon, or created by self-sacrifice. This one was not that kind of witch. Verbena Flock is what Luke said she was called, though her true name could have been something different when she was born. Her kind of magic requires blood, pain, or a sacrifice—but not one of her own."

"Mama said the witch forced Callaway to promise not to kill me, after. He gave me her name, to force a connection between us."

"If I didn't know what an idiot your father was, I would think what he did was very clever. He honored the vow he made to give you her name, in a way. From what I can piece together, the witch your father contracted was the leader of her coven. She expected to break a bond, but your presence in your mother's womb complicated the spell. Perhaps she sensed your strength, even then."

The whole room had grown quiet, everyone listening to him. "Changing a name is no small thing, especially if it's done through the power of blood, and with magic. If you'd been born Verbena Flock, and the witch had survived trying to break your parents' mate bond, she would have had a hold over you no one could break. You would, in effect, have become a vessel she could pull from, and use." I shivered at the thought, and he held me a little tighter. "She could have found you no matter where you might be hidden. Even after her death, it's possible her coven could have pulled strength from you to do their spells."

I laughed, a little hysterically. "But because my father was an idiot—"

"Yes," he said with a smile. "And you and your mother were strong. The witch died, in any case, and your father fulfilled his promise to name you for her, more or less."

"Where did the name Wills come from?" Bradley was very carefully not looking at Grigor when he asked, but at my mama.

She whispered her reply. "Rose Willow was the name of my best friend when I was a little girl, before we had to run. Mama said we needed a different last name, once we got out of the packlands. They'd kill me if they knew I was..."

"A Rain, one of the descendants of the Alpha Mothers," Grigor finished for her, when she had to stop for a moment.

She nodded. "Willow was still too close to the pack names, and my mama said Wills meant protector. Resolute protector," she whispered. "She used her power to change my name."

"So we really are Wills. I like it. I like knowing where it came from."

Mama didn't reply; she'd fallen back on the sofa, obviously in pain. Grigor stood, setting me down on the chair, and approached. He held a hand out to Mama, waiting for her to acknowledge him. "May I? I can ease your pain."

"No... blood magic."

"I have sworn to my brother mate, Brand, not to harm an innocent. I would never harm you, Alpha Mother."

After a long, measuring look, she took his hand. "I'm not really an Alpha Mother. I never had a ceremony."

"You never needed a ceremony, little blade. You were born an Alpha Mother, and earned the right to the title by fighting without cease for your whole life. You're one to the shifters in your rogue pack; there's no other way they could have escaped death, if you hadn't been the mother they needed to help them battle their madness."

"Tenebris," she breathed. "I wish I could see those boys again."

"I can help you heal, so you can try."

With a sigh, she closed her eyes. "Call me Mama, then."

His gaze flew to mine, emotions swirling so fast, I wasn't certain how he felt. After a few heartbeats, he smiled. "Yes, Mama." Then he closed his eyes, and I felt— almost saw—the magic moving from him to her.

"Blue," Brand muttered, moving to my side. "The magic. It's blue."

"You can see it?"

"Yes. You can't?" He wrapped his arms around me.

"No. I can feel it in here, but I can't see it." I pressed a hand to my heart. "I don't have your eyes."

Those silver-white eyes moved over my face. "You have every part of me, little one."

We watched as Mama's features softened. She fell asleep, smiling, and Grigor rose, a little shaky, as Margarette carried Mama to the bed and laid her down. Once she was lying quietly, Brand murmured, "We need to talk. Outside." He led us all into the hallway.

To my surprise, Bradley and Margarette rushed to me, and before I knew what was going on, they'd enfolded me in a group hug. "Oh, Flor, we're so glad to see you again. We just wish it weren't under these circumstances," Bradley said, before Margarette cut him off.

"I wish I could tell Glen how happy it makes me that he has you—that you all have each other."

My eyebrows flew upward. I wasn't sure what had changed, but something had made her get onboard with the multiple mates thing.

"And if you need us to help you disentangle from *that one*..." Bradley said. "He may have saved my life, but that doesn't mean he gets to ruin yours."

Someone growled softly, and everyone went quiet, but when we all looked to see who it was, the growling one wasn't my wizard mate.

It was Brand. "We are together. Flor, me, Glen, Finn, Luke... and Grigor. Treat him with respect. We need him; she needs him. There will be no more discussion." His pale eyes bored into Bradley, and it had never been clearer who had more power.

Bradley's shoulders dropped a split second after his gaze did, and Margarette hmphed. "Well, we'd better discuss a few things before morning. When the moon rises tomorrow night, we won't have the chance. We need to figure out what weapons we have, both non magical and magical, it seems. We need to plan what to do if..." Her eyes moved from me to each of my mates, and I shook my head.

"Don't say it. It's not going to happen."

"Flor. It's hard enough with one mate. When Bradley was dying..." She swallowed audibly, but went on. "I would have gone with him. You need to be prepared."

"I am," I declared. "I'm prepared to kick witch ass from here to the Atlantic if I have to, maybe see if water really does make them dissolve."

I thought they'd laugh, but Grigor just mused aloud, "Water, no. But salt could be useful, depending on how much we could lay hands on." His fingers started moving, like he was doing some mental calculations.

Margarette swallowed again, looking like she was trying not to cry. "I just can't see how it'll be all right. If that bitch gets her hands on even one of you—"

"We'll just have to hope that doesn't happen," Finnick interrupted.

"Hope?" she scoffed, and it was so much like the tone I'd had in my voice every time I'd said that word in my life, up until now, that I couldn't help but smile.

"Yeah, actually. Del always told me to use every weapon I had. You know what I figured out since I left Northern? One of the strongest ones I ever had was hope, even if I didn't know it. I always had hope that I'd get out of Southern, so I never gave up running when the bastards hunted me. I hoped that I'd find a place that was safe, so I kept fighting, and hiding, and taunting Ivan when I was kidnapped from your packlands. And I found that place, at Mountain."

She winced slightly, probably remembering how she'd promised me that safety at her pack.

I gave her a half smile in return. "I even hoped for the impossible. That Brand could be Alpha of his pack, but not have to kill his father to get there. And that came true." My gaze captured hers, and I saw a dawning understanding. "I hoped for friends, and I found them in the last place I'd ever imagined. My own shitty pack. I never knew that all those years, while I was struggling to stay alive and away from the males, that the girls, the women, were helping me in secret.

"And I'm *their* hope, Margarette. Without me, without my mates, there is no good world for them. So, I'm going to run with it. I'm gonna let that hope fuel me, and give me the strength to fight for a world they deserve."

I felt Brand's eyes on me, then Grigor's arm slid around my waist. "Let's find a quiet room and rest for a while, my little blade."

"We'll watch your mama," Brand promised, gently escorting the Hilliers back into the room. I blew him a kiss before Grigor led me down the hall and away, Finnick following behind.

CHAPTER 25
YOURS ALL ALONG
FLOR

We traveled down one dimly lit hallway after another, until finally, Finnick stopped in front of a door. He pressed his hand to the locking mechanism, but nothing happened.

"Show our mate what you can do, brother," Grigor encouraged.

"I can't do much," he argued.

"Show off for her," Grigor whispered, with a wink to me. "She'll be impressed."

To my surprise, Finnick ducked his head, then pressed his hand back to the keypad. Small electrical sparks flew out of his hand, and the door clicked open.

"Magic? I am impressed," I admitted as I moved beside him, letting my fingers trail across his chest, loving the way he shivered just the smallest bit. Even though I hated the uniform he had on, he looked like a model from a fashion magazine, lean muscles filling out the jacket, and above the open collar, all high cheekbones, flaming auburn hair, and bright green eyes. He filled out the fabric of the trousers, too, I noted, and bit my lip at the substantial bulge that my simple touch had created.

He blushed, but when he ran one hand over my shoulder and tucked a lock of hair behind one ear, it was my turn to turn red. I had to clench my teeth to keep from whimpering, moaning, or something equally dumb at the way his hand lit up every nerve. He could feel my reaction in our bond, and his shoulders straightened as the air filled with the slightest hint of warm cinnamon and jasmine.

Inside the room, a combination of less pleasant scents met my nose. Electrical burning, spilled whiskey, and strangely, peanut butter. The lights were dim, and the room more well-furnished than I would have expected in a prison. One wall was lined with shelves that held a mini-fridge, a microwave, and a basket of snacks. Close by was a small table and chair with a reading lamp and a tablet, and in the center of the wall to the left was a bed.

"Someone slept here?"

Finnick shook his head. "This is one of two rooms the tech crew that worked down here was assigned for breaks. No one's ever actually used the bed that I know of."

I sat on the edge of it, bouncing a little. It was small, twin-size, but the mattress was firm, and the only scent was laundry detergent. "Tech crew?"

Grigor answered for him, as Finnick stepped into a small room—an adjoining shower and toilet. I heard water running. "I'm afraid they're still at their posts, locked into their little office."

My gaze flew to the camera in the corner of the room. I didn't think it was working, but who knew? "Are they in there spying on us?"

"From the afterworld, perhaps," Grigor muttered, as Finnick rejoined us. When Finnick frowned at him, he shrugged. "I told you before, I needed fuel. I didn't even torture them." He turned to me. "Don't worry, my queen. They were not innocents. They were bad men. I checked."

He checked? I wondered how, as I fought to keep from smiling. Grigor's bloodthirstiness didn't bother me one bit, but it would probably be a mistake to joke about it. I took a turn in the bathroom next, cleaning up as best I could, and taking off everything but my too-large, borrowed shirt before returning to the bed.

"So, are we resting then?" I unbuttoned the collar and lay on top of the soft gray blanket, the loose shirt covering to the middle of my thighs.

"Rest. Ah, yeah. I guess you're tired," Finnick choked out, though Grigor was shooting him an odd look. He kept glaring at Finnick, then cutting his eyes to me, even tilting his head, like *go on.* It was funnier than it should be.

"I should be tired," I said, stretching. My boobs were still small, but they had a little more curve to them now, and they showed through the shirt—the nipples, especially —as I stretched. Two sets of eyes landed on them, hungry, then fell to the bottom hem that was now resting at the very tops of my thighs. The air in the room grew charged with desire. "I'll just get comfortable." I lay back on the bed, hoping I looked sexy, but more than a little insecure. I may have bitten a handful of mates, but I wasn't some sort of practiced seductress.

But honestly, these two were meant to have some skills. Instead of joining me, Grigor pretended to examine the snacks, holding up a package of peanut butter crackers like it was a lost treasure of the ancients. Finnick was looking anywhere but at me.

"I didn't know getting laid was supposed to be this

difficult," I grumbled, yanking the edge of the blanket up over my face.

Grigor's whisper carried even through the covers. "All right, pup, get over there before she really does fall asleep."

"I can't." Finnick's reply was agonized. "Not down here."

My breath caught as I realized what he meant, and when the blanket was pulled away a moment later, my eyes were stinging. Damn, I was thoughtless. This was where he'd been tortured as a child. Maybe not this room, but this place. "Finn, I'm sorry."

"No, Flor," he said, shame etching his features. "I'm the one. I... I lost so much of my innocence down here. I don't deserve you—no, don't argue. It's not your forgiveness I need. It's my own, and my wolf's. We know we haven't earned the right to be with you. But even if we had... I couldn't bear for our first time together to be here."

"But we will have a first time," I said carefully. My own wolf was pacing. This was the mate who'd tried to turn us away before. The one who'd hurt my wolf, in a way I hadn't realized until now, when she was so close, just under my skin. Agitated, and ready to burst forth. "You're not rejecting me."

"Never," he swore, gathering me into his arms. His mouth landed on mine, kissing me thoroughly, the embrace deceptively gentle. His lips were soft and almost reverent, but his arms were bands of iron around me. He was not letting me go. I fell into the sensations of his mouth on mine, his tongue exploring me. I nipped at the top of his tongue, where my first mating claim lay, and shuddered when his wolf answered my teasing with a low growl. He pulled back a few inches, and his eyes shone with bright fire, blue sparks swimming in the depths. "I'll never let you go, mate. I have so much to show you. So much to give you. But first, I have to earn back my place at your side."

He pulled me close again, devouring me with his lips, his hands moving on my back and shoulders, leaving trails of sensual fire everywhere he touched. I pressed my thighs together, trying to ease the building ache there. At last, just as I was wondering if I might come just from his kisses, he broke away.

He licked his lips, his canines too sharp to be human as he stared fiercely, silently, down at me. The hunger in his gaze had me thinking I'd been wrong. Maybe I was a seductress after all.

Slowly, I unbuttoned my shirt and let it fall open. "You sure you want to wait, Cityboy?"

"I do not. But I must." I would have sworn a spark flew from his eyes to the bed, and I blinked. By the time I opened my eyes again, he was at the door. "Grigor? Your mate needs you."

"*Our* mate, pup," Grigor purred as he stalked closer, taking off his stolen uniform like the fabric had offended him. "Keep watch?" Finnick's reply was a grunted yes, before he stepped outside.

Before the door closed, Grigor's last piece of clothing fell to the ground, and he stood still, his eyes devouring me while I took him in. He was lithe, and his skin was slightly darker than Luke's, with muscles that flexed and shifted sinuously as he circled the bed, almost like some sort of jungle cat. His sharp jawline flexed, too, as if he were forcing himself not to leap on me and claim me. Every line of his body was sculpted, as if the centuries of his life—*centuries, for fuck's sake!*—had perfected, rather than aged him.

He was a legend, and the only one of my mates I hadn't

bitten. The one I knew the least, and the one who seemed the farthest out of reach for a Southern pack reject to be with. The small, faded scar on his chest reminded me that he'd also loved someone else first. My insecurities flooded back with a vengeance.

"So, it's just the two of us," I babbled, when he stopped at the right side of the bed. "That's... nice?" I fought to keep my eyes above his waistline, but I couldn't. His cock was almost at my eye level, and it was rock hard and long enough to make my mouth water, curving up in a smooth arc to press against his stomach.

"Nice? The things I want to do to your body could not be described that way. I want to *own* you. I want to leave my mark so deeply inside you, in your body and your soul, that you will feel me there for the rest of your life. I want to make you whimper with need, and scream with pleasure." His gaze was filled with a blend of lust and compassion as I blushed so hard, I probably would've passed out if I hadn't already been on the bed. His tone was solemn when he finally asked, "But what I want isn't important. Do you truly want me, little blade? Are you certain you want to be bonded to me?"

I relaxed at the slight tremor in his voice. Somehow, he was just as insecure as I was. "So certain," I said, knowing the truth was all he needed. I reached out and took his hand in mine, pressing it to my heart so he could feel it beat. "I've wanted you since the forest at Northern. You made my heart race then, and it's never slowed down." We both smiled as he felt the evidence of that. "It feels like I've been yours all along, Grigor. That this is just the final step in some dance we've been doing since we met."

"Since long before that, *moya koroleva*," he whispered, running the back of one hand over my cheek, then down my neck and shoulder, over one of my tight nipples, and to my stomach. My abdomen trembled. "Where shall I claim you, my perfect mate? Where shall I put my mark?"

He leaned over the bed, tracing my other mates' marks slowly, so lightly it felt like a feather moving over my skin, the electric feeling of his hands shooting into my core, making me gasp.

"Here?" He touched Brand's mark, then Luke's. "Here?" He teased the skin around Finnick's mark, sending a little power into the place. Whatever he was doing, it felt amazing, and I heard a muffled groan from outside the door. Finnick had felt that, too.

Grigor winked. "Glen left a gorgeous mark. I plan to taunt him with it every time I feast on your delicious pussy." He leaned over and kissed my mouth, a surge of power moving with his tongue over mine, and his hand resting on Finnick's mark on my neck again. I felt a series of sparks connecting those two places, then travelling down my body to land and go off like miniature fireworks... in my clit.

I whimpered. Had I just come?

"Damnit, Grigor!" Finnick shouted from outside. "I don't have any other clothes to change into."

Grigor's wicked grin had me laughing. "Did you just make him come? In his pants?"

"No, little blade. *You* did." His hands moved to Luke's mark before he shook his head. "Best not to distract that one."

He distracted me instead. He moved his warm body next to mine, his hands and tongue free to explore, as mine were. I'd kissed him before, at Southern, and he'd tasted me then. More than tasted: he'd wrecked me, moving his tongue at speeds I was almost certain required magic.

But I'd never been able to take my turn, never had the freedom to explore him. I was more than a little nervous to try out my brand new skills on such an experienced mate, but what if I didn't get another chance? We were heading into a battle we might not survive.

And the jobs weren't going to blow themselves.

I grinned at my terrible humor, tucked one foot behind his calf and, in a quick move, flipped us so I was on top and he was beneath me. My hair fell over the sides of my face as I instructed, "Keep your hands on the sides of the bed."

He blinked, then obeyed.

"Now, don't move." His body practically hummed with tension as I slid down the bed, my tongue tracing patterns, until I reached his cock. The skin there was smooth as velvet, and I took a moment to run my hand over it, then dropped my mouth to the tip, drawing in just the end. "Mmmmm," I hummed as I moved lower, one hand exploring a little farther back, cupping his balls. I let a finger stray even farther back, and he stiffened.

"Flor!" He sounded almost shocked, but a droplet of pre-cum had beaded at the tip of his cock, so it wasn't a bad thing. I lapped up the drop, surprised when it tasted almost minty. It wasn't cold, but the sensation on my tongue was the same as when I'd drunk from a stream in the Northern packlands. Bright and bracing.

"That could get addictive," I muttered, before drawing more of him between my lips. He was just the right length and width for this, and after a few attempts, I was able to get my lips to the base without choking.

"Flor," he repeated, then let out a string of words in some strange language. "I can't... You can't..."

I stopped. "Is it not good? I haven't done this a lot."

He hadn't moved his hands, but I could tell he wanted

to. "My beautiful, perfect mate, every touch of your hands is a fire that burns me alive. Your tongue is more pleasure than I can bear."

I tried to figure out what he meant. I felt Brand's amusement in our bond, and noted the deepening flush on Grigor's cheeks as it sank in. "That good, huh?" I wiggled my eyebrows, sliding my mouth back down over him, loving the way it made him tense up.

After only a few more strokes, he broke. In a movement so fast I couldn't tell how he'd done it, he was on top of me again, his eyes flashing. "That good, my love."

"Fuck me, Grigor."

"Anything you ask." He slid one hand up to my hair, pushing it out of the way, his eyes snagging on the metal tag in my ear, emotions moving over his face too rapidly to make them out. He balanced over me and pressed the smooth tip of his cock to my entrance, then surged forward with his hips, filling me in one deep thrust.

I'd already come, so I was more than ready, but I came again when he lowered one hand and set a fingertip vibrating directly over my clit, never hesitating, even though he was still fucking me.

Something was wrong, though. He was moving smoothly, never breaking his cadence, but he was holding back. "Grigor," I whispered, pleasure zinging through me as another climax approached. "Grigor, please. Let me in."

His hips slowed. "My queen?"

"Claim me. Let me in," I repeated, lifting a hand to his hair and pushing it behind one ear. "I want to hear you in my thoughts." My wolf rose inside me, whining for her mate, for Grigor's wolf.

His rose as well, his dark eyes shining less with magic, and more with a wild darkness that called to me. He was dangerous, but never to me. His canines slid out to show over his lower lip, and somehow, it made him look almost boyish. Eager.

"Anything you ask," he repeated, and began moving more slowly. His lips pressed gently on my shoulder, opposite the one where Brand had marked me, just below Finnick's mark, and he kissed the skin softly. Then he opened his mouth and bit down.

"Grigor!" I gasped. The bed was shaking beneath us, the objects that had been on top of the table and shelves clattering to the ground.

"My mate," he replied with dark satisfaction, and the bed shook even more violently. No, not the bed. The *earth*. The whole house above us was moving, as was the ground below.

"*My* mate," I replied, feeling my own teeth become longer, sharper. I tilted my head and sank my teeth into his firm, smooth neck, tasting fire and ice. Power and darkness. Pure love and an eternity ahead of us to share it with one another.

"My love," he half-shouted, as he emptied himself into me, then opened his mind. I fell into his thoughts, into his memories, drowning in a storm of love, madness, and desire.

CHAPTER 26

OPENING UP
GRIGOR

I t was more difficult than I had dreamed to keep my power from reducing the house above us into rubble as I surged into my mate's body. The pleasure was a maelstrom that caught me, the overwhelming bliss nearly blinding. Power from the connection filled me, healing me from the silver poisoning and beginning to refill my magical reserves.

At long last, my wolf had claimed his mate. He wanted the world to know what had just happened, wanted the earth itself to be as transformed as he was by the connection that lit up his weary, feral soul. I felt such compassion for that part of me, the side that had made certain we stayed alive, though it was a punishment at least as horrific as the life I'd lived, to suffer through all those years alone.

But *now*. Now, she was here, asking to be let inside. So we turned our attention from shaking the world on its foundation, to doing something far more difficult: allowing the one we loved most to see exactly who it was, what it was, she had claimed.

Her wolf walked into my spirit on small, dark paws. Her

coat was every bit as dark, though it glinted red, and her eyes were amber fires that warmed me as she moved through my memories, exploring. Searching. What was she looking for?

Not that it mattered. I'd trespassed on my beloved's thoughts many times, before I had any right. As she ran through my past, through the threads that made up the tainted web of my magic, sniffing and sneezing once when she approached the oldest memories I had, I knew I had no choice. I belonged to her. She owned my body, my mind, my soul itself.

The earth stood still, but inside, I quaked to think of what she had found when her wolf stopped running.

"Oh, Grisha," she whispered, and I knew she'd seen my earliest memories. "I'm so sorry you had to wait for so long. I'm glad you lived. Glad you survived... everything. We'll be together from now on. Your wolf and mine."

Tears slipped down my cheeks, and I opened my eyes, wondering. I couldn't remember crying since... since I was Grisha, and my mother held me. I tried to clear my mind, to think of what my perfect mate needed most.

My wolf growled low in my chest. *Ah, of course.* "Your wolf is ready to emerge. Would you like to shift, my queen?"

"Can I?" she asked, but before she'd finished her question, I'd used the connection between us—a wide, amber bridge of power as thick as my wrist, and a hundred times stronger—to help her slip into her wolf form.

She was as small as I remembered from her one disastrous shift after the battle at Southern. I'd thought the red on her coat back then had been blood, but if it was, it had soaked into her wolf's form somehow, tinting her a rich ruby hue. Her snout was narrow and perfectly shaped, her ears dainty, with the circle of metal still pinned to the left one, though the tufted fur along the edge obscured it somewhat.

"You are magnificent," I praised, as she turned a circle on the mattress, trying to see herself. "My wolf would like to come out and meet her in fur." She yipped in agreement, and I changed.

We tussled on the rumpled bed, the scent of our love-making pleasing to both our wolves. She lifted her tail in the air enticingly, but I nipped her flank playfully. There would be a time for our animals to mate as well, but I could feel others approaching.

Damn, it was good to have enough of my magic back to extend my senses. Soon I'd have enough to break down the doors, if we needed. Enough to protect my mate, and my brothers, and level this whole tainted building if necessary. I wasn't there yet, though, even with the fresh mating bond. But soon.

A soft knock at the door had her jumping down and sniffing at the handle. It opened, and Finnick and Brand stood there, gaping at her beauty from the doorway as she preened.

"There you are, wildflower." Brand stripped out of his clothing. His shift was like a droplet of water falling as he moved from one form to the other effortlessly.

"By the moon, Brand, when did you grow into a bear for real?" Finnick muttered, backing up to make room for the monstrously large wolf to pad into the room. My own wolf was impressed, but not threatened by him, not even when he turned those silver-white eyes in my direction.

Well, perhaps a little. He was the largest wolf I'd ever seen, a dark chocolate brown that reminded me of a grizzly bear, though he moved with a far more sinuous grace as he nuzzled and licked at our little queen's darker coat. She scraped her teeth along his shoulder, where her mark lay, though it was hidden under his fur. I could sense it, though, my own fresh claiming bite somehow connected. We were *all* connected now, invisible cords running from me, Brand, Glen, Luke, and Finnick to her, our center. They were all strong, except one.

Finnick stood at the door, his hands gripping the frame so tightly his knuckles turned white as he stared inside, his expression heartbreaking. It was deep love tempered by an equally deep loss, an ocean of regret and shame.

Pup? His damp green eyes met mine before he dropped them to the floor. I spoke into his mind, though it was harder than it should be. He was keeping himself shut off from the shared bonds. *Pup, let it go. She has forgiven you. Shift, and greet your mate.* I could tell he was planning to say no, so I put a thread of command in my inner voice. He needed to be reminded that he was no longer who he had been. *You will not punish your wolf for your own choice to push her away. Let him greet her, Finnick Dimitrivich.*

A wave of gratitude shot from him to me, as the command calmed at least some of his turbulent emotions. Already sprouting fur, he stripped off his clothing and finished the shift. His wolf was also larger than mine, and lean, his russet coat shining even in the low light. He stepped silently into the room, but Flor immediately whirled to meet him.

She growled low, circling him, and the rest of the wolves in the room went still and silent, waiting to see what she might do. Flor was forgiving—sometimes too forgiving for my tastes—but her wolf was an unknown. Hackles raised, fur bristling, she stalked up to Finnick and sniffed the place on his shoulder where her mark was hidden under gray fur. Then she stared directly into his eyes and stuck out her tongue.

Finnick blinked, uncertain what to do. He glanced at me and Brand. I had no idea, but Brand seemed to understand. He let his own massive tongue hang out.

A wave of shame rushed out of the poor pup as he understood as well—not only what Flor's wolf was demanding, but why. I listened to his thoughts, seeing flashes of what had taken place. This was the part of him that had touched another. The place where Flor had marked him, and the same place where his own misguided feelings of betrayal were concentrated.

I saw flickers of memories, his wolf rising, forcing Finnick's human side—the weaker half of his soul, from the wolf's point of view—to lie dormant.

Back then, his wolf had tried to chew off his own tongue. He'd almost succeeded before Finnick had regained control of their body. But every time he slept, the wolf woke, until Finnick had been forced to lock him away, using too much of his strength to do so.

Now Finnick's wolf struggled to be still, but managed, keeping his legs stiff and his tongue out as Flor approached, growling and sniffing at his muzzle. Was she going to bite the tongue off for him? A part of me approved of the idea. But it would hurt her, if she did. I readied my hold on the bonds, in case I needed to protect her from his pain.

She pressed her nose against the tip of his tongue, lapping the small mark where she'd claimed him. Then, she bit down, gently, carefully, pressing her teeth into the same marks she'd left the first time, before pulling back to stare directly into his eyes. They had never been physically intimate, and I knew that this bite would strengthen their connection further, but after she withdrew, the low growl in her throat almost playful, I realized that her bite had healed him. Healed his wolf, through blood. His spirit was energized, and the bonds between us all sang with new power.

Blood magic? I wondered, but didn't see any red sparks.

Moon magic, Brand's voice thundered in my mind.

I wasn't certain what he meant, but I accepted it. Though I wasn't certain how comfortable I was that the Mountain shifter had been able to enter my thoughts so easily, and without me noticing his presence. I lifted my lip, showing my sharp teeth.

His wolf let his tongue hang out, lolling in obvious amusement, before he nuzzled Flor once more and trotted away. A moment later, Finnick followed, his spirit obviously lighter. I hopped back up on the bed and shifted into my human form.

Flor stood on four legs, the cutest, disgruntled look on her furry face. I had to bite my inner cheek not to laugh, since she was concentrating so hard, she'd crossed her eyes. I didn't help her this time, though. She needed to know how to shift without any interference, and in another minute, she did just that, sneezing and shifting almost at the same time. Somehow, the sneeze made her do a half flip and while she was human-shaped in the end, she was also upside down. One leg was propped on the wall behind the bed, and the other had almost smacked me in the face.

"Don't say a word," she warned.

I mimed zipping my lips, and she unfolded herself, curling in to hold onto me. She slept for an hour or two like that while Brand and Finnick shared their thoughts with me, sketching in the details of our plan.

When that conversation ended, I checked in on Glen, who had escaped whoever had been chasing him, at least for the moment, and was safe. Then I reached for Luke, who was resting. We were all gathering our strength for the coming fight.

When Flor awoke, we made love again, slowly, staring into each other's eyes the entire time, as if we couldn't bear to look away. Or at least I couldn't.

"I have to leave soon," I said quietly, tucking her hair behind her ear, and tracing the circle of metal that still marked her. But now that I knew how she felt about it, how it reminded her of Del and learning to fight for her own survival, I no longer found it unattractive.

She sat up. "Where are you going? Are you planning to just... kill everyone?"

How she knew me already. "I had thought of doing just that. But I'm still not at my full strength, and Luke is in their hands. He needs to face his father and gain his rightful place as Alpha. Finnick feels a deep need to confront his own Alpha and make him pay for his crimes. The witch is not here, not close."

"You're sure?"

"As sure as I can be without seeing her in front of me. She was using a spell to hide, but let it fall. I can feel her through her blood, now that I know she's one of my line." I scowled, still incensed that I'd allowed a witch like her to capture me.

I'd used some of the energy I'd gained during our mating to send tendrils of my magic out to search for my blood. Other than Finnick and Elina, I was certain there was no one else alive with even a drop of it. Not on this continent, in any case.

"You need a little revenge, too," Flor teased.

"Maybe," I agreed, and kissed her thoroughly. "In a better world, we would stay together for many days, with nothing to do but learn the heights of pleasure. I would have no goal but to explore the mystery of your perfect body. Even if this wasn't how I pictured our joining." She ducked her head, but I lifted her chin before the thought could take hold. "No, my queen, *you* were perfect. It was only the setting that left something to be desired."

She arched her eyebrows. "Oh? Where had you pictured this moment?"

I stood, pulling on my clothes reluctantly. "Perhaps I'd planned to make a bed for you, for us."

"A bed?"

"Yes," I said, not bothering to hide the truth of it. "I'd hoped to make a strong, sturdy bed from the bones of everyone who hunted you. Everyone who hurt you."

Her laughter filled the room as she rose, unfolding her perfect, lithe limbs. By the moon, she was distracting. "Grigor, tell the truth. Did you keep all the bones from the toadfuckers who hunted me?" When I didn't answer, she went on, muttering to herself, "I saw lots of guts. A few fingers, but not many bones."

"I may have collected some of them," I replied, trying not to reveal the location of the cache in my thoughts. I wasn't sure if the idea of a bed made from the worthless males' bones disgusted her or appealed. Even if I didn't make a bed, they could come in handy as benches, or chairs. A suitable throne for my little *behrserker* queen.

"You could make something with them," she agreed, tapping me on the nose before she covered her perfect body with clothing again. Then she grabbed a package of peanut butter crackers and headed to the door. "Maybe Brand would join in. He's a carver, you know. It could be a bonding thing."

I would never have imagined I would be fighting

laughter as I left my soulmate in a prison to sneak away. But I never would have imagined being so... It was such an unfamiliar emotion, I had to search for the word.

Happy. That's how I felt as I followed Flor and bid goodbye to her mother and the still-wary Hilliers, shaking hands with Finnick and exchanging nods with Brand. When I cast a quick look-away spell and walked right past the Enforcers at the secret entrance to the lower levels Finnick had shared with me, I was more than content. I was hopeful and happy as I left the lower levels to find the witch, ready to end her before she could do any more damage to one of my own. The emotion itself was a distraction.

A dangerous one.

CHAPTER 27
TRUE MATES, TRUE MONSTERS
FLOR

For the first few hours after he left, Grigor's happiness bubbled up inside my own chest, like a soda can that had been shaken up, and might explode at any moment. His joy at being mated to me was contagious, though his emotions tasted like rage, too. He was going off to kill the wicked witch, after all. I thought he might have found her, but when he caught me checking in on him, he sort of turned down the volume of the connection. Probably needed to focus.

I worried for him, but knew he was strong enough, now that we were mated. And he believed in me, as well as Brand and the others. He knew we could win our fight as well. Even with all the bad surrounding us, somehow it felt like good stood a chance.

I sat beside Mama on the bed as she rested, trying to ignore the funk that rose from the sheets. It was my father's awful scent, but it seemed to soothe her. I kind of understood it now; I couldn't get enough of my mates' scents. I sniffed subtly at my arm, taking in a little of the cold, clean scent of Grigor.

Maybe I wasn't all that subtle. "I did that for years after I mated Bradley," Margarette murmured from the chair, exhausted but amused. Bradley had gone with Brand and Finn to guard the doors at the same time Grigor had left to hunt down Elina, so it was just the three of us left in the room. "I couldn't get enough of his scent. I still can't. I just hide it a little better."

"Ah, sorry," I said, but she shook her head.

"Never apologize. I'm the one who needs to do that, for so much. I got stuck in my way of thinking about rank and rules—you showed me that. I never thought I could be just as wrong about mates. I spent so much of my life learning about them, studying them to see if I could help strengthen our pack. But seeing you with Brand and Finnick, and even that Grigor…" She shivered a little. "You're changing everything. You're special."

Was I? She might believe that, but I didn't. "I don't think so. I think the world just got bad enough that it had to change. If I hadn't been here, the moon would've found some other way to force the shifters here to stop their bull-shit." I could tell she wasn't convinced. "How many weapons are in this room right now, Margarette?"

"Your mother's sword," she said instantly. "And our wolves are weapons, of course." I waited, and she looked around. "I suppose you could use the silverware on the table. You taught the women at Northern that. And at Southern, from what your mama told me."

Del would have had a field day teaching Margarette. I grinned. "There are at least fifty things in this room I could use as a weapon." I pointed to a crumpled peanut butter cracker wrapper. "Even that could be a way to disguise traces of scent." I nodded to a few other things I could see— the chair legs that could be taken off and used as clubs, the sheets that could be used to strangle or bind limbs, or even made into a slingshot in a pinch. Glass bottles that could be broken and swung as clubs, beer cans that could be ripped and reshaped into knives or throwing stars. "But the most important weapons, you can't see. Endurance for running. A mind that sees clearly, that can stand up to pain and pressure. Training."

"I miss training." She stood and stretched, her movements stiff.

"Me, too." I slid off the bed, moving over to a cleared section of the floor. I sank into the first *tae kwan do poomsae* Del had taught me when I was young, and Margarette followed my lead. Both of us whispered our *kihaps* softly, so Mama wouldn't wake up, and moved on through the familiar stances.

After a half hour, we were both warm. "Wish we could spar," Margarette panted, taking a drink from a glass of water. I didn't want to say what I was thinking: that she needed rest and food more than exercise. That we would be fighting for our lives soon, and she needed to conserve her energy. She knew all that.

"Let's spar after we get out of here. Or fight as wolves, even. I shifted, you know."

"I heard. I can't wait to meet your wolf." She smiled, then tilted her head. "Why did you ask me about weapons?"

"Because I need you to understand something. I'm not the reason things are changing. I'm not special. I'm just the weapon that came to hand, when the Moon Goddess finally got pissed enough to step in." I held up the peanut butter wrapper. "Maybe She needed one that would be overlooked, counted out. One that no one would be afraid to let in their guard."

"Flor, you have five true mates. I think that makes you pretty special."

I shrugged. "You know, I never thought I'd take even one. Mama made me promise not to, for obvious reasons."

Mama's crackly voice came from the bed as she slowly sat up. "That's because my own true mate was a monster." She accepted the glass of water Margarette carried to her, and smiled at me. "You were the best part of him. The only thing he ever got right. Come here, baby." I kneeled on the floor at her feet, waiting. "I need you to know a few things before moonrise. And I need to give you my blessing and pass on my legacy." I had no idea what she meant, but she was as clear-eyed as I'd ever seen her.

"The sword?"

"No. I need to bless your matings. All of them."

I didn't get it. As far as I knew, matings weren't formally blessed, they just happened. But Margarette sucked in a breath.

Mama put her frail fingers under my chin and lifted my head. I stared at her familiar scars, her red-rimmed eyes with dark circles like crescent moons beneath them. "Grigor tells me I'm the last Alpha Mother, and he may very well be right. But he won't be after tonight."

"It's forbidden to speak of that," Margarette began to protest, but she stopped when Mama lifted one eyebrow.

"The moon can't be overruled. This is the old way, warrior. Listen and remember." It sounded like Mama's voice, but there was a thread of power woven into it.

Margarette went silent, her mouth still hanging open.

Mama stroked my cheek gently. "My own mother was dead by the time I met my mate, and sometimes I've felt that was a blessing in itself. But I am so glad to have known yours, all of them. I taught you that true mates were monsters. I was wrong, my baby girl. Yours are no such thing."

Tears streamed down my face. "Grigor might be," I half-joked.

"That's true. But he's the perfect type of monster for you. He'll stay in the shadows, and guard you better than he could otherwise. Some of the moon's children weren't created to hunt in the daytime." I didn't know what that meant, but she had half-closed her eyes. "I learned these words when I was little, but no one has spoken them in so long..." She moved her thumb to my forehead and traced a crescent. "May the moon watch over your heart, daughter. May you and your mates honor Her above all, and follow Her laws from your first howl to your last hunt. May your matings be fruitful, and your pups strong, and when the evening of your life grows dark, may you run on spirit feet with your true mates, and return to Her in the sky as one." She pressed a kiss to the place she'd touched with her thumb. She nodded at the sword. "Now, hand me that."

To my surprise, Margarette handed it to her. "Alpha Mother," she whispered.

Mama's eyes narrowed. "So you know what that means."

Margarette dropped her gaze. "We have a collection of books at home, all to do with true mates. Some of the books are old, with notes in the backs and the margins. I think I understand some of it. I never wondered what happened to the Alpha Mothers they wrote about. I was too worried about how few young were being born, how few mates were being found. I was trying to discover where they'd gone."

"Many of your pack's true mates were exterminated," Mama said, the thread of steel stronger now. "Your pack, and others around the world, may never recover, not for generations."

Margarette closed her eyes and fell silent again, her brow furrowed.

"The moon didn't make Alphas to lead the packs," Mama said. "Not alone. She balanced them, as she does all things. Light and darkness. Wolfcraft and witchcraft. Healer and destroyer. The Alpha Mothers in my pack were wise, strong women who balanced their counterparts. You remind me of them, Margarette." I thought it was a compliment, until she continued. "You're wise and strong, and blinded by prejudice. Easily led to your own destruction by the very ones who betrayed all the packs."

"At the Conclave," I whispered. "The last one at Southern, forty years back. The Betrayal."

"Yes. My uncle told me more, on our journey here. The young girl at that Conclave, the one who was supposedly attacked by a Western shifter, wasn't from Southern, but a smaller pack."

Margarette spoke hesitantly. "The Southern Alpha was killed, and the one from... your pack... executed for the crime." It was still hard for her to speak of Western, and I could tell that made her angry.

Good. More females needed to be angry at the males who'd talked them into giving up their power. More males should be afraid of what was coming for them, once the females rose up and demanded justice.

She coughed, and I told the part of the story I knew. "No, the other packs had already planned to strip Western of its rights before the Conclave began. Sergeant said that's why they call it the Betrayal. Because the Western pack didn't use magic at that Conclave to begin with. They'd vowed not to."

She nodded. "The girl. The one from the small pack— she was the one who claimed she was attacked by Western, and when other shifters retaliated, Alpha Hollis *was* killed by magic. But not ours. My uncle believes it was by *hers*."

"The girl," I said, putting it together. "She was Finnick's mother, wasn't she?" Elina was old enough to have been there, though she must've been a teenager.

"He thinks it could be." I wanted to ask more, but Mama started coughing, flecks of blood spraying into her hand. When I handed her another glass of water, she was obviously much weaker. "Help me put my sword on," she whispered. "Quickly. The moon is rising."

My wolf howled silently in grief and agreement, and I knew the final battle was almost here. Margarette wrapped Mama's sword in a cloth and helped her tuck it into her shirt, along her spine.

Footsteps pounded toward us from both ends of the lower levels, and I felt my mates moving closer. Not just Brand and Finn, but Luke as well.

Mama rasped the last few words just as Brand shouted through our bond, and out loud just outside the door, for us to be ready. "My daughter, Florida Witch Wills, you are the Alpha Mother of the Occidens Pack. Serve the moon with every breath, and She will give you Her wisdom and Her strength." There was no weird feeling, no magic or mystery. Except my own mama's eyes on me, clear as day, shining with pride.

"I love you, Mama."

"I love you, too, Flor."

CHAPTER 28
DISTRACTION
GRIGOR

J ust outside the exit to the lower levels, I smelled the witch's blood. But she was far away, and I assumed the closer scent was a distraction. I slunk along the tree line to the rise anyway, to see what was there. A large clearing ringed by pines, almost a small valley, took up half of the land inside the fences. A raised lip of grass-covered earth made up the meeting place, with a dirt ring in the center for the fights, or the speeches.

The scent of her blood was all around the area. Old blood that had soaked into the earth, as well as salt, as if the witch had done some spell there, and tried to cleanse it. This was where the Council would meet, but it was already teeming with Enforcers and servants.

The earth was shadowed around that area, but Elina McDonnell was far away, and old spells weren't my main concern.

She'd been away from the Mansion since the day she'd dropped me in her dungeon. Once I'd regained enough of my strength to seek her, I'd felt her presence moving away from the packlands before stopping to the northwest. I'd thought she might return, but instead, she'd stayed away, distant enough that perhaps she felt safe. Now, her blood was a pulsing beacon, calling me to her, to kill her.

I almost couldn't believe that her coven hadn't taught her how to hide her presence from other magic users. But then, there were so few witches left alive, and most of their knowledge had been lost. The only ones I'd sensed nearby were drained, like Finnick, almost to the point of losing their witchcraft entirely. She clearly assumed I was still bound by silver, helpless.

There was no doubt in my mind where the witch was now. I followed the pulse of her blood, the rank, familiar scent of her. I ran for hours, until I could taste her blood magic as well in the air, fresh traces of it mingled with violent death.

She hadn't run from the Mansion to hide. She'd gone here to kill, to gather more power, preparing to come back to her home and harm my mate. My brothers. I would not allow it.

My rage gave me speed, and I ran faster, invisible to the humans as I leaped over their roadways and dove back into the shadows of the trees on my way. The witch might have used an automobile to travel to her destination, but I could channel my wolf's power—and his speed—into my human form, and move just as fast.

I stayed as far from the roads and the stench of exhaust as I could, keeping her scent in my nostrils instead. I ran north and west, crossing roads and streams, seen only by the small creatures of the woods, who sensed my wolf and froze in place as I passed.

Before long, I slowed, within a mile of where my wolf's

nose insisted the witch had stopped. I wasn't scenting blood *inside* a body, but spilled. There was something flat, almost stale about the odor, though it grew more intense as I approached. Had someone else found her, killed her, before I could?

No, she wasn't waiting for me, wounded. This was something else, and the witch was somewhere else.

Incensed, I dropped the look-away spell as I stepped out of the cover of the trees. My wolf wanted nothing more than to return to our mate and guard her, take her out of the hands of her enemies. But I had to see what this was, understand what the purpose was.

In the clearing was a dark spell circle, the taint that rose up in the late afternoon almost as visible as the steam drifting from the spell's focal point. Six dead shifters, rogues from the state of their clothing and starvation, lay in a circle around a flat wooden platter of still-warm blood. There was an empty space around the circle, and a trail in the leaf mulch leading into the nearby forest. The seventh sacrifice, perhaps dragged into the woods after they were killed, or perhaps consumed.

I leaned down to examine the spilled blood. What spell had she done? Something to strengthen her own blood, which was in the platter, or something to bind the other shifters' blood to her own. Or both.

I covered my nose, offended by the reek of the spell circle and everything around it. The dead shifters carried the familiar stench of feral wolf, and must have been half gone before she'd gotten her claws into them for the spell. There had been at least four dozen other shifters here, though. An army almost, none of them among the dead. I examined the entire scene, noting traces of semen on the ground, before catching a scent I'd come across before.

Ivan, the silver-poisoned, half-mad shifter who'd attacked Flor. My wolf raged that she might still be in danger from that madman. I'd looked for any trace of him, magical or otherwise, before I'd followed Flor away from Canada to make sure she was safe from him. Then I'd tracked Sergeant all the way to Southern.

I'd known I would need to make sure Ivan was dead someday, but now I was cursing myself for letting it go. He was not one of the dead, but he had been here. I turned to face the Eastern packlands, knowing where he had to be headed, and with whom.

A slight tug at my senses from that direction, the connection of my blood to hers, had me cursing again. I could feel her as she moved away, back to the Mansion, and my feet itched to follow her. It would take much of my energy to do so. She had to be in a car, going that fast.

At the other end of our bond, Brand's wolf lifted his nose. Ah, I'd forgotten to mute those connections. Even though the distance I'd run would soften my emotions somewhat, they would all sense my unease. Gently, I pinched the bonds closed and turned my full attention back to the spell.

Just as I did, a sharp, frigid breeze cleared the air around me, carrying the stench of corruption and death away, and a more potent scent to me, of living blood. *It won't be living for long.* I followed the scent into the woods and, a few dozen feet later, the slight wheeze of labored breathing, finding the missing shifter.

Or what was left of him.

This one wasn't a rogue. I knew him well, though the last time I'd smelled him, I'd been at Southern. He'd spilled his seed on the floorboards of the Pack House, while I hid underneath the bed, keeping Luke alive. If Elina McDonnell had been this one's lover, and she had left him here, like this, then all the others were in more danger than I'd feared.

She wasn't an untrained witch. She had to know what she was doing, if she'd known not to go into the battle against Brand and the others without mustering more strength, and an army as well.

She'd known what the cost for a spell that would make her impossible to defeat would be. Which also meant... the salt and blood back at the Eastern Mansion may have been something else. Something far more dangerous than I'd imagined one witch with no coven could create.

Run back, my wolf insisted. *Kill him and go. No time.* I had a terrible feeling he was right.

I cursed as I approached the dying male. "Torran."

It was the wretched shifter who had tortured so many of the Southern pack, killing males and brutalizing females. Someone had taken all of his clothing, and most of his skin, and left him a shivering, dying mess on the cold forest floor. I approached with no pity at all, only a small regret that I was not the one who had done this to him, and a pinch of gratitude that his death would fuel my return to Eastern.

The male struggled to turn his head to me when I spoke, and made a garbled sound when he saw me. A laugh?

"Who?" I demanded, pushing power into the question, though I wasn't sure if the male could still speak. His cold eyes focused at last, bloody tears streaking down his raw cheekbones, and his mouth drew back into a terrible smile.

"My... mistress..." he croaked before he let out an odd, rattling wheeze and went still, that victorious smile stretched across his frozen face.

Fuck. I'd waited too long. But maybe I could drink some

of his pain. He had to have been in agony, given that he'd been skinned alive. I had a feeling he'd been in his wolf form for that, too. Just another indication that the witch knew what she was doing.

I leaned down to sniff at the bloody, mud-covered corpse. There was almost no residual pain, or fear on Torran's corpse. She had to have consumed it before she left.

How strong would she be now? My wolf howled, and I loosed my own rage-filled cry into the cold, darkening sky.

It didn't matter. Thanks to my bonds with the others, and with Flor, I was stronger now than when Elina had captured me at Southern. When I returned to Eastern, I would bathe in the blood of everyone I scented here who still breathed, starting with the witch.

I felt like a fool for a moment, for allowing myself to be lured away, separated from my new mate. But regret was one of the least powerful emotions.

Revenge was far sweeter.

With a flick of my hand, I set the remains of Torran and the other shifters on fire, and reached for my brothers with my mind. For some reason, the only one who heard me was Glen.

He was with Sergeant, and his reply to my report was immediate, though he sounded exhausted. *Join us here. We'll attack the compound when the Council meets.* He sent a mental image of the grove of ash trees where he was hidden with the Tenebris pack. *Can you defeat her?*

I will destroy her. It was a vow to the moon. *Are the others well?*

You can't reach them? Glen's mental voice was brittle. *They went into the Council ring a few minutes ago.*

I started running back, my heart racing, my mind spinning. What was Elina planning? Salt could be used to break a spell, or contain one. The salt around the ring could mean she'd performed some spell there long ago, or was preparing one for tonight. She could keep power contained in the ring. Or...

Halfway to Eastern, I had my answer. A strange sensation ran down my limbs and pooled in my heart, the center of my power, like my bonds had been numbed. They remained, but felt like they were underwater, or deep in the earth. I called out and received a general sense of anticipation and fear from all of them, but no pain.

As I stopped to tear off the shredded remains of my boots, the soles worn through, my mother's voice whispered in my ear, an echo of an old lesson on basic witchcraft she'd taught me long before I was old enough to attract my father's attention.

"Remember, Grisha, the balance must be kept. Above and below. Inside and out. Dark and light. Hold in, let go. Every spell has a push and a pull." *She held a gray pebble on her palm, demonstrating the small magics as it moved with her voice.*

I sprinkled a handful of table salt on her palm to make the pebble go still, a new trick I'd learned the week before. She laughed and poured more out, daring me to try and take the pebble away with my own magic. It had been the first time my strong magic had failed me.

"Even salt can be used to break a spell, or make it close to unbreakable," *she explained. I asked how it was possible to make a spell that strong, and her eyes shuttered.* *"With salt and blood, and the kind of magic I have chosen not to use. But even blood magic can be overcome, with enough time and effort. The only magic that can never be defeated is the moon's."* *She stared through the small window in the direction of my father's castle.* *"And even that can be locked away, though not forever."*

Locked away. That's what she'd done. She'd locked them inside the Council ring.

And I had no idea who else was in there with them.

I sped up, using too much energy to track Elina's blood, the beat of her heart. The Mansion was many miles away, but that was where she was now, or close to it. Close to the circle of salt she'd laid around the Council ring, a spell using blood, her own blood. It would have created a cage, keeping prisoners contained... or a protective barrier, keeping out those who might want to harm her. Or both.

It would be unbreakable, except for her own blood.

I would be the only one who could tear it down. But I'd taken myself off the board, chasing her old spell across the county for hours. Even if I returned on a straight path, and channeled every scrap of energy I had into returning to Flor, it would be well past moonrise.

Hours. I had run for hours, and now I had minutes, my strength still not where it should be.

Brand. Brand had the strength of the Mountain pack. I opened the bond to him and called out a warning, a plea. It was like screaming underwater, nothing but an ominous stillness left when my mental voice gave out.

Unnerved, I ran faster and reached out again and again, fruitlessly, to Brand, then Flor, Luke, and Finnick. None of them answered, and I knew why.

Glen! As the moon sailed above the tree line of the forest where I ran faster than I had run in my long life, Flor's whispered scream in my mind froze my blood, and set my feet ablaze.

I ran and ran, my own blood draining into the earth as the rocks and thorns underfoot took their toll. It was a price I would pay a thousand times, if I could only get back to my little queen in time. *Take my blood,* I thought to the moon as she shone dimly behind a low cloud. *Let me suffer, but save them.*

The moon slid higher in the sky, its cold light shimmering, wavering, as if it were deciding whether to grant my prayer.

CHAPTER 29

LITTLE ROGUES
GLEN

"Drink some water, pup." Sergeant patted me on the back as I panted, lying in a heap on the forest floor. It was semi-dark in this grove, the sun having given up hours before, and the moon almost ready to rise. I didn't have time to rest, but even with the extra power that had surged through me hours before, when Flor and Grigor had claimed each other, my body was screaming for rest. "We don't have long, but you'll need to rest. Gather your thoughts, and breathe."

Breathing should have been impossible. I'd been running from Eastern Enforcers for what felt like days when Sergeant and the Tenebris boys had signaled me. Though I suspected the only reason I'd gotten away was that the Eastern Enforcers' attention had been diverted to the crowds that had begun arriving at the front gate. Hundreds of shifters had been pouring into the Eastern packlands, circling the Mansion to fill the area behind the house, around the Council ring.

Taking the canteen from Sergeant's hand, I managed to take a few sips while I collected my thoughts. I didn't have long; Grigor had spoken into my mind only a moment before, and I had bad news.

"How far'd he run?" Bo murmured from a tree branch ahead of me as I caught my breath.

"How long's the question," his friend Leroy replied. "He kept them Eastern shitheads runnin' in circles until they pulled back."

Sergeant grunted. "He's been running since yesterday morning. He drew the Enforcers away from the pack protector so she could get inside. You two need to run now, get some distance from the fence line. Remember your training." They both nodded and scampered off, their movements far quieter than they had been the first time I'd found them blundering through the forests at Southern. Sergeant waited, sniffing the air, until a distant call—the unmistakable hoot of a great horned owl—let him know they were away and hidden.

Sergeant didn't relax. He didn't like that the Enforcers had stopped chasing me. I didn't like it either.

I'd shot away from the Mansion when they'd found us, my heart in my throat, my wolf howling at me to draw the predators away from our mate. The howling had only stopped once I realized Flor had gotten inside without being spotted. At least, I assumed that's where she was, since every Enforcer had focused on following me. It had been almost impossible to keep tabs on her while I ran myself ragged inside the fence line, searching for the moment I could escape.

There had been Enforcers doing something all around the clearing where the Council meetings were held on the full moon. I'd thought they were cutting the grass around the edges, but they'd been pouring something out in a wide circle, maybe fertilizer, though it hadn't smelled like it.

They hadn't been armed with clippers or weed eaters, but walkie-talkies and what might have been surveying tools, until they spotted me and joined in the chase.

I'd finally managed to get close enough to the fence and climbed over, using my claws. Then I'd led the two dozen Eastern shifters on an even longer chase in the woods, some of them carrying guns. The stench of silver had tainted the air when they'd shot at me and gotten close enough for me to catch the scent. But instead of freezing with fear, I ran faster, rage at the way the Eastern pack broke our laws with impunity giving me speed.

That rage, and the calm in my bond with Flor, had kept me going for miles. Most of the Enforcers quit chasing me, and when night fell, I'd climbed trees and picked off the last three, giving them quick deaths with my claws. It was more than they deserved. Then I'd looped back to the acreage behind the Mansion, looking for Sergeant.

He and his boys had been running, too. They'd sent two or three of their pack out to test the boundaries of the compound, taking out any drones or cameras they found on the way with slingshots. When Enforcers had chased, they'd let them, luring them into brushy, dense patches of forest, then falling on them en masse. Sergeant told me they'd stopped hunting close to the fence line when there was some kind of earthquake.

If I'd had the breath to laugh, I would've. *Earthquake, my ass.* I'd been in the middle of fighting the last Enforcer, twenty miles away, and felt the ground move. Distracted, I'd almost let the shifter get his claws into my eye. But the enormous surge of Grigor-flavored power had told me precisely what was happening, and I'd channeled that strength into finishing my final battle, then running back.

Sergeant handed me another container, a small can of

apple juice. I hated the stuff, but needed the calories, so I popped the tab and drank it in one long gulp.

"Did it work, Glen? Flor got in safely?"

I pressed a hand to my chest. "As far as I can tell. She bonded with Grigor, and it felt like she settled something with Finn, too? I can't tell what's up with that, exactly. But Flor's alive." I tried to stand, grabbing onto Sergeant's arm for balance. "Grigor had bad news. Just now. He's on his way here, from the north." I tapped my temple when Sergeant's thick eyebrows lifted.

"Ah, I see. He's not with them?"

"No. He chased after Elina, but she wasn't there."

"Wonder what she was doing," he murmured, just as a breeze cut through the grove. His nose twitched, and he inhaled deeply. "Smells like blood. A lot of blood. And magic."

I shivered. Grigor had warned me she could be near, though he was on his way. "That's her. She's got to be close by."

"So close, you wouldn't believe it, Glen Hillier." The voice slid out of the nearby bushes from every direction.

We both froze. *She's here,* Sergeant mouthed, his breath a small cloud in the deepening cold. He hooted three times in a row, and waited until leaves crackled in the distance. The boys had heard.

Letting go of his arm, I focused on the feeling of dread emanating from in front of me. Sergeant silently unsheathed his sword, waiting. No, it was Flor's sword, I realized. She'd left it with him, having only taken her steak knife into the Mansion. Sergeant held it like he'd won a thousand battles with it, though. He may very well have.

Stay here, he mouthed, and stepped toward the danger. But that wouldn't be where she was, I knew. If she'd managed to fool Grigor into chasing the wind, she wouldn't expose herself like this. I opened my mouth to whisper a warning, but felt something dull and cold, no larger than a thumb, press against the base of my neck. It had to be a gun, and even though I couldn't smell it, I knew in my soul it was loaded with silver ammunition.

Wait. I couldn't smell *anything.* I couldn't shift my eyes, or cry out. I was frozen, as a hand wrapped around my throat, and four sharp-tipped nails plunged into my neck.

I knew from the moment she stabbed her claws into me that she was stronger than me. But she wasn't stronger than all of the mates in my bond. I took a shallow breath, ready to call on them to help me defeat her. Or at least escape her hold.

"Shhhh," she whispered, turning my head to see the four shifters who were perched in the trees around us, guns aimed at the back of Sergeant's head. If even one of them shot him from here, he was dead. "Good boy. He doesn't need to die just yet."

Then, in the distance, one of the boys cried out. "Bo!" It was Leroy's young, high voice.

My blood went cold as the witch continued. "But that one might. All the others, all your dirty little rogue friends could die, if you don't cooperate. Be still, mmm?"

It wasn't like I had a choice. If it meant protecting those boys, that young pack and Sergeant, I had to let her hold me, even if I could get free. *The pack protects,* my wolf whispered in my mind. *They are pack.*

Sergeant hadn't heard Elina, and when he glanced back, he didn't act like he could see her either. He pointed to me to go to one side and around. I nodded with my eyes, unable to move my head. His own eyes flared wide for a split second before he turned back and crept into the brush, sword ready. Had he realized something was wrong? I hoped so.

"Good." Elina's voice was louder when he finally disappeared. The four shifters leaped down soundlessly from the trees, and I realized she'd used some kind of magic to make them blend into the foliage. The stench of silver and blood was almost overwhelming as she let whatever magic she'd held over the area drop.

One of them snapped out a question in Russian. Elina answered in the same language, though her words had an odd accent. "Now, little rogue, it's time for us to go and set a little trap for that dirty Southern whore you're all obsessed with."

Flor! I screamed in my mind as loud as I could. I heard my name echoing back, as if it had bounced off four other souls.

But one answered, a tinny, muffled shout. *Glen!*

And then the world went dark.

CHAPTER 30

THE COUNCIL MEETING
FLOR

My blood still hummed with the power Grigor had shared, and my heart with the knowledge that he loved me in his own dark, perfect way, when Brand burst into the cell. "They're coming to take us above. Flor, you cannot be separated from me, do you understand?"

I knew he wasn't afraid that he couldn't overcome any number of shifters; he practically glowed with power right now. His eyes really did shine, lighting up my face as he stared down at me. No, the one he was concerned about was Elina. I glanced down at his arm, where that bitch had tried to leave her mark. There was nothing there now, not even a magical trace, but even the memory of her scratches pissed me off, and made my wolf bristle with rage.

She's not here, I reminded myself as Margarette and Bradley helped Mama up and out into the hallway. I couldn't hear anyone but us moving in the corridor, but I could feel the presence of at least a dozen shifters ahead of us, and above. *Grigor said he'd felt her, hours away.* Unnerved for some reason, I said out loud, "All we have to deal with are regular wolves, right?"

Bradley replied as we walked toward the exit that led up and into the Mansion. "Eastern Enforcers are no such thing. They'll be armed with silver, all of them. After he locked us away, Aidan bragged about how much silver he'd stockpiled here, weapons from the end of the war and contraband his Enforcers collected."

"Isn't that against pack law? To have a shit ton of silver weapons, I mean."

Bradley sighed. "Yes and no. Council Alphas were the only ones allowed to keep silver on hand, ceremonial blades, mainly. Eastern asked for a dispensation, to keep a small cache of silver weapons, in case the Russians attacked us with their own again. Of course, it was meant to be locked away, not used against allies."

I managed to keep my mouth shut, though I wanted to cuss about the leaders of the whole damned nation somehow being above the law. I was on Brand and Samuel's side; this whole "new way" with an elected Council was absolute bullshit. Silver was the one thing the moon had made it clear shifters weren't to fuck around with.

"Even without silver, these guards would be a threat," Brand said, though he didn't sound too worried. Faking it for my benefit, I suspected, since I could feel his concern through our bond. "They've been trained to withstand pain, and to follow orders with complete obedience, even if it means their own death."

I swallowed hard, trying not to think about death right now. I knew how dangerous this night would be. If any one of us died—me or my five mates—we could take the rest with us. We might be stronger for being bonded like we were, but it was also our greatest weakness.

I shook away an odd sense of foreboding and focused on Bradley's words. "...but Aidan's careful to follow the law's letter, if not the spirit. They may truly believe he is in the right. That the rest of us are the ones who subvert the law."

"Pack law needs a little subverting," I muttered. "Where's Finn?"

"He's still at the other exit," Brand whispered. "He'll join us at the last minute."

I opened my mouth to ask what minute that might be, just as the door at the end of the hallway opened wide, and a shifter came down. "Luke!" I called out, remembering myself when I sensed the others at his back, a group up the stairs and stretching into the hallway beyond. He was acting like he was on their side, so I had to pretend, too. "Why're you helping these assholes?"

"As opposed to helping the assholes you've sided with, *mate*?" he snarled, playing along.

Right behind him was a shifter I'd never met, a narrow-shouldered, mean-eyed one who stank of silver. The scent was so intense, I almost sneezed, but I didn't want to close my eyes around these fuckers, not even for a second.

He held a gun in one of his heavily gloved hands, a bunch of thin metal cables in the other, and had a silver knife tucked in an open sheath at his waist. He shoved Luke forward with his other hand. Luke hissed in pain, and I saw why when he reached into his back pocket and pulled out an equally heavy set of gloves before taking the bundle of cables from the guy.

"By the moon, they're all silver," Bradley whispered beside me. "There's so much."

"Tie them up, Southern." The asshole tried to shove Luke again, but he moved to one side, ignoring the gun.

"If I'm not moving fast enough, you can do it, Niall," Luke said, slowly pulling on his gloves. I couldn't hear his voice in my head, but I could feel his emotions. He was terrified, but trying to hide it. The last thing he wanted to do was put that silver chain on any of us.

"The girl first," the asshole demanded.

Wait. Niall. I bristled, realizing now who this rat's ass was. He was the guy who'd tried to force Finn's little sister into a mating. He'd beaten my mate. I was going to return the fucking favor, lifting my fists to *dare* him to bind me, but my Bearman stopped me with a look.

"No," he replied, stepping in front of us all. "Me first." His tone left no room for any other option.

"Not a bad idea," Luke said, stepping toward Brand. I could tell they were communicating somehow—though I wasn't certain if Brand could hear Luke's thoughts, or speak with him like we could with Grigor—and Brand stood still, his gaze locked on Luke's as he held out his massive hands. *Sorry,* Luke mouthed as he looped half of the chains around Brand's wrists again and again. Behind him, Niall's smirk grew wider, his shoulders relaxing. I steeled myself to sense Brand's pain through the bond, but I should've known better.

"I hardly feel it," Brand said, and the truth in his voice shocked everyone but me. His silver eyes softened as he winked down at me. When Luke finished, he kneeled down and looped more silver cables around Brand's ankles, forming shackles, though I could tell he was trying to keep the silver over the fabric of Brand's jeans. My Bearman stood quietly, allowing it, and I didn't pick up even a hint of discomfort, though his eyes grew brighter with every loop.

Finally, when Luke stepped back, the stench of silver filling the air until my nose itched painfully with another sneeze, Brand straightened. He should have been weak from the silver, and Niall stepped closer, his fear less obvious. A few more Enforcers crowded into the hallway behind him, their own guns already drawn.

"Now the girl."

Luke stiffened. "The males—" he began, and Niall lifted his gun to point it at Luke's back.

"The girl, I said."

"No. I think you'll need to chain me again first," Brand said quietly. "Bradley? Back everyone up please."

"Shit, yes." Bradley pulled me back, trying to push me behind him as well, though I peeked out around him to see. Brand nodded at Luke, who returned the gesture grimly, and stepped back as far as he could.

"Wha—" Niall wasn't able to get the word out before Brand lifted his tightly-bound wrists up to the dim light, then flexed his arms. The silver cables creaked like ice breaking on a lake, then shot out to all sides, small pieces of silver flying like bullets out from the cables.

Niall screamed. "Fuck!" A piece of the cable had just embedded itself in his cheek. One of the other Enforcers wasn't as lucky; he'd gotten a larger chunk that had slid across his neck, acting as a flying garrote. The hallway was slick with blood in seconds, and Niall slipped, still screaming. His gun went off, though I wasn't certain he'd meant to fire it, the bullet ricocheting off the concrete walls, and ending up—

"Brand!" I gasped as I smelled his blood, and felt a hint of his pain at last. He leaned over, and I was afraid he'd been wounded somewhere vital. But all he did was grasp the cables around his ankles, and pull them away like crepe paper at the end of a birthday party.

He held them out to the cursing Niall. "See? You'll need to tie me again. Or you could accept our vow to walk peacefully to the Council meeting outside. I'm not sure you have enough silver to contain us all." His eyes narrowed. "Or enough Enforcers."

"Son of a bitch," Niall shouted, lifting the gun again. I squirmed around Bradley and planted myself at Brand's side, my wolf howling for vengeance. I wasn't sure where he was shot, but I knew Brand had been hurt.

Brand growled at Niall and held up his arm. The bullet had gone in there, blood oozing from the entry hole. He flexed his muscles, and it popped out, falling to the floor with a quiet clink. "That's Alpha Son of a Bitch to you. Now, do you want my vow to the moon, or do you need to waste some more silver?"

The Enforcer at his feet let out one last rattling breath and died. The others had already retreated back up the steps. Niall looked around and realized he was alone, with only Luke on his side.

Just then, Finn sauntered up the hallway behind us, calling out, "You know, Niall, I did you a favor when I helped Tana get away from you. Not just because you're a pathetic excuse for a shifter, but you're so stupid. You would've felt bad, being mated to someone so far above your fucking station and beyond your limited intellect." Finn had somehow fixed his clothing and hair, so he looked like he'd just woken up from a refreshing nap and was ready for a trip to the Enforcer yacht club, or whatever shit rich people did.

Niall snarled, but I could tell he was shocked to see his Alpha Heir looking fresh as a daisy. "How did you—" he began, but then wrenched his attention back to the group when Luke nudged him.

Luke cleared his throat. "Shall we? The moon's rising." He winked at me. "Brand, Flor, Finnick, Bradley, Margarette, and Lily? Do you all swear before the moon to come peacefully to the Council ring outside this pack house? To do no harm within its walls to any who do not offer harm to you, and to present yourself for judgment before the moon and the gathered pack?"

Brand grinned. "I swear before the moon," he began, then repeated all the words. I could feel him laughing in our bond, and when I repeated the words with the others, I knew why. We were only promising not to hurt anyone inside the Mansion, and the vow only covered those who weren't trying to hurt us. And the judgment part seemed wishy-washy as well. Whose judgment?

When Brand turned his moon-bright eyes on mine, I knew what he'd vowed to. The only judgment he would accept, which was not Aidan Fuckface McDonnell's.

A few minutes later, we were crossing through the opulent house, a dozen Enforcers with guns trained on us, all of them stinking of silver and fear, hemming us in. I didn't see any servants this time, though I heard one or two people moving in the direction of the kitchens. It was odd, like the Mansion was deserted. It was even odder finally having the heightened senses of my wolf. I only wished I could have spent our first shift together outside, running under the moon.

Soon, I promised. *We just have to get out of here first.*

As we walked through the Mansion, I let myself take in my surroundings, since this time I wasn't hiding under a catering cart. It was so lavish, it triggered a new kind of rage. My pack hadn't had this kind of wealth, not even close. Not even the Alpha and the assholes who'd lived in the Pack House. The shifters in the smaller packs that I'd seen at the Conclave had been almost as poor as Southern. This was the closest pack to us, geographically, and the place where the current Head resided... and he was, what? A billionaire, I'd bet.

I'd heard a radio show once where someone had been joking that regular people should "eat the rich." The people on the show had been humans, so they'd meant figuratively. But my wolf side licked her lips now, thinking it might be time to see what fat, wealthy city wolves tasted like.

Bradley and Margarette were clinging to each other, and I knew that of all of us, they were the weakest physically, maybe even counting Mama. They'd been imprisoned for far too long, and the food they'd gotten in the lower levels hadn't been enough.

When I noticed Becca and Vanya peering out wide-eyed through a crack in one of the doors that I figured led back to the kitchen, I touched my mouth, then pointed to the Hilliers. By the time we reached the end of that hall, a pewter tray with cups of water, juice, and a board covered with cheese cubes and fruit was sitting on a side table.

One of the Enforcers who'd been escorting us snarled, "They're all supposed to be outside," and barged through the kitchen door, ordering whoever was still in there to go to the ring. I wasn't sure what that was about, but it couldn't be good.

"Gotta pee," I announced, and Finn stopped in his tracks ahead of us. I wasn't lying.

"This way," he said, pointing to a door.

Niall snarled at him, but Luke lifted an eyebrow. "Even at Southern, we don't want shifters pissing on our floors."

"I mean, I could just go in the corner..." I gestured to a plant.

Luke stifled a laugh. "It's a hell of a lot cleaner than our latrines."

Finn ran a gentle hand over my arm as he opened the door for me. "Take your time."

"We don't have fucking *time*," Niall bitched, but my mates stared him down, while Bradley and Margarette snuck juice and handfuls of fruit and cheese behind his back. I slipped into the bathroom and peed, then washed my hands and face, giving the Hilliers and Mama enough time to gather strength, I hoped.

When I came back out, Margarette and Bradley each took turns in the bathroom. Margarette whispered, "We're just delaying the battle."

I half-smiled, though my nerves were making me feel a little sick, but Brand answered for me. "Good. The moon should be high in the sky for what's ahead." He gripped my hand, though for some reason, that made the Enforcers around us tense up.

Still, no one shot a gun or attacked us in any way as we exited the Mansion and started walking down a wide, crushed-granite path to the area a quarter mile away, where Glen had told me there was a ring for fighting like we had at Southern. Well, he'd described it as more of a giant circle, hundreds of feet across, with edges that sloped slightly higher, almost like an amphitheater, and a fighting ring in the very center. So like Southern, but bigger and fancier.

Brand stopped walking for a long second, his nostrils flared. "What is it?" My breath made a cloud when I spoke, and I suppressed a shiver. It had to be close to freezing, and nightfall wasn't even here.

"Blood," he replied, but started walking again. I tried to smell it, but the stink of silver had seared my nostrils.

Over the hill ahead of us, an eerie glow shone along the upraised lip of the Council area, from a ring of electric torches planted in a giant circle, like miniature streetlights set low to the ground. I couldn't see down into the ring yet, but I could hear a constant murmur, and see the backs of an enormous crowd. There were hundreds of Eastern shifters gathered inside the circle, most of them in human form, engaged in hushed conversations.

When we crested the low hill and a few of them spotted us, something odd began to happen. Almost all together, the crowd turned. The shifters in human form faced us on their feet, their expressions growing angry. Ugly. They didn't smell feral, but they looked it, like there was something twisted inside them.

The shifters who wore fur, though, reacted very differently. Almost as one, the wolves dropped to their bellies. I wasn't sure what was happening, but Brand seemed to know. His bright gaze fell on the closest wolves, and they began whimpering and whining, backing away.

"Eastern! Make way," Aidan shouted from the center of the ring, and the lines of troops parted, opening up a path for us to approach.

I spotted a few groups of women, dressed in the black and white uniforms of Eastern's maids, and lifted my chin to Becca and Vanya, whose chests heaved like they were out of breath, and scared out of their wits. What were they doing here? I supposed a Council meeting could be open to any shifter, right? But every single one of the Mansion's maids was out here, shivering in their thin uniforms, and shooting wary glances at the Enforcers that hemmed them in.

As I stepped over the rim of the hill, I noted something else odd: a thick double stripe of something white on the ground, or in it. A ring of chalk or stone, buried in the dirt an inch down? I wasn't sure, but there wasn't time to examine it.

"Bring them here, Niall." The Eastern Alpha was dressed in a black suit, like he was about to run a board meeting for humans, rather than a shifter Council. Almost all the others closest to him, the ones in clothing at least, wore Eastern Enforcers' uniforms, black on black.

There were a few shifters standing beside him dressed in odd uniforms, though. Without looking at me or Brand, Luke muttered, "A true High Council meeting. He's called in the smaller packs," before he broke off with Niall and went ahead.

I peered at them curiously. Had they been at the Southern Conclave? Would they recognize me? At least one of them did, from his reaction, and he began whispering to the shifter on his right. The whispers rushed around the pack, until all of the oddly-clothed shifters were staring at me... until they noticed Brand, and his eyes. Then they fell silent, their faces shining with awe and fear, one or two of them even bowing slightly.

Brand walked just ahead of me on my left, and Finn on my right. Bradley and Margarette were behind us, one on each side of Mama to help her if she needed it, but we all entered the ring within a few steps of each other, and over another line of chalk, though it was gritty when my boot scuffed against it, and pinkish. Salt, maybe, though this one had been mixed with blood. That couldn't be good news.

I peered around, taking in the groups just in front of a huddle of maids. It looked like there were far more foreign pack members here than there ought to be. I counted heads the best I could, and thought it could be a solid third of the crowd. Where had they all come from?

My ears popped just as I stepped onto the packed earth. For a split second, all I could smell was blood. Then, I couldn't smell anything but silver and sweat, along with the hundreds of shifters who milled nearby. Something was wrong, and the hairs on my neck stood up.

It felt like I'd entered a bubble, and I was cut off from the bonds that connected me to Grigor and Glen. No, not cut off. They were muted, like they were on the other side of a canyon, and so was the power I'd felt buzzing in my veins up until now.

As I stared at Aidan in the ring's center, Niall at his left and Luke taking up position on his right, I reached for my missing mates. They didn't answer, though I could sense their presence at the end of the cords that bound us.

I didn't like it. The foreboding got stronger as the moon began to peek over the trees to the east. Brand was feeling it, too, I could tell. His unease was almost overwhelming, until he realized I was starting to panic.

I went still, a whisper echoing in my mind. *Grigor?* It seemed like he'd tried to speak to me... No, to one of the others. Even though I didn't think he was hurt, he was raging. Struggling, somehow, or exerting himself in some way. Was he fighting Elina?

I glanced up at Brand, whose brow was furrowed as his gaze jerked from the ground to the sky and back again, like he was trying to figure out what was going on. Listening to something, though no one around was speaking, at least not to him.

Aidan straightened his shoulders and called, "Under the full moon, and before the witnesses gathered, I, Alpha Aidan McDonnell of the Eastern Pack, and current Head of the North American Council, call the gathered packs to order. I call the moon to watch over us all, and for the packs to know that the judgments made here are lawful and true."

Brand snarled silently toward the moon at those words. I looked up as well, and shivered. What in the hell was going on? The full moon had been a pain in my ass during the nights I was hunted at Southern, but even then, its light had felt pure. I didn't know what was going on now, but I knew what Brand had been looking at. The muted feeling in the ring extended to the sky, somehow. The moon itself felt... cut off, from us. How in the hell had this been done?

"Such bullshit," Brand muttered, then raised his voice. "As if any shifter can call the moon. As if any judgment but Hers is true."

Aidan pointed at Brand. "You have not been given a voice in this Council, shifter. You have made no pledge, and have no rank here. Be silent. You may not speak until instructed." It was an Alpha command, carrying the force of all the North American packs. Well, all of them except one. Mountain.

Brand blinked for a second, then burst into the loudest laughter I'd ever heard. It almost hurt my ears, and Aidan flinched at the sound. But when Brand stopped laughing to reply, all the shifters, even the Eastern Enforcers, were thrown into a near-panic. "If you weren't such a worthless bastard, it would be cute to watch you try to command me. I'll speak when words are needed. And I'll only honor the judgment of the moon, not of some weak Alpha attempting to break our deepest laws in order to grasp at power." His voice didn't hold even the tiniest hint of strain as he shucked Aidan's Alpha command, on his own packlands, like it was a piece of dead grass.

You could've heard a pin drop. I did hear a few clicks, maybe safeties being switched off on guns, all around us. Brand must have heard them, too, since he stepped back. All of my mates except Luke moved slightly closer, so I would be protected from the bullets, if they came. Luke's expression was tortured, as if he wanted to break away from the role he was playing now and run to me as well.

Such bullshit. They obviously hadn't put it together that we were all the weak links now, not just me. "I'm not the only one that needs protecting," I breathed.

"You know we don't see you as weak. But our wolves won't be able to resist defending their mate," Brand whispered.

"Sure, sure," I grumbled, just as something sliced into me.

A bullet? No. *Claws.*

There were invisible claws in my neck, piercing my skin. I choked, stumbling to a stop when Finn caught me. In less than a second, Brand and Luke were sprouting claws as well, and Finn was snarling through a mouth with sharp teeth.

"What's going on?" Bradley demanded.

I didn't know. I hadn't been injured, but someone had. *Glen!* I cried out inside as I heard him scream my name, then vanish.

A wave of anger came from outside, from Grigor. He was sending emotions toward me, but I couldn't hear his voice. "Why can't I hear Grigor?" I whispered.

"Because there is something wrong with this place, and because he's far away," Brand answered just as quietly. Sniffing the air, he peered around us with eyes that glowed bright as the night grew dark. "Though the witch is not."

CHAPTER 31

THE FIRST ALPHA CHALLENGE

FLOR

G len was outside the ring, hurt, and I was almost certain he was in the hands of that bitch, Elina. But we had plenty of other problems standing a few feet away.

"You break pack law if you refuse to honor my position and our rules for Council meetings, Brand Becker. You and your pack may not be a part of the North American Council, but if you don't intend to join and follow my leadership, then you have no place here. No vote on the decisions we'll make." Aidan's voice rang with truth, and the strangers from the other packs murmured in assent. He had a point.

Brand delivered a sharp look to Finn, who stepped up. "The pack law is clear. Alpha Becker is here as a guest, so you can't force him to leave. And he may have no vote... but then who does? You've had Bradley and Margarette imprisoned in your dungeon for weeks, bound with silver, waiting for this meeting, to vote on whether or not they betrayed their own. To decide on their possible execution. If Bradley can't vote, then are you prepared to make the decision on your own?"

"If I have to," Aidan spat. "I am the Head of this Council."

Finn leaned forward almost eagerly, like he was on the hunt. "*Interim* Head. Your position is to be decided here as well. If no other Alpha stands here to cast a vote, then there is no Council. In the fourth amendment to the North American pack law, the decision made at the first Conclave at Eastern after the war, it was decided that no serious matter could be brought to a vote without the presence of at least three Alphas of the larger packs, or their Heirs voting as proxies." He curled his lips in a humorless smile. "No proxies here, Father? Did their invitations to this Council go astray?"

The ring had gone still, the only sound the hum of the electric lights set around the perimeter. I didn't understand all the politics, but it seemed pretty clear that Aidan was fucked. He needed at least one Alpha he could depend on to have his side.

Of course, he had one. Just a worthless, toadfucking, rat bastard, piece-of-shit one.

"I'm Alpha," Callaway slurred from the edge of the ring, the bloody-faced Niall dragging him forward. Dear old Dad was still wearing the clothing he'd had on when he left the lower levels, though it looked like someone had tried to wash out the bloodstains on his shirt. His thick chestnut hair fell over his face in a greasy curtain, almost hiding his bloodshot eyes.

The nearest shifters stared at him with derision and moved back a few steps. He had to smell worse than ever, from their reactions. I heard the word *feral* muttered more than once.

No one seeing him now would bet a dollar on him winning this fight, but I was still worried. He was a tricky bastard, and Luke was honorable. Though maybe he'd picked up a little of Grigor's moral flexibility when they'd bonded. I sure as heck hoped so, because I had a feeling we'd need every advantage we could get soon.

I glanced over at Mama, noting how straight she was standing now. She'd pulled her sword out from under her shirt and held it in her hand, her eyes fixed on her mate, like she was watching a rattlesnake that had slithered too close.

"I'm Southern Alpha now, and I'll still be Southern Alpha when you're dead in the dirt, boy. You're not even from our pack, you know? An adopted wolf from a weak pack." He staggered forward when Niall let him go, then turned on Aidan, spit flying from his mouth as he ranted. "Aidan, I can't believe you're letting this foreign wolf try for a place on the Council. Haven't I always voted the way you said? Even back when Bradley was Council Head."

Aidan's lips went tight. "I never told you how to vote on a Council matter, not one time." It was true.

Callaway sputtered. "But... but you made sure I knew... you said how you were votin', and you promised—"

"Nothing. I never promised you anything for your votes, for any Council vote. That would have been unethical in the extreme, possibly illegal."

I watched Callaway figure it out, could almost hear the gears turning in his brain. He sneered. "Tricky fucker, ain't ya? Look at what's happened to the packs since you took over, hm? Heirs running off like that Glen Hillier, taking whores and calling them true mates. Sharin' their mates around like a tray of fuckin' party mints. Disobeyin' their fathers, disrespectin' the moon." He coughed up a wad of mucus and spat it at Aidan's feet. "I fuckin' pledged myself to *you*, Aidan. Not even your Council, but you, like you

demanded. You said you'd make sure I got back to Southern. Got what I deserved. And this is how you do me?"

The shifters around us were getting angrier at every
word Callaway uttered that had the ring of truth, and
Aidan's face was growing redder.

Luke interrupted his tantrum. "I pledged myself as well.
Alpha McDonnell gave me one promise in return, a vow on
the moon. That the Alpha challenges would take place first,
before any decisions were made, so I could finish the fight I
won once before on our packlands. You should remember:
you were there." His lip curled. "You didn't speak a word
against the idea then."

His words were also true, but they enraged Callaway. Or
it might have been Luke's tone. He must have been taking
lessons from Finn on how to sound cold and unbothered,
but still annoyed, like he'd been served the wrong drink a
second time.

Callaway tore his shirt off, exposing his distended
stomach, which looked more like the bloated beer gut some
human men had, rather than the honed physique of an
Alpha. "I thought I beat that disrespect out of you a long
time ago, boy. Guess you need another lesson."

At that very second, the moon sailed above the treetops,
and a shaft of light fell on Luke's face as he stepped
forward, unbuttoning his shirt. "I challenge you, Calvin
Callaway, for the position of Alpha of the Southern pack.
Again. I challenged, so you choose the form. How will we
fight?"

"I'm gonna choke the life outta you with these two
hands, you little piece of shit."

Luke nodded and dropped his shirt on the ground, then
toed off his shoes. His silver mate mark, the scar from my
teeth, shone in the moonlight. But so did the dozens of

scars that striped his back, and the healed-up stab wound that I'd made in his gut the day he'd told me we were true mates, so I wasn't sure which one the gasps I heard from the crowd were for.

It was hard to focus on their movements. My father was weak, but still fast, and he managed to avoid some of Luke's first strikes. They didn't have weapons, and they weren't supposed to shift, so this would be a brutal fight. A few seconds later, Luke made it past Callaway's guard and delivered a series of punishing hits to his ribs. He had to have broken at least one, and the old Alpha twisted backward and fell to his knees, coughing blood.

Luke waited for him to rise before beginning the fight again, and I cursed internally. Had he forgotten who he was fighting? This fuckface didn't have an ounce of honor. I tried to send a sense of urgency into the bond I had with Luke, but he didn't even twitch. I didn't think he could hear my thoughts, but I tried to picture Callaway on his knees, and Luke using both hands to twist his head off and then spit down his neck—

Brand's hand landed gently on the back of my own neck as I fumed. "We're not like them, wildflower. We have honor."

I had to fight not to roll my damned eyes. Of course Brand would be the one to pick up on my thoughts, or maybe he'd just read my posture. "Sure, babe, you keep thinkin' that. But we need this to end, so we can get to Glen."

Maybe Luke heard me, because from then on, he started fighting in earnest, his moves faster, his intent to knock his adopted father to the ground apparent in every blow that landed. The old Alpha was shit talking the whole time, though, and I had a feeling he'd shifted his claws, from the small knicks and cuts that appeared on Luke's side. But even when the Alpha fell again, Luke waited, rather than going in for the kill.

What the fuck was stopping him? Pity? It had to be something else.

I felt a pang of remorse in the bond that I knew wasn't directed at my father, and then Luke's eyes flicked to my side.

Mama. She was standing between the Hilliers, the two of them holding her up now as she shuddered, like every blow that landed was hitting her.

I felt like I might be sick. I hadn't even thought about her as Luke fought. She was connected to Callaway, like she'd always been, but with him close, it was so much worse.

A ripple of love, tinged with deep sadness and pity, moved across my soul. Luke didn't want to hurt my mama, didn't want to be the reason she died. Just like I'd done in the lower levels, after I'd stabbed Callaway, Luke was waiting.

And just like when we were down there, Mama called out, "Do it. Do it now."

Luke's gaze swung to me, and I nodded, mouthing one word. *Please.*

Callaway was on his hands and knees, and Luke leaned down to grab his head. Only, just like when they'd fought before, the asshole shifted. It was a bit slower this time, and had to be painful. Luke let it happen, though. He was more than confident he could defeat the Alpha, in any form. No one around us protested the shift, either. It was obvious to everyone watching that the fight was all but over.

Callaway's enormous wolf howled in misery when his transformation was complete, and swung his grizzled snout up to Luke. I wasn't sure if he was looking for mercy, or even what mercy would mean to his wolf. The creature practically radiated shame and rage, in equal amounts.

"I'm not sparing you. Not you or him." Luke extended the hand that wasn't on the wolf's neck, transforming the nails smoothly into deadly, long claws. He stared the wolf down until Callaway dropped his gaze, waiting. Quickly, Luke pulled back his claws and stabbed the old wolf in the side of the neck, piercing the artery that I knew lay beneath the fur.

It was a clean death, or would be, in a matter of minutes. Callaway slumped to the packed earth, bleeding out, his eyes fixed on the spectators in the circle. Looking for something.

No, someone.

"Lily?" Luke called out to Mama, and she broke away from the Hilliers and stumbled to him, her sword hanging limp at her side. Luke caught her before she fell to her knees, and helped her kneel beside her bleeding mate.

She stayed still for a moment, her silver curls covering her face like a veil, until she moved one hand to rest on the wolf's flank. He twitched, letting out a soft, pitiful whine. "Oh, Calvin. It would've been so different if you hadn't been afraid. Look at these children, standing up to all the wrong that's been done in the name of the moon. You were afraid to lose your power more than you were to lose your true mate. And now look what you've gone and done. You've killed us both, and for what?"

The spectators close enough to hear gasped as they realized who she was to Callaway. What they were witnessing.

She shook her head and lifted the sword, or tried to. Luke wrapped one hand around hers and helped her set the blade to the beast's neck. Luke's eyes stayed on my face, in case I changed my mind, I supposed. But I was frozen in place, Brand's hand on my shoulder the only warmth I could feel.

Mama grunted, then lifted the sword with Luke's hand over hers, helping steady the movement. I thought she might say something, but all she did was raise her head to the full moon, the light illuminating the scars all over her face, and the tears that ran in twin rivers down her cheeks, as she brought the sword down. Luke must have given her strength, because the blade descended all the way to the ground.

Both of them had done it, had delivered the moon's judgment, and pack justice.

Mama's dead. I heard a keening sound in my mind, a pitiful howl, and knew it was my own wolf, grieving the mother she'd never met. I hated Callaway at that moment more than I ever had. He'd stolen so much from me, and now, even in his death, he was stealing more.

Mama took one last breath, her eyes searching, until they landed on me. *Love you,* she mouthed. Then she fell to the earth, her form shifting in those final seconds, until she lay in her wolf form, half-curled around her mate.

I'd never seen Mama shift, so I'd had no idea what color her wolf was. But I stuffed a hand over my mouth to keep from crying out when I realized her fur was the same red as my hair. Bright, not dark red like me when I shifted. She shone like a flame under the full, silver moon, and I'd never seen anything more beautiful in my life, or anything more heartbreaking. "Love you," I whispered back, just before the crowd began to press forward. "Love you, Mama."

I couldn't be sure she heard me, but her wolf seemed to shimmer for a moment before she went completely still, and a cloud sailed over the moon. In the distance, I heard a muffled howling. It sounded like dozens of wolves, far away, mourning.

"Tenebris," Brand murmured, squeezing my shoulder.

The first Alpha challenge was over. Which meant the danger had only begun.

CHAPTER 32

STEALING POWER

FINNICK

The fading moonlight spurred my father into action. While Luke and Callaway fought, Niall, along with some of Eastern's most vicious Enforcers, had surreptitiously flanked our small group, separating those of us who had been locked in the lower levels even farther from the circle of observers. I kept some of my attention on them, knowing they would make a move if they saw the opportunity.

My mind worked frantically, as I tried to predict what gambit Father would attempt next. It had to be something to do with our pack's place in the shifter world. Some new grasping at power.

He'd brought shifters here from other packs in North America, but also from abroad. It was their presence that had tipped him off to my involvement in Tana's disappearance. He'd had his driver take us to one of the hotels our pack used to house guests when the Mansion was full, and I'd been shocked at the foreign presence. There had been dozens of shifters milling in the lobby, and when one of them began speaking Italian, my heart had raced. I'd thought for a moment that perhaps Tana's rescuers hadn't gotten her safely away, and I'd sucked in a sharp breath.

My error had drawn Father's attention at just the wrong moment, and when he'd asked about my most recent involvement with the Italian packs, I hadn't found a conceivable lie or diversion in time. He'd used his Alpha command to force me to admit to helping her escape. But that was all I'd given him. He hadn't been able to beat her whereabouts out of me, though he'd tried.

It helped that I truly didn't know where she was.

All of the shifters from the hotel were here tonight, and a few more. I recognized two from a Hungarian pack who'd visited a decade before, and a few more who I thought might have been a part of a German business contingent in the city a few years after that. He'd brought them here for a reason, to attend this Council, but I still had no idea why.

To watch as he executed the Hilliers, perhaps, so he would have "impartial" witnesses to their deaths? That couldn't be his reason, or not all of it. Foreign packs were only invited to witness Council meetings when the outcome would affect their packs as well. It had to be a far-reaching decision with international implications.

It was a risky move, though. The scent of silver was overwhelming, and some of the foreign packs had even stricter laws about its use than we did. The obviously displayed guns were the most shocking part of the whole evening, and I noted the appalled expressions worn by many of the smaller packs' Alphas as they took in just how many of our Enforcers wore them on their hips.

The Long Hunt, my wolf murmured. I agreed. There was something coming. Something bigger than Father being named Alpha, or the Hilliers or Brand being punished, or accepting Luke as Southern Alpha.

Something that involved Mother. Where the hell was she?

I had a terrible feeling the spell that had been laid where we stood—though I had no idea how such a thing would have been accomplished—had something to do with what was taking place tonight. I'd felt the rasp of salt under my shoe as I stepped into the ring, and seen more circles of the stuff even farther out. The way our bonds had been stifled when we crossed into the final ring, and the way even the moon's light was muted, it was all planned. It was an enormous trap. But for whom? And how would they spring it?

As if in answer, a cold breeze started up, and I scented something over the silver that had my heart racing. Blood. Not fresh, but days old... and I knew whose it was.

My mother.

I wanted to cry out, alert the others to what she'd done, what my father had done. But even though my connection to my father had grown less... central, after Grigor had given me his name, and Flor had marked me again, the decades of Alpha commands not to reveal our family's secrets was still there, making it impossible to reveal the truth to anyone outside my bonds.

I didn't have time to think through what the scent of Mother's blood meant for anyone inside the circle. My father had stepped into the center of the ring, gesturing for Enforcers to haul off the remains of Callaway and Lily. "Get rid of them."

Before anyone could touch Lily, Flor spat out a curse and flung herself toward her mama, steak knife in hand. Brand moved forward as well, murmuring to Flor as he lifted the dead, red-furred wolf gently, then carried her a few yards away to set her beside Margarette. Someone in the crowd offered up a shawl, and Flor lay it over Lily's body, while Brand stood watch.

Two Enforcers picked up Calvin's corpse, but my father didn't wait for him to be carried away before he announced, "Luke Callaway, you are Alpha of the Southern pack."

Luke blinked. "No, I'm not." A wave of tension ran through the crowd, as the truth of his statement was felt. "Why am I not the Alpha?"

That was a very good question. I'd never witnessed Alpha power moving from one Alpha to another, but Brand had shared some of his own transition when we waited in the lower levels, and this was nothing like that. Luke was no more powerful now than he had been an hour before. The visiting Alphas in the crowd began to shift restlessly, moving away from my father.

He smiled. "The Council has to give you the power." Another truth, sort of.

"That makes no sense," Brand called out. "When an Alpha loses a challenge, the moon gives the winner the power of Alpha, not some committee." He strode forward, towering over Aidan. "When I fought my father, the power was an avalanche, and instantly moved into me. Why isn't the power of Southern moving into Luke right now?"

"I'm the Head of this Council. He'll receive his Alpha power when I give it to him."

The tension in the gathering became a deeper unease as the heresy of what he said was understood. One or two voices murmured loud enough to hear their dissent.

"Those are not the old ways, or the new." Brand straightened, staring up at the hidden moon. "Our strength comes from the moon, and returns to Her when we die. Who are we to try to steal Her power? Aidan McDonnell, I challenge you."

My father's jaw dropped, but I knew better than to believe the shocked expression. His left fist was clenched in the way it did when he'd made a winning move on the chess board, or clinched a victory in a boardroom.

"You cannot challenge me, Brand Becker. You ask who I am to steal the moon's power? Look at you, with your eyes shining with strange magic. You're the one with power you have no right to." His voice rose over the crowd, and they went quiet again. "Too much power. Six thousand shifters in your pack alone, and yet you're not satisfied. You come here, unwilling to pledge to the Council, challenging me for the leadership of the entire North American pack. What could your end goal possibly be? To take over this continent? Or would you be content with that? Perhaps you have your eye on a greater prize: another continent, or even the world. Do you see yourself as another Alpha of Alphas, perhaps? I look at those eyes, filled with forbidden magic, and wonder where they came from."

He held out a hand and pointed at Flor. "But I shouldn't wonder. You're bonded with a witch whore, aren't you? You, and the Hillier boy, and Luke as well, and who knows how many more." He gasped for effect. "Could the moon have judged Luke as unworthy to receive the Alpha power, because of this unholy connection? Or is it the Moon Goddess's way of protecting the pack from your influence, from another despot who would rule over us all?"

None of what he said rang as false, but only because he phrased all his accusations as questions. It was a ploy he'd taught me when I was a child, and a way of leading the gullible that was too often successful.

It worked now. The mood of the crowd shifted quickly from awe and unease to anger. Brand's eyes became, not a miracle, but a threat.

But my father was not done. "Brand Becker, you cannot challenge me. You've broken the deepest laws we hold sacred, and I will defend the pack law with my last breath if it means keeping you from tainting our packs with her filth."

Flor only lifted her chin, standing beside Brand. "Well, this filthy whore knows how to read, and you're the one breaking laws right now, asshole."

"Silence!" Aidan commanded. Flor wrinkled her nose and sneezed twice.

Then she wiped her nose and took another step forward. Her hair was pushed back over one ear, revealing the metal ear tag she still wore. "I can't believe you think that'd work on me. You really are a weak-ass Alpha."

The crowd roared in disbelief, but an icy cold finger of dread worked its way down my spine. Many of the shifters here would see her ability to talk back to my father not as a sign of her strength, but as evidence of her witchcraft.

Someone would attack, and soon. But who?

My wolf snarled. *Niall.*

Where was he? I couldn't find him in the group standing behind us, and I stepped closer to Flor. He wasn't the most physically imposing shifter in our pack, so he could easily slip in and out of this crowd, but he was clever and twisted, taking more pleasure in torture that anyone I'd ever met, with the possible exception of Torran.

My blood went cold. Niall was evil, but Torran was worse. I hadn't even thought about where he might be, not for days. He'd vanished from Southern after the fight, but where had he gone? I wasn't fool enough to think Mother had let him slip her leash. He was more than her primary informant and torturer. He'd been her lover for years, although what he felt for her seemed closer to addiction than affection.

Flor kept going, ignoring the dark looks that were leveled at her from all around. "I've read the old law books, at the Mountain pack. All it says is an Alpha challenge has to be offered with witnesses, and take place under a full moon. A fight to the death, and the winner is the one who survives. That's the old way." The cloud that had been over the moon moved away, and Flor's hair lit up like a flame. "The moon's ancient, Aidan McFuckface. Your new ways are like that cloud, blocking out the light for a flash, then gone. The old ways will still be here when you're a patch of bloody fur and a few bones." She arched an eyebrow and nodded to the ground, as if to indicate that moment was about to happen. "How about you man up, or wolf up, and fight."

"No!" "Becker's power hungry!" "He's trying for a coup!" The shouts were planted, voices I knew, but the crowd responded, surging forward, intent on keeping Brand from challenging again.

Brand roared at the noisy crowd in return, and whirled around, trying to keep himself and Flor safe in the center. I glanced at Father. Enforcers were holding Luke's arms now, and a gun at his temple. The Hilliers... *Shit.*

That's where Niall had gone. Bradley and Margarette had guns in their faces as well, both of them snarling but unable to fight. Silver ammunition at this range would mean death, with the moon's power—their pack's power— somehow cut off.

"You cowardly piece of shit," Flor shouted, ignoring the Enforcers who were circling her and Brand, trying to find an angle to attack, though none of them were able to get past Brand's long reach.

Father sneered at her. "The Alpha challenges are over. It's time to begin the Council meeting, and the sentences for these traitors."

"Too chickenshit to fight?" Flor called out again, her voice cracking.

Father laughed. "Who would I fight? You?"

"No," Bradley Hillier shouted, his voice raw. "You'll fight me, Aidan. You stole my position. I'm going to make you give it back."

CHAPTER 33

THE STRONGER MATE
FLOR

My heart was still beating, but I wasn't sure how. It felt like someone had torn it out when Mama had died, and stomped it flat. The bonds that connected me to my mates, even muted, were all that was keeping me on my feet right now. Well, that and Brand's strong arm. He was trying his best to take some of my pain away, but there was nothing that would do that, nothing except time.

And maybe killing a few of these toadfuckers before the moon set.

"Stole your position?" Aidan's calm reply had me jolting to attention. Flanked by two tall Enforcers, the red-haired Alpha was staring down Bradley Hillier like he was no more threatening than a bug on his windshield.

I was worried that if they fought, he might wipe Bradley out just as fast as a bug. Glen's dad was wrecked, weak not only from the past few weeks of starvation and silver exposure in the lower levels, but the previous ones spent in a coma at Northern. It was brave of him to challenge Aidan, but foolish. He might win, but it was by no means a sure thing.

"No, Bradley, I'll do it," Brand said, at the same moment Finn replied, "I'll challenge him."

Aidan's face began to turn red as he focused on Finn's words. "You already betrayed your pack once, boy. I was merciful and let you live. I won't make that mistake again."

Bradley faced Brand and spoke earnestly. "We both know you're not some power-hungry Alpha, but Aidan's done a good job riling up the crowd. If you win, there's no way they'll see it as anything other than the world's strongest Alpha trying for more power." Bradley's lips tipped up. "The world's most honorable Alpha, as well. I... am proud to know you."

I didn't like that pause. Like he'd been about to say, I *was* proud to know you.

Finn interrupted. "Bradley, no. Let me challenge him. I deserve to give him back some of what he gave me."

"No, Finnick. It's my place to fight him." Bradley's voice rose, before he pressed a kiss to his mate's hair and stepped away. Margarette's expression was grim, her eyes haunted as she watched him walk into the center of the ring. "Aidan stole my position while I was recovering from illness and injury. He used that role to accuse me and my mate of being traitors to our own pack, in an effort to hold onto that power."

Aidan scoffed. "Or so you'd like to believe. Do you deny what *you* did, Bradley? Do you deny slaughtering a large number of your highest ranked Enforcers, executing them when they only followed your leadership, your pack laws?"

Bradley stiffened. "I don't deny killing them. And I don't deny that the rules we had in place not only caused suffering to our unranked, our most vulnerable, but created an environment where the most reprehensible urges of many of my Enforcers were given the chance to be expressed, and harm our pack."

Aidan blinked in shock. "You admit you don't deserve to be Alpha of Northern? Then how can you pretend to be fit to challenge me as the Head of the North American Council?"

Bradley's voice cracked as he replied, "I may not be worthy of any role. My Heir is Patrick Hillier, and I believe he will far surpass me as Alpha of Northern."

Aidan's face went comically red, and Brand smiled. "Nice one, Alpha Hillier." When I shot him a questioning look, he leaned down and murmured, "Bradley just named his Heir in the Council ring, before witnesses. Pretty sure Aidan was hoping to vacate the position without an Heir and place one of his shitheads in the spot." Finn nodded in agreement.

"I may not be worthy," Bradley repeated, lifting his chin. "But you definitely aren't, Aidan. I challenge you now as Alpha of the North American Council. How shall we fi—" Before he could finish, Aidan had already attacked, leaping forward and delivering a brutal roundhouse kick to Bradley's chest.

Margarette cursed as her mate skidded across the dirt, a cloud of dust rising up from his fall. I nudged Brand, and we slowly worked our way closer to her as the fight went on. If this went to shit—and from the first few exchanges of blows, it was going very wrong for Bradley—she would need us close.

Aidan and Bradley fought without speaking, and even though I didn't want to see anything to admire in the elder McDonnell, his fighting style was impossible not to appreciate. Every move was efficient, every response to an attack measured and calculated to use the least energy. He caught

Bradley's fist and turned, pulling the Northern Alpha in a circle and rotating his right arm. There was a sickening crunch, and Bradley cried out, the first sound besides heavy breathing and grunts either had made.

He broke away, his right arm dangling loose at his side, the shoulder dislocated, or something in the joint broken. He didn't have time for it to heal, and I wasn't sure it would anyway. It was our connection to the moon—or an Alpha's connection to his pack—that gave us our quick healing. The moon's power was shut off somehow, and there was only one other Northern pack member for him to draw strength in the closed circle from.

I glanced up at Margarette, who had moved a few steps away from Mama's body, and was staring intently at her mate, probably trying to channel into him whatever power she had left after their imprisonment. I was pretty sure it wasn't working.

Before I could check to see if Luke's cuts had healed from his fight—*don't think about Mama,* I reminded myself as my wolf whimpered. *Don't think about it now, we can grieve later*—Aidan had attacked again. Bradley was thrown across the ring entirely, and I knew Aidan had to be pulling on his pack's power to strengthen his blows. This time, though, Bradley landed at Brand's feet, lying only a few feet away from Margarette and me.

No one approached Brand, not even Aidan, for a moment, as Margarette dropped to her knees and crawled toward her mate, cupping his battered face in her hands. He didn't have the strength to do more than lift one hand. "I'm sorry, my love," he rasped.

"No," she half-shouted, pressing her forehead to his bloody one before staring into his face, wild-eyed. "No, Bradley, *no*. You can't—"

He pressed two fingers against her lips, and smiled somehow. "My love, I need you... to promise me..." He coughed, and a dribble of blood fell from his mouth to the ground. He gasped a few more times, trying to speak, but the only sounds that emerged were those of his lungs wheezing. Had a lung collapsed? He groaned in pain. Behind him, Aidan slunk closer, and Brand snarled a warning.

Finally, Bradley drew a small breath and whispered, his voice as quiet as leaves falling, "Love, promise me... you'll go on. Fight on. For Patrick. For our pack. We... have so much... to make right."

She pressed kisses against his mouth, then his cheeks, his eyes, everywhere she could reach. Frantic, as if she could create a shield formed from her love, to carry back into the battle. To protect him, when she couldn't. "No, Bradley, you have to live. I can't go on without you."

He smiled again, though his eyes were already clouding. "My love, you can. You were... always the stronger... of us. You made me... a better—"

His head fell, but before I could tell if he'd died, Aidan was there, dragging him back into the ring by one leg. Brand dropped to one knee, holding Margarette back when she tried to throw herself over her mate.

It seemed cruel, but I saw why he'd intervened. All around us, Enforcers had their guns in hand, barrels pointing at her. They would love the excuse to kill her for interfering with the Alpha challenge.

Though the challenge was already over.

In a second, Aidan had Bradley on the ground in the center of the ring again, the bad arm twisted farther behind his back, tearing it so thoroughly, I was almost sure nothing but skin was holding it on.

"Bradley!" Margarette screamed, trying to crawl toward him, intent on reaching her mate even if it meant she pulled her own arm off to get away from Brand. I dropped next to her, taking that arm, both arms, and wrapping my own around her. If she interrupted now, she would die, too.

"You have to stay strong, Margarette. You need—"

She snarled up at me, her eyes bloodshot, her wolf ascendant. "Why? *Why* do I need to be strong?"

I wanted to tell her all the reasons. Because she was my mate's mother, and losing her would mean he'd lost both of his parents in one hour.

Because I'd just had that happen to me, and I didn't know if I could bear to feel that pain again, through my bond with Glen, and in my own breaking heart.

Because she was the first woman who'd ever approved of me. Who'd thought my fighting and training was commendable, and not some sort of failing.

Because she had a pack that at least for a while would have no Alpha, and the women and girls there didn't deserve what would happen to them if Aidan and his pack were allowed to hold onto their rule.

Because even after all the shit we'd gone through, I loved her, and I couldn't lose the only other woman I thought of as a mother tonight. I needed her. Our world needed her.

None of that would convince her wolf. But I knew what would.

I bared my own teeth, allowing my wolf's growl to fill my voice. "Because I don't know if I can kill them all without your help."

Her eyes lit up with a fire deep within, her decision made. "I'll stay. I'll stay until every last one is dead."

I held her hands as tight as I could as Bradley's final

whimper reached our ears. Then a howl went up from the ring, followed by an answering one from the wolves in the crowd, then a few scattered half-hearted human cheers.

"He's dead," Brand breathed. "May the moon light his journey to the other side. May he run with his pack from now until we join him in the skies."

I grunted as Margarette crumpled in my arms. Had she fainted? She was still alive; I could see her breath in the frigid air, her pulse moving under her skin.

"The moon's justice has been served!" Aidan's voice was a crow of victory.

I was on my feet, my steak knife in my hand, before I knew what was happening, the familiar, uncomfortable buzzing in my head that had started at Southern long ago filling my senses. I would kill him. I would cut off his head and—

"Flor." Brand's voice was as filled with despair as I'd ever heard. I blinked, noticing his hands were on my arms now, holding me like I'd just held Margarette, keeping me from throwing myself toward Aidan.

Aidan, the snake, had won. He stood, his teeth bared in a maniacal grin, with one foot on top of Bradley's neck, and a fist in the air, like he'd achieved some great victory, rather than defeating an opponent who he'd tortured and starved beforehand. He called out to someone, asking for... a sword? Why? Bradley was dead.

His laughter split the night as he lifted a sword—it had to be silver, from the stench that wafted from it on the wind. He was going to... cut off Bradley's head? That was the death reserved for shifters who died without honor, who betrayed their pack, or dishonored the moon.

And this fucker thought he was going to do that to Bradley? To Margarette and Glen?

A rage began building inside me that didn't resemble the fuzzy madness that I'd felt in battle, and I pressed one hand to my chest.

But the rage wasn't coming from me, or not just from me. It was Brand, and Luke, and Finn, their emotions echoing through me. Growing in silence, only requiring one breath of wind to fan the flames of rage into a firestorm so destructive, no one would survive it.

Aidan could not be allowed to do this, but how could I stop him?

Del's voice echoed softly in my mind. *Surprising your enemy won't give you a lot of time. But it might give you enough.*

I couldn't move, not with all those guns on me. But maybe. I took a chance, throwing back my head, and let loose a howl of equal parts pain and threat. It worked. The sound was high and haunting, a wolf's promise of death made with a human throat, and Aidan's arm wobbled just long enough.

Then another voice split the night. "I challenge you, Aidan McDonnell!"

CHAPTER 34
NO FATHER OF MINE
FINNICK

Flor's eerie howl gave me time to shake off the stunned Enforcers who had me hemmed in, but I knew not to wait even a second longer to act. I vaulted myself over the one who'd tried to stop me with his now-broken arm, as I shouted my challenge.

My father's reaction was predictable. Scorn, and dismissal. "What did you say, boy?"

"I said, I challenge you, Father. You're not fit to lead the Council, or any pack. Bradley was no traitor. You, on the other hand..." The words stuck in my throat, and our gazes clashed. He tried to force me to drop mine, and for a moment, as his fists flexed and his eyes went a darker shade of green from his wolf, I was tempted to do just that. Crumble under his power and disdain, as I had every time before.

He had always been my worst nightmare, my abuser, and my primary torturer. It was second nature to fear him, to flinch.

As he trembled with suppressed anger, I was back in the lower levels as a child, under those fists—which had seemed incredibly strong, hard, and large—as they beat down on me again and again. Hearing his voice in my memories. *"This is how you get strong, Finnick. You learn to take the pain and transform it. Own it. You have to be hurt again and again, and only then will you conquer that weak part inside you. Only then will you have nothing left but strength."*

I could almost feel it now, the pain that had buried me alive, not only when Father had punished me, but when Mother had come afterward, to run her hands over, and often through, the wounds he'd left. I'd thought it was her attempt to comfort me. I knew better now. They had made me weak, and as he lifted those hands that had tortured me for so long, daring me to come closer in the ring, I knew that familiar, broken piece of me would never be healed.

It had to let go of my deep longing for a father who would love me. Not one who made sure I knew love was the weakness I needed to have torn out of me, one slice, one stab, at a time.

Finn.

Flor's voice was the faintest whisper in my mind, and I blinked away the remembered pain. Was I hearing her, or imagining her voice? We were bonded, but the magic here was cut off, and our bond wasn't complete, not in every way.

But maybe... Grigor had given me my birthright. My mother wielded magic, but according to Grigor, I did, too, now. Wolf true mates could pull power from one another. Maybe magical ones could do something similar?

You're my mate, Finn, and you are strong, and kind. You're a protector. Protect your pack now, from him. Her soft inner voice, filled with confidence in me, with something that might even be love, had me straightening. It didn't matter if it was my imagination, or her inside me. She was right. I was strong, and I had lived my whole, broken life as a protector of my little sister.

My father wasn't strong on his own, not without calling on the pack's bonds at least. I'd grown taller than him years ago, and bonding with Flor and my brothers, and Grigor, had given me an even deeper core of power. Why was I still afraid of him? It was time to put aside the Finnick I had been—Finnick McDonnell, son of a weak Alpha.

I was Finnick Dimitrivich, brother mate to the most feared of all shifters.

Father flinched as I allowed my wolf to peek out through my eyes, assessing him. "You dare?" he hissed.

The crowd around us was growing quieter again, the drama unfolding here more than they'd believed possible. I was almost certain half of Eastern was laying bets on my death. Why wouldn't they? I'd laid down for Father like a dog for my whole life, to protect others. Now, I had to do the opposite.

A cold burst of wind whipped through the crowd, and Father's eyes went wide, his fist clenching twice at his side. His trap, whatever it might be, was about to be sprung. I tensed, but replied firmly. "I do dare, at last. How shall we fight, Father? In skin or fur?"

For some reason, more than one shifter in the crowd coughed, and it sounded like someone stifled a laugh. Father's eyes cut across the gathering, forcing them to silence, and when he turned back to me, his face was as red as his hair. Was he *ashamed*?

What the hell?

My mind spun. Father almost never shifted into his wolf in public, and hadn't for years. He wasn't the most physically imposing shifter in his human form, not a behemoth like Brand, but he was strong. His wolf hadn't been weak either, or at least I didn't remember it being so. Though it had been years since I shifted with him, at least five years now.

Why would anyone in our pack dare to laugh at that simple question? I blinked furiously as it dawned on me. I'd assumed he'd taken fur for pack runs during my absence, but maybe he hadn't. Maybe his wolf had grown weak. I thought of the time I'd walked in on Mother with two lovers, and it clicked. Their infidelities had consequences, it seemed.

"I don't need my wolf to kill you. You're a weak fool." Father stripped off his shirt, then gestured for help. "You two, drag this trash away," he spat, meaning Bradley.

Flor snarled from where Brand held her in the circle of Enforcers, but the two who came to take the dead Alpha away lifted him respectfully, one of them dropping his eyes to me as well, though he made sure Father didn't see.

For some reason, he wasn't paying attention, instead strutting past the gathered Easterners. I was instantly suspicious. He was stalling for time, and I knew why when I saw a dozen shifters sag as he passed them, pulling their power into himself. Shit, he was draining his Enforcers... *Wait.* It wasn't just his Enforcers who made up the first line of gathered shifters. As he passed by a second time, more than one young woman in a maid's uniform was pushed forward. Some of them fell to their knees as he walked in front of them, their energy fully drained. One of them passed out, and was kicked behind the row by a burly guard I knew well from the lower levels.

A small whimper from one of the other maids reached my ears. "She's dead. He killed her."

Fuck. Shifters could heal from almost anything, under the full moon. But the moon didn't reach inside this spell.

I needed Father to get angry with me and start the challenge fight before he could siphon enough power from the gathered pack to defeat me, or before he drained the vulnerable past their ability to heal inside the spell.

"Stalling, Father? Are you afraid?"

He scoffed. "You were born a fool, and you're about to die one. This pack will never be yours."

"Maybe that's for the best. This pack is almost entirely corrupt," I replied calmly, pulling off my own shirt. "Maybe I should burn it all down and start over, once I've put you in the ground." His eyes widened in shock when he saw the bite mark Flor's wolf had put on my neck, close to my collarbone.

"The whore's fucking *you*, too?" His question was a hiss, but the shifters around us heard.

"Flor, you mean? No, never," I answered honestly, and swallowed hard. I needed to fight his control, so at least the shifters nearby would hear the truth in my next words. They needed to doubt him.

I am Finnick Dimitrivich, I reminded myself. *He is not my Alpha.* To my surprise, I realized it was true. The Alpha bond was a wisp of a connection, nothing more.

Of course it was. After an Alpha challenge was made, the Alpha could not draw on the challenger's bond, if they were from the same pack, which meant... *Holy shit.* The commands I'd been burdened with, not to share what went on in my pack, my family, were nothing but thread, easily broken.

I could speak the truth out loud now, and let everyone hear.

I raised my voice. "Though you would ask that kind of question, wouldn't you? I've walked in on your true mate fucking more than one other male how many times now? At least three, and from the sounds and smells in the Mansion, Mother has been unfaithful for a good decade. As have you."

That was all it took. My father's eyes blurred into a mixture of his and his wolf's, and he readied himself to attack.

"Now, now, dearest son, is that any way to speak of your mother?"

Brand whirled on his toes, snarling as he faced the source of the words, and I saw just where Niall had gone.

He marched in front of Mother now, escorting her to Father's side. But not just her, a group of males I recognized, though two of them shocked me. Armed with a gun in one hand and a sword in the other, Niall sneered as he approached, but my gaze was on the shifter behind him. One with silver teeth that glinted when he lifted one lip as he passed me, then carefully concealed them again, ducking his head.

Ivan, the Russian wizard. She'd brought him into the heart of our packlands. Behind him marched four dozen shifters dressed in strange camouflage, with Cyrillic writing on the shoulder patches. They smelled of silver and blood, and the rest of the crowd shrank back as the stench grew thicker.

The air itself grew warmer, as if the weather outside had been cut off again. *Wait.* It had been. The bubble that kept the moon's power from reaching us, that had kept Luke from taking on his father's Alpha strength, had opened for her, then closed again. I needed to break that spell, somehow. But first I needed to understand what she'd done to create it.

Wearing the black vicuna wool pantsuit she loved best, with heeled black boots and an odd, ragged fur stole I'd never seen before, her hair done up in an immaculate bun, Mother stopped in front of me, assessing. Her lip curled, at the state of my clothing, I assumed. Or maybe it was at the mate mark on my neck. She didn't speak, though. She'd taught me that the first one to break a silence was the loser of the battle of wits.

I didn't care. I wasn't fighting her way anymore, not measuring myself against my parents' bloodthirstiness or intellect. What mattered was my heart, the bonds to my mate and brothers. What mattered now was saving them, and all the shifters in our care, from this Long Hunt. The vulnerable and the young who were not here now, and who could never stand up to her innate evil or magic, were what I fought for.

"How?" I asked. She tilted her head, waiting for me to elaborate. "How did you cut the Council ring off from the rest of the world? What kind of sacrifice did this take?"

Her smile was the one she had given me so rarely, when I'd done a particularly thorough job of torturing one of the shifters she'd assigned me during my training, as her tool. As part of her evil. "Always such a clever boy. It took time, and blood, of course. Almost too much of mine to recover. But I had to have the power to forge a new future for our family, after all."

Her voice was strangely muffled, and I could tell no one heard her words but me. Then she flicked a tassel at the neckline of her black stole. It was fur. *Wolf* fur, and I recognized the scent that rose from it when she touched it.

"Torran?" I managed to ask, though bile rose in my throat. "Your lover?"

Her lips curled into a smile, but her eyes were pained. "A true sacrifice has a real cost, son. As you'll discover soon enough." I had no idea what she meant, but I knew I had to do whatever it took to make sure I never found out. "Hello, Aidan, darling. Sorry to be running late. Are we dealing with traitors and rogues yet? Because I found one that our Council has been looking for, lurking right outside our pack's border."

Niall snapped his fingers, and two of the Russians stepped from the back of the newcomers, hauling Glen between them. He was unconscious, blood running freely from small wounds on his neck, but still breathing, from what I could see and hear. There didn't seem to be any other obvious wounds, but the ones on his neck were enough.

"Give him to me!" Brand snarled, and the Enforcers did just that, half-throwing Glen onto the bloodsoaked earth of the ring where Brand and Flor were being guarded. Flor started cursing as she crawled to Glen, her hands moving over his body, hissing when she noted the blood that ran from his neck only to vanish. It was the same type of wound Brand had worn; it was feeding Mother's power.

"Bearman?" Flor asked, her voice strained.

Brand growled louder and lifted Glen off the ground, cradling him in those massive arms like a baby. Flor stood at their side, her teeth bared as she stared Mother down.

My own wolf was beyond rage, entering the cold, calcu-lating place I'd built from years of torture and harsh lessons. My only goal was to kill every one of my enemies. Every hand that had been lifted against Flor, or Glen, or any of our loved ones.

I thought of the "arrangements" Grigor had described. I understood it completely now. *We'll have flowers for the rest of our lives*, I promised my wolf silently, waiting. Watching the most dangerous enemy, the one who needed to die as soon as possible, and who would be the hardest to kill.

Mother. The sacrifice she'd made had given her evil a strength that was sickening. To my wolf's eyes, she glowed with power like a dark moon. No, like a red moon, pulsing with stolen blood.

I couldn't take her on alone. Not even with Brand by my side, and the others. Cut off from the moon's power as we were, trapped in this circle, surrounded by silver and enemies, we had no way to win.

Mother was a psychopath. But she could channel her power into Father, now that she was here, and help him in that way in the fight against me. I could defeat him, possibly even after he'd juiced himself up on the strength of our gathered pack. But both of them, when Mother was bloated with magic, wearing her own lover's pelt on her neck, and carrying his strength in her veins?

Fuck. I'd waited too long to start the fight.

We needed our own unhinged brother, and fast. I reached in my mind for Grigor again, pushing at the bubble that cut us off from him. I could almost feel him, racing toward us, reaching for me. Listening to my thoughts—no, my heart. He couldn't read my thoughts right now, but maybe my magic, our shared blood, would cross the divide.

I sent a call out in my blood—*run, run, run*—each beat urging him to go faster, filling the command with urgency so he would know.

"What is that?" Mother sucked in a breath and peered up at the sky above us, then back at me in suspicion. She stepped toward me, greed twisting her features. Hunger.

I blinked once, then dropped my eyes, even stooping over as I used to when she was doing what I now knew was feeding off my power. I let my hands tremble and tilted my head to one side submissively.

I needed her to think I was as weak as ever, though I

could feel the strength in my blood now. Her gaze flicked back to Father as the crowd began to grumble, even our own pack's Enforcers uneasy with the introduction of our sworn enemies in the middle of what was meant to be our most sacred place.

"I brought some unexpected allies with us," she announced, dropping a cool kiss on Father's cheek and taking up her place at his side. "Ones who have sworn themselves to the North American pack, under your leadership. They want nothing more than to move past the ugly history we shared, and forge a strong alliance for the future. I would like to introduce General Ivan, our newest ally."

The general, dressed in fatigues I'd seen before when he'd struck me with magic outside the Northern packlands, marched across the clearing to kneel at my father's feet. No, he kneeled between both my parents, his gaze moving between them. "I come willingly, Alpha, with no purpose but one: to join with you and your Council and lend you my pack's power in your time of need."

I'd known he was working in collusion with my parents, but seeing him march into the very heart of our packlands, boldly passing through the crowd to appear before the Council Head? My own shock was echoed in the deep, fearful silence that came from all those around us. Not even the whisper of a breath could be heard as the general bowed his head. From one side of the shallow bowl of the Council ring to the other, the entire gathering stared at the two of them, wondering what was happening.

When my father reached out a hand and helped Ivan to his feet, a stern, benevolent expression on his face, no one but me could see the glint of victory in his eyes. "I welcome your assistance, General Ivan. *Alpha* Ivan." He clasped the man's arms and pulled him close, both Alphas staring into each other's faces. It was an even match, and when Ivan dropped his gaze to the ground, the gesture was obviously perfunctory. "Who did you bring with you to our alliance, Alpha Ivan? Who can we count on for assistance as we root out the true danger to the North American pack? The power-hungry, lawbreaking shifters in our midst?"

"I bring the East, Alpha McDonnell. I bring a final end to the old war, and a true alliance with the pack who have been reaching out to you for over ten years, hoping for a partnership." His voice rang with truth, but he had to shout over the crowd to be heard as he finished. "I come on behalf of the Alpha of Novosibirsk, to offer any aid you request, in exchange for a permanent alliance."

A piece of the puzzle clicked into place. Of course he was working with the same Alpha my parents had sold Tana to. The Long Hunt meant they had made promises and forged connections at least a decade ago that were only now coming into play.

"That alliance is a gift. In return, and as a sign of our new relationship, our daughter Tana will join your pack as Alpha Mate." For a split second, I feared she had been found, but the sour pursing of Father's lips betrayed the truth. She was still safe, though perhaps not for long. If Ivan knew Tana had vanished, he was careful not to react.

Niall made some sort of complaint, but fell silent. The crowd exploded into noise for a long moment, but it was no louder than the sound of my own heart beating. I understood what this was. The Hunt was over. My father had gained control over the North American packs, made certain there was no one to challenge him, and then delivered us into the hands of our enemies. His secret allies.

The gathered pack members, even our own Enforcers, were clearly horrified, but there was nothing that could be done. The Alpha's rule was law, and they listened helplessly as Father went into detail about how this was possible, *legal*, quoting obscure changes to pack law that had made it so. Changes he had quietly, consistently introduced over the past two decades as minor amendments, ostensibly to protect the North American packs. But put together, they subverted the intent of the law to keep us from allying with the Russians. I'd known the changes were part of his Long Hunt, but had never once imagined the depth of his treachery. Or his stupidity.

The Russians could never be trusted, not even if there were a thousand mate bonds connecting our packs. As Ivan slid his eyes to me, his teeth carefully hidden beneath his lips, I suspected there was another, even more repugnant deal that had been struck, one that would not be announced. Mother was a magical ally, and with so few witches left alive, her spells must have been delicious bait for the insane, revenge-hungry general.

The only thing that kept despair at bay was knowing that Tana was safe, somewhere in Europe. Well, that and the voice of my brother mate, Grigor, who was whispering —not into my mind, but into my blood itself—as the Russians bowed, giving their vows of allegiance to my father one at a time. *I come. Delay. Prepare.*

I whispered the words into Flor's mind, and to my great relief, her head dipped slightly, though the Enforcers tightened their fingers on the triggers of their guns at even that small movement. She *could* hear me. Brand was holding still, his wolf enraged, but perfectly in control as he protected Glen. He wouldn't do anything to risk him, or our mate.

But it wasn't only her in danger. Grigor had whispered to delay, but I could feel my father's power increasing as each Russian vowed to follow and protect him and join our pack.

When they were done, Father turned to Luke. "Now, you can join us as well, and bring the impoverished, beleaguered shifters of Southern into this powerful alliance. Luke Callaway, you have earned the name of Alpha of the Southern pack. Come and make your pledge, then receive the power of Alpha as well." His words were carefully chosen; this was a transaction, the power conditional on Luke's vow.

Luke's hands trembled at his sides as he stepped closer to Ivan, though not with fear. He was so filled with righteous rage, he couldn't contain it. But when he bared his teeth and drew in a breath to reply, Mother cut him off.

"I'm not sure that's the best idea, Aidan. He's bonded to a witch. One who's ensnared more than one hapless Alpha Heir, claiming them all as her 'true' mates. As if one could hold that sacred bond with more than one. She's here now, possibly controlling them all for some wicked reason." She called out over the crowd, "Isn't that right, Florida *Witch* Wills?" Father's outward expression was one of deep sadness, but I could almost smell the satisfaction as one more trap was sprung.

"You callin' *me* a witch, bitch?" Flor replied every bit as forcefully. The shifters around her were backing away more frantically than they had when Ivan had entered the ring, which I found ridiculous, though my wolf approved. She was far more dangerous than any Russian army.

"Aren't you?" Mother replied, shrinking back in mock fear, even stepping slightly behind Father.

I should have known what would come next.

"This may be painful to hear, Elina, but look at our son. He challenged me, and made terrible accusations. I'm afraid her corruption has struck at the heart of our family, our pack. Perhaps if she is taken care of, we can still save him."

Somehow, Mother managed a tear. I watched it roll down her face, as false as the moonlight that shone without any power on us all.

CHAPTER 35
RIGHTEOUS FIRE
FINNICK

Help was coming, though not from the moon. I could feel Grigor pushing himself as my own blood thrummed in my veins, my own mouth opened to pant.

But he might not arrive soon enough.

My eyes flicked to the full moon sailing over the pines, and my mind to the puzzle it presented.

The absence of its power filled me with confusion and fear. Of course, nothing made sense in this damned ring. Not the way Bradley had died, or how many shifters Father had brought in to witness his rise to power, including our house staff, or the casual way his Enforcers were revealing their weapons.

Guns? Silver-laced blades? The smaller packs and visitors were doing the best they could to slink to the fringes of the circle. I could sense their growing panic and horror as they realized there was no escape. Some of the foreign shifters were showing how dishonorable they were, grabbing the Eastern maids and holding them like shields in front of them as they tried to flee, though they could only go so far before they were stopped by an invisible force.

That also made no sense. The dome that stopped them from leaving the clearing was a magical spell, or at least it felt the way I imagined one would. But what was powering it?

Grigor had given me a first lesson on perceiving magic when he taught me to open the locks in the lower levels. Spells and magic were as different as cars and gasoline. "One is the power, and the other the vehicle used to contain and use it." He'd let me feel the power inside him, and then, through our bond, showed me his intention to break the lock. "Some witches have to use incantations. Others need an object, a stick or a blade. All you and I need is our fuel— our magic—and our intent to use it, which is the 'spell.'"

This bubble was a spell, growing stronger as the minutes ticked on. As if it were somehow getting more fuel from somewhere, or someone.

Mother.

It was her power amplifying the energy inside it. When she'd entered with her new ally, the panic and noise inside it had increased. But I didn't know how to confront that magic.

Father had to be stopped as well, even though the moon's role in the transfer of power from one Alpha to another was obviously being shielded against in here. It didn't matter. He had to die for the crimes he was committing, the betrayal, all under the cover of his position.

I glanced over at Brand. The guards had herded him, still holding an unconscious Glen, along with Flor and Luke, to the center of the ring. Brand looked on the edge of shifting, fur rippling over the backs of his hands as he cradled Glen to his chest. Even so, he still appeared calm, somehow.

Flor, though... Her face was flushed with anger, or power, maybe both. Her rage was like a living thing as it rose inside her, a red sun moving higher inside her soul. Or a red moon.

Maybe we weren't completely cut off from power after all?

But I didn't have time to wonder.

Father was spouting some more nonsense about Flor having corrupted me, as I waited for my chance to attack, when the air shifted. Someone else was taking his shot. Without warning, Niall was at my side, snarling and reaching for me.

My wolf licked his lips as I ducked away from him easily, slipping through the crowd. I might have trouble defeating Father, with his links to the Eastern pack bonds, but this fucker? If I could get him far enough away from my parents, I could kill him, though I regretted not having time to mete out at least a few of the tortures I'd planned for him. He needed to suffer, though hearing that the Alpha's daughter he thought he had some right to had been promised to a Russian oligarch must have wounded his pride at least.

Sending a prayer up to the moon, even if I knew it wouldn't be heard, I drew Niall closer to the edge of the crowd. I stopped in front of a group of maids who had moved as far away from the center of the ring as they could go, though a line of young Enforcers stood beside them. These weren't the worst of Eastern's males, though, and I could tell they were more or less protecting the females. In fact, more than one of these males had been Niall's targets, if the disgust and fear that shone in their eyes as they gazed behind me was genuine.

I felt the air move and knew Niall was striking for my back, and I wondered if one of them would muster the courage to call out to warn me. But they were all frozen in fear, only one of the females making a squeaking noise, her mouth opening. I turned at the last second, ducking underneath his swing, the blade in his hand stinking of silver. I didn't bother talking to him. I'd heard everything he had to say the month before, when Father had confined me to the lower levels for this asshole to torture.

All I wanted was for him to die painfully.

All he wanted to do was chat, apparently. "I've wanted to kill you for years, Alpha Heir. I'm almost glad you turned out to be a traitor to the pack. You never deserved to be next in line to lead," he sneered, lunging again with his silver dagger. It caught the edge of my borrowed black uniform, searing a line down my bicep, but I moved before he could bring it around for a second parry.

A grating sound—metal on the dirt at my feet—had me glancing down for an instant. The female who'd squeaked, or maybe one of the Enforcers nearby, had kicked a sword my way. I snatched it up, spinning to avoid another slice of silver, and met Niall's next strike with one of my own.

The fight lasted only a few minutes, and Niall got in more blows than he should have been able to, even with his training. I was faster and stronger, and his eyes grew wild. But the bonds that tied me to Brand, Glen, and Flor kept reacting every few seconds, and the anger swelling inside me distracted me long enough for him to use his silver blade.

But I'd learned to ignore pain far worse than silver, and my strikes grew faster and harder as I sensed the others in my bonds needed help. Brand, in particular, was being overwhelmed with sheer numbers.

The moment arrived, and time seemed to slow down as I saw the opening. Niall slipped on a smear of my blood, and as he wobbled, I delivered a sweep to his leg, the kick bringing him to one knee. Then, a jab with my fist to his temple, and a 360-degree turn that brought my sword hand back to his neck, before he could recover his balance.

He'd lifted one arm, and I sliced through that as well, though it was his head that flew farthest, sliding across the ground to land at the females' feet. The closest of them didn't wait for the light in Niall's eyes to die before they pounced on the head, and lunged for his fallen body as well, taking out years of vengeance on his corpse, now that they could.

"Shit," one of the Enforcers whispered, backing up from the wild-eyed women at his feet. "They've gone crazy."

I let my eyes find his and spoke the truth, though I was panting with exertion. "You know he probably brutalized every one of them at some point. This isn't insanity. It's justice. If you did the same, justice will find you." I didn't wait for his answer, but waded through the crowd toward the greater battle that was being fought. To Brand, and Flor.

I never made it that far. A circle of soldiers formed around me out of nowhere, all of them in Russian uniforms, save one.

"You useless sack of shit. You'll pay for killing Niall." Father had chased after me as well, and stood directly in front of me, holding a sword I'd never seen before.

"Why?" I asked, truly curious. Father blinked. "He was a broken tool. You'd promised him Tana, and didn't deliver. I wonder what the Alpha of Novosibirsk will think when he learns you can't deliver her to him either? She's gone," I said in Russian, just in case. "I helped her escape, but not even I know where she is now. She's safe from you and your deals. Not that it matters. I'm sure you wrote some back door into the contract with him. You always do."

The Russians' eyes moved to Father, all of them narrowing with suspicion. One of them asked me, "This is true?"

"It is. He is not a wolf, but a fox. Very careful to make agreements he can easily escape. I should know; he taught me how to do it as well, and I used all I learned to make sure my sister is far beyond his reach."

Father shrank back for a split second when the tallest Russian growled at him. Then he lunged for me. "I should have drowned you as a pup," he snarled, just before his sword met mine.

"You tried," I reminded him, almost laughing at the weak blow. I'd grown stronger than him long ago.

"You're a traitor to your pack. To the Council." He backed away, looking for a better angle to attack. The Russians had widened the circle, to give him room.

"No, I'm a protector," I replied, remembering Flor's whispered thought. "Killing you is protecting this pack. Taking back the Council you stole is justice for all the packs. The moon's justice."

He laughed out loud. "I tried to beat that sentimental, sanctimonious shit out of you, but it seems I failed. You were born a fool, and you're about to die one. This pack will never be yours."

I wasn't sure what he'd been waiting for, but all I could think was *good.* Something hardened in his gaze, and he lunged forward.

Even if he wasn't as strong as me, he was fast, and

exceptionally skilled as a fighter. We hadn't sparred in years, though, and he hadn't been practicing, or learning new skills. His moves were predictable, and I avoided his first strikes without breaking a sweat. I was faster, having learned a few things at Northern—and at Southern—he wouldn't be ready for. I pulled out a series of kicks Sergeant had taught me, with a spinning roundhouse that connected with Father's knee.

The crack of the patella breaking was louder than the grunt he let out as he hopped back on his good leg. His eyes narrowed, and as he inhaled, I could tell he was pulling on the pack bonds to heal. He shook his leg out and attacked with a series of open hand strikes so fast, I couldn't track them, only use what I knew of his style to avoid most of the hits.

Neither one of us spoke as we fought, though I had a feeling I'd need to land a few more mental blows before he would make a mistake severe enough for me to secure the advantage. But distractions were all around. When Father broke away after I'd landed a blow to his face, blinding him for a split second with the blood, I lost focus as surely as he had, but not from a strike.

"Brand!" Flor's scream came a split second before Glen's shout for his mother, and at the exact moment that a gut-churning wave of agony tore through the bond inside me.

Back in the ring's center, Brand was being attacked. I barely held onto my sword, staggering drunkenly as the pain started and stopped in the next instant.

Fuck. Fuck! He had closed off the bonds so that we wouldn't feel what was happening.

I had to get to him, had to save him. Save all of us.

I wrenched my focus back to the fight I was in, and

swiped out in front of me with my sword... to find no one there. Father was fleeing, leaving a trail of blood and cowardice as he retreated behind the Russians. None of them moved as they watched my father's retreat, their eyes filled with disgust and judgment as they heard his call of, "Finish him."

It was too much to hope that they would let me chase him down and finish the fight, though. As one, they stepped forward, nodding and unsheathing their own blades.

I had one hope of winning this fight. I called out to Grigor, sending a demand through my blood.

I needed his power, all of it he could spare, and I needed it *now*.

CHAPTER 36
LINES CROSSED
FLOR

As Finn's father talked himself hoarse about how his son had failed him, something had happened. I'd started to feel... stretched inside, like an over-filled balloon. What was filling me wasn't air, though, or water, or anything so safe or neutral.

It was rage in its purest form, similar to the feeling that had blanked out my mind and made time stand still in battle for me before. My head pounded, my eyes ached, my vision grew red-tinged, and my gums burned as my fangs descended slightly.

Kill them all, my wolf encouraged. *Use me again.*

Use me again? Those three words had me hesitating. So it had been her, during those battles. Her wildness, her strength and fearlessness. Her magic.

Yes. Kill them all. She was so certain she could do it, cut down every one of the shifters who stood in this circle with us, beginning with Ivan and Aidan, and ending with Elina like the cherry on top of a murder sundae. But that single-mindedness was something Del had trained me to fight against. He'd taught me to think about battles before I fought. Run when I had to. Hide. Plan, so that I would walk away, and my enemies would not.

A soft, muffled sob caught my attention. Vanya had fallen to the ground when Aidan strutted past like a fucking power vacuum, jabbering like a pompous fool in front of the Russian general, and stealing almost every scrap of her energy with a careless wave in her direction.

Del and Sergeant had taught me to plan so that the innocent didn't get caught in the fighting.

Use me!

Not yet, I replied to my wolf's silent urging, as the *behrserker* rage ballooned. *But soon.*

It was almost impossible to hold still, to keep from shifting into my wolf form and tearing into the shifters around me. But I managed, knowing the moment hadn't arrived. We weren't all here, and I forced my wolf to acknowledge that. Grigor wasn't here yet.

She settled reluctantly, and the scar on my chest burned with liquid fire as the ballooning rage began to disperse, traveling down the arms of the scar somehow, and out. To my mates? Maybe. Whatever my wolf was up to, my vision returned to normal, and the stretching feeling eased a bit.

As I caught my breath, I noticed Vanya being pulled away from the front lines of the circle by hands—Becca's, maybe. Then silently, as Niall stepped toward Finn, the servants who'd been closest melted back into the crowd, far enough back that I couldn't see them.

We were surrounded entirely by enemies now, but my focus was a hundred percent on Elina. The Russian general, the Eastern Enforcers, that fucker Niall, even Aidan—they were all nothing compared to her. She'd gone too far, and she had to pay.

"Is there nothin' you won't do, Elina?" My voice was a

growl as my lips moved almost without my permission. My wolf wanted to take charge, use a weapon? One of my best was my sassy Southern mouth, and I gave her the reins. "You got all these pack members nervous as cats in a room full of rockin' chairs, can't you see that? Bringin' that creepy Ivan here and smilin' like you didn't just drop a turd in the punchbowl. You just gotta suck up every scrap of power, dontcha? I'd say bless your heart, but I wouldn't mean it, and I ain't all that sure you've still got one. Is there any line you won't cross? Any crime you won't commit?"

Elina tilted her head, like I was a monkey who'd done a trick. Curious like a wolf, though her eyes remained fully human. "Isn't that what I should ask you? You've even ensnared my useless son, and for no reason that I can tell other than to add to your own power. Why did you claim them all? How could you do it? How *did* you?" The last question was the only one she wanted answered, and she waited as she held out a hand to the nearest Enforcer, who handed her his sword, moving like he was in a trance.

Wait a sec. She'd said that all out loud? I let my eyes flick to the guards around me, suddenly realizing they weren't looking at her, or me. Aidan was talking behind her to the crowd as she approached, graceful even on the uneven ground. *Ah, fuck a duck.* She'd done some magic shit.

None of my mates were looking at her either, except Brand, who had Glen in his arms. He began to put him down, and I thought, as hard as I could, *Don't. Keep him safe. I've got this.*

I hoped he couldn't hear the lie in my voice. I *so* did not have this, but my wolf was raging that Glen had to be kept away from Elina. She'd done something to him to knock him out, and had a hold on him through the wounds on his neck, which meant he couldn't defend himself. Brand was the only one in the world I'd trust to keep him safe right now. Well, him or Grigor.

Elina moved even closer, no one reacting as she did, so I figured she was using a look-away spell. Power practically poured off her with every step she took, and I wondered how she'd managed to hide it all these years. Might as well ask. I needed to stall for time, and if there was one thing a villain liked, it was the opportunity to monologue.

"How did *you*?" I let my eyes go wide, like I really gave a rat's ass. "You're so damned strong. How did you manage to fool your pack, *all* the packs, for so long?"

She stopped moving, and another odd bubble formed around us as she smiled, the air between us and everyone else going weird and wavy for a split second. "It's all about bloodlines, of course. I'm a direct descendant of the greatest coven that ever existed, and the Russian Alpha of Alphas, who was the strongest wolf ever born."

She paused, and I sucked in a breath. *Keep talking, keep talking.* "Wait, that means…"

"Yes. You mated into my vastly powerful bloodline. You see why I can't let you live."

"M-mated?" I didn't have to hide my shock. She knew I was mated to Grigor? That had just happened today. *Those fucking cameras in the lower levels…*

"You think I can't smell you on my son? You marked his neck, but I could sense you'd claimed him before now, though I couldn't tell how." She waited.

"Ah. The tongue," I said, like I was sharing a favorite recipe. Inside, I was cheering. She didn't know about Grigor, thank the moon. "I bet you didn't check inside his mouth."

She blinked, then laughed out loud. "Very clever. I almost hate to kill you."

"I almost hate to die," I snapped back, circling a little as she stepped almost within arm's reach. "I thought you came from some weak little pack in Florida."

Her lip curled. "You're not altogether wrong. My wolf father was a weak Alpha. My witch mother was the powerful one, though he never saw who she was. Well, not until she drained him."

I didn't ask what that meant, but I had a suspicion it was the same thing Grigor had done to the guards in the lower levels.

I let out an exaggerated sigh. "Seems to be a common failing of shifter males, I guess. They can't see past their penises to recognize how strong the females in the packs are. Stronger than them, a lot of the time." Her smile changed, almost genuine now. I rushed on, stepping casually to the side. "Your mama was descended from the Alpha of Alphas, then. I've read about that guy. He was the father of Grigor Dimitri—"

She cut me off with a hiss, as her eyes flicked toward the Mansion. She still thought he was in there. She didn't know he'd gotten out. "Do *not* speak his name."

"Okay, okay." *Lady,* I wanted to say. *I'm not just speaking it. I'm screaming it, in my mind.* Though with her this close, and the bubble of silence, I couldn't tell if he was still on his way. What if he'd been hurt, or trapped again? What if he was just too far to get here in time?

Nothing will keep me from you, he'd promised before he left. I had to hold onto that. That, and my own damned skills at bullshitting and fighting, if it came down to it.

I let out a low whistle. "Yeah, but you're descended from that guy. No wonder you're so strong. But your mother, she was Verbena, right? Verbena Flock."

A flicker of what might have been pain moved through

her gaze. "Yes. She taught me everything she could before she died foolishly. One of the most important lessons was how to hide your true self. Your true name. It's the only thing that kept *you* alive all these years." She sneered, her arched brows moving into a scowl for a moment.

I shrugged. If her mother had been outwitted by my stupid fuck of a dad, then she'd deserved what came next. Not that I said that out loud, of course.

Elina was obviously still pissed about it. "When I learned what he'd done, I wanted to rip his head off to see if his brain rattled around like a peanut inside that skull. The only way he could have circumvented that vow was if he truly believed he'd fulfilled it. *Florida Witch*. What kind of an idiot names a baby Florida Witch?"

I still hated my name, but I might've liked it a little more now, witnessing how mad it made this bitch. But she was getting closer to attacking, I could tell. I needed to delay. I thought about what Del had taught me about bait, and distraction. I needed to give her a little fresh meat to keep her talking.

"You're tellin' me. Yeah, Callaway wasn't the sharpest nail in the box. Good thing my mom was a badass, bein' an Alpha Mother and all that."

She went still. "That's how. That's where your power came from! She was from the Western pack, I discovered that. But now, it all makes sense. She was the last Alpha Mother. By the moon, I'm sorry she died before I arrived here. The power of her death would have fueled me for a year."

This bitch here was talking about devouring my dead mom? She couldn't die fast enough.

But it wasn't time. I forced my wolf down, shoved the growing pool of power and incandescent rage back inside me, knowing if we attacked now, we'd lose. We were still too close to Glen, who was helpless right now, and she'd put up that second bubble, keeping us hidden away from everyone but Brand, it seemed like.

I also had to figure out exactly how I was going to take her down on my own once she got sick of talking. I had my steak knife, but I was pretty sure she'd have some spell that could melt the steel before it broke her skin, or something equally fucked up.

Elina swiped at me with the sword, giving an annoyed grunt when I ducked her quick stroke. But she wasn't trying all that hard to kill me. Why not? "You would have killed Mama, then? Not just drained her, like you did your own children?"

"Oh, has Finnick been whining about that? And here I didn't think he'd ever figure it out." Her smile grew savage as she pulled a four-inch-long silver dagger out of an odd, dark arm sheath. I hadn't scented the silver at all, though that may have been because there was so much of the stuff around already.

We'd circled to where my mother lay. I'd covered her up, but someone else had slid her sword under the shawl at some point. I'd noticed it earlier, though the cloth had obscured all but the very edge of the hilt. I could almost hear Del's voice in my head, talking me through what came next. I would have to pick the right moment to grab the sword, and I couldn't go for her throat. I had to be unpredictable.

"Perhaps I would've kept her alive. Mother taught me not to waste power."

There it was. She didn't want to kill me. She was hoping to capture me, turn me into a shifter battery for her magic. "My mama did the same. When you're poor like we were, you learn to make do with less. To put up with hunger and pain. She gave me so much, lessons on how to keep going when you don't think there's any hope left."

"So tragic." Elina lifted her sword, turning so the silver dagger was slightly hidden. I knew I had to lay out my own bait, and hope it was enough to stop her from trying to chop off my head for at least a couple seconds.

"Ya know, she wasn't the last Alpha Mother." I dropped to one knee and placed a hand on Mama's chest for an instant, hoping Elina hadn't noticed Mama's sword under the shawl. "She gave that honor to me before she died."

"*What?*" Elina breathed the word with amazement, like I'd just given her proof Santa Claus was real. She had to have heard the truth in my words. Even if I didn't think anything had changed in me when Mama said it, I could tell it meant something huge to this bitch. "You, an Alpha Mother?" She lowered her sword slightly. "Put down your little knife, and come with me. I won't kill you; I swear it."

"What, so you can suck me like a crawdad head for the next year? I was born at night, but not last night. No fucking thanks, lady."

Her eyes narrowed. "If you die, my son could as well. And possibly Brand, Luke, and Glen. It's a waste of so much potential." There was no mistaking what she meant. A potential power source for her to feed off of. "Come with me back to the lower levels. I'll let you live, and your mates."

"You know somethin'?" I chewed at my lip and screwed up my face in thought, acting as dumb as she obviously thought I was. "My mama was crazy as a June bug almost her whole life. She never taught me much. But there was a guy who worked in the kitchen named Del. He taught me plenty."

She had no idea where I was going with this. "How to cook?"

"Nah. But he did make sure I knew how to take out the trash."

I snatched up the sword and drew my steak knife in the same instant, leaping away from Mama toward my enemy. I struck fast, almost knocking the sword out of Elina's hand and avoiding the quick, perfect parry she executed with the silver knife.

"Ah, shit. You can fight, too?" I grumbled. Was it too much to hope I'd only be fighting a witch, and not some kind of a trained warrior one?

Apparently so. She struck out again, her moves as fluid as Finn's had always been, but each one that connected, our swords and knives clashing, sent a shock up my arm that almost numbed me.

Was she stuffing her blades with magic? Probably so. Maybe I could... I almost laughed. I might have magic, and I might be bonded to more than one magic wielder, but I didn't know how to use it. We parried a few more times, the crowd around us moving away, still seemingly unaware of the battle going on in their midst, until I managed to score a hit on her arm with my steak knife.

The scent of her blood filled the air, and I smelled... *Glen*. Glen, and a little bit of Finn, and a dozen other shifters I didn't know. And not one hint of wolf.

"You're not a shifter," I gasped. "You don't have a wolf?"

Her laughter was the only pretty thing about her as the realization hit. "Oh, I have a little wolf left. Just enough to keep Aidan alive."

The cloud that had been over the moon moved, and the light that fell on me felt like a warning, and a command. What she had done was a crime against nature itself. I

314

thought of the things my great-uncle had written in his diary about the imbalance between witchcraft and wolfcraft, and how that had been the reason all shifters were suffering. The North American packs had swung one way—exterminating any wolf who had witch magic, and cutting off the Western pack to keep their packs "pure."

Elina had done the opposite. She'd nearly killed off her own wolf, giving her witchcraft all the power.

My heart ached for a moment. *Her poor wolf.* "Why would you do that?"

She cracked her neck. "You believe I should have let my weaker half rule me? I may have been descended from magical royalty on my mother's side, but I was sired by the weakest Alpha alive. His weakness in me was like an infection. I flushed his blood out of me one drop at a time, little girl. If you weren't such a fool, you'd see it's the only way for a female to get to the top in this world."

She really believed it. More than that, she hated her wolf side—so much that she'd suffocated it somehow. The fight between witchcraft and wolfcraft had been lost a long time ago in her soul.

As clouds passed overhead, beams of moonlight flickered on her face, sending ominous shadows that made it look like she was rotting on the inside. She was, I supposed. Half of her, or more, was dead.

Flor, Brand whispered in my mind. My heart leaped to hear him, though his voice was faint. *She's draining Glen.*

Can you stop her?

Maybe.

I could tell he was worried, but I believed in him. I sent my faith in him, to take care of what needed to be done while I fought, down the bond. *Do it.*

He sent back a ripple of love and rage. *Make it fast.*

"Shut up and fight, Elina," I snarled, shifting my stance. I had to end this bitch, and I couldn't wait for Grigor to return.

For a moment, she had the same glint in her eye Finn had when he'd challenged me at Southern months ago, in the ring. Eager, and excited. She dropped back into a fighting stance, the sword in her left hand, the silver dagger in her right.

I mirrored her, glad that my wolf had finally settled down, the rage that filled her not pressing quite so hard on my insides. I could tell that Brand was about to blow a gasket, though, but he'd moved away enough that Glen wouldn't be in danger.

Glen was moving, his head shifting in the corner of my vision, and my heart felt the tiniest bit lighter, though I knew better than to give him more than a sideways smile. I was facing a skilled, psychotic, magical opponent, who was watching me like a hungry hawk. If I lost my focus for even a second, I could land us all in a heap of steaming shit.

I gripped my steak knife and my mama's sword tighter, and prepared to fight for all our lives.

CHAPTER 37

USING HIS MAGIC
BRAND

Flor was all I could focus on, though doing that was more difficult than it should be. My gaze wanted to slide off her, so I knew she was hidden under a spell. No one around even glanced her way, though she was a marvel.

My brave mate, squaring off against the hag who'd already managed to trap or trick every one of us, including Grigor. From what I could tell, no one besides me had heard what she'd revealed to Flor about her wolf.

She'd eaten it, devoured her own wolf's magic to feed her witch side. This was the evil the pack Alphas had warned against, and for a moment, I wanted nothing to do with it.

But my mate's eyes glowed with her own inner magic as she whirled and fought, avoiding Elina's strikes, taunting her. She drew blood, and the magic the witch had used to keep everyone from realizing what was taking place in the middle of the ring wobbled and fell. The other shifters backed away, leaving the two females fighting and me standing with Glen, not too far from Lily's shrouded form. I couldn't see Margarette or Bradley's body, and I hoped she had found a place far from the center of the battle. Luke and Finn stood only a few steps away from Aidan, who was shouting something at Ivan.

All eyes were fixed on the fight between the witch and Flor. My heart raced with fear for her, but the battle gave me time to focus on Glen, who had just woken in my arms. When his blue eyes met mine, I didn't bother asking him what had happened. I needed to know what was going on now.

"How do I help you?" I whispered, trying not to attract the attention of the closest Enforcers.

"She's... pulling," he croaked. I understood. It was what had happened to me, when she'd clawed me in the Mansion. It had taken magic to close off the bond, Luke's bite along with Grigor's power.

Magic. Moonblessed. Was there any difference?

I stared up at the moon for an instant, not expecting an answer, not certain what I was looking for. The moon shone down with the same light that I wore in my eyes now, though, and that realization was answer enough.

I'd hated magic my whole life, assumed it was unnatural and wrong, and the way Elina was using it on Glen was truly evil. But the only way to fight it was to accept that I had magic as well, and use it. Resolved, I turned Glen in my arms and nudged his tangled hair aside. Then I set my teeth around the back of his neck, directly over the bloody claw marks Elina had made, and bit down, sending a plea to Grigor for help in directing my intent, as well as a prayer to the moon.

His blood was hot and salty on my tongue, and I could almost taste the tainted magic Elina had left in him. I tried to remember what it had felt like when Luke bit me to stop the drain from the witch, picturing it in my own mind like a fountain being cut off.

Elina cursed aloud, stumbling just enough for Flor to land another hit, with her sword this time. Elina screamed louder, and the Enforcers around me surged forward. Glen struggled against me.

"Can you stand?" I asked, allowing my claws to extend past my fingertips, but not daring to fully change.

"Stand? I'm alive. If you want, I can fly." It sounded like a movie quote, but there was no way he was teasing me right now. He was in pain, and we were in danger. No shifter would choose this moment to joke. Then he grinned at me and added, "Mate."

Almost no shifter.

"You fucker," I grumbled as I let go, just in time to launch myself forward and smack a gun out of an Enforcer's hands before he could fire it. Beside me, Glen did the same, though he moved more slowly, still weakened. I wanted to tell him to stay behind me, but there was no behind: we were surrounded. At least one fool of a guard was using his gun like some sort of action movie villain, aiming at us, but hitting the guards closest to us as I ducked and weaved to avoid the shots. Soon, the stench of silver blanketed the air, small particles of it in the dust and gunpowder making it hard to breathe, panicking everyone.

"Stop shooting!" someone yelled.

The asshole didn't stop, and his next bullet traced a line of fire across my bicep. I roared, my wolf side bursting free, and transformed into the half-man, half-beast form Flor had seen once before at Northern. Only this time, I could feel that I was far larger, and I towered over the males around me on my oddly shaped wolf legs. I was a larger target, but I could see farther. Maybe I could get Glen to

Luke and Finn, and tear a hole in the spell that blocked us from our power, and Grigor from us all.

But now I could see that where they fought was no safer. Aidan and his Enforcers were battling them a hundred feet from the center of the ring, using swords and claws, though the bullets seemed to have stopped for now. Before I could plan anything else, before I could even see if the screech of a woman from the fight was Elina, or Margarette, or someone else, the crowd crashed like a wave over me, carrying Glen off to one side, and me directly toward the silver-toothed General Ivan.

"You," I snarled, shaking the males who had dragged me to him off like water after a swim in my lake.

"Yes, me," he replied, his gaze filled with wonder and avarice. He now held a rapier in one hand, though his other hand was hidden behind his back. I assumed he had some additional weapon there, torn from the nightmares of every decent shifter. "Shift before I kill you. I want to wear your fur as a coat."

I didn't bother replying. He'd been concealing a wand, one that was now pointing directly at my head. This wasn't the wand he'd used before, but its twin. Dark wood that seemed to draw the light of the surrounding air and smother it.

I ducked the first blast of red sparks that poured from the end when he waved it at me, knowing what would happen if I let myself be hit. I'd felt so helpless, back at Northern, when he'd surprised me with it. Helpless, motionless, unable to go to my mate and protect her. Ivan didn't expect me to move as quickly as I did, and he was sloppy at first, allowing one of my arms to swipe him, tearing long, jagged claw marks into his side.

But he was a seasoned warrior, learning quickly from

his mistake. The next round of sparks landed on my left leg, and the entire limb blazed with fire before going numb. *Shit.* I wasn't going to be able to dodge any more of that evil fire balanced on one leg; it was hard enough to avoid the magical round that was now whistling toward me. But my arms were long, and I moved as gracefully as I could, managing to rip into his shoulder this time.

Though he twisted his head and tore a chunk out of my arm with those fucking silver teeth of his before he staggered back. Neither one of us took a moment to breathe, but fought on. He was a bloody mess, but I was losing the fight to the magic. One arm numb now, one leg, and the side of my face.

Shifters massed behind me, and I could hear Glen screaming for his mother, Luke howling Finn's name, and Flor... I couldn't hear her, but I felt her, in our bond, still fighting.

Then I heard her voice. *Shift, Bearman.* A whisper, there and gone. Slightly impatient, like a thump on my head.

Of course. Shifting into my wolf could heal normal wounds. Maybe it would heal me now, enough to fight.

I transformed instantly, my wolf roaring to be set free, and the numb places burned as the sensation returned to my limbs.

"Perfect," Ivan said with a wild grin, lifting the sword.

No. The wand *and* the sword, in one hand. What was he doing?

He dove forward, the sword's blade lit up with a swirl of the red magic, like a snake's tongue licking out from the point and wrapping around me, around my enormous wolf form. The magic scorched my fur, burning straight to the skin, like chains of silver. This time, I wasn't numbed, but held motionless, feeling every bit of the agony the red fire caused. I bellowed, trying to break free, but struggling against it just seemed to make the invisible chains tighter.

"Brand!" Flor's desperate cry as my lungs filled with liquid fire, as my vision hazed red with blood, forced me to struggle on, fighting to stay on my feet. Fighting, and failing.

I fell to my side, tied with magic, as Ivan leaned down, his lips brushing my ear. "I've always wanted an Alpha coat," he murmured. His breath foul in my nostrils, he slid his open mouth down to the base of my throat and set his silver teeth over the very place where Flor's mark lay.

Directly ahead of me, Luke was fighting to get closer, raging and battling the shifters who held him back, uncertain what to do with him, whether he was friend or foe. He was my friend. My brother, and I felt a deep surge of gratitude that I'd let him into my heart. All of them, even Grigor.

Especially my wildflower.

But now, it was time to let those bonds go.

I had just long enough to reach deep into my soul, to close off the bonds that connected me to the others, to her, so they wouldn't feel this pain.

Then Ivan opened his jaw wide, and began to skin me alive.

CHAPTER 38

A MOTHER'S SACRIFICE

GLEN

T'd closed my eyes on what had felt like a disaster. Captured by a witch, surrounded by enemies, immobilized by blood magic. My only comfort was that Flor was with her other mates, and that Sergeant and the Tenebris pack had escaped.

I woke to a deeper hell than I'd ever imagined could exist. When consciousness returned, I was as weak as a newborn pup, my thoughts muddled and my gaze unfocused. Brand's bond with me made it clear just how bad our situation was, even before I opened my eyes. He always felt steady to me, through the bond with Flor. But now he felt like a mountain of despair was crushing him, and my own wolf whimpered under the agony. Something more was wrong as well, a deep loss carved into my being, as if at least part of the foundation of my soul had been carved away while I was unconscious.

Still, I made a joke, like I did in the worst times of my life, and the temporary lightness in Brand's burdened soul, attached to mine, was a relief.

Then he set me on my feet, my legs unsteady even with his support, and I understood his despondency.

I'd thought I was surrounded before. But now, there were hundreds of enemies hemming me in, along with the others. Russians in their camouflage, calling out in their language, possibly every Eastern Enforcer and ranked shifter alive, and oddly, even Eastern staff from the Mansion, who were ill-dressed for the cold weather, and even more ill-equipped for battle.

Luke and Finn were across the crowd, or at least I thought I saw Finn's red hair for a moment, and heard Luke cry out. Flor... *Fuck.* Another flash of red hair and a silver whirl of blades drew my attention. Flor was fighting for her life against Elina.

Before I could decide where to go, or even how to defend myself with my limbs so weak and my vision blurred, I was torn away from Brand by a wave of Enforcers, and carried dozens of feet across the fighting ring to another battle.

There, a female shifter defended a small patch of the fighting ring as if it were the heart of her own packlands, though she was a Northerner.

"Mom?" I cried out, shocked to my core. She leaped up, limbs whirling, as a male wolf lunged for her and she struck back at his snout, slicing off the tip of his nose. Then, in another fluid motion, she returned to her spot, crouching like a feral beast over what looked like an injured shifter.

No. The shifter wasn't injured, but dead. And he was my father. This was the loss I'd felt, the missing part of my soul. My Alpha was gone.

Dad.

Images, memories, of all our years together, flickered through my mind like a book falling shut, the pages fluttering as it slid to the ground. I saw him teaching me to hunt rabbits as a young boy, and then showing me how to dress and prepare the meat over a fire, when I turned up my nose at eating the raw flesh.

A few years later, he'd drawn two lines on my face with the blood of the first deer I'd taken down on my own, declaring me a "Pack Hunter" to all of the gathered males, as if there were such a title.

When I'd finally reached the age when I could shift, but was afraid I wouldn't manage it with the whole pack looking on, he'd whispered the story of his own first shift, when one of his feet had refused to take the form of a paw for a half hour, and his father had sat on top of it and given a long, boring speech to keep the pack from seeing.

"I'll sit on your foot if you need me to," he'd promised.

Now Mom sat beside his motionless, bare feet, her pain and loss practically vibrating in the air around her. She guarded his body as if he were still alive, and though I wasn't certain who had killed him, it didn't matter. Any of them who tried to touch him, or her, would die.

Mom held two blades, both of them taken from Eastern shifters, I presumed, as they were the same kind their Enforcers fought with, and at least two of those were dead a few feet away. A half-dozen Russian soldiers in human form were bearing down on her, coordinating their attack.

I snatched up a fallen knife from the ground and ran the last few steps to her side, adrenaline making my legs move far more smoothly now, cutting through two males in wolf form who were unaware of my presence, the knife slicing through fur and severing their spines like they were made of butter.

I didn't know where all the extra power in my strikes had come from, though I had a feeling it was the strengthened bonds from Brand and the others that were planted in my soul. But I used it to fight beside my mom, my power and her blind rage forging us into one undefeatable force, until we found ourselves facing a new opponent.

The guards had fallen back and grabbed hold of a group of females, all of them dressed in maid's uniforms and trembling with fear as well as the cold. There had to be two dozen of them, in messy rows of five or six. They were being shoved toward us by a solid wall of Eastern Enforcers.

At least one of the males held a gun to their backs as he snarled, "Fight!" and the girls stepped forward, tears and snot running down the face of the one closest to me. They held weapons, some of them grasping blades that might have been silver-edged, though the stench of the metal was so strong in the air, it was hard to tell. But they were not trained fighters.

"Cannon fodder," Mom snarled.

I agreed silently. They were obviously hoping to exhaust us with these opponents, or distract us. "We can't kill them," I muttered.

Mom leveled a scathing glance at me. "Of fucking course not." One of the Eastern males laughed, a short brutal sound. Mom lifted her chin in a sharp gesture at one of the females, a plain woman with silver-brown hair and a scar down her face that was the mirror of the one Mom had gained in her fight at Southern. "Do you want to fight?"

"Not you," the woman spat back.

Mom's face creased into a savage grin. "Good answer. Get behind me."

The woman's eyes widened for a split second before she did just that. The rest of the women followed suit, forming a circle around my father's body, their backs to him and their weapons held up in defense. Mom and I didn't wait to attack, leaping over the females in the back of the group to reach the most dangerous males.

Mom grabbed a guard who had shot one of the younger girls in the back. Before the guy knew what was happening, she'd choked him, yanked his arm back and torn the whole thing off. She threw it toward me. "Get the gun."

I let the limb fall to the ground, the moon-damned weapon still clutched in the disembodied hand. "No." Mom bared her teeth at me. I snarled back. "No guns."

She didn't have time to argue with me, as the males had already realized their error and moved into the empty space left by the maids and kitchen workers. One of the maids darted out and grabbed the severed limb, though, taking the gun.

Mom shouted, "Good girl," to her, and began killing again.

Not fighting, just killing. I'd only seen this once before, when Flor had gone into her rage at Southern. Mom's face was frozen in a feral mask as we fought side by side, her arms and legs moving too fast for my eyes to follow. Far faster than the males who came against us were prepared to face. Every Enforcer who confronted her died for his trouble.

I did my best to keep up, tapping into what felt like a well of my own mad power, the pooled strength all the bonds funneled into me. The bonds and some odd, red-hazed energy that I was almost certain was coming from Flor.

I didn't grow tired as quickly as I should've, though I was breathing heavily after only a few more minutes. But the sheer number of bodies that stacked up around us made it harder after a while to defend the women and girls who circled my father's body. More than one guard made his way through the fallen, trying their luck behind us.

Trying it, and failing. The girls may have looked help-less, crouching low on the ground, but as soon as one of the males turned their backs on them, they swarmed, driving him to his knees, then to his face, in the dirt, dying under their weight and the dozens of wounds they made all at once with their small knives. One or two of them had somehow transformed their jaws into wolf muzzles, and were... I swallowed, not wanting to see what they were doing when they tore into the exposed abdomens of the males. These males deserved it, and the females deserved their chance to taste victory, literally.

I thought we *might* have a chance until a cry of triumph came from the Russians, and a shocking spear of agony ran through my heart, the center point where all the other bonds lay. It was the same agony I'd known at Southern, when I'd thought I was dying, but somehow even worse. Like I was being eaten alive.

We all felt it. Flor, Finn, and Luke screamed out loud, and Grigor's rage-filled cry filled my mind.

But Brand was silent, sending only a flood of pain, until the bond went numb.

The Enforcer I'd been defeating when the shock hit noticed my second of distraction, and like the well-trained warrior that he was, took the opportunity to launch a flurry of blows. He knocked me back, and my own blade fell to the dirt. He rose up over me in a flash, his sword dull in the oddly muted moonlight.

The strength that had filled me from Flor and the others, the righteous anger and need to defend my father, my mate, my friends, evaporated. I lifted my head, hearing my mother's scream, knowing it was for me. I had to move, had to rise and defend myself. I couldn't let her see both her mate and her son die on the same night. But I didn't know how I could stop it from happening.

Of course, Mom did.

She met the blow, her entire body interposed between me and my death, twisting in the air as she flung herself to intercept the blade, though she didn't have time to lift her own stolen swords to meet it. Her face turned, her blue eyes meeting mine for a split second as she sailed through the air, before the sword pierced her through.

"Mom!" I screamed for her, but it was too late.

CHAPTER 39
YOU HAVE TO DIE
FLOR

The moon was still sickly, the ring filled with screams of pain and fear, and the scent of sweat, blood, and silver.

I wasn't winning the fight with Elina, but I wasn't losing either, when everything changed. I was bleeding from a good number of cuts and nicks, most of them closing up as fast as my wolf could heal me, but some of them stinging like silver, slicking my limbs with blood. I'd blocked out everything but the fight, until invisible teeth tore at my shoulder, at the same place where Brand's mating bite lay.

It was agony like nothing I'd ever known, and I cried out for my mate as I fell. I reached for him down the bond, but he slammed it shut faster than I could dive into his soul and send—well, I wasn't sure if I could send healing power, or anything. I didn't know how to do all that fancy bond magic stuff he and Grigor seemed to think was easy as pie.

But I sure as fuck was going to try. I battered at the wall between us, howling for him, my eyes searching for him, and not finding, because he'd fallen.

And then Glen cried out for his mother... and a wave of terror washed over me as I saw her, Margarette, just for an instant, through Glen's eyes. Saw her fling herself between him and a killing blow, saw her take the blade through her own abdomen, and felt his shock and pain.

My knife fell to the ground, and the now-familiar *behrserker* haze dropped over my eyes, my wolf foam-lipped, my mind welcoming the madness. If I was going to save my mates, I needed to embrace that side of me that was wild, feral.

Time seemed to stop, as it had before. But this time, I wasn't alone in the frozen moment. Elina was there with me, her arms already around me: one hand holding my hair, and the other wrapped around my neck, pulling my head back. Her small silver blade pricked the base of my throat as the haze subsided, leaving me dizzy, my head pounding, like I'd hyperventilated.

"So much rage. I can feel it swirling in you like a hurricane. I almost don't want to do this," she muttered, her breath warm on my ear tag, the blade just nicking the soft skin where my pulse throbbed. She inhaled like she'd sprayed her favorite perfume, humming at the aroma of my blood in the cold air. "You're such a rare thing, Florida Witch Wills. I'm tempted to keep you alive. The pups you could bring into this world, the spells their deaths alone could power!"

"You'd kill *babies?*" I choked out the words, trying not to accidentally slit my own throat on the blade. But if it meant saving myself from a lifetime of giving her babies to torture, I'd knew I'd do it.

"I've done worse." She leaned down and licked my temple, tasting my blood and humming like she'd just had her favorite flavor of ice cream. Bile rose in my throat. "And

I will again, when I have your death inside me. You're so powerful, little fool. Such a waste."

"You won't win," I promised.

"You're still hoping for a miracle? You've lost. You've all lost." She sounded truly confused, her hand tightening around my hair.

I didn't blame her. I had no weapons left but hope. Hope, and... *Grigor. Grigor, help. Help us.*

I might have imagined it, but I heard a soft, breathless reply. *I'm coming.*

I closed my eyes, and on the back of my eyelids, glimpsed a shadow wolf almost flying, its four dark feet a blur. *If you're gonna get here for the party, you'd better hurry. I'm afraid they're about to turn the lights off and lock the doors.* I waited a second, then thought, *I want you to know, I love you, Grigor Dimitrivich. Even if you killed half the shifters in the whole world, I'd still love you. Does that make me evil?*

No, beloved. It makes you perfect. Hold on...

He went silent, and I opened my heart, all my bonds, or tried to, and sent the same words to all of the males I loved. *I love you. I love you all.*

Elina gave a disgusted grunt. "You're reaching for them, aren't you? Which one? Luke, or Glen? That idiot son of mine? I'm almost certain your Mountain mate is dead, or will be soon. Whoever it is, say goodbye." Elina's blade sank in, and I froze. "You know, if you weren't bonded to those four fools, you could've lived to see how I'm going to change this world. How it'll be with a witch who deserves to rule it in control."

I had to be dreaming it, but I could have sworn I heard Del's dry laugh. *Keep 'em talking, girlie. Time can be a weapon. Ego can be, too.* A swirl of dust rose up from the ground, and I knew something had changed. But Elina didn't know it yet.

"Rule?" I managed to rasp. "You'll be an Alpha?"

"Nothing so limited."

"A queen, then. Queen of all the shifters. What are you planning? What are you going to change when you rule the world?" *Keep talking, keep talking.* She yanked my hair harder, and I looked up at the suddenly cloudless moon, praying as hard as I ever had in my life. The full moon glowed down on me brighter than it ever had. I could feel its beams landing on me, cooling my injuries, healing me. A breeze kissed my cold cheeks.

"...you have to die," Elina finished at last.

But I wasn't listening anymore. I was doing everything I could to contain my emotions, and failing.

"What... Why are you laughing?" The blade cut deeper at my throat, but I let it, knowing hope had arrived.

"You said..." I wheezed as the moon seemed to pulse in the sky. "You said," I tried again, a hysterical giggle creeping out with the words. "Four. *Four* mates." I moved my gaze from the moon to her face and let my wolf peek out at her. "You left one out."

Her thin eyebrows rose high, then higher as a shadow flew across the crowded ring and landed right behind her.

"Boo."

CHAPTER 40
LATE TO THE PARTY
GRIGOR

I'd never run as fast as I did, returning to Eastern. At times, leaping over roadways and gullies, I was certain I flew.

"Help me to be what I should have been all along," I whispered to the moon as I felt the blows my brothers were taking in that cursed ring. "Help me to be a protector. Give me the power to save her, save them, and I will devote my life to your children."

I wasn't certain if She heard my plea, but I knew that if we all lived through this night, I would spend the rest of my life trying to fulfill that promise. My feet bled, and I let the drops fall on the earth as a sacrifice to the moon. Tears streamed from my eyes in the cold wind, and I gave those away as well.

Maybe the moon accepted the gifts. All I knew was that as I ran, power began to flow into me directly from the full moon in a way I had never felt before. Clean, pure power, that seared my blackened soul as it healed me, and fueled me. I channeled every scrap of it into my race to save my mate, my brothers.

My pack.

In far less than an hour, I crossed into the Eastern pack-lands, drawing strength not only from the moon, but from tainted patches of land where evil deeds had been done, and left their stain on the earth. Healing the earth as I consumed the darkness.

An odd sensation began at my throat, like an echo of pain—someone else's agony. Someone was shredding him. I knew it was Brand when I felt the powerful mind clamping down, cutting off the bonds, protecting us all from feeling the torture with him.

My gums burned as my teeth extended, rage filling me. No one touched my brother and lived. If he died... *No.* I refused to think of it.

Another few seconds, and I saw with my magical sight the powerful shielding spell Elina had created and triggered. It reflected the moonlight in a giant dome that arched above the trees and glittered against the sky. It was the reason I hadn't been able to speak clearly to my bonded ones. I needed to tear it down.

Ahead, between me and the spell, however, there was an army. Hundreds of shifters, hiding just inside the tree line that stretched around the Mansion and Council ring. I prepared myself to cut a swath straight through them, obliterating any who stood in my way, beginning with the two who stepped out from the tree line. My arm was extended, claws out, red sparks already flying from my hands, as I realized my mistake.

"Leroy! Get down!" One of the shifters screamed the words and threw himself over the other, hiding him with his body, as I skidded to a stop and whipped my hand skyward, releasing the stored magic, almost too late.

In the next second, Sergeant was there, right behind them, his own claws out, his eyes burning. "Magician."

I froze, my power making it hard to focus. "Alpha."

"You're hers."

I was drawing a breath to answer when Flor whispered in my mind, her thought as soft as a butterfly's wing as her anguish, and her love, managed to filter through the spell. *If you're gonna get here for the party, you'd better hurry. I'm afraid they're about to turn the lights off and lock the doors.*

I snarled at Sergeant, and at the hundreds of shifters who'd begun to emerge from the shadows of the tall pines, backing him up. "Let me pass. I do not want to hurt you."

"The witch put up a spell, behind a barrier, a salt circle. I've been trying to get in, but these damned tattoos..." He indicated the patterns all over his body that cut him off from his magical birthright.

I didn't have time to pity him. Flor was there, whispering to me. *I want you to know, I love you, Grigor Dimitrivich. Even if you killed half the shifters in the whole world, I'd still love you. Does that make me evil?*

No, beloved. It makes you perfect.

I exhaled, the moon's magic still pouring into me, my own rage giving the pure energy a sharp, bloody edge. My little *behrserk*, evil? Never. But evil was what I was prepared to do if these well-intentioned shifters didn't get out of my way. I held out a hand and gently picked up the two Southern boys who had fallen and were still holding on, waiting for their grisly end.

"Your magic would never work. I'll tear it down," I promised, already moving. "Follow me inside."

Hold on, I told Flor. She was now professing her love to the others, and I could hear her desperation in the silent words.

I leaped over the trees and landed at the edge of the dome, cloaked in shadows. The spell had been made with the witch's blood, but was being fueled by the ones inside. The innocents, the Enforcers, the Alphas... and my bonded pack. Their strength flowed through the ground and sky and into the dome, making it unbreakable. It was a diabolically clever, balanced spell, and would have worked, except for one thing.

Their blood was mine, too... as was Elina's. And blood was the key.

I bit the palm of one hand savagely, then pressed it to the invisible surface, holding the other up to the moon. I opened up my tainted, murderous soul, let the moon shine her light into every dark corner, let it fill me... and then I let it flow through me.

The dome was there in one blink, and gone in the next. Without hesitating, I stepped forward into a world made of pain, none of it my own.

My bonds flared, and I was awash in sensation, my skin being scoured away by it, screaming in my mind at the intensity of it all. Brand's physical pain at being mutilated. Glen's grief for his parents. Finnick and Luke's agony as they were held back by sheer numbers from Brand and Flor's sides.

But my little queen was in the center of the pain, her soul bristling with courage, her heart thumping with a relentless beat. *Hope. Hope. Hope.*

I was at her enemy's back before the next beat, freezing her in place before she could finish cutting into my beloved with her silver blade, and whispered a greeting worthy of the boogeyman of all shifters.

"Boo."

The witch would have jumped, if I didn't have her

immobilized by the shadows I'd flung around her. Her fear filled the air around us, her whimper as I crushed the air from her lungs, a sweet, high sound in my ears that sailed over the roar of the crowd.

I disentangled her hand from my queen's red hair. "It's time to die, witch," I hissed, as I noted the strands she'd ripped free, and the blood on my little mate. "I only wish I could make it last."

Before I could kill her, my feet shifted, or perhaps the world did. One last, wispy cloud moved away from the face of the moon, and I was jolted by a wave of energy. Where had that come from? My answer came quickly.

Flor. She'd come into her power, and the moon was acknowledging Her daughter. Flor's eyes glowed with bright amber fire, her hair floating around her face like she was holding onto an electric current, sparks of silver light racing along her skin. She was transformed.

She was a goddess.

In the next breath, my bonds with the other males went wild, the combination of power and pain almost over-whelming me as they drew on the power to heal and fight. I had to help them, but how could I leave Flor? This close to the witch, even with her trapped, I couldn't afford to lose focus. I wouldn't be drawn from her side again.

I tamped down the connections, tearing my gaze from Flor. "Time to kill a witch."

"There's no time. Leave her to me. Help Brand," Flor gasped. "Save him." She was absolutely right. The Mountain mate had closed off our bond, but here, I could smell his death on the breeze. I may have waited too long already.

"Yes, beloved," I replied, sending a burst of healing energy through Flor before I popped up at Brand's side.

"You." Instantly, I flung more shadows around the magic thief, Ivan, wrapping his limbs in dark cobwebs. He fell to his side, his jaw wide, silver teeth coated with blood. His entire body was soaked, and Brand... I swallowed hard as I knelt beside my brother, who lay on his side in his wolf form.

I'd done worse to my enemies than what the silver-toothed fiend had done to Brand, but not by much. I blinked away something—was it tears?—before I used my hands to try and fold his fur around him. His heart wasn't beating, only quivering, and I had no idea how he was still alive. His blood was everywhere but inside his body, the dirt around his matted fur turned to mud with it.

I didn't waste time on the magic thief, who lay struggling at my side, or on the others who milled around us in shock. I didn't hesitate. I pressed my still-bloody hand to the heart of my beloved's first mate, and sent my own blood into the wolf's trembling muscle, pressing down gently.

My healing powers had never been as strong as my destructive ones, and I knew I might fail. But I had to try. I forced more blood from my body into his, extending my fangs and tearing into my lower lip to allow more to drip down into the gaping wound.

Live. Live, brother. Live for her, live for us all.

There was no answer. My beloved's heart still beat with hope, though, and I let myself listen to that cadence as I squeezed gently, moving the fresh blood into the chambers of Brand's heart. I fed her hope into my soul, and my blood into his body, and felt something in my own innermost spirit change.

There was always a price for great magic, a balance that had to be struck. Now, I sensed the price that was being extracted, one drop at a time. Brand might live or die; I still wasn't sure. But to make this attempt, I would lose something I'd taken for granted. My immortality.

My wolf had kept us alive for the mate we knew waited for us. He had kept my heart beating during the years when I'd killed indiscriminately, lost to pain and rage after Anya's death. When I'd been able to listen, to hear him again in our shared soul, he'd assured me that another mate—a wolf mate—would come.

Wounded, I'd harvested power from the light and the darkness for centuries, hoarding it so that I could stay alive for him, for *her*. Waiting for that promise to be kept. It had been worth the wait.

She was worth waiting an eternity for.

But now, eternity was the cost of living with her and my brothers. I would pay it gladly, to save the most honorable shifter I'd ever known.

"Take it," I whispered to the moon, then bit deeper into my lip, the cut I'd made there already healing. *Take it, and save him.*

I didn't remove my hand from his heart. Not when his fur began to shrink back, lying in place more or less, on his wolf form. I didn't stop squeezing until I felt the heart resist my hand. Then, and only then, I withdrew from his chest cavity, still bleeding into him, pulling the shredded fur over the savaged torso. The moon spilled down on us both as I knelt at his side, unsure if he was alive.

Dizzy from my own blood loss, I waited, hazily aware of a battle going on around me. Shouts of "Mountain!" and "Tenebris!" split the air. Guns rang out, and swords clashed. Wolves howled and barked, and shifters cursed, but I didn't take my eyes off of Brand.

Not until he turned his own head to me and opened his eyes. *Brother,* his wolf spoke into my mind.

Brother, I replied, before I lay beside him, my hand on his side.

I felt... old. My muscles were sore, my heart aching like it had been torn out and reassembled. My arm trembled, and when an Enforcer raced toward us, I wasn't sure I could rise to protect either one of us.

But I didn't have to.

"Fight me, ya ratfuckin' piece of cougar dung!" It was the boys from the forest, the one named Leroy and... Bo, I remembered. They had been the youngest of my queen's hunters, and were the weakest of the Tenebris pack.

But they had the most valiant hearts. Together, they flung themselves at the Eastern Enforcer, Bo rolling himself like a bowling ball at the male's legs. Not a second later, Leroy leaped on his shoulders, biting his ear and howling like a banshee.

The Enforcer wasn't some young pup, though. In an instant, he'd thrown the one on his shoulders to the ground and had his sword raised, ready to strike.

I lifted a hand, hoping whatever magic I could muster would be enough, but the first boy stood, though he wasn't a boy anymore. He was a midnight black wolf, skinny and lanky, with enormous paws and a shaggy head, his trousers still hanging in tatters around his furry middle.

Bo had shifted, though from the dazed expression in his deep brown eyes, and the unconscious shiver of his new, dark fur, I was almost certain it was his first time. To my surprise, he shook off the confusion and bared his teeth, leaping silently for the Enforcer's hand and tearing it off with a giant crack. The sword fell to the ground, and the wolf rose to the male's throat, ripping it out as cleanly as he had torn off the hand.

Leroy was up in a flash. "Bo! You're a wolf! You got your

wolf!" He danced around his friend, who yipped proudly, rubbing his bloodstained muzzle on his friend's pants leg. They both turned to me as I rose on one shaky arm. "Your Unholiness, sir. Mr. Flower Arranger," Leroy stammered, pushing Bo behind his legs. "We, ah, didn't meant to stop you from, uh, havin' your dinner, sir."

Bo grabbed the severed hand and carried it over to me with a low whine, like he was presenting me with a choice cut.

"The hunt isn't over," I groaned as I rose. I meant for them to go and kill a few more Enforcers, but from the sheer panic in their faces, I knew they'd misunderstood.

"Sergeant, save us!" Leroy screamed and ran off, leaping around small groups of fighting shifters.

Fighting. *Shit.* My power had diminished, and that meant the witch might have gotten loose. *Flor?* I reached into my bond and saw her power shining red. She was in her wolf form, fighting Elina.

Well, if being thrown around the bloodsoaked ground could be called fighting. Luke had fought his way to her, and was watching the battle carefully, alert for bystanders who might shoot at her or attack once she'd beaten the witch. Not that any shifter would dare approach. He practically glowed with power, his father's Alpha dominance combined with our strengthened bond sending any wolf he looked at to their knees.

Do you need help, little behrserk? I asked Flor anyway.

I've got this, Flor thought. *Go check on Glen and...*

Ah, yes. My heart sank. Glen's parents. And Finnick was across the ring as well, his father still alive. "No rest for the wicked," I murmured to Brand.

He chuffed and stood, his wolfish head at the same level as my chest. His fur was a patchwork quilt of thick silver scars almost the same color as his eyes... though his eyes had a slight red tint to them now.

Across the crowd, Glen cried out, and the pain in his voice echoed in our bond. I shoved as much power as I could spare toward him, feeling Brand do the same, and then we both ran to help.

CHAPTER 41

TAKING HIS PLACE
GLEN

Time stood still.

"Mom!" My scream seemed to go on for hours, Mom hanging in the air in front of my eyes, the sword jutting through her abdomen. She didn't speak, though her mouth dropped open as the pain hit, but her eyes said everything.

I love you. I love you. I love you.

Pride and sorrow, pain and even joy—that she had been able to save me. It flickered there as she fell, her swords dropping from her hands. I lunged forward, catching one of them mid-air, spun, and sliced across the neck of the Enforcer who'd struck her. His own eyes went wide with shock as his body and head were separated in the suddenly bright moonlight.

I tried to catch Mom, too, before she hit the earth, but at that very instant, a rush of power electrified me from head to toe. I opened my mouth in a silent shout as connections to a thousand wolves rushed into me. No, it was two thousand, and each one was a shifter I knew. I'd trained with them, fought beside them, protected them.

It was my father's power, the Alpha power of the Northern pack.

How was this *possible?* I was a rogue. I'd abjured my pack. I'd left them...

An answer to my unspoken question flickered in my mind, a memory from one of the others, perhaps? Brand, or maybe Grigor. I wasn't sure. Patrick had been declared the Heir, but the moon's power had been blocked from this hellish place when Dad had spoken the words.

Somehow, I was Alpha. I fell to my knees, stunned, until a soft hand landed on my leg. Mom's hand, the nails bloody and cracked, her fingers bruised and raw.

"Mom, be still." She was alive, though the sword was still wedged in her body. I stooped lower, cradling her head in my hands, careful not to move her. The bonds kept rushing into me as I held her, and I trembled. I felt her, too, as part of the pack, inside me.

She smiled gently and mouthed the word *Alpha*. Her vow bound her to me, her fading power connecting with mine as that one word served as her pledge.

Her love filled my mind in a way I'd never felt before. I didn't just know she loved me without condition—I felt it in my marrow, in my blood.

Connections kept pouring into me, every shifter in Northern being tied to me, to my soul, and I shook under the intensity of it. "How?"

She mouthed the word *Alpha* again, her hand going slack, eyes closing.

"No!" I shouted, desperate to save her. "Don't go to sleep, Mom," I demanded, and a hint of Alpha command was in my voice.

Her breath rattled in her lungs, but she obeyed. No, her wolf did. She blinked up at me, dark irises glowing slightly, the full moon that sailed above reflected in her pupils.

Command her, my own wolf snarled. *The pack needs her.*

Command her to live? I could. I was her Alpha; she had made her pledge. I could command her to do anything, though I wasn't certain she would forgive me for it.

We need her.

"Mom. Keep breathing," I tried, but I didn't have enough Alpha power yet to stave off death, and she was truly dying. A part of her wanted to go, to be with her mate.

But my wolf insisted. *The pack needs her still.* It wasn't clear what pack he meant, but he howled at me to act.

"Breathe," I shouted, but the light in her eyes, still fixed on me, was fading.

Shifters poured into the ring all around me, and I recognized their howls as they began to fight. Northern was here, or at least some of them. Mountain as well, their outsized wolves tearing into the guards who had circled me and Mom.

Bullets whined, and bones snapped. The screams and snarls of battle surrounded us.

I heard Patrick's howl of agony as he encountered our dad's fallen body, and felt his rage deep inside me, in our pack connection. Patrick was the one who should have been Alpha. I called his name, and he was there beside me, kneeling, shock coursing through him as he saw how badly Mom was injured. Our eyes met, and a whole conversation passed in an instant.

I didn't mean to take your place, little brother.

His wolf snapped. *Alpha, it was always yours. The moon doesn't make mistakes.* Out loud, he said, "Alpha, I am yours to command."

The connection was instant, his strength flowing into

me... and trickling to Mom. Her chest rose again, the light in her eyes flaring dimly.

I needed the pack. "Pledge!" I shouted. "Northern, to me. Give me your vows!"

Instantly, pack members began appearing, shouting their allegiance. "Alpha, I pledge!" "Alpha, I am yours!" "Alpha, you are mine!" They fought their way to me, some of them touching me with one hand, each contact like a defibrillator, shocking my body. Mom jolted, too, though, and blood gushed as the blade shifted inside her abdomen.

I turned my head toward Patrick, though I couldn't focus my eyes. "Take the sword out." He did so carefully, quickly staunching the blood with a cloth that appeared in his hand, given by one of the Eastern kitchen staff who dared to come close enough to help. In the distance, I could hear shrill screams as other girls and women were injured and attacked. They had to be cannon fodder, warm bodies that Aidan had brought to the fight, and he was most likely using them just now as that.

I felt Finn's rage and knew he was fighting his own father, trying to wrest control of the pack from him, and save the girls—save all of us. He was surrounded by enemies, even though reinforcements had arrived.

But I had my own fight to win.

More Northern pack members appeared, giving their pledge before flinging themselves back into the melee, forming a protective circle around Mom, Patrick, and me. There were at least a few dozen, and a few of them had true mates back at Northern, though it didn't seem to matter that they weren't here in body. Those distant mates whispered their vows through the bonds, each new strand a stream of pure energy filling me.

The vows made the power that had entered me with the

moon's brilliance flow like a turbulent river in a spring thaw. It felt as if the power was destroying a part of me inside as I channeled it, funneled it into Mom, chanting, "Live, breathe, you will stay for the pack. I command it." It was like reaching into a flood to pull her out by one hand, or her hair, and instead of rescuing her, I was drowning myself.

Dying, alongside her.

But suddenly Grigor was there, in my soul, anchoring me. Grigor, and then Luke, Brand, and Flor. Even Finn, who I had been so angry at, for hurting Flor, but whose soul I could feel was fully devoted to her.

All of them tethered me as I fought to withstand the pull of power, and death, and grief. I let them hold on and used every scrap of the Northern flood to push life into Mom, as Patrick held the cloth to her stomach.

"Live," I commanded again, my voice a crack of thunder in the night. I set my hands next to Patrick's on her chest, envisioning the power that I'd been given, even if I didn't deserve it, flow into her. "Live for the pack."

Her chest rose and fell once, twice. Then, in a flash, her eyes snapped open. "Alpha." There was accusation and allegiance in her tone.

I knew why. She'd been close to joining Dad, almost in his arms again. But I knew how to force her to live. "Mom, they're killing the girls, the servants. The women. They have no one to protect them. There are too many enemies, and not enough protectors." The words felt cruel on my tongue as I spoke them, but I had to. "Get up, and protect the pack."

She let out a rage-filled scream and rose, her face pale, the scar that stretched across it as silver as the glint in her light eyes. I blinked, wondering if her eyes were like Brand's now. But then she'd turned her face away, swords retrieved from the ground, and was wiping her own blood from the blade that had eviscerated her on her trousers.

She snarled at my brother, who blinked up at her, tears streaming down his cheeks. "Defense, the way we trained with pups this fall. We need to get them together here, then take them... there." She pointed to the edge of the ring, with two tall pines that had grown together. We all knew what she meant. The trees would act as protection from rear attacks, and if we formed a double circle, a shield of warriors, in front, the girls would be safe behind us as we traveled to that patch of relative safety. In the fall, Flor had worked with our youngest on climbing and hiding in the treetops. We all knew this drill.

Reaching into the pack bond, I sent a command out to Northern. "Protect the girls, the women. Gather the vulnerable. They are pack." I pictured the twin trees and called out, "Follow the Alpha Mate."

There was slight confusion as the wolves stumbled, unsure. *Oh, shit.*

Flor was the Alpha Mate now.

"My mother," I repeated. "Go! Follow my mother!"

Someone shouted, *"Alpha's mother!"* and the wolves all swiveled their heads to her.

Mom snarled again, like the phrase hurt her. I growled back. There was no time to argue. My pack members darted into the battle, then Patrick and his fighters whistled for Mountain troops to help. They began working in tandem to trip up the Easterners—and even some of the strangers— who had grabbed girls and were using them as shields. As soon as the fighters tripped, smaller shifters, dressed in ragged clothing, darted in and grabbed their fallen weapons. Even the guns.

"Tenebris! Tape the guns!" I knew that voice, though the order made no sense. I nearly smiled as I grabbed a fallen dagger. Sergeant was here, fighting with his Tenebris boys.

Well, fighting or doing a craft project. I watched one of the rogues peel up the end of a roll of duct tape he wore on one skinny wrist, and wrap it around the gun a dozen times, until the weapon was useless, trapped in a ball of dull gray tape. While he did that, another two boys did the same thing around the fallen Enforcer's ankles and wrists, ending the job with a solid strip of tape around the cursing Easterner's mouth.

"Sergeant!" I called, but just as he turned to me, something punched me in the back once, twice, then a dozen times.

It was agony, but one I'd felt before, and with my newfound power, I wasn't in any danger of falling. I screamed in anger and turned, knowing what I'd find: a shooter, standing close behind me.

I was wrong. It was a firing line, three Eastern Enforcers, holding their guns on me, still firing. Half the bullets were hitting me. The other half flew wide, peppering the Tenebris boys and even the crowd of girls who'd been huddled together.

The night split with fresh cries of pain from young throats.

The rogues flung their bodies over the girls, some taking the bullets in their backs, others grabbing the maids and running with them toward the trees. Then, as suddenly as they'd begun, the bullets stopped. A giant shadow fell over the gunmen, and another smaller, darker shadow appeared beside them, wrapping around their throats and slitting them all in the space of two seconds.

My brothers. They stepped up to me, each one placing a hand on one of my shoulders. I looked up. Brand was... changed. His skin was patched together like Frankenstein's monster. I wasn't sure how he'd survived what had been done to him, but then I saw the way Grigor gazed at him. Protective and with a warmth that was unusual and unexpected.

Brand's silver eyes glowed so brightly, it almost hurt to look at them. Grigor's were red as blood. *Creepy little fuck.*

"Little brother."

"Hey, Joaquin," I replied weakly, the silver inside me making me tremble. "Know any magic tricks for making silver disappear?"

"As a matter of fact..." He sent a pulse of power through my body. All the bullets that had been caught inside me were ejected suddenly. It hurt like fuck, before the power of my pack rushed through me, healing me instantly.

"How is Margarette?" Brand asked. "Where—" But Mom had loosed an unmistakable howl from the edge of the fight, drawing the enemy to her, while the others got the girls of Eastern and the boys of Tenebris to safety.

"She's angry but alive, and I'd like her to stay that way," I replied, before shifting into my wolf form.

"We'll make sure of it," Grigor said gently, but then went still. "Brand? Help Glen. I may need to assist Finnick." He was gone before Brand could reply.

I nudged Brand with my snout. He responded by shifting into his own wolf form, massive and dark brown, like the loamy soil of the deep forest, but with silvered scars intersecting all over his coat. Proof of what he'd suffered to protect the pack so far.

I howled my promise to do every bit as much, if I needed to. The abuses, the imbalance—it had to end here tonight. And it would start with us keeping the smallest members of any of the packs from suffering even one more injury or injustice.

Thirty wolves howled along with me, through muzzles as well as human-shaped mouths, and the battle began to shift as Northern did what it had failed to do for years.

It protected the weakest ones.

CHAPTER 42
FOOL ME ONCE
FINNICK

I was pushing myself to the outer limit of my endurance and strength as I fought as many of my parent's new "allies" as I could at once, desperate to protect the innocents huddled near me. The two Russians I faced now both held silver blades, which meant they had no honor. I responded in kind, dropping to my knees and grabbing handfuls of dry earth. Fighting dirty, I'd accused Flor when we first met. Southern tricks.

These two were no more ready for them than I'd been, and when I leaped up toward them, flinging the dust in an arcing cloud into their faces, it flew directly in their eyes.

The first died on my claws before he could react. The second was still blinded and coughing when he died on his own blade. Their fellow soldiers stood around us, frozen at the speed of my attack.

That shock was the last thing they'd feel.

Just then, the moon brightened, bathing us all in its light. It felt like holy fire, racing across my skin and pouring into me, filling my veins with magic. I soaked it up like a desert landscape in an unexpected rain, and bloomed with violence.

The spell was down.

I tapped into the power that poured like a spring flood from Grigor and my bonds, and from the moon directly into my blood, and fought like a creature possessed. I sensed my brothers and my mate fighting their own horrific battles, carrying their share of the moon's power and Flor's red rage along with their own strength as we all threw ourselves against the enemies.

To my surprise, I was not alone in my fight. The same females who had leaped onto Niall's corpse rose up at my sides and my back, grabbing every weapon they could find and protecting me from more than one strike, even though they suffered for their trouble.

They fought like Flor had back at Southern, as if they had nothing to lose, since they'd lost it all anyway. No hope, no future, no dignity. They fought with stolen blades, clawing silver bullets out of the packed earth and jumping onto the swords that were being used against them, getting far enough inside the soldiers' guards to shove the silver into their mouths, forcing them to swallow, even as the girls bled out in the attempt.

They died bravely, escaping the trap of living in my father's corrupted pack at last, and each death was a match on the fire that burned in my chest. I fought harder, trying to keep them all safe, though it was futile.

Until Grigor was there, clapping a hand on my shoulder. "Did you save any for me, pup?" His grin was terrifying, and even though the Enforcers facing us didn't know who he was at first, every one of them flinched when I replied.

"Grigor Dimitrivich, you know I'll always share."

The scent of urine filled the air as Grigor whirled to face

the tall, battle-hardened soldiers. To their credit, they gave a half-hearted effort to raise their weapons against him. But none of them stood a chance. He spun, almost flying, his shadowed form appearing just long enough to pluck out an eyeball or two, or slit a throat. In seconds, the ground around us was a thick mud that smelled of iron, piss, and despair.

But for once, it wasn't the despair of the innocent. No, those females had risen again, and were doing creditable impressions of the boogeyman themselves, showing a savagery that had me blinking. Everything seemed to be going right, but my wolf was clawing at me, urging me to break away from this fight, insisting the true danger lay elsewhere.

My father. He had fled, but I knew better than to dream he'd left the battle entirely. He would know there was nowhere on earth he could hide from what he'd done.

Though he hid from me as I ran from one group of fighters to another, taking in the various contingents who were fighting, shame rising in my heart and bile in my throat as the Eastern Enforcers showed they all had silver, and used it without compunction.

Finally, I spotted his head bobbing near the edge of the crowd, his red hair a beacon. He was running toward an area that seemed to be clear, which was odd. Unless it was magic that held the others back... or a battle.

Of course, it was Flor. My mate, and my witch of a mother, swords cutting the air in a deathly dance, though Flor was laughing as she fought.

But she didn't see my father running up behind her, no more than thirty feet away, a knife in one hand.

Fuck. I ran as fast as I could, sending a burst of awareness through the bond, shouting, "Behind! Look back!" I hoped she'd understand. I ran as if she might not.

She didn't turn, too busy fighting Mother, and I knew I wouldn't reach her in time, but then Father tripped on a bowling ball. It sent him skidding across the ground a few feet before he jumped up.

It wasn't a bowling ball, but the small, midnight black wolf had flung itself at Father's legs in a move no warrior had ever been taught. There was no dignity to the attack, no style. It was... I found myself grinning. It was a trashy Southern move, and when another one of the skinny boys from that pack leaped at Father before he could kick out at the black wolf, yelling something that sounded like, "Yee-haw, motherfucker! You're about to find out what a whole can of whoop-ass tastes like," I knew it was one of Flor's.

"Father!" I yelled as he lunged with his blade at the dirty-faced boy. "If you want to fight a child, start with your own." I thought for a moment, then added, "You ratfucking chickenshitter son of a rattlesnake bastard." I raised an eyebrow at the boy, who wiggled his hand in a so-so gesture.

"We'll work on it," he promised, then ran off with the black wolf, using their small size, speed, and utter fearless-ness to trip as many of our enemies as they could.

Father's disgust was etched in every feature of his sharp face as I approached. Revulsion, indignation, and disbelief at what was happening.

"Did you truly believe you could force every wolf in North America to roll over for you?" I asked, wondering at his ego. "Did you believe there would never come a day of reckoning, that an Alpha as weak and craven as you would ever hold power over so many better, stronger shifters?"

"Don't talk to me about strength," he spat, circling

around, watching my hands. I held no weapons, but he and I both knew I didn't need them. "You were weak when you were born, and stayed weak, even with—"

"Even with Mother's blood in me?" I narrowed my eyes. "Her magic? You think she had that much power?"

"I know she did. Does." He shifted his knife to his other hand, then back, in a move he'd taught me when I was six. I didn't bother watching the blade, just his eyes.

"But she wasn't strong. She stole that power. Did you know she drained it out of me, since I was little? Did you know she drained me and Tana both, eating our magic?" He flinched. "Did she eat yours, too, Father?" His cheek twitched. "By the moon, you weren't a weak Alpha when you met her, were you? You were stronger before; I would bet on it."

"I'm not weak now," he spat out, lunging. I spun to one side, ducking the sloppy swing easily, but when I inhaled, I could smell the lie in his words. His pack, the source of his strength, was being slaughtered around him. He himself had almost nothing left to fight with.

My gut churned at the thought of what she'd done, though I felt no pity for him. He'd planned the Long Hunt right beside her. He'd damaged his children, sold us off again and again. He'd destroyed our pack and its legacy.

"You know she feeds on pain, don't you? Did she feed on your pain, over these past decades? The pain of your wolf, and hers? That's how she grew fat with power. She stole it from her family. Just like you tried to steal what wasn't yours from Bradley." The absolute stark truth of my words hit him harder than any blade could, and he staggered. "You could've been a great Alpha. A decent father. A leader worth following, with a legacy that his pack would sing to the moon for generations. Instead, you're a cautionary tale."

Father sneered. "And what legacy will *you* have? If you kill me, you'll be nothing—just Finnick McDonnell, who killed his own father."

I smiled. "Wrong again. I have a legacy, but not as your son. I'm Finnick Dimitrivich, descendant of Grigor, and true mate to Florida Wills, which gives me more pride than any business deal or alliance ever would. And you're the one who'll be nothing." I finally gathered myself to attack, pulling power from the moon as well as through my bonds, but he defended himself so slowly, so carelessly, I suspected he'd given up. Shame had a stench of its own, and I'd never smelled it on him, until now.

I struck out with my claws extended from human-shaped hands, knocking the knife away. It skittered across the ground, into the shadows that stretched from the pines over the edge of the ring. Many of the foreign shifters and visitors from the smaller packs had fled now, and watched from the trees, with a few Tenebris, Northern, and Mountain pack members guarding them from the occasional fleeing Eastern or Russian Enforcer.

I struck quickly, slicing his carotid artery with one swipe, and stabbing into his femoral artery with the next, giving him a far kinder and quicker death than he deserved. He looked small as I stood over him, small and weak and pathetic, though to my shock, he transformed as he died.

He gave a soft whimper, a whine that almost sounded grateful, as he laid his furry head down on the bloodsoaked earth. Not two seconds later, his Alpha power sank into me, welding itself to my limbs. I felt taller and stronger, though the bonds to the other members of Eastern were frayed and strained. Eaten, as if moths had been at them.

Not moths. Magic. My gut churned at the knowledge of what had happened not just to me, but to all of us. She'd been devouring our whole pack from within, for years.

I sighed and bowed to my father's dead wolf, the part of him that I did pity, though not to him as my fallen Alpha. Then I strode across a battlefield that grew quieter by the second as my pack realized they had lost, leaving only the Russians as our adversaries. The Easterners moved away from me, parting as I approached, dropping their weapons when I snarled. Some of them tried to slink toward the shadows, but a few turned to fight the Russians. I took careful note of the shifters who held onto their arms and stepped in beside me.

There weren't many to remember.

Margarette and Sergeant were leading the charge against the remaining Russians, who still fought viciously, probably because they had everything to lose now that Ivan was dead. Perhaps they hoped my mother would whisk them away to safety if she won, or escaped.

But Flor wasn't going to let that happen. She fought like she was born for this night, for this battle. Her steps were sure and quick, her strikes vicious and clever. Her amber eyes glowed like yellow moons as she leaped and spun, every hour of her training obvious in her moves.

She was a fucking miracle, and my wolf's mouth watered watching her, knowing she would be ours someday in every way. I stepped closer, keeping an eye out for any fools lurking in the shadows.

Most of the torches that had helped light the area of the shallow bowl had been knocked over or extinguished, and now all that lit the figures of the two women was the moon. Mother's hair was half-torn from her usual tight bun, dragging over one swelling eye, her clothing in tatters.

She held her head up, but her usual haughty expression was nowhere to be seen. She was facing down her death, and knew it. That meant she had never been more dangerous. She had nothing to lose.

I nodded to a Mountain shifter who was standing on one side of the loose ring around the two, his gaze on everything but the fight, hands resting on the hilts of two long, wicked daggers in his belt sheath. I was shocked when he bowed to me. "Alpha, if you would like to watch your mate's battle, I will guard your back," he said, straightening, still keeping watch on the shadows.

I blinked, recognizing him. This was the warrior who had been Brand's father's Head Enforcer, or the Mountain equivalent. "Dean, thank you. Where is Brand?"

"He's with..." He swallowed hard. "The little, ah, the newest mate. They're making sure the girls and the Southern rogues, the ones they call the Tenebris boys, are healing."

"Grigor." I relaxed. I knew Brand had been injured to the point of death, and Grigor had saved him, but I wasn't clear on how it had happened. "There's a full medical room in the west wing of the Mansion. Once we're sure it's safe here, I'll take anyone who needs care inside. There was a lot of silver in this fight, and far too many young girls whose wolves can't heal them yet." He nodded, and I stepped past him, trusting him to guard my back while I guarded Flor's.

Not five seconds later, Luke appeared on my left. He hadn't grown taller, but his newfound power made him seem more substantial. "Alpha," I greeted him. He dipped his chin in reply, and we turned together to watch the fight. We both hummed in appreciation as Flor cut a long line down her opponent's arm, then spat a bloody wad into her face, blinding her for just long enough to carve a matching one on the other side.

"Dirty," he said of her technique.

"Effective," I replied. "Can you believe we thought she was a boy when we found her in the woods?"

Luke chuckled. "As Flor would say, it's a good thing you're pretty."

I found myself smiling, until Mother's lips started moving, though no sound emerged. Was she trying some kind of spell? I wasn't sure. She could just be whispering. Flor was watching her lips, though, and her face went pale as the seconds ticked on. Then Mother dropped her sword.

This was it. Her move.

My teeth lengthened, and my claws extended as I narrowed my focus, readying myself to shift if I needed to cross to Flor fast. I was good at seeing strategies and patterns, knowing what an enemy was thinking sometimes before they did. It looked like Mother was surrendering, but my wolf ran purely on instinct, and right now, something had him panicking.

Luke stiffened as well. "She's up to something."

"Can you hear her?"

He snarled. "Not well enough. Was that sword her only weapon?"

Fuck. "Not a chance."

I knew Flor believed that almost anything could be used as a weapon. Mother had often expressed a similar sentiment, sometimes jokingly, often when she was wearing a provocative cocktail dress that left nothing to the imagination. *"No one would ever guess how many weapons a shifter like me can carry,"* she'd bragged. No one ever would guess, because no one would believe just how many deadly items she kept on her person.

"She'll know." Luke grabbed my arm when I took a breath to shout, or run to Flor; I wasn't sure which. "She'll know it's a trick. Don't distract her."

"I have to save her," I snarled. If I had to tear out my own mother's throat to keep her from hurting Flor— however she was doing it—I would.

Luke's grip grew tight on my arm. "She's saving us, you idiot. She's saving you. Let her." He sounded certain. Proud, if pained.

"What?" When I couldn't shake free of Luke's grip, I reached for the newly strengthened bond between me and Flor, trying to understand what she was thinking.

Her thoughts were filled with regret and sadness. A few words made it through. *Fool me once, shame on you.*

Amber eyes met mine across the dark-stained earth, and I realized what she must be remembering. The pain I'd given her, only a few weeks before. It was still there in her gaze, still a bruise on her soul.

Fool me twice...

Shame filled me, then horror, as Mother pulled a long silver wire from her hair and looped it over Flor's neck.

CHAPTER 43
FOOL ME TWICE
FLOR

There was a moment in every fight when you won or lost, and it had nothing to do with what moves you made or which strikes connected. Del had told me over and over that the real battle was in a fighter's heart. The memory of the last time flooded my mind.

"That's why you'll never lose, if you don't give up. Even if you're trapped. Even if they get you down. You will get back up." Del held a cold cloth to the goose egg swelling over one eye, while I squeezed a five-inch gash on my left bicep closed with a clean kitchen towel.

He'd found me a few minutes before inside one of the kitchen trash cans—shoved inside, with trash covering me almost entirely, my arms and legs bound with duct tape, and a piece over my mouth and half of one nostril—when he came in to do his shift. He didn't bother to ask who'd done it. It was the same shit, different day. I still smelled like old coffee grounds and rancid meat.

I was feeling sorrier for myself than usual. Mama had been running around naked by the fence line, yellin' about hidden treasures, and I'd been stupid. Instead of keepin' my head down,

I'd run after her, tryin' to get some clothes on her. She'd slapped my face for my trouble.

That had hurt more than the wolf's claw that caught my arm when Trevor Blackside's gang of fucknuggets had jumped out from where they'd been starin' at Mama.

"How many times am I supposed to get back up, Del?" I sniffled as he got the kit out to stitch the deepest gash. "Is this all life is, being shit on a thousand times, waking up to worse every day? Why should I even bother?"

He let out a long sigh, then turned back, wrapping his arms around me as I sat on the long table and cried. "Girlie, here's why. This world needs you. It may seem like it doesn't; you may not believe it now. But I've never met a shifter with a heart as big as yours. With as much fire in her belly. All you gotta do is wait for your day to come. Or your night, under the full moon. Someday, you'll look around and see that everyone in spittin' distance will be looking at you, maybe not all of them with love. But with respect."

"Maybe you knocked your head, too, Del. Nobody'll ever respect me. I'm Southern trash."

"You're Southern steel, Flor. You may not be the strongest on the outside, or the fastest—though we're gonna start training with more weights. You gotta get faster at outrunnin' those assholes." He pulled back and stared into my eyes. It was kinda itchy to meet his gaze, but he was proud of me when I didn't drop my head. "Your spirit is pure steel, Florida Wills. Pure steel, and as bright as a sharp blade. You're gonna cut the rot outta this world, just wait."

He let me go, and examined the cut on my arm again. Somehow, it had stopped bleeding already. He grunted, getting up to put the medical kit away. "But first, you're gonna need to cut the rot out of fifty pounds of old potatoes."

My arms had been sore after I'd peeled and chopped all

those potatoes. No one had noticed the extra salt in them from my tears, though the whole table of males who'd thrown me in the trash had somehow gotten the squirts that night. I'd figured out how, when I saw the empty box of human laxatives in the dumpster.

My arms were even more sore now, though I could draw power from the moon since the dome had fallen, and power from my mates, too. But my heart was what I worried most about, and not just my own.

Glen had watched his beloved father die. Luke and Finn had both killed their own shitty ones, though I would've taken my mates' places in a heartbeat if I could've, so they didn't have to live with those memories. No matter how awful your dad was, there was still that connection to mourn.

Not that I was going to let myself think about that right now. Maybe not for a few years.

But now I was going to have to kill Finn's mother right in front of him. I'd felt him end his father a few minutes before, and thought it might be the moment when Elina would falter as well. I'd hoped it would be, since Finn hadn't been close enough to see her fall. But she'd only stumbled once, cursed, and spat a little blood. Her wolf had to be dead for her not to react at all to her true mate's death.

Or maybe not.

"Please no. Don't make my son see this. Not like this, not while he's watching," she whispered as her eyes darted to him, hovering anxiously on the edge of the loose circle that stood by, witnessing the fight. The onlookers were mainly Mountain and Northern fighters, though there were some powerful-looking shifters I didn't recognize, big wolves that I hadn't seen at the Southern Council. Maybe they were from some other country, but they weren't Ivan's Russians. No, those fuckers were all across the ring, getting their asses handed to them by Grigor, Brand, and Glen. My boys had some aggression to work out, it seemed like, though when Grigor felt my mind touch his, he immediately sent me a thought.

Do you need us, little flame?

Nah. But Finn might. I was about to make him an orphan, after all.

I jerked my attention back to Elina. She was doing a damned good impression of a defeated woman. The faint scent of ozone I'd smelled earlier beneath the silver, when she'd been moving faster than she should have been able to, was gone. Her narrow shoulders drooped, and her hair fell around her face. Well, around part of her face. A hairpin or something was keeping half her bun from collapsing, and her long-ass hair from becoming an easy handhold for me to slit her throat.

I wasn't about to fall for her hangdog routine. "You think I should give you more consideration than you and your mate were going to give Bradley and Margarette? You think you've earned a death with dignity?"

"I suppose not," she whispered. "You're the same as me, after all. A witch, flush with power. Why would you be any more compassionate?"

"You think I'm like you?"

She sighed. "I know it. You'll see. The power makes your heart *cold*. It keeps you from feeling what you should. If I had another chance..." She hung her head, letting her sword fall to the ground. A few of the shifters watching let out shocked gasps. "Please, let him look away. Please, don't let him see this." I wasn't sure who she was talking to, or praying to, but I knew what she wanted.

"Fool me once, shame on you," Mama had said more than once when I was a little kid. It wasn't until later that I learned there was a second part to the saying.

I turned my head away from Elina, sending Finn a look of apology. His expression was stricken, though Luke, who stood beside him, holding him back, seemed to have figured out what was going on. I liked that. He believed in me. Finn, well, he'd take some training.

I let my head stay turned for one second, two seconds... *Fool me once, shame on you. Fool me twice—*

Elina fell for my bait and reached into her hair. I thought she might be grabbing a hairpin, but it was far cleverer than that. From the corner of my eye, I saw she had a garrote that had been holding up her bun, a fine silver wire running from one dark wood tether to another, tucked around the bun in a clever arrangement. She held one end in her hand, then sent the loop flying over my head, in a flash.

But I was ready for it. I had my steak knife already on the way up, catching the wire on the serrated blade just as it dropped over my head. With a hard yank, I tore it out of her grip, the silver stink in the air making my stomach churn.

She let out a scream of rage, but I was already using my leg to knock her off balance, hooking a foot behind her knee and driving her to the ground. One of her arms had landed behind her with a sickening crunch. The other I pinned with a knee as I kneeled over her torso. She knew she was defeated, and threw her neck back, though her eyes still sparked with a few defiant flickers of red.

"See? You're the same as me." Her Southern accent was back, and her voice sounded far too close to the way mine did.

One wooden end of the garrote was in my hand, the other wrapped around my steak knife. I moved the knife, thinking. I wanted to twist the wire around her neck, to let her feel the burn of silver, like so many of the innocents on this battlefield had. More than any other shifter I'd met, she deserved to have her head taken as well.

But I couldn't do it. As she watched, I unwrapped the wire from my knife and threw the silver away.

Finn shouted, "No! Flor, don't let her—" The sparks in her eyes flared up, into a bright fire, and I knew she was planning to use magic against me.

Let her fucking try.

My focus on my five-pointed scar, I tapped into the power that waited inside me, the *behrserker* rage that I'd first felt at Southern no longer making me a mindless killing machine. Though I expected Grigor was helping me somehow, or maybe Brand, or both of them, as I was now able to channel that strength into my arm.

She managed to say one word. "Fool—"

"—me twice, shame on me," I finished for her, though I wasn't sure that was what she was saying. I drew my steak knife—not silver, just plain Southern steel, swiped off the Alpha's own table at Southern—across her neck. "Oops." My wolf had channeled all of her strength, and Grigor had sent a burst at the same time, so the knife had more than done its job.

Elina's head fell to the earth and rolled away.

A split second later, I was lifted up into the arms of my mate. I smelled two of them close, bright ginger and cold, sharp magic. A shadow moved on the ground behind me, and Grigor was in my mind whispering, *Well done, little behrserk*, but I was cradled in Finn's arms.

"Thank you," he whispered as he pressed his face to my

hair. "Thank you for doing that for me. I know she was evil, but... it would have been hard."

I swallowed hard. How had I not put that together? That if I hadn't killed her, Finn would've had to kill both parents in one night. My heart ached like it was breaking in a way that would never heal, and I wasn't certain if it was my own pain I felt, or his. He'd grown up in a pack every bit as bad as mine, just in different ways. Alone in a way I hadn't realized until I stepped foot onto these packlands.

At least I'd had Del to show me what love was supposed to look like. Finn had only had Tana, and she was gone. I prayed we would be enough to help him heal.

You're more than enough. His thought was feather-soft, but his pain was still sharp and fresh.

I didn't know what to say, so I just took his face in my hands and leaned up to press a soft kiss to his mouth. It tasted of blood and salt from his tears, but his gingery scent warmed, covering the stench of the battlefield, and my spirit warmed with it. When I saw the moon shining on his face as he lifted his head, silver beams illuminating his red hair, his eyes sparkling with blue specks of magic among the green, I wondered how such a sweet, quiet moment could exist in this cold, angry world.

"Quiet," Finn whispered. "Listen." We both held our breath. He was right. The battle was over. No more swords or knives clanging, no more wolves howling for blood. Shifters began to creep out of the trees, fear keeping their footsteps silent, but hope bringing them into the moonlight.

"Little flame? Brother?" Grigor's soft question had Finn turning. My other mates stood there, Luke, Glen, and Brand, all in their wolf forms. Luke's wolf was a shimmering pewter gray, with black tips at his ears and paws.

He was as handsome as he was in his human form, and with the same blue eyes. Glen's wolf was grinning with sharp white teeth and gave a short yip of greeting, but Brand... The vicious scars that marked him now had my throat tightening.

"Let me down, Sparkles," I said, squirming to get to them.

"Really? Sparkles?" Finn grumbled, but let me go.

My arms were around Brand's neck first, his fur soft on my face as I hid the tears that wouldn't stop flowing. "I thought..." Guilt swamped me. I'd encouraged him to shift into his wolf form, thinking it would save him. But it had just given Ivan the chance to torture him.

Brand changed in my arms, instantly holding me to his broad chest. "Shhh, wildflower. Shush, no tears. I'm alive. We survived." He didn't say we'd won. Victory had come at a cost none of us had wanted to bear, that would haunt us all for the rest of our lives. "We're still alive."

"How?" I asked, pushing back and placing my hand gingerly over the massive scar that began at his neck, where my mating mark had been, to his chest. An enormous, roughly star-shaped scar sat over his heart, and I blinked. It was so much like mine, but bigger and with raw edges. "How?" I repeated. There was no way he should be alive.

"Grigor gave me his life," Brand answered, though his voice was rough, and he sounded... confused about it. "He gave up his—"

"Something I had no need for anymore, brother," Grigor interrupted.

"Oh, yes. I see," Brand murmured, his silver eyes gleaming brightly.

"You see?" I asked, swallowing hard, not understanding.

"He gave up his immortality." When I gasped, Brand cupped my chin in one massive hand and smiled sweetly, though the fresh scar that ran from his temple across one cheek made me think of a pirate. "I wouldn't live a single day without you, beloved. None of us would. What use is forever, if you're not there?"

Though his eyes shone like twin moons, his words fell onto my sore heart like a warm ray of sunlight. "I love you, too." I smiled back at him, then let my eyes move over every one of my battered, tired, perfect mates. "I love you all."

CHAPTER 44
CONSUMING EVIL
GRIGOR

No one in the clearing besides me knew what could happen when a powerful hybrid witch died. I'd killed dozens over the years, from weak ones who'd preyed on humans, to a coven who'd slaughtered the very last of the bear shifters in Russia for their pelts and power.

One like Elina McDonnell—who'd committed evil deeds for decades, who had sacrificed her own lover that very day for more—would still be filled with tainted energy for weeks or months after her death.

Unless someone consumed it.

My wolf side recoiled, remembering the ones we'd hunted before. The feral beasts who'd preyed on the innocent, and whose remaining power had needed someone to hold it, rather than let it seep into the land and end up feeding more evil. I didn't want to be the one to swallow Elina's death. Didn't want to go to my little queen oozing residual corruption.

But already, Elina's magic was leaching into the earth. If I didn't act quickly, she would make an indelible mark on the packlands, situated as her corpse was at its very heart.

Its *dead* center, such as it was.

Though I tried to make light of the task ahead, my wolf still struggled as we moved to stand over the corpse. I'd never been particular about my meals, and I was hungry. But this whole battle had made me and my wolf sick at heart. I'd watched young girls fall under blades held by full-grown males. Watched unarmed women throw themselves over boys to save them from bullets the only way they could, with their bodies. Hundreds lay dead, dying, or grievously injured.

It made my stomach growl. The death that surrounded me, and not only Elina's, was a lure to the darkness inside me.

I let myself look at Flor, her bright hair somehow still shining in the fading moonlight as Finnick embraced her. She was all that kept me sane now, if I could ever be called that. Her presence, her fierce goodness, kept me from drinking it all in, bloating myself on the darkness.

Night covered the battlefield, inky shadows stretching out from the trees. My brothers had begun to move around the clearing, calling out orders to the Mountain and Northern shifters, looking for any of theirs who might be saved, and beginning the terrible work of counting the dead.

As I hesitated, two or three lean wolves crept out of the shadows and slunk toward Elina's still-steaming corpse. These were shifters who smelled of the old world, and who might know what lay at my feet. Power, going to waste, trickling into the earth.

I hissed them back into the forest, but eyes gleamed from the shadows, and the next few who ventured out of the tree line belonged to this pack. They were famished, their bones birdlike and cheeks gaunt, their spirits sputtering like half-blown candles. A few of the girls from the Mansion had been starved witches, and the sight of all the power she'd stolen from them was turning them feral. They seemed confused, uncertain what was drawing them toward the one who'd tortured them.

"Grigor, fix it," Sergeant called out, stepping in front of the females. I narrowed my eyes at his command, but obeyed when Flor nudged me along our bond. I kicked Elina's head closer to her body, then kneeled to press one hand to her cold face, the other to the closest part of her body I could touch, her arm.

This was going to... How did Flor say it? *Ah, yes.* This was going to *suck.*

I closed my eyes, needing to think of how best to do this. I was no longer immortal, and I was tied to my little queen as well as my brothers now. That meant I could not be careless, or cleaning up the witch's mess could damage us all. I lowered my head, inhaled, and allowed the heavy weight of her stolen power to seep up my fingers, to my wrists, then elbows. It came sluggishly at first, then faster, like a mudslide flowing downhill, gathering speed. Coating everything it touched with a filth so deep, it was suffocating.

I kept drinking it in, packing it down, away from my bonds. It hurt, like drinking shards of glass mixed with burning liquid. Maybe because she was of my own bloodline? I wasn't sure. It didn't matter.

I didn't matter. Only my mate, only that she was kept away from—

Brother. The word was a command, and my eyes flew open. Brand stood in front of me, in his wolf form, the scars on his pelt and his eyes gleaming silver. *You matter. You don't need to do this alone.* He nudged my hair with his enormous muzzle. *This is what it means to be pack. To be family. Share your burden.* He opened his mind to me and, before I could stop him, reached into me and grasped the thick sludge of contamination I had been consuming. His snout wrinkled. *Eh. Tastes like shit.*

I closed my eyes again. I wanted to laugh, but the pain was too sharp, the pressure of keeping Elina's evil away from my center too intense—until he lifted his head to the moon and howled softly. Nearby, others began to howl as well. Flor, Glen, Finnick, Luke, all of them shifted into their wolves, wherever they stood on the battlefield, entered my mind, and took up the singing along with Brand.

Sing with us, brother, Luke murmured. He stepped up on my left, and Glen on my right, both of them taller than I was in this form. For the first time since my mother had died, I felt... protected. Finnick was behind me now, and Flor joined Brand, her dark red wolf like a drop of midnight blood, her eyes still blazing amber fires. She pulsed with power in perfect balance: the moon's pure, clean light, and her own red rage that flowed from her wolf and through her five-armed scar, fueling me along with the rest. I was in awe of her, of the perfect balance between witch and wolf magic that she'd attained in the past few hours. She was a miracle, and she was, somehow, mine.

Sing with me, Grigor.

My heart raced. I was theirs as much as they were mine. Their pack. Their responsibility and their joy. I lifted my head and let loose a dark howl of my own.

The pressure eased, though the power was still sliding into me from where I touched the corpse, even faster now, as if it were being drawn from me at the same rate as it entered. *Where was it*— I gasped as it became clear. Brand was funneling it somehow, out of me and into the sky.

To the moon itself.

I gaped at him as his wolf glowed bright, turning silver, his howl so loud my ears ached. How was he doing this? My wolf trembled, not with fear, but awe. This was a holy moment.

When Brand's howl died off at last, the earth around us was clean, and I was no longer tired. I felt energized, as if some of the power had remained inside me, but was puri-fied now. Brand shifted into his human form, and the others did likewise, standing beside him as we all stared down at Elina's remains.

Emotions swirled inside me, so many that I felt almost dizzy. The worst of them came from... Finnick. He was not dealing well with this.

Luke laid a hand on Finnick's shoulder, and Flor laced her fingers with his. "You okay, Sparkles?" she asked gently.

His voice was raw. "Yeah. But I need to..."

Flor nodded to Luke. He understood immediately; Finnick didn't need to see this. "We need to get the injured ones taken care of. Finn, come with me and Flor?"

Yes. Help Sergeant, and... get her some clothing, I thought at Finnick. He was stunned, his expression that of a lost soul. *No one but us deserves to see her perfection.*

A little of the desolation eased in his gaze. *Agreed.* If he realized that I'd wrapped a weak look-away spell around her nudity after she shifted, he didn't speak of it. No one was allowed to see our glorious queen but us, and the task gave him a reason to leave the scene of his mother's death.

The three of them moved toward the Mansion, until it was just Glen, Brand, and me who remained. No other shifters came anywhere near us, though that may have been because I was using a stronger look-away spell to keep from having to interact. No one spoke, until Glen finally said, staring down at Elina, "The *fuck?*"

Brand made a disgusted sound. "My thoughts exactly."

I blinked, confused. "No. No one should fuck that."

I ignored the groans of the others as I nudged what was left of the witch with my toe. Her head lay on the ground, though the skull had been squashed, somehow. All that was left was the mummified skin of her face, her hair covering most of it. The body was a shriveled husk, her clothing more substantial than the remains.

Glen squinted at the mess and mumbled something that sounded like, "Flat as a pancake." He wasn't wrong. "Where'd they go?"

Brand just straightened and crossed his burly arms. I suspected he was trying not to let the way his stomach was churning show on his face.

Glen turned to me. "Where'd her bones go, Joaquin?"

I chewed at my lip while I checked for residual magic in the dust that spilled out of what was left of her face. Elina's magic had been bone deep—removing all of it meant that I'd had to draw it out forcefully. Though if I was being honest, I hadn't taken much care to leave her intact. I'd *wanted* her to be pulverized. "All her magic has been dispersed," I assured Brand when he growled. He wasn't glowing now, but I could still feel the thrumming of magic in him. "Given back to the moon."

"Makes sense to me. She was bad to the bone." Glen hummed a few lines of a song, for some odd reason. Had he sustained brain damage from the fight? Brand and I exchanged concerned looks. "You two worked together really well," Glen went on, ignoring us. "What are you gonna do with the rest of her?"

The scraps of Elina really were clean, not a shred of magic or intent left. Safe to use, though Brand was a sculptor.

A *sculptor*, of course. I cringed. No wonder he was disturbed—I'd taken an artistic opportunity from him. "I apologize. I should have left some bones for you to carve."

Glen chuckled, and Brand rubbed a hand over his beard. "Why would you think that I'd want to carve her bones?"

"Flor suggested we might participate in some kind of joint artistic effort with the bones I kept back at Southern." I shrugged. "We could have made something to remember this night by as well. A souvenir."

"You're not serious." A thought drifted through my mind. *Not a single point of any fucking kind on his moral compass.*

He wasn't wrong, but perhaps he couldn't see the possibilities. "I apologize for the lack of bones to carve. But there's enough left to make a purse. I could even make a backpack." The idea had merit. I wasn't allowed to kill shifters indiscriminately anymore, which meant I might have more time on my hands than I was used to. "I might need a hobby of some kind," I mused aloud. "I've never done leatherwork."

Now Brand covered his whole face with both hands. "No. Just... no. Remember?" He pictured Finnick in his mind.

Ah, yes. Of course. "I apologize again." I sent a burst of magic toward the remainder of the witch, and it burned up, leaving only a slight stench in the air that the night breeze wafted away quickly. Brand relaxed, dropping his hands, and I looked up at him. "Thank you, brother."

"For what?"

"For being my... moral compass. I would never want to hurt one of our pack, but I might do so inadvertently. Killing is second nature at this point."

He nodded once. "Perhaps you do need a hobby. Have you ever tried whittling?"

"Or music," Glen added helpfully. He was gathering up fallen silver weapons, including the garrote, though he'd wrapped his hands in a length of fabric first. "You're already a decent guitar player, Joaquin. And I don't mean to brag, but I can play the tambourine like a pro. We can court Flor with duets."

I nodded, but cautioned, "You do need to provide a few more courting gifts of your own, if you don't mind me saying so. Not just songs, pup. Our queen enjoys more substantial offerings."

"The heads of her enemies? Their entrails?" He curled a lip, but his eyes sparkled. "Thanks, but I've got it covered. I'm giving her the boxed set of the 1995 *Pride and Prejudice*. We'll watch it by the lake, and I'll wear a white shirt, fling myself into it, then ardently declare my affections. She's gonna love it."

"Moon save us all," Brand muttered. He shifted back into his wolf form, moving across the battlefield, sniffing at dead shifters, and making sure there were no more magical surprises left for us.

With a smile, I wrapped my hands to gather silver alongside Glen, though I answered Brand in my mind. *The moon already did, brother.*

CHAPTER 45
HURTING AND HEALING
LUKE

Flor was pretending. I'd watched her for far too long not to know the difference between a real smile and one she plastered on to cover up what was really going on inside. She was doing a good job, and I knew why she felt like she needed to. If the Eastern girls and women hadn't felt safe before their Alpha and his witch wife died, they felt even less so now. They didn't know who was safe, who to trust with their injuries, or who might be every bit as bad as the Eastern Enforcers we'd locked in the lower levels, until we could sort them all out.

Flor needed to rest. We all did, but I could feel how close she was to the edge of collapsing. I could see her hands trembling as she barked out orders to make sure everyone got food, water, medical help, and a place to sleep inside.

"They don't want to sleep in the Mansion," a young woman explained, indicating a group of girls who were huddled together, sharing some blankets that had been taken out of the house. "It's full of strange males, and... we've been locked up in there for so long."

"Of course not, Vanya," Flor said, pasting the smile back on after it slipped. "How about in the forest?"

She shook her head. "Maybe in the garage..."

"The laundry room?" Flor suggested. "Turn on a dryer?"

Vanya smiled for some reason. "Too small. Twenty of us are still alive."

"Only twenty?" Flor's smile trembled. "Okay, lemme think."

The woman waited, looking to my mate for the answers. She was the only one they would listen to, the one they felt comfortable with, which didn't surprise me. She'd wiped herself clean, more or less, and her wounds from the battle had healed, leaving some new silver scars on her arms and one on her face. She still wore her mother's sword and her steak knife, now tucked into the belt of a new pair of clean black jeans, her hair tied up with a length of string. Her ear tag glimmered in the light of the torches some of Brand's shifters had relit so we could see who needed help.

That tag drew every eye, from the smaller pack shifters to the Eastern unranked servants, to the wounded foreign visitors, its existence turning everything they'd thought they knew on its head. But it was the shifter who wore the tag that no one could look away from.

She'd left the Mansion powerful, but the battle had transformed her. The balance of witchcraft and moon magic she'd achieved made it feel like she had her own gravity, pulling others to her. She was by far the most powerful female shifter on the continent, and her strength radiated around her like a force field. Not one shifter could meet her gaze and hold it, except her mates.

But maybe... I had an idea, and broke away from the group of Enforcers I'd been assisting to look for the one who might be able to help. Some of the smaller pack Alphas were making calls home, letting them know what had happened, and asking for supplies. We couldn't use human medical help, and Eastern's supplies were already running low. Finn had called on his pack members—the ones who didn't reside in the Mansion or on the grounds—to bring what they could from their homes, and to make their pledge to him, though I was almost certain he wanted nothing to do with his pack.

But none of them had shown up yet. A few stacks of blankets and bags of food had been dropped at the gates, but not one shifter who lived outside the Mansion had tried to enter. Finn was inside, making a video call to the Alpha of Novosibirsk, with Brand and Grigor both there to make sure the Alpha knew exactly who he would be dealing with if he decided to try and retaliate for "losing" Tana, or for the deaths of the Russians who'd allied with the McDonnells. We were fairly certain they were connected, some possibly even members of that Alpha's pack, but even if they weren't, he had to be put in his place.

The Mountain pack was so angry at what had been done to their own Alpha, they were ready to travel across the world to take revenge. Brand had been calm about the possibility when Dean had suggested it. "The only one who might need killing at some point in the future—but not until we take care of our own messes—is their Alpha. He's a very bad man," he'd said, then winked at Grigor.

Grigor had smiled like it was his birthday, but stayed silent.

The shifter I was looking for now was staying quiet, too, but I knew just where to find her. A grassy place behind the Mansion, as far from the battlefield as you could get without leaving the fenced area, was where the bodies of the fallen had been moved. The enemies had been stacked and covered with large tarps on one side, but the ones I walked toward were our own. Each one, whether they'd died in wolf or human form, was covered with a clean tablecloth or blanket, placed in lines with enough space to walk between them. The moon had almost set, and a few grieving wolves paced the edges of the area, but allowed me to pass.

"Margarette?" A blanket in the center shifted at my voice. I approached slowly and saw her lying under the cream-colored fabric, her arms wrapped around her dead mate, her head resting on his chest as she wept. I kneeled next to her. "Margarette, we need you."

She stared blankly up at me, and I almost dropped my gaze. Glen's mother was in excruciating pain, and there was no one to fight now, no place to find her revenge. All that was left was the emptiness of missing her true mate. I had a feeling her wolf would follow Bradley to the moon, if she didn't see a reason to live.

I tried again. "Margarette, the girls of Eastern are scared to death. They won't go back into the Mansion; it's the place where they were tortured. They don't feel safe in the woods. Some of them are too young to shift, others are too weak to even walk that far. They want to sleep outside, but there are too many strangers, too many males."

"Flor," she whispered after a long moment. "Flor can help."

"She's breaking, Margarette. She's strong, but she's only one shifter, and she lost her mother tonight as well. Can you help, just for one night? So Flor can sleep a little. So the girls can."

"Get someone else."

"There's no one they trust. No female strong enough to protect them if they're attacked again. They watched you kill the ones who hurt them. They know you would die for them."

Her voice cracked. "I want to die, Luke. I want to die, and be with my mate. My Alpha."

"I know." I waited quietly, slightly queasy at what I was about to say. Every shifter knew how painful a true mate's death was. Even if the pain itself didn't kill the survivor, it was nearly impossible to entice the wolf side to stay alive. If Flor died... I shook the thought away. I was doing this for her. "It would be easier to die, to let go. To not have to protect the pack anymore."

Margarette growled slightly, her wolf offended.

That was good. I could work with anger. "But you've never taken the easy way, have you?"

Silence.

"I remember when you picked Flor up off the ground at Southern, and promised to protect her. Promised to be her mother. You broke that promise." She gasped and raised her head, but I went on, my voice rising with each word. "You broke that promise, and if you don't help her now, you're breaking it again. You and Bradley both owe her for any honor your pack has left. She saved your lives in battle at Southern. She showed you the error of your ways at Northern. She broke into the lower levels here to save you. She gave Bradley, moon be with him, a chance to die with honor instead of being executed like a criminal.

"And now, she's heartsick and exhausted, and the only female with enough power to protect the others. Do you think *this* is what penance looks like, Margarette Hillier?" My voice was a shout.

She jumped to her feet, her face a mask of rage and pain. "It hurts!"

I yelled back, "I know! You're still breaking your promise, Margarette."

"You don't know *shit!* How can you be so cruel?"

"I had excellent teachers," I answered quietly. "And years of watching my true mate being beaten and starved, tortured and hunted and hurt, but I wasn't able to protect her then. I made a promise, too, you know. I promised to do everything I could to protect her from now on. To say anything, to be as cruel or as kind as I need to, to make up for all the times I couldn't save her."

"You wretched little shit," she croaked. "I *want* to die."

"I know what that feels like as well. You think I didn't want a way out? But the only way out of this kind of pain is through. You get up, and you do your damned best to fight for the pack, for the weak and the scared, the children and the unranked. You get the fuck up and you move, even when it feels like surviving one more day will kill you. You stand up and you spend every breath making this world a place safe enough for your children to bring new pups into it, Margarette."

"Flor...?"

I shook my head. Flor hadn't once spoken about children, and I knew it could be many years before she would be ready for that conversation. There was no rush on my part. "You have two sons, and from what I hear, they've both found their true mates. You have reasons to live that haven't even been born. Come back to the pack. Help the girls."

I went quiet, watching as her whole body trembled. I thought she was quivering with rage, but when she took a few steps away from Bradley and shook like a leaf, I wasn't sure.

Would she fall? Of course not. Still, I walked behind her

all the way back to the Mansion, where the girls were gathered by a torch, still peppering Flor with questions. Sergeant and the Tenebris boys were watching from the edge of the pines, closer to the back gate.

One of the women was in the middle of a panic attack, her head hanging between her knees as she tried to breathe, while another held onto Flor's arm. "They might not have caught all the Russians, you know. They've been taking calls from them for years, Flor, I heard them talking when I was in the bastard's room—"

"Enough!" Margarette stopped at the back of the group. Every single female fell silent and turned to her, mouths hanging open as she plowed through them and laid a hand between the panicking girl's shoulder blades. "Breathe," she ordered, and counted a few breaths with the girl, who relaxed slightly. "Now, listen. We're sleeping in the woods. I'm going with you. Take fur if you can." She narrowed her eyes at the group. "Some of these girls can't shift yet. What do you have for bedding, Sergeant?"

He stepped up. "It's a clear night, no rain. We have blankets in the van, plenty for the girls. My pack can patrol and sleep in the trees. I'll set some boys to digging a pit latrine."

A few boys broke off with yips of, "Yes, Alpha," at that, and ran toward the back gate.

"Thank you, Sergeant." They exchanged a long, pain-filled look, before Margarette faced the girls again, who were grumbling about strangers. "Do you believe that I would put you in harm's way?" she asked one of the girls, just as two more women came out of the Mansion, pushing a cart loaded with food. Margarette lifted her face and let them all take her in. She was nothing like the woman I'd first met, years before. Her face was scarred, her hair short.

New lines of pain and fatigue etched her cheeks, and her eyes had gone dull. But her voice had all the power it ever did, and when she pulled a dagger out of her belt and held it up, no one could look away.

"I have left the body of my true mate, your rightful Council Head, to lie alone under the moon, so that I could come and live out the promise we made to the pack. I will protect you with every breath I have, every drop of my blood. I have sacrificed for you, because it is my duty and my privilege. I will keep you safe. Now, follow me." She turned on one shaky foot and strode to the gate. The girls all followed her instantly, mesmerized by the web of comfort and power she'd spun. The women with the food thanked Flor, then followed as well.

Flor blinked up at me, swaying a little on her feet. "Luke?"

"Time for sleep, little one," I murmured, lifting her into my arms. "Forest, or bed? I had a guest room with a down—"

She almost sobbed out the word. "Bed."

"Bed," I agreed, carrying her into the Mansion. She was asleep long before we reached the room.

"GOOD MORNING." I opened my eyes to find Flor sitting up beside me, drinking a cup of what smelled like hot mint tea, and wearing chocolate cookie crumbs on her face. She'd showered at some point, and changed into a roomy t-shirt, her hair still damp. She screwed up her nose, and I smiled. She looked far too young to have defeated the world's wickedest witch on her own. "Well, I suppose it's technically good afternoon."

I sat up. "I slept all day?"

She grinned. "Yeah. Finn snuck in around seven and brought me fresh clothes and towels. Brand came in around nine and brought breakfast." She waved at the bedside table, where a tray sat piled with cookies and carafes of juice, water, and a pot of tea. "Then Glen showed up a half hour ago and caught me up on all the latest. You snored straight through." She put her teacup down.

I couldn't believe it. "How...?"

"Brand said it was because you were with me and felt protected." She fluttered her eyelashes.

"Protected? Who'll protect you from me, though?" I laughed and grabbed her around the waist, tickling her and nibbling the cookie crumbs from her face and chest, until she begged me to stop.

"I'll pee!"

I kissed the tip of her nose. "Whatever you're into, little mate."

"Ewwww!" She threw herself off the bed and ran to the bathroom. I was debating whether to follow her for a quick shower—there were a million things to do today, and I needed to help the others—when she walked back out, nude.

My mouth went dry, and suddenly, I needed a glass of water more than I needed anything else. Except, perhaps, my mate's body under me.

"By the moon, you're perfect. No, don't roll your eyes at me." She had more scars than before, all of them made by silver weapons the night before, but they looked years old. She climbed back up on the high, soft bed and lay beside me, so I could trace them all with my fingers. "You'll have as many as I do if you don't slow down."

"I'm done with silver," she said, stretching her arms over her head. "If I could get rid of it entirely—like, make every pack swear not to use it—I would."

"If you were the Council Head? Is that all you'd do?"

"First thing, maybe," she mused, then swiveled her head to me when I hummed. "Don't even think it."

I just shrugged. "You'd be great."

"Are you nuts?" She flipped over so she was straddling me, and held my hands over my head, pressed down on the pillow. She kissed me thoroughly, intently, as if she were trying to memorize my mouth, pulling my taste and my scent into her own. Breathless, she pulled away at last. "Council Alpha. I'd be an absolute despot. Mad with power. I'd force you to lie still while I licked every inch of your body..."

She started doing just that, moving her clever hands and mouth down my neck and chest, toying with my nipples, pressing soft kisses along my own fresh scars and making her way down to my cock. I'd never been so glad to have taken my own shower and stripped down the night before, as when she closed her lips around the tip and sucked firmly. But gently.

Too fucking gently. I bucked my hips up, and she pulled off. "Nuh-uh-uh, you have to hold still. I'm the Alpha, remember?"

I wasn't sure if she realized what I did: that there wasn't even the slightest scent of a lie in the air when she stated that. But if she did, she let it go, and let me slide into her mouth again. Her lips and tongue moved slowly, soft as satin and maddeningly tantalizing.

"You're torturing me, aren't you?"

She gave a muffled giggle. One of her hands slid down under my balls, cupping them while she tasted me, a small finger dropping even lower. I pushed her away slightly then, the sensation of her soft, slow mouth with her naughty finger pressing against my ass apparently being the magic combination to unlock an instant orgasm. I didn't want to come yet, though the idea of her swallowing me down as I filled her mouth...

I reached one hand to her hair and gently pulled her off, my breath sawing in and out like I'd run a marathon.

"You don't like it?" she asked, her lower lip jutting out.

"I think he likes it a little too much, princess," Glen said from the doorway, then sauntered inside. He wasn't alone. Finn stood right behind him, holding a basket full of what looked like women's clothing.

"Ah, I'll just drop this here—" Finn began, but when Flor made a disappointed sound—her mouth around my cock once more, but one hand rising to make a *come in* gesture—Glen reached back, grabbed him by the shoulder, and shoved him into the room.

"Don't make the lady beg." Glen approached the bed and stripped his own shirt off. "Luke, do you mind?"

"I'm not the Alpha in charge here. She is," I told him, grinning as Glen's mouth formed a little o of surprise.

Flor still didn't notice, or at least I didn't think she did. She was concentrating too hard on making me come faster than I wanted to, though her cheeks had gone red at the appearance of an audience.

"Little one," I groaned, grasping the headboard in an effort not to reach down and twist my fingers through her hair, and fuck her mouth until I spilled.

"Hey, Dream Girl." Glen was standing at the end of the bed, his clothes shed. "Can I join you?" She nodded her head, never letting go of my cock. He crawled onto the bed and ducked his head, burying his face in between her thighs. She squealed, then moaned around me. Glen echoed her sound, and went to work.

Whatever he was doing made her own movements more jerky, taking me deeper into her mouth, until I cried out. "Yes... Flor, yes!"

I hadn't even finished coming when she was shuddering, pulling her mouth away, and screaming out her own climax. She went boneless, slumping down on top of me, her head turned to one side and her face on my abdomen. With a happy sigh, she licked the scar she'd made there with her knife, back at Southern. "So good."

"Gonna get even better, princess," Glen said, crawling up over us both. My eyes flew wide, but he winked, and flipped her off of me, onto the mattress. She tried to push him away, her blush so deep, it matched her hair.

"Glen, Luke's *right here*."

"He is, isn't he? I mean, how bad would that be, for me to fuck you right next to him, while he watches? No, maybe he should do more than watch. Hold her hands up here, brother?" he asked, as he lifted them both over her head.

"I'd love to." I turned onto my side, rearranging myself so I could pin her hands over her head, like he'd asked me to do. She chewed at her lip, and I whispered, "This okay?" She nodded once, a jolt of excitement zipping through our bond, and Glen chuckled darkly.

"I think it's more than okay. I think she likes it. Our princess likes getting dirty and doing dirty things with her mates." When she sputtered something unintelligible, he kissed her thoroughly, then notched his cock at her entrance. "Luke's going to hold those hands up there. All you need to do is lie back and feel it." He surged forward, plunging all the way into her with one long thrust. "Lie there and take your mate's cock." He pulled out and thrust again, then started a slow, steady rhythm.

I'd only been with Flor once, and that had been back at Southern. I wasn't sure if she was blushing harder, or me, as Glen narrated his fucking like some sort of porn star.

"Luke, when she comes, she gets so tight it's almost hard to fuck her at first. She's gripping my cock like a glove, it's—ah! It's the best feeling I've ever known. And look at her, those perfect nipples. Luke, I can't stop, but I need to see those nipples getting sucked. Would you lean down and... ah yeah, like that. Suck a little harder, make her arch her back." Flor whimpered as I bent forward and followed his instructions. "Shit, she just clamped down on me like a vise. Are you sucking hard? Yeah, pinch the other one."

He slid a hand down between her parted thighs and rubbed her clit, thrusting more gently as he did, his voice a low rasp. "Come for us, princess. Come with my cock stretching out your pussy, and his mouth on your sweet nipples."

My cock was hard even before she did as he asked, arching her back and crying out as she tumbled over the edge. At that very moment, I felt Grigor and Brand in my mind, heard Grigor's laughter and Brand's consternation.

I wanted to laugh, too, when I realized what had happened. *Both of you?*

Shut up, Brand thought back.

At least I'm not the only one to come so damned fast, I replied.

Well, I tried to direct my thoughts their way, but Flor giggled, too, and Glen coughed. Maybe everyone had heard? I didn't care.

"Looks like you're ready again," she murmured, then

squealed as Glen started fucking her harder. I rolled off the bed to give him room to move, and watched from the side. The expressions of pleasure, natural and pure, that painted her face were the most glorious thing I could imagine. Every once in a while, though, she would open her eyes and glance across the room.

A whisper came from the far wall, where her gaze kept straying. "She's so beautiful." Finn's face was etched with longing. I walked over, wondering why he couldn't see what I did. Couldn't feel it.

She needed him.

"She's your mate, too," I replied. "Go to her." He shook his head, and I whispered as quietly as I could, "Finnick Dimitrivich. Don't punish yourself any longer. She needs you. Needs to know you want her. Love her."

He made a small, broken sound, but moved to the bed. He didn't take off his clothing, still dressed in the business suit he'd changed into after the battle, but he settled on the edge of the bed, and Flor grabbed his hand with hers when he did.

"Finn? Do you want…"

"To kiss you while my brother makes you come again? While he gives you the beginning of the pleasure you deserve? Yeah, Wills. I want that."

It was almost heartbreaking to watch Finn, who'd always seemed so cold and self-assured, especially around women, fumbling for the right place to put his hands, the right angle to kiss her. But he lowered his face to hers, and none of us mentioned the tears that fell onto her cheeks from his eyes.

Healing took time, and we all had a lot of healing to do.

CHAPTER 46

FUTURE PLANS
FLOR

If someone had told me I could live the rest of my life in that guest bedroom with my mates, I would've jumped on the chance faster than a duck on a June bug. All that was waiting outside that door was a shit ton of work, a buttload of butthurt shifters from all over the world, and a field piled high and wide with the dead who needed to be sent on to the moon.

I sat at a table in what Finn had called a "conservatory" but was really a fancy glassed-in porch, and ate my third sandwich of the afternoon. This one was a ham and pickle thing on some kind of bread I'd never tried. Not bad.

Of course, I'd eaten frogs and even rats before. Thinking of those days in the woods, I flicked my ear tag and listened to the others around me make the endless to-do list for the combined pack leaders. I'd never been gladder not to be an Alpha, relieved that my part of being in charge had ended with the fighting. But I admired my Alphas as they spoke.

Brand, Finn, Luke, and Glen had all gotten dressed in clean sweats. They sat with me, across from Sergeant and Margarette, the late afternoon sun warming our faces through the wall of glass windows. Finn had found me some clothes that fit somehow, even though it seemed like everyone in his pack was six feet tall. The red wool sweater and black trousers felt expensive, and had fancy French tags, but the new tactical belt that held my steak knife and sword at my waist was the best part of the outfit. The sun would go down soon, and we knew we had to figure some shit out before the moon rose again.

Sergeant was talking with Finn. "The other packs, the smaller ones and the foreign visitors, are demanding to be let go, and take their dead with them. For now, we've barricaded the gates—"

"Why?" I butted in. Didn't we want everyone to go home? "Why not let the door hit 'em on the way out?"

Luke explained. "We don't know which ones were colluding with Aidan, and which ones he was going to force into his new 'alliance.' If we let them go, they could come back to challenge us, even bring an army over to try to attack our Council's member packs before we've recovered from this fight."

Margarette scoffed. "Take their dead. Idiots. The funeral pyres are already being built. They'll be given to the moon where they fell, not hauled in car trunks and body bags across the country."

Sergeant nodded. "I tried to talk to their Alphas, but..." He wore dark shadows under his eyes, and his tattoos stood out on his arms and neck, some of them red and raw, like he'd been scratching at them. I wasn't sure he'd slept at all since the battle.

Glen broke in. "But they see you as a rogue Alpha, and your pack—"

"It's not an official pack. No Council has named it. They won't listen to me, and some of the smaller pack Alphas said outright that when both Bradley and Aidan died, their own allegiance to the North American Council died as well."

I tapped my chin while they kept arguing, trying to figure out how they were going to sort out the good from the bad, and how to put a new Council Head in place, or even if they should.

Finn flat-out refused to put himself forward. "My pack won't even come to the Mansion to help the wounded. I felt dozens of them leaving today, probably defecting to a pack overseas."

Brand growled. "You're their Alpha. You can command them to stay."

"I don't want them," Finn stated baldly. "I'm letting them go. I don't want shifters who learned the lessons my parents taught about what it means to be pack. I don't want to force shifters who were traumatized and abused by their pack Enforcers and Alpha to stay when they finally have the chance to be free." He finished in a whisper, "I don't want to be Alpha." My heart ached for him, but I understood.

Glen felt the same way, I could tell. He reached out and patted Finn's shoulder, but didn't say it out loud. His eyes went to his mom on his right.

Margarette shifted in her chair restlessly, staring at the food on her plate like it repulsed her, and she might jump away from the table and run screaming into the woods. Or grab a knife and run down to the lower levels to kill every one of the remaining Eastern Enforcers.

At some point in the night, she'd shaved her hair off entirely, and changed into a plain black shirt and pants. A maid's uniform, it looked like. Somehow, she looked even more badass than usual, though it was impossible to meet her eyes without wanting to cry myself.

"They'll become rogues. Shifters need an Alpha," Margarette reminded Finn.

"His shifters have one. What they need is a kick in the ass," Glen suggested, placing a few blueberries on his mom's plate. They were her favorite, and she eventually picked one up and ate it. But only one.

I knew Finn's runaway shifters might be some of the worst pack members, but I kept my mouth shut. It wasn't like they could hide from the boogeyman, and if any of them had hurt the maids here, or Finn's sister, I'd let Grigor take a field trip to hunt them down.

Grigor wasn't in the porch with us—he was off looking for magic stuff in the Mansion and on the grounds. If Elina had made one evil magic wand, she'd probably made a dozen, according to him. He needed to make sure her influence was completely gone from the earth as well.

But he spoke into my mind. *Time to speak up, my queen. Step up into your rightful place.* He sent an image of me wearing some fancy crown and holding a scepter, on a throne I was almost certain was made of the bones of my enemies.

I rolled my eyes mentally. I was no ruler. I was a *reject*. His laughter when I reminded him of that went on for far longer than it should've.

Finally, I got tired of listening to the others farting around. I stood abruptly, and the room went silent. "So, we need a Council Head, right? For tonight. We need to meet before or after the funerals, right?" Everyone stared, but I went on when they all took deep breaths to argue. "I mean, the Council meeting never was adjourned, or whatever. So who's the leader now?"

For some reason, that shut them up. But why the fuck were they all blinking at me?

I tried to keep my patience. "You could vote, I suppose. Heck, all the Alphas could. The smaller packs, and the four main Alphas. Luke, Glen, Finnick, and Brand. Choose one of y'all to be the leader." I waved at Finn and Glen, who were both already shaking their heads.

"I'm not planning to stay Alpha here," Finn said quietly. "I won't leave just yet, but... there are too many bad memories. Too many years of pain. I'll need to find someone else to take my place." The others didn't seem at all surprised, and I didn't ask what he planned to do, or who he might be able to sucker into stepping in here. If it was up to me, I'd bulldoze the whole place, and rebuild somewhere else.

"Maybe when it's safe, you could bring Tana to Mountain?" I suggested. "I'd love to meet her."

"She'd love you." Finn's smile was a flicker, there and gone in a blink.

"I'm turning Northern over to Patrick," Glen announced softly. Margarette flinched, but he went on. "It'll take some time to get him up to speed, but I want to move to Mountain, spend every night in Flor's arms, and get fat off Ida's cooking."

Brand grumbled about having no peace, and tossed his napkin at Glen's head, but he winked at me.

"Okay, not you two. So, Luke or Brand."

"Nope," Luke said. "I don't even think Southern should remain a recognized pack. I think Tenebris and Southern should be folded into one, and Sergeant should lead." Everyone turned to him in shock, but he was already nodding to Sergeant, who didn't seem surprised. When had they talked about this?

"That's kinda drastic. Sergeant, would you lead a

combined pack?" His chin dipped once. Curiosity itched at me. "What would you do, Luke?"

"Be with you," he replied instantly. "Stay at your side, wherever you are."

"Gonna need to build a bigger bed," Brand muttered.

I blushed. "Yeah, but like... for real. What do you want to do? At my side." Glen laughed and started to say something rude, but Margarette pulled herself out of her stupor for long enough to snap him with her cloth napkin.

Luke grinned. "I was in charge of Southern's investments, and Sergeant has no desire to take over that. I could still take care of the accounts, as a friend of the pack. But I've heard you talking about the library at Mountain, Flor. I want to see it, and I'd love to read all the pack laws I never had a chance to. Callaway brought me over here as a child, and made sure I never knew what rights and responsibilities I had as an Enforcer, or even as an Heir."

He fiddled with his own napkin, looking down. "I'd want to study the old ways in depth. I think I'd like to learn all I can, then teach the younger members of any of the packs, or ones like me who should know better, but were kept from the truth. We're going to need to unravel the mess Aidan and Callaway made."

"I love you too damn much," I said, wiping my eyes. I turned to Brand before I got any more emotional. "So, looks like you're it, Bearman. You're the strongest Alpha left in this Mansion, at least—" I shut up when the slight scent of a lie filled my nostrils.

My own lie. A chill ran up my spine. "What? Wait, who's a stronger Alpha than you?"

Brand's mouth twitched. "I'm pretty sure it's you, wildflower."

"*Fuck* no." I shoved away from the table, silverware

flying, my empty coffee cup tipping over. "That's impossible." Nobody argued, but they all stared with varying degrees of patience or pity, or so it seemed. "Okay, sure, I had powerful relatives. And I know I got a level up, or whatever, when we all bonded. But that's not my power, that's yours—it was you guys. I'm just the—"

The guys all spoke at once. "The center." "The throne." "The focus." "The heart."

The queen, Grigor whispered.

I swallowed, my heart pounding somewhere close to my throat. "The fuck."

"Why are you so shocked?" Brand asked. "Your Del taught you all about strength. You know it's more than a powerful body, or wolf. Strength comes from within."

"Not that much strength. Not Head Alpha power!"

"You're an Alpha Mother," Sergeant said. "What did you think that meant?"

Was I hyperventilating? I felt my mates send soothing waves of comfort through our bonds, and suddenly, I could breathe again. "I really didn't know what it meant. I thought it was ceremonial, or something."

Sergeant took a deep breath. "I was a member of the Moonblessed Warriors. One of the youngest, but I had the same training. One of the first lessons we were taught was about balance—that the moon gave us witchcraft and wolfcraft, Alphas and Alpha Mothers. But the truth is that all of it comes from one source, and it's only our understanding of the moon's power that makes it seem like there is a distinction." He took his own empty coffee mug and a juice glass from the center of the table. Lifting a pitcher of water, he poured half of the water into one, and the rest into the other. "Is one of these coffee, and the other juice, just because of the shape of the containers?"

What was he saying? My mouth was suddenly bone dry, but I sure as fuck wasn't going to drink either one of those containers of water.

I looked around the table at every one of my mates, and Margarette, and even Sergeant. They were all smiling now. "No. Not just no, *hell* no." I put a hand over my heart, wondering if a shifter my age could die of a heart attack. "Not in a million years."

Grigor! Get me out of here. I needed him; I didn't think my legs were gonna work. The fucker just laughed in my thoughts, though I felt him grow nearer.

"Don't fret, wildflower," Brand murmured, stepping closer. "You don't have to lead the Council. You don't have to do anything you don't want. You owe them nothing. The women and girls at Eastern, the rest of Southern, the Tenebris boys—they'll be fine. Surely they'll trust decisions made for them by strange males."

He grinned as I bared my teeth at him. "And Grigor thinks you're the role model? That was low."

Margarette shook her head. "You all have to stand together. The Alphas won't listen to a woman as young as you are, no matter how worthy or strong. How old are you, Flor?"

"Twenty," Luke answered for me. "She turned twenty on July thirtieth."

"Ah, wildflower. I missed your birthday?"

"We all did." Finn stood and walked to my side, dropping to one knee. "I'll make it up to you next month, if you'll let me. I'll take you out, and show you the best part of living this close to a city."

I swallowed. "Take me out? Like, a date?"

"Dinner at my favorite rooftop restaurant, maybe the ballet, or the symphony. Dancing, if you like."

I wasn't sure why I was blushing. "A date. I've never been on a date before." In the background, the other guys were groaning and cursing softly, but Finn's green eyes had my complete attention.

"I'll be honored to be your first."

"I can't wait," I whispered, leaning forward to kiss him.

"Enough romancing the girl," Sergeant snapped. "It's time."

Brand murmured into my ear as we walked down the hallway, his hand on my arm all that kept me from running away, "Remember, wildflower. I love you above all else. Everything is your choice."

Pretty words, but I knew that sometimes the world made the choices for you.

CHAPTER 47
THE STRONGEST ALPHA
FLOR

S ergeant and Margarette led us out to the back of the Mansion, striding ahead of me and guys to the battlefield. The landscape had changed over the course of the day, thank goodness. There was almost no mud now, like someone had sucked the blood straight out of the soil. I had a feeling I knew who was responsible for that, since Grigor's bond was practically buzzing with energy.

The Mountain and Northern shifters had taken on the task of organizing the dead. All the Russian corpses, including Ivan, were piled up on the far edge of the ring, on top of some wooden pallets. No one stood near them, or spared them more than a glance.

"So much for the alliance," I muttered, feeling eyes on me from every direction. I would have stuck out my middle fingers at the dead Russian bodies, but I had manners. Not a lot of manners, but at least that much.

The dead Eastern Enforcers, with Aidan's body wrapped in what looked like an old tablecloth, were in a separate pile, and their two dozen or so mourners were far fewer than I would have thought. Finn hadn't been kidding about his pack not coming back to help, not even to send their own to the moon. I shivered at the coldness of their behavior, more than the chill in the air.

"Some of them are too frightened to come. Most of the ones who would mourn these are still in the lower levels," Finn reminded me.

Ah yeah, waiting for judgment. My heart ached for Finn, but his jaw was clenched, so I stayed quiet. I knew how it felt to have a shitty pack. There was nothing I could say to make it better, but I grabbed his hand and squeezed. When he squeezed back, his shoulders dropped just a little.

The dead from the overseas visitors and the smaller packs were stacked carefully, with nicer cloths covering their bodies, and even some pine branches and a few hothouse flowers spread around the wooden platforms. Their surviving pack members stood by, anger etched in their faces, some of their fists clenched as if they were grasping at invisible swords. Anger surrounded them like an invisible cloud.

Brand leaned down and whispered in my ear, "We've asked everyone to stay in human form for the meeting, until the pyres are lit, and then shift to run." He stepped behind me, his massive form casting me into a shadow that felt safe, somehow. He laid one hand on each of my shoulders, squeezed gently, then let go.

I relaxed slightly. I'd never run with Southern for a pack funeral, but I knew how it went. When the sparks rose into the sky, the wolves shifted and ran through the forest toward the moon, howling the way for the spirits who'd gone on.

Luke moved up on my left, and Glen on my right, Finn stepping around all of us to stand in front. It looked like some kind of honor guard, and the thought sent a hysterical laugh into my throat that choked me slightly. Me, the pack reject, marching into the middle of the gathered packs from the whole continent and more, like some sort of queen.

Grigor's whispered, *You thought it was a term of endearment? Little queen, I recognized you from the beginning,* had me choking in earnest.

Luke shot an amused glance my way. "Need a cough drop?"

I scratched my nose with my middle finger, but stayed quiet as we began to move through the crowd, the shifters parting in silence, surrounding us as we drew closer to the dead that had been placed in the center of the field, near to the place where I'd killed Elina. I'd wondered if the ground there would feel tainted, but it was clean, as if our blood had never stained the earth.

The wooden pyre there was smaller than I'd expected, and a lump rose in my throat as I noticed what someone had done to the two shifters on top of the carefully arranged wood.

Only one of the Northern members had died from silver gunshot, and none from Mountain. The Northern Enforcer lay in his wolf form next to Bradley. Someone had placed Bradley's hand on the top of his pack member's shoulder, and the picture it made had tears springing to everyone's eyes.

"He would have liked that," Glen choked out, just as Patrick came to greet us. The two hugged. "You did that?"

Patrick nodded. "Dad was his Alpha to the end. They'll run together to the moon."

Ahead of us, Margarette stumbled and let out a heart-breaking whimper. Sergeant wrapped his arms around her, before two of the maids ran up and escorted her a few yards away to where the rest of them stood, near the twenty smaller, covered bodies of the Eastern maids. Margarette, Sergeant, and the Tenebris boys stood between the groups, and the kitchen staff who'd helped me sneak into the lower levels were there, or most of them.

One of the Tenebris pack was holding hands with Vanya, who had a stunned expression on her face. When her eyes met mine, I shot her a silent question.

Her cheeks flushed slightly, and she mouthed two words. *My mate.* The bearded male beside her was one of the older Southern rogues, and had seemed the most feral in the cave in the woods. But now, his eyes were clear, though he held an unsheathed sword in one hand, clearly ready to kill to protect his true mate if anyone tried to hurt her again. I smiled at Vanya, happy that something good had come out of the battle.

Brand hummed. "Their bond is beautiful."

"You can see it?" I squinted, but I didn't see what he meant.

Finn answered, though. "It's so bright. Their bond, and the ground beneath them. What are those other threads, Brand? The ones that are spreading from—"

Brand hissed for some reason, but just muttered, "Later."

"Not too much later," Finn urged. "They should know before they go back to their packs."

I didn't know what they were talking about, but I could tell they were both shocked, in a good way.

"None of the Tenebris boys died?" I asked, taking in the hundreds of shifters that began to move out of the trees, ones from the visiting packs who wore still-bloody clothing and expressions of distrust and fear.

"Not one," Luke replied. "They fought like demons after Lily..." He sighed, and I squeezed his hand. I hadn't let myself look to the pyre where she lay, though when Luke said her name, I let my eyes fall on the small stack of wood near Bradley's.

Mama's pyre was almost beautiful. The wood had been stacked carefully, with evergreen branches woven together like lattice around the sides, her still form covered with a gleaming white cloth. Around the edges, small items dotted the fabric: a pocketknife, a folded up heart made out of duct tape, a small pile of limestone fossils, and another of shiny agate stones like the ones in the creek that ran through the Southern hunting grounds.

A few pieces of paper held down by a small, stuffed bunny caught my eye, but before I could ask, Luke explained. "Some of her boys wrote letters, poems. They loved her so much."

My eyes burned with unshed tears. "I'm glad they all made it. She loved them right back." She'd been their mother, too.

I fought to control my emotions, surrounded on all sides now by quiet shifters. Once the last wolf had emerged from the pines—though I spotted one or two of the Tenebris boys in the treetops still—Brand squeezed my shoulder again and spoke. "Tonight, we come together to mourn our fallen, and to run as a pack. But the Council meeting was never adjourned, and decisions must be made."

"The Council's dead," someone shouted.

"Fuck the Council," someone else added.

Brand waited for the crowd to quiet before continuing. "Luke Callaway is Alpha of Southern. I am Alpha of Mountain. Glen Hillier is Alpha of Northern, and Finnick of Eastern. The Council is still formed, and the bonds of your packs, and the alliances created, remain. For the moment, at least."

The crowd was silent, as he spelled out—mostly for the visiting shifters—how the War Council had been allowed to continue. How it had been meant as a temporary solution, but had been kept in place out of fear and anger.

"It is our belief that the new ways of governance caused much of the death and pain on our continent, and led us to this." He gestured at the stacks of dead. "The new ways are not the moon's ways. The Alphas of the four main packs have spoken, and we would return to the old ways, where the moon's law is all."

A young Alpha stepped forward. "The moon's law?"

Brand nodded. "Where the strong protect the weak, and the Alpha protects the pack."

"Protect which pack, Brand Becker?" The Alpha who'd been brave enough to speak was missing a hand, his wound made with silver. "Mountain? That's what this is, isn't it? A coup. You want to be an Alpha of Alphas, like McDonnell said?"

I'd never seen this guy before, but I liked his spark. Finn's voice in my mind supplied a name. *He's Cilian, Alpha of a smaller pack between here and Northern. Honorable. And brave.*

Cilian bared his teeth at Brand. "You want to rule all the packs, because you're the strongest Alpha. Well, we want out. My pack may be small, but we never had a choice to say no before. Look at what you've done to us. Silver weapons? Guns? We want nothing to do with any of you; we never did. Just leave us alone, and pretend we don't exist."

My heart ached. I'd felt like that for most of my life. Like staying out of a fight could keep me safe. Like I could run away from the pack, and live alone, be content.

"I'm not the strongest Alpha," was all Brand said when the crowd's muttering had died down. *Get ready, wildflower.*

I'd never wanted to kick him in the shin more than I did right now, and I would've, if Glen and Luke hadn't held me back.

Cilian bristled. "Who is, then? Finnick, son of the witch and the dead Alpha who made sure my pack never had enough to thrive? Or Grigor Dimitrivich? You want us to accept one of *them* as our leader?" More than one shifter shouted angrily at that.

Brand gazed around at all the gathered shifters, many of whom flinched when his silver eyes turned their way. "No. None of those are the strongest of us. The strongest Alpha here was seen as the weakest by nearly everyone, even their own pack. They were hunted and abused, for no other reason than that it was allowed by the Alphas who could have stopped it. This Alpha doesn't want to rule, and that's what makes them the very best choice to lead."

His voice was loud, and rang with truth. The moon rose over the trees at that exact moment, painting him in golden light, as he turned and kneeled, bowing his head at me. Glen and Luke dropped to their knees at my sides, and Finn did the same.

The Mountain pack was on their knees without another word spoken. Their eyes shone up at me from where they kneeled all around the rim of the bowl, guarding.

I'd never hyperventilated before, but I was pretty sure I was about to. "This is absolutely batshit crazy," I choked out. "I'm—"

"The strongest Alpha on this continent," Sergeant called out, as his pack kneeled as well. "Before you came here, you traveled from pack to pack, howling for change, and bringing the moon's justice to the oppressed. We watched you fight an enemy who imprisoned you, one who would have enslaved us all and forced us into an unholy partnership with our mortal enemies. We watched your mates draw on your power, given by the moon and by your righteous anger, to overcome an army. Then, after the battle, you protected the vulnerable and cared for the wounded."

His voice was so loud now, I was almost certain he was using magic to amplify it. "You are more than an Alpha. You are the daughter of the former Alpha Calvin Callaway of Southern, and Lily Rain, Alpha Mother of the Tenebris pack. You are Florida Wills, Heir of the Occidens Pack, and their only living Alpha Mother."

For some reason, the words Alpha Mother changed the atmosphere. The smaller packs seemed confused, but the foreign packs, the visitors, all slowly bowed their heads to me as well. They didn't kneel, but it was obvious they felt some kind of way about the term.

Glen called out, "Northern will follow your guidance, Florida Wills, as Alpha or Alpha Mother." The Northern pack all kneeled as well, leaving only the smaller packs to stare, uncomprehending, at me.

I let out a shaky breath as the moon flew higher, and the assembled packs all waited for me to speak. Del's laughter echoed in my ear, so loud I could have sworn he was standing right there beside me. *If you can't run, fight. If you can't fight, then talk your way out. The most important weapon any shifter has is a brain. Use it.*

I still wanted to run, but I knew it was time to stand my ground. I'd spent too many years running, letting the pack chase me. Even if I wasn't anywhere near sure I was the right one to do this, the moon hadn't sent anyone else. So it was time to stop running, to turn around, and encourage them to acknowledge a few things.

Force them to, if it came to that. I had the power, like Finn and Grigor had said. It flowed through my blood, rested in my bones. My wolf knew it, and so did all of these wolves.

I was the Alpha. Now all I needed to do was act like it.

"A girl?" Cilian called, interrupting my thoughts. "A female can't be an Alpha." His nose wrinkled. "Wait."

I took a deep breath. "You know what that is, right? The smell of really old, outdated bullshit. It turns out all the things we thought we knew were a load of it. But even if I'm somehow the strongest we've got—which makes me pretty fuckin' terrified for y'all, if it's true—I don't want to be Alpha. All I want to do is help them." I pointed to Vanya and the girls around her, then the Tenebris boys. "I want to help the ones who've been shit on for decades finally get to live without being afraid of those who were supposed to protect them."

I waved at Cilian's missing hand. "I was raised by a shifter named Del, who had one leg. My pack stripped his rank and told him he was worthless, that he couldn't be a warrior because he didn't have all his limbs. That was bull-shit, too. I want all the packs to get it—that strength isn't about how many you can kill, or who you can force with Alpha commands, or coercion."

The guy blinked. "What else?"

"What else? I want the packs to stop dying from their own damn stupidity. You see this?" I pointed to Vanya. "She met her true mate, who was a rogue until he landed in my Mama's makeshift pack. She'd never have met him if she'd stayed locked up in the kitchens here. I want the Conclaves to stop being for political bullshit and be about this:

bringing shifters together to meet their true mates. So more babies get born, and we stop dying."

I glared at the dead Easterners. "I want no more guns, no more silver. I want any shifter who so much as picks up a silver knife to know it's the fastest way to find himself stacked up like firewood." I softened my tone as I gazed at the maids, or what was left of them. "I want no more putting one wolf over another. No more keeping females under an Alpha's thumb, and calling it protection. The moon doesn't see rank, She just sees Her children. Why should we think we know better?"

"No rank?" someone called out. "Packs make their own decision about rank, not the Council."

I shouted back, "Then maybe before the Council disbands, they make one more fucking rule! All that rank is used for is to keep someone under your heel. To put shifters in their place." I sneered. "The Mountain pack doesn't have rank, besides Alpha, and look at them. They're huge, the most powerful pack in the world, and they have pups on their packlands. Their pack isn't dying, but they'd be even stronger if they had their true mates. I'm talking about some of you." I waved a hand to the crowd. "Think about this: your mate could be right here, right now, standing on this field." I pointed to the stacks of the dead. "Or there, about to be sent on to the moon. So why the hell would you fight each other?"

One of the foreign Alphas stepped up, a guy almost the same height as Brand, and said in heavily accented English, "You are female; you cannot be Alpha. You are witch wolf. You should not even be alive."

Behind him, I saw Grigor slipping through a shadow, no one even glancing his away. He had his hands almost around the guy's throat when I shook my head and thought, *Stop.*

I pulled the neck of my sweater down, so they could see my scar. "You're right, I shouldn't be. But not because I'm a witch. Because I was almost killed by one. A witch tried to murder me before I was born. From what I understand, that ripped my soul into pieces. The moon kept me alive for some reason, but it means I have five true mates, instead of one."

The guy's bearded jaw dropped.

"I know. Miracle, magic, I don't know how it worked. All I know is that I'm damned glad. Have you found your true mate yet?"

He shook his head.

"Well, I promise you, the way you'll feel when you do will change how you think about rank, or power. Who taught you that females were weak anyway? My guess is some male with a tiny dick and self-esteem issues." A chorus of feminine laughter rose from the crowd. "You see this tag?" I flicked my ear. "My pack gave this to the shifters they thought were the rejects, the trash. But my mates saw past that. We need to go back to the old ways. No rank, no tags, no believing that being weaker means you're less than. Weaker means you get more of the pack's protection, so you can grow strong."

Brand had stood quietly and was moving through the crowd as I spoke. In the middle of the kneeling Mountain shifters, he stopped and held out a hand to a female shifter. "Alpha?" she asked, standing. She was at least six feet tall herself, with long dark hair twisted into braids. She wore a black leather bandolier lined with knives, stretching from one shoulder to her waist. I wanted it.

I will get it for you, Grigor answered.

Damnit, was I not going to have a single private thought from here on out? I cringed when Finn replied, *Probably not, Wills.*

Don't steal my packmate's pretty weapons, Grigor, Brand thought. *I'll make my flower her own set.* Then he said aloud, "Sarah, come and meet your true mate."

Her brow furrowed with disbelief, she followed Brand as he strode to the foreign Alpha. The two stood, face to face, for a long moment, before the male reached out a trembling hand and touched Sarah on the cheek. The air around them seemed to shimmer with moonlight and magic, as they both gasped out, "Mate!"

As they embraced, Brand moved to one of the Northern males and led him across to the tree line, where one of the few Eastern Enforcers who hadn't been locked away stood. He might have been handsome before the battle, but now he was missing an ear, and his face bore the marks of silver dust. Brand didn't have to encourage them to touch; the second they did, they fell into each other's arms, crying quietly.

True mates.

It felt like a spell had been cast over everyone who stood in the ring, and all around it, but this time, not one made of blood and salt.

It was of hope and possibility.

"No more killing," I said when I could speak again. "No more being afraid of what's different, or unusual. No more ranked and unranked. No more Council. Just the moon and the pack, joined under Her, running together. Hunting and howling and protecting each other."

Every Alpha stood and shouted their agreement. Every single one. Then, only seconds after Brand talked me through calling an official vote to do away with the Council on the next full moon—once every pack had a chance to receive a copy of the old laws from the Mountain library—a wind whipped through the clearing. It was like the world had let out a breath it had been holding for a long while.

Someone in the crowd howled.

Someone else sobbed.

Then, a pulse of light poured out like a wave from the moon, and every shifter fell to their knees, heads bowed. Well, every shifter but Brand, who stood at my side, his face upturned, smiling at the sky.

Without a single match being lit, the pyres all exploded into flames at the same time, their smoke rising straight into the sky, gray and black shadows in the shape of wolves running higher and higher, going back to the moon.

Without thought, or intention, or even a hint of pain, every shifter alive in the ring, no matter their age, shifted into their wolf form. We ran through the night, together, singing.

Healing.

CHAPTER 48

THREADS

A day later, the leaders of all the North American packs sat around talking about what exactly it meant to have no rank. Except for Alphas and Alpha Mothers—a title they all agreed needed to come back —they were more or less agreed on doing away with the separations, and all of them swore to stop marking the unranked with physical signs, like ear tags.

Three days after, as they decided about what to do with the silver weapons that were left, and how to punish or rehabilitate the Eastern Enforcers who were twisted in ways that could never be fixed, shifters in the Mansion began to whisper about what had happened in that ring when the fires had lit, and after.

Sergeant took some of them into the parlor and began teaching them about the balance of witchcraft and wolfcraft. About the Western pack, and what had happened to cause the war, and the eradication of the most powerful magic-wielding shifters in the world. Not all the smaller packs allowed their members to sit and listen, but some did.

A week later, the foreigners had gone home with new treaties signed between all the North American Alphas, from the smallest pack to Mountain, and scribbled on by me as well, though it made me feel like the biggest faker to see my name on the documents. Even worse was how the strangers had treated me before they left, making sure I knew their names, where they came from, and even inviting me to their packs.

"Why the hell would they want someone like me as a guest?" I asked, when the last one—a gorgeous, dark-haired guy from Italy—had dared to bring flowers for me to the front parlor. I sniffed them now, enjoying the heady scent of jasmine and gardenias in the bouquet.

Finn was staring at the shifter's back as he exited the room, like he was deciding on the best angle to stab him for a mortal wound. Brand was trying to incinerate the bouquet with his gaze.

"What?" I grumbled. "I can't like flowers?"

"I gave you a bouquet," Glen muttered.

So did I, Grigor added. *Whole arrangements. Maybe you need another one.*

Don't kill the Italian! I warned, but he didn't answer.

Glen cleared his throat. "I'm pretty sure it, ah, has something to do with the stories about Alpha Mothers."

I scowled at him over the bouquet. "What stories?"

"Mom told me there was something about... fertility boosts?"

I was horrified. "They want me to have sex with them?" All my mates howled so loud in my mind that my temples pounded.

Glen rushed to explain, though what he said wasn't much better. "Fuck, no, princess. Supposedly, having an

Alpha Mother even as a visitor can increase the chances of conceiving a pup by a factor of ten."

Ew. They wanted me to, what? Sit around and send out some kind of woo-woo fertility vibes in the middle of an orgy?

"You're not planning to go to any of their packs, are you?" Luke asked. He'd been the one taking notes on the meetings, and had a list of invitations.

I hesitated. *Do I owe it to the world's shifters to help them have more pups?* The silence from my bonds as I pretended to ponder the idea was... okay, it was hilarious. "Of fucking course not. They can get their own Alpha Mothers. I'm gonna spend the rest of my life at my lake." I sent the guys a mental picture of some of the things I wanted to do in the little cottage at the lake, or even on the shore, and they all relaxed.

When the last foreigner had left, and all that was left were our own North American packs, the whispers about what had happened on the pack run under the full moon became stories. Vanya and some of the other ex-kitchen staff loved sharing the best ones to me in private.

Brand was supposed to be some kind of avatar for the Moon Goddess, and Grigor was his alter ego, the shadow that drained the blood from the evil when they stepped away from the moon's light. "Like two dark gods," Vanya had giggled. "And you're the blood-red wolf goddess herself, calling them to do miracles and murders. One of the Tenebris fellas is making a comic strip about you." She held her hands out over her chest. "Your boobs in it are enormous, and it looks like some monster ate half your shirt."

"I heard there's a bloodsucking shadow god draining the lower levels like they're his personal juice bar," I teased Grigor that night as he started what was becoming a nightly ritual: a kiss for every year he'd waited for me, a soul-shattering fuck, and then the lullaby he'd sung me since we met, before he slid away and left me to sleep with my other mates. "You told me you weren't a vampire, Grigor."

"I'm not," he said with a placid, creepy-as-fuck smile. "And I'm only drinking the very bad guys. I always check, I promise."

I didn't ask how he checked, and I didn't want to know what he meant by drinking. I wasn't going to fuss on behalf of the assholes in the dungeon.

Vanya had admitted that Grigor let her and the others accompany him some nights, so they could "get closure." Becca in particular had gone down there with him more than once, Vanya said, and the older woman was looking a solid fifteen years younger.

Now that the Council had been disbanded, and the Alphas of each pack had their own rules, the ban on speaking about Western had vanished. Becca's mother had been from a smaller pack close to Western, and she wanted to go back and see if any of her family, or her mother's friends, were still alive. Sergeant had spoken to her privately, and I had a feeling both of them were feeling a pull to their familial packlands.

Sergeant would be tied down at Southern, though, and we weren't certain what would happen when Luke tried to give his Alpha power over to my great-uncle. As far as we knew, no Alpha had even voluntarily disbanded a pack and given his mantle to another. But Brand knew who to ask about that.

A month later, after Brand's grandmother Verona had traveled from Mountain and brought copies of the old laws with her—books which Finn scanned and printed out for each of the packs—all the Alphas went home and took copies of the old ways, and about twenty true mates. Brand had given the foreign shifters a gift, when the full moon magic was still showing him what he and Finn called the "threads" of the mate bonds. Some of them had true mates already, but a few of them had what looked like threads stretching in different directions. Brand showed them where they led, or at least the direction, and they left happy and eager to follow his guidance.

But in some cases, he'd seen too much. Three of them had lost their true mates in the battle, before they'd ever met. He couldn't bear to tell them, though one of them had guessed it somehow. Brand and all of my mates had spent a night drinking with the poor male, finishing off far too many bottles of expensive whiskey.

"I told 'im about my little buddy Rebin back at Mountain," Brand hiccupped. "Rebin and Annalise. S'good to know we don't just have the one time to get it right."

Becca had been helping me get Brand into bed, and she'd pestered me for the story afterward. When I'd told her about the true mates who'd met that year at Mountain, and their wild story of falling in love forty years before, when Annalise had been a teenager, Becca had gotten starry-eyed.

"Are you saying that if we miss our mate in this life, we might find her in the next?" If hope had a face, it was hers right then.

"Yeah, I am," I murmured. "The moon loves Her children. You'll find her, Becca. I know it."

The smaller pack shifters who'd stuck around for the whole month tried to get Brand to do his magic with them, too, but once the moon waned, he'd lost the threads.

Luke had suggested having some dances instead. The

smaller pack Alphas invited all of their unmated shifters to attend, and Finn emptied the Eastern coffers to make it possible, flying and bussing them in from all over the continent. Margarette had set up a whole tent city on the grounds, and she and Sergeant stayed out there with all the most vulnerable.

Every night, we'd filled the Eastern ring with music and laughter, replacing some of the terrible memories with good ones. Watching the square dancers swing past each other, one after another, and then stopping all of a sudden as a mate bond formed, did something to heal everyone who watched. Even Margarette, whose eyes I still couldn't meet without wanting to burst into tears.

"I have to go," she said one night, after two more females had found their other halves. This time, one had been a mature shifter from Northern who hadn't ever left her packlands. Her mate had been part of Cilian's pack, just over the border. Something about the two middle-aged shifters meeting like that had sent Margarette into a tailspin.

"Where are you heading?" I asked after I'd finished hugging her and gotten myself under control. Glen stood at my shoulder, listening. Her eyes lingered on us, then moved to the shifter from her pack, who was smiling so brightly, the nearly full moon couldn't compete.

"Western," she answered, shifting her backpack over one shoulder. Her hair was long stubble, and she wore a knitted cap Ida had sent her for the cold. "I was wrong about so much, for so long. I have to assume everything I learned about your mother's pack was just as wrong. I'm going to look for what's left, or who."

"All you have to do is call," I told her. "We'll come, if you need us."

"I need you to stay, to build this new pack on the ashes of the old." Her voice broke, and she gave Glen a fierce hug, whispering something in his ear for a moment, sobbed at his reply, then turned and jogged into the forest.

"What did she say?" I asked that night.

"She told me I'd made the right decision, to give up being Alpha. That the only thing worth fighting for in this world is love." He kissed my head. "I told her I'd learned that from her."

That full moon, Glen transferred the power of Alpha to his brother, and no one died, though Patrick's face when he got a call the next day from Northern, made me think someone had. "Kristin left," was all he said, before he shifted into his wolf form like a total idiot, and ran straight to Canada.

Sergeant had made a deal with all the Alphas, that any rogues they found be duct taped and shipped to my old pack's front gate, for him to rehabilitate. When he heard some might already be on the way, he left, too, taking the Tenebris boys and their mates back to Meridion—nobody called it Southern anymore—to rebuild.

We would follow soon enough. With Verona's help, Sergeant and Luke had patched together a ceremony of sorts to perform under a *new* moon, weirdly enough, that they thought would work to combine the remains of my old pack and the Tenebris ones. As long as the old Southern pack members wanted to belong to Meridion, and were willing to give up their ties to Luke, Sergeant said, it would be a bloodless transition.

"By the time you get there to consolidate the packs, I'll have them straightened out," he promised. "By hook or by crook." I didn't know what that meant, but it didn't sound entirely bloodless.

"Good," Brand agreed, scowling at Sergeant's slightly bloodthirsty grin. "We can't lose any more."

"I can't lose my only great-uncle either," I warned him as we said our goodbyes. Bo and Leroy were waiting in the van, grinning like idiots, glad to be going back to the hellhole. I grinned back. "Say hello to Iris and Delia and the girls for me. Tell 'em I'll see them soon." I wasn't about to let Luke and Sergeant do some experimental ceremony without me there.

"You're coming back, too? You promise, Miss Flor?" Leroy asked, eyes wide.

I laughed. The one place I'd never wanted to go back to kept pulling me in. I guess even if it was a shithole, it was my shithole. "Yeah, I promise. I gotta check on my flower arrangements, don't I?"

Sergeant grumbled the whole way home about those arrangements, according to Bo, who texted later.

And the month after that, I had my very first real date.

CHAPTER 49

FIRST DATE FORGIVENESS
FINNICK

I peered across the darkened private box at my mate, taking in her profile as she listened to "Vissi d'Arte," my favorite aria in the world. I'd wondered if she would enjoy the opera—she'd seemed slightly hesitant when she found out where we were going.

"First for dinner at Skyline, then Tosca," I'd told her when I brought her gown to her room that afternoon. The others had all made themselves scarce, but her friend Vanya and one other maid were there to help her dress and do her hair. "Just the two of us."

It wasn't exactly a lie. The others had promised not to join us in the box, but I knew they'd all followed us into the city.

"Opera is fancy," Flor had admitted in the limousine on the way to dinner. "I'm not sure I'll know how to act."

I'd loved her even more for the honest admission, but I'd assured her we'd be in my pack's private box, and there was no need for acting. "People like to think opera is sophisticated. But it's the purest, rawest form of emotion I ever encountered growing up. Talented opera singers can take pain and turn it into the most beautiful music. I think you'll like it." I hoped she would.

She will, Grigor had assured me. He'd insisted on staying close, though out of sight.

He'd been giving Flor and me lessons in wielding magic, and didn't want to leave us without a magical chaperone. He'd shared before the date that he had confidence in us, but we'd been working on setting and extinguishing small fires.

"When you're first learning control, mistakes can be frightening. And with the levels of power you both have, there's the chance you could burn down the city without meaning to. My own mother didn't let me leave her side for three months after I learned the spell for fire. Good thing, too." He hadn't shared more, but I'd accepted his shadowy presence for the evening without needing to know.

Flor had been grateful. After the battle—or perhaps after she'd mated Grigor—the magic she'd inherited had become obvious, giving her a... presence. She was still slight and short, and wore an ear tag, but there was no mistaking her for anything but shifter royalty. Every shifter could feel her power, and they unconsciously dropped their gazes and even bowed when she ran past, not that she noticed.

She looked like a queen now, as I sat across from her in the box. She suited the dress I'd chosen for her, a deep blue form-fitting, floor-length crepe gown. The neckline dipped low enough that I could see her décolletage, with flowing tulle sleeves that belled out and met at a satin band at her wrists. Scattered crystals all over the sleeves gave the impression of the night sky, and the crescent-shaped diamond necklace I'd given her hung like the moon above one of the points of her scar.

Her favorite part of the ensemble were the long slits on

the outer side of each leg, starting at her thighs and running to the bottom of the gown, of course, and the butter-soft leather knife sheath I'd had made for her steak knife.

She liked the dress, but I could tell she didn't like the opera. She *loved* it. Tears fell freely down her cheeks as she listened avidly, her hands gripping the rail in front of us as if she were moments away from rushing to the stage and comforting the soprano.

When the curtain fell, she was the first on her feet, clapping so hard it had to hurt her hands. "Finn, how does anyone think opera is boring?" she asked, wiping her face with the backs of her hands until I handed her the clean handkerchief from my pocket. "It's tragic and magical and... oh, Finn." She threw herself toward me, jumping up to wrap her arms around my neck. I caught her and held her face to mine as she rained kisses on me. "You were right; it was like a transformation, all that pain turned into pure beauty."

I pressed my lips to hers, trying to tell her everything I felt with my kiss. How perfect she was, how happy it made me to know she saw what I did, how much I loved her. I kissed her, holding her to me, through the final curtain call. While the rest of the patrons shuffled out, I lost myself in the feeling of her lips on mine, her arms around me, her soft, small curves pressing on—

Glen asked me to tell you to... get a room? Ah, yes, get a room. Grigor's voice was rich with laughter in my mind.

Our minds. Flor pulled back, her expression sheepish, and a little hesitant. "Yeah, we should probably... get a room?"

I knew what she was asking. Over the past weeks, we'd done many things together. I'd watched her with the others, I'd held her for Glen and Grigor as they lavished pleasure on her and filled her, and I'd grown addicted to her small, perfect nipples.

But I hadn't been inside her. I hadn't tasted her. I wasn't sure if I'd forgiven myself enough to do that now, but the uncertainty in her eyes, and the chorus of growls from the other mates in my mind, made it clear that she needed me to try.

It was a good thing I'd reserved the penthouse in the hotel across the street for the weekend. "One room, coming up." She grabbed my hand, and we practically ran across to the hotel, smiles on our faces, drawing judgmental glances from the other guests.

"We should behave," Flor whispered in the hotel elevator as I leaned down to nuzzle her hair, sneaking a hand behind her back to discreetly cup her ass while I was at it. The operator, a stern-faced human in his sixties, had his eyes on the floor, but two older women I vaguely recognized from the society pages were standing in front of us, obviously aware of us. Flor's blush was almost as bright as her hair.

"Why?" I whispered. "I've already made my mind up. I'm leaving the pack to Cilian, and the city for good. We'll never see any of these people again."

"But what about the opera?" she asked, with what might have been a tiny whine in her tone. "I want to go back. I loved it!"

I dropped a gentle kiss on her lips as the older women exited. "Then we'll come back. Cilian won't care. He hates the city anyway."

"Thank you," she whispered, nuzzling my neck, nipping slightly at the place where she'd bitten me.

As soon as the doors opened, I scooped her up and ran

to the room. It was enormous, the wall beside the door sporting a table draped in satin, vases of white roses, jasmine, and ivy, and carafes of water, wine, and covered plates with food. The opposite wall was entirely made up of windows that looked out over a city shining like diamonds in the cold, clear night.

The best part of it was the bed, large enough for a half dozen. I ignored the soft laughter in my mind, and shoved the others out. They'd been jealous of my claim on her first date, but that was their fault. And this was my night.

Her night.

In less than a minute, she was lying on the massive bed, the full skirt of her dress piled around her, her crystal-covered ballet flats on the floor. Her eyes hooded, she reached under her skirt and took off the knife sheath, dropping it onto the carpet as well.

"Finn, you have too many clothes on. Take them off."

"Yes, Alpha," I murmured and did just that, slowly removing each part of my tuxedo, the heat in her gaze warming me as she so obviously approved of my body. I wasn't as muscular as Luke or Glen, or as huge as Brand. I wasn't some ancient master magician, like Grigor. I was the one of her mates who had been unfaithful, and even if my reasons had been pure, I was afraid it put me in last place in her bed, and maybe even in her heart.

But as she unzipped her dress down the side, then held it out to me, kneeling on the soft linens in nothing but a scrap of blue lace and a diamond necklace, I decided there was one thing I could do to feel that I'd earned this moment, that I deserved to fully claim her.

I could use the skills I'd learned in darkness, and turn them into worship.

I dropped to my knees at the foot of the bed, pulling her

by her slender ankles to the edge of the mattress, and bowed my head, kissing and licking my way up the insides of her thighs as she shuddered. Her thighs were muscular but small under my long fingers as I spread her open, a feast for all my senses. I drew a breath of her scent into my lungs, letting it out on a moan as I slid the lacy panties down over her legs.

"I love you, Finnick Dimitrivich," she murmured.

"I love you more," I replied. Then I lowered my face to her mound and began to beg forgiveness with my whole heart... and my lips... and my tongue. I spelled out my love, writing letters on her swollen clit as she arched her back, crying out once, twice, three times.

I flipped her over onto her front and dove into her from behind, letting my tongue cover every part of her, my fingers and tongue working in tandem to take her to the edge and over four more times before she sobbed into the pillow, "Finn! Get inside me before I die!"

I hesitated, blinking. "Are you... Are you sure?"

It was her wolf who answered. "Yes, mate. I am sure of you. Join with me."

"Yes, Alpha," I replied.

A dark chuckle sounded in my mind, her wolf pleased with the term, though Flor herself usually complained when we called her that.

I'd been able to hear Flor in my thoughts since she reclaimed me in the lower levels, but her wolf had rarely spoken. Now, she padded softly through my thoughts, inspecting them. No, my emotions. She took in the guilt, the worry, the self-hatred, and tore at it with imaginary jaws, spitting it to one side.

No more of that. Only love, mate.

My own wolf howled his agreement. *Only love.*

My heart overflowing, my wolf close to the surface so he could experience this moment, I slid up and over her. I nudged her thighs apart, then pushed her up onto her knees, notching my cock at her entrance. She groaned in relief when I pushed forward, and began to thrust.

CHAPTER 50

A SPECIAL GLOW

FLOR

Finnick was a machine. He'd licked every inch of my body, and a particular few square inches enough times that I wondered if my bones had turned to liquid. Then he'd started fucking me, and... never stopped. I was half-sobbing as he held me close, his chest to my back, his cock moving inside me without softening, and without coming.

Why wasn't he coming? I'd had a hundred orgasms, it seemed like. But he hadn't come once, though I could tell in our bond that he was loving the process.

My other mates had taken care to introduce me to more kinky stuff than I'd ever imagined could exist over the past few weeks, promising it was just the tip of the iceberg of fun. So I wasn't inexperienced anymore, and I knew this level of stamina was... unusual. Was something wrong?

Somehow, I gathered the courage and the breath to ask.

He huffed against my ear, his lips teasing the too-sensitive flesh of my neck where two of my mating bites lay. Bites he had worked on for long enough that it felt like each one of them had turned into a clit, or something. I'd come twice just from him nipping at them, and felt my mates' groans echo in my mind as his actions had obviously had a similar effect on them, wherever they were.

"I can fuck for days without coming," he growled in my ear. "I can fuck forever. I can give you more pleasure. I *will* give you more, until you order me to come."

Wait. I had to order him? If I'd had the energy to laugh, I would have. Had he been waiting for an invitation? "Come, Finn. Please, fill me up, I need you to come inside m—"

Oh, thank the moon, someone said in my mind, though I wasn't certain whose voice it was, as Finn's release had triggered my own.

It was a tidal wave of pleasure and power, and I could have sworn the lights went out as Finn came and came, his shouts echoing in the dark. My face was buried in the pillow when I finally returned from whatever plane of existence Finn had fucked me onto.

"Oh shit," he muttered. Somehow, I mustered the strength to turn over and saw he was...

"Glowing?" I sat up. No, more like sparkling constantly, blue shimmers and a few red gleaming like glitter all over his skin.

The room was dark, and the city lights that had been glimmering outside the window were dark, though as the seconds ticked on, they started to flicker back on, one building at a time.

"Are you—"

"I don't know," he muttered, staring down at his own torso. He had a gorgeous, smooth chest, with small, dark pink nipples, and ridges and valleys of solid, lean muscles all the way down to his long cock. Which I should not be able to see, given that the lights were all out.

"You *are* glowing. What did you do?"

"I don't know!" he answered, slightly panicked, jumping out of the bed. He grabbed a pillow and rubbed at the glow. It didn't come off, of course. *Grigor?*

Yes, pup? Grigor's easy laughter had me relaxing, though Finn didn't stop pacing the room until he slid out of one of the shadows. "Looks like you two had fun on your date," Grigor said, carrying a bowl of warm, floral-scented water and a soft cloth to the bedside—who knows where he'd found them. Perching on the side of the bed, he began to clean the sweat and cum off my body. He took special care with my inner thighs, lingering on Glen's mate mark there until I moaned. "Are you sore, little queen?"

Grigor had a thing for what Finn had told me was called "aftercare." Almost an obsession, really. He patted my pussy gently now, blowing cool air across it and tutting as he inspected me one last time, running the warm cloth over all of me. He had no trouble seeing in the dark, and the lights were coming back on as he looked around the room.

"I mean, I'm a little sore," I admitted, but mainly I just wanted him to keep up the kinky sponge bath. I kinda liked aftercare myself, and sometimes it led to more fun.

"Grigor," Finn interrupted. He'd wrapped a white towel around his waist and ran a frantic hand through his red hair, pushing it back from his shining face. "What do I do? Why am I glowing?"

"Sparkling," I whispered. "He's sparkling like a vampire, right?" Glen had forced us all to sit through a movie marathon of his favorite vampire flicks. Grigor had laughed every time the one with the "skin of a killer" came on screen, muttering slightly concerning things that made me wonder just what other creatures walked in the world with us.

I'd ask him later, though. Maybe a few decades later.

"They do not sparkle." Grigor winked at me, then turned with a serious expression to Finn. "Pup, you're young, so you may not know this, but good sex can give some shifters a special glow—"

"Fuck all the way off," Finn snarled.

I giggled when Grigor stifled a laugh and apologized. "It's your magic, I think. You'd never reached your potential until now, from what I can tell. You're not in pain? You're just powerful then. Maybe this is normal for someone whose magic has been drained for years. I don't know." When Finn scowled, Grigor set down the cloth and stared at me. He shook his head, then studied Finn for a long moment. "That's... unexpected." Grigor's dark eyes flashed with excitement before he explained, "You know that our magic needs fuel."

"Blood, pain, death," Finn whispered. "And the moon."

"And it's strengthened by our bonds," I added, wondering what Grigor was seeing when he looked at Finn.

"It seems that what you needed to unblock your potential was another source of power. Joy."

"Joy?" Finn blinked. I found myself laughing again. "I'm sparkling with... happiness?"

"A special glow," I whispered. "I hope it never stops."

Finn was not amused. "What if it doesn't?"

"I'm not worried. Even if it lasts, it'll just make you sexier to me. Like Brand's eyes." Finn's lips curved upward. They all knew Brand's eyes did it for me. "We'll go live at the lake, hunt, fish, and fuck every day. It was already the retirement plan, right?" All of the guys had agreed we'd move to Mountain as soon as the mess was cleared up here. That was only a few months away, maybe less.

Grigor grumbled something about his own eyes. "It's

diminishing a bit at a time. By morning, you should be back to normal—though I think you may need to meditate, focus on... Come on, here." He stood and grabbed Finn's hands, pulling him over to a chair. "Shut your eyes. Hands closed on your lap." He pressed a hand to the center of Finn's forehead, and the other to his heart. "Sit here and focus on the power. By the moon, you're leaking all over! Yes, see this? Right, just..."

Their voices got quieter, and I drifted to sleep, only waking to find myself lying next to Grigor. The windows were curtained, and Finn was still in the chair. It was dark outside, but at least most of the city's lights were glimmering again.

Grigor was sitting beside me on the bed, staring at me like the creeper he was. Apparently, he didn't need much sleep at all, and wanted to take advantage of every moment we had together. Such a grandpa thing to say, though he'd swatted my butt the last time I'd teased him about acting old.

"Is he done leaking?" I murmured.

Grigor shook his head. "Not yet. But he paid through the weekend, and I've put a spell on the door. He's deep in meditation. No one will disturb him."

"He's going to be okay?"

He snorted softly. "More than okay, little queen. He blew open the channels to his power, the passages through his soul that magic runs along. It's hard to explain, but he's not hurt. He's just exhausted, and he should be. When he wakes, he'll be as powerful as I am, or close to it."

"Jealous?"

"Not at all. More protection for you, and for our pack, is never a bad thing." His teeth were slightly sharp as he smiled. "And I have the advantage." When I lifted my eyebrows, he explained, "More experience, and far fewer of those pesky morals that trip the rest of your mates up." I rolled my eyes, but we both knew it was true.

And it was one of the things I loved most about my murderous, oldest mate. The others were all amazing in their own ways, but Grigor was the only one who would whistle happily while he plucked the eyeballs from the sockets of anyone who gave me so much as a mean look. Though he would always claim to check to make sure they were bad guys first.

Was it his fault the world was so full of bad guys?

Grigor pulled me from my thoughts, and out of bed, leading me to the bathroom, where I took a few moments alone before he wrapped me in a robe and my crystal flats, then pulled me to the exit.

"Where are we going?"

"Hunting," he replied, with a dark twinkle.

"Bye, Sparkles," I whispered as the door closed behind us.

"This isn't hunting," I accused a half hour later. The night had been cold, but running with Grigor had warmed me up.

Especially because we were running from the human police. Well, not the humans, but their dogs. Grigor had carried me into the zoo in the center of town, and when I'd gotten sad seeing the animals in cages, he'd decided to let them out for me, as a "belated mating gift." I'd had to shout over the screaming of seventeen monkeys and the roar of a disgruntled lion before he'd paid attention, and by then someone had called security.

"It is hunting," Grigor insisted as he grabbed me and wrapped me in a quick spell just in time, leaping to the top of a light post to watch the chase below. The two lovely, fierce German Shepherds, followed by the officers, came running around the corner only a half a minute later, the dogs sneezing as they ran through some magical thing Grigor must have put down while we slipped away.

I sighed as he carried me bridal-style to a bridge over a small stream in the city center, pulling out a box of hand-made chocolate truffles from the dark cloak he'd begun wearing after Glen had binge-watched *The Witcher* with him. He hadn't liked the way I'd eyed up the lead actor, though Luke didn't mind. "Looks like me," he'd whispered in my ear as Grigor and Glen made fun of the hot Englishman.

"I suppose it was a hunt," I admitted to Grigor when the last chocolate was gone, peering around the park where he'd carried me. "But I thought you meant *we* would be doing the hunting."

"Oh, no. We're not hunting." He stepped back. "*I'm* hunting."

I blinked and let out a startled, "Oh," as I understood. Heat started at my feet and raced to my hairline, setting everything between the two points on fire. "Hunting me?"

His reply was a sweet threat, wrapped inside a dark promise. "Yes, little queen. I will hunt you."

My core tightened, and the air around me went sweet with cinnamon and jasmine, surprising me. I would've thought my vagina needed at least a day off after Finn had finally finished.

But no, apparently, I was every bit the hussy I'd started

437

out as on the streambed in the Southern woods. "What do you get if you catch me?"

"Whatever you want," he replied, crouching. I felt a thin sliver of his magic fall over me, a look-away spell, probably woven with protection as well, knowing him. "The hunt starts in three minutes."

Whatever I want? "Don't you mean whatever *you*—" I started to ask, but he'd vanished already, and a thrill zipped through me. If I could keep him from finding me, I could ask for the moon.

Sounds fun, my wolf purred. *Let me play.*

Absolutely. I slipped into my wolf's fur in a blink, lifting my head to the moon before I slipped silently into the brush.

The hunt was on.

CHAPTER 51

THE HUNT

GRIGOR

My little flame burned wherever she ran, even in the darkness, but it wasn't the red of her coat that made it impossible for her to hide from me. It was the unquenchable fire of her spirit.

I'd heard Glen and Finnick a few days before talking about how much she had changed since they'd first met her. They'd been doing some combat training with the Eastern females who'd inexplicably chosen to stay with the new pack. Or the old pack. Cilian Malloy would be the new Alpha after the next full moon, and he'd decided to rename the pack. Very wisely, he'd chosen to call it Oriens, and to set up his pack with no Enforcers or ranks at all, using roles in their places. He would have pack artists, pack chefs, and pack warriors, as well as pack nurses and historians.

They needed the historians most of all, in my opinion. A pack that lost their history was forced to run the same trail again and again, until they learned.

I'd been in the forest with Luke, double checking the females' camps there. They still lived close enough to the Mansion to use the kitchens and bathrooms, but none of them could sleep in the place. I didn't blame them, though I'd done my best to cleanse the building of the residual foul magic that had seeped into the walls.

"They think our little flame has changed," I'd remarked to Luke as we walked in the shadows of the tall pines.

"Flor hasn't changed at all," Luke had said with a slight smile. "She was born just like she is now. Fierce and strong. The same foolish courage, the same loving heart. You should have seen her when she was a toddler. She would walk right up behind the cruelest Enforcers and swipe the food off their plates when they weren't looking. And then she'd scamper off and hand the stolen food to someone even hungrier than she was. Once it was an orphaned baby raccoon."

Luke had suffered alongside her, and her fire had been all that kept his own burning. And now, though her wolf was a clever quarry in this playful hunt, that fire—my North Star, my full moon, my lodestone—led me straight to her.

Led my wolf to hers.

I padded into the clearing, past a stack of boulders that threw deep, irregular shadows in the moonlight across the rabbit path she'd followed, knowing she was crouched on top of one of the rocks, waiting. I stayed low to the ground, pretending to be scenting her, hunting her, and waited. I would be ready for her when she— "*Oof!*"

I let out a very un-wolflike sound as Flor pounced far more quickly than I'd anticipated, her small form landing squarely on my back. In the same move, she managed to flip me over onto my back, then froze. She was splayed on top of me, her forelegs around the sides of my ruff, her jaws clamped gently on my throat. The sharp pricks of her teeth were a warning never to underestimate her.

I never would.

My hunt, her wolf laughed into my mind. My *prey.*

My mate, I replied, using my back legs to flip her over my head, knowing she would let go, and not rip my throat out.

Or if she did, I would die happy, gazing into those amber eyes that were now filled with mischief and laughter. She leaped for me again, and I mock-growled, losing myself in my instincts. Her jaws were wide as she nipped and spun, teasing me, slapping my snout with her tail before darting away, then diving back under my neck, marking me with her scent. She peeked over her shoulder, those eyes blazing as she enticed me. Invited me.

I hesitated for a moment, though my wolf snarled at me. We had made love dozens of times since the battle, but never in this form. Never as wolves. *Little queen?*

I had never seen a wolf blush, but I would have sworn her red-black fur went a deeper shade as she whined a soft assent.

I gave my soul over to my wolf, who had waited so long for this mate, who had kept us both alive when I would have given up. I gave him the moment, and he took it— took her—biting gently into her neck as he entered her warm, willing body. She panted beneath me, waves of bliss pouring through our connected bonds and out into the others where they waited, all of them awake. Through Brand, who was crafting a message to Dean, planning the expansion of the Alpha's Den for the new occupants of the Alpha's family.

Through Luke, who stopped in the middle of cataloguing the library at Oriens, taking note of which books and journals needed to be copied and which would need to be brought as originals to the library at Mountain, the handwritten notes revealing which Alpha and packs in the wider world were true friends, and which were threats for us to address over the coming years.

Through Glen, who stood watch at the edge of the city park, just in case. None of us took our mate's safety for granted, or each other. He was in human form, but his wolf was yipping to be let go, to share in the mating dance under the moon.

Through Finnick, who cursed softly as he began to glow brighter in the hotel room when I pressed deep into our mate, giving her wolf side a pleasure she hadn't known with any of the others yet, as the thick base of my wolf's knot pulsed and thickened, locking us together.

She tied us all together as she hunted and found her bliss. And every one of us knew we'd found ours as well: our purpose and plan. Our joy and our salvation.

Our queen, who ruled us with a heart filled with hope.

CHAPTER 52

GRAND

FLOR

Late summer, Mountain Pack

"I think we should go with Brandor," Glen mused from the middle of the lake. We'd paddled out here in a small rowboat to fish, supposedly. But I think Glen had been running away from the others, since he'd been teasing them hard enough to deserve a little payback, and he hadn't even cast his line out into the water.

"Brandor?" I raised one eyebrow, or tried to. It was harder to raise just one eyebrow than the romance novels Glen and I had been reading aloud to each other made it out to be. Both eyebrows? Easy. Just one? That took practice.

It was a good thing I was retired, and had plenty of time to devote to things like that.

"Yeah, Brand plus Grigor, for their ship name," Glen said, dragging one hand over the side of the boat through the water. He'd read some online story about "bromances" and decided that was what Brand and Grigor had going on. He wasn't wrong. The two of them had been almost inseparable since we came to Mountain. Most shifters were naturally wary of Grigor, and back at Eastern, no one had been brave enough to speak to him besides Becca and Vanya.

But here at Mountain, when Brand was around, they at least acted like his shadowy presence didn't worry them. Yesterday, while Brand had been accepting the pledges from the shifters who'd been too late to make their vows before the battle at Eastern, Grigor had been lurking in the closest shadows a few yards away, alone... until two of the pack's toddlers had decided "Boo Man" was their new favorite playmate. I stifled a laugh, thinking about how natural Grigor had looked with one toddler pulling at his pants leg, and another climbing up his back.

Of course, he'd had a child before, a long time ago. What if he wanted more?

My heart raced, until Grigor spoke into my mind. *Little queen, I only need you. My life is full and perfect. If you want pups someday, your mates will do our best to give them to you. If you don't, or if you want to wait, then—*

Brand's mental voice broke in. *Grandma Ida has already sent to the witch who lives in our packlands for herbs to make sure it's your decision. No one will ever take your choices away again, wildflower.*

I peered around the lake's edge, wondering why their voices had sounded so close, but Glen was still talking. "I mean, Brandor even *sounds* cool."

"Why not Boo Man and Bearman?" I murmured, admiring Luke and Finn, who were on the bank, and who might, if I encouraged them, be convinced to take off their clothes. Finn had just come down from the house, and was still in his usual dark suit, since he'd been doing some sort of online video call with a pack in Italy. Well, a shifter organization, rather than a pack. They were some kind of religious order, if there was a religion where the priests and priestesses were all badass assassins.

This branch of the order was taking care of his sister Tana, and she'd even enrolled in a local school. No one else over there knew who she was—a good thing, since the story of their mother had been shared all around the world. We were all worried about what other packs might do to exact some sort of revenge on the family, now that Finn had shared how many visiting shifters and humans had been killed and drained for their parents' evil plans. Tana needed to stay hidden, and go to school where she felt safe, but Finn was having a hard time letting her go.

I had a feeling she was going to be fine, and Grigor had promised to check in on her after he went to "visit" the Alpha of Novosibirsk.

As I stared, Finn started to strip out of his suit. It was hard to tell from here, but he might have winked at me while he did it. I heard Luke say something about it being hot, before he took his own shirt off.

It's so hot, I thought at them. *Far too hot for any clothes.*

Their laughter rippled across the lake, but they both began removing their remaining clothing slowly, like one of the videos I'd scrolled past on the phone Brand had provided. Lots of the pack had phones now, though we kept them put away when Samuel was around. He was every bit as old-fashioned as before, but Brand had convinced him that pure isolation was more dangerous than connection, even if it meant using human tech.

I was wishing I had my phone now to take a video of my two hot mates stripping. But a second later, I was very glad I'd left it in the cabin.

Glen was still talking when the water rippled behind the boat, and it wasn't because of a fish. I grabbed hold of the sides, trying to keep a straight face as Glen muttered, "Boo Man? Come on. I'd go with 'Grand,' but that's already a word. And honestly, both of them have egos big enough to sink a boa—"

Suddenly, the arm he'd been trailing in the water got a bite. Or a tug, at least.

"Whaaa?" he screeched before vanishing over the side and falling into the water. I barely managed to stay inside when I leaned over the edge to see. Brand and Grigor were swimming like sharks around Glen, who was cursing and spitting, his blond curls falling over his eyes. "Not cool, guys!"

"Oh, you're not cool enough?" Grigor smirked. "I think I can fix that. I know where there's some very cool water." He dove down and grabbed Glen under the water—it was so clear I could see him gripping Glen's ankles—before pulling him down. They vanished into the deep blue, and Brand's smiling, bearded face popped up beside me.

"Want to cool off, wildflower?"

I shook my head and nodded toward the bank. "I was kinda ready to go back in. Maybe heat up."

"Sounds fun." He reached over the stern and grabbed the tow rope, pulling me to shore as fast as any motor. I heard Glen and Grigor surfacing behind us, then more yelling, but I didn't look back. Luke and Finn met us at the pebbled shore, tying the line to the enormous driftwood log that was our makeshift dock.

They were doing things with blankets and pillows near a tall pine, but I was mesmerized by the way the sunlight shone on their bodies. Finn and Luke were obviously aware of my focus. There was no way they needed to flex every single muscle, unless the pillows they were arranging were made of lead, and both of them had semi-hard cocks already.

"Making the bed?" I called. "I could use a nap."

Finn raised one eyebrow, making it look easy. "You'll need a nap when we're done with you, Wills."

"Oh, you think you can wear me out this time?" I teased back. "That'll be a first, Sparkles."

He mock-snarled. It was true that every time we'd made love since the battle, he'd had another power surge, and needed to spend the next few hours meditating to be able to control his sparks. Glen liked to tease him about his post-coital "naps," though.

Honestly, I thought it was cute. Finn didn't like how much energy it took out of him, but Grigor reminded him that his magic was growing stronger, and to think of it as training for a new kind of fight.

I'd hoped we were done with fighting, but we all knew better. There were small pack Alphas and Enforcers on the continent who had chosen not to follow the old ways, having grown too used to being in power, and packs who still believed the only good rogue was a dead one.

More than one pack had clung to the misguided belief that true mates could only be male and female pairings, claiming that same-sex pairs weakened the packs, even when some of the strongest shifters found their other halves, proving it to be sheer bigotry.

But for now at least, for this one summer, we were having what every Mountain true mate had: a season of peace, with nothing to do but learn each other's bodies, and explore how much pleasure and love we could share.

It turned out, when you had five Alpha-powered lovers

to share it with, there didn't seem to be a limit. All we needed was time.

"We have all the time in the world," Brand said.

"Well, not all the time—" I began, when I noticed an odd, muted spot in our bonds. They were hiding something from me. *Grigor?* I growled.

He didn't reply, but Finn did. *We have more time than most, my love. Grigor may have given up his immortality, but I'm... well, hybrids like us have longer lives anyway.*

A flicker of thought from Luke—*Another two hundred years with her will still not be enough*—had my mouth drying up.

"Do you really think we'll live that long?"

Brand hummed as he waded out of the water, the water on his back sparkling like diamonds in the sunlight. "When you live in the balance, when you honor the moon, anything is possible. Even miracles." He peeked over one shoulder and grinned again. "I'm looking at one right now."

I groaned, but I knew he was telling the truth as he saw it. He always did.

"Now, enough talk. I think we should all dry off and rest." Brand pulled me up against him as I stepped out of the boat, his lake-cooled skin brushing against my sun-warmed body. He kissed me until I was almost as soaked as he was, then carried me over the rocks toward the blankets until my feet touched soft grass. His wild pine scent surrounded me, mixing with my own warm cinnamon and jasmine as he reached around to my front and began to unbutton the damp, blue-checked shirt I had on.

"Rest?" I murmured as the shirt fluttered to the ground and he moved his hands lower, removing my steak knife from the sleek new leather belt Luke had fashioned for me, then opening my shorts. They dropped to the grass as well, and I stepped out of them, loving the feeling of the warm sun, the slightly cool breeze, and Brand's body heat as he held me close, his arms wrapping under my arms, and his face nuzzling against my hair.

Both Finn and Luke had stopped flexing and gone still, wearing the hungry looks they always did when I was naked.

"I think we should all rest," Brand murmured, his lips and teeth grazing the side of my neck, lighting up the mating marks there.

"She might need some help relaxing, brother." Luke prowled toward me and dropped to his knees, wrapping his hands around my thighs and pressing his tongue to Glen's mating bite on my thigh, before dragging it up in a long stripe to my clit.

"That's not relaxing," I moaned as he spread my thighs wider. My knees wobbled, but Brand had caught me under my arms and was holding me up, presenting me like a feast for Luke to devour.

I trembled, my climax already approaching. Luke may have been the least experienced of my lovers when he claimed me, but he had taken to learning every technique that existed—and inventing a few more—when it came to using his mouth on my body.

Brand growled in my ear as Luke dove lower, thrusting his tongue inside me before nibbling his way back to my clit. "You're so close already, aren't you, wildflower? I can feel it, you know. Feel what it's doing to you. How close you're getting." His cock pressed into my spine as I leaned back, letting go completely. "Open those eyes, mate. Look at Finn."

I obeyed, my eyes snapping open. Finn stood a few feet

away, his eyes glowing with his wolf's energy and his magic, blue and red sparks swimming in the green. He had one hand on his cock and was moving it slowly, the thumb gliding over the tip. I licked my lips, wishing I could have a taste of him.

"When Luke finishes, Finn isn't going to be able to wait, is he? He's going to fuck his tongue into you." Brand's voice was driving me crazy, and my core clenched hard, almost painfully. I was so damned *empty*.

Luke pulled back. "Brand, she needs you, inside her. Now." He backed up until he was kneeling on the improvised bed they'd made on the rocks. Brand's wicked laughter rumbled along my back as he carried me over, then dropped to his knees on the blanket, setting me on my feet, though he was still holding me under my arms.

"Brother, a hand?" he growled, his cock pressing against my thighs, the angle not quite right.

"Of course, Alpha." Luke winked at me when I shuddered—he knew how kinky I found it when my mates called each other Alpha during our lovemaking—then parted my knees and reached between my legs, helping position Brand's cock. Brand thrust slowly, his girth always requiring a little more time to make sure I was ready.

I was *so* fucking ready. Luke had his fingers on my clit, circling slowly as Brand found a teasing, slow rhythm from behind. Then he dropped back down, licking and sucking at my clit like it was his favorite candy, Brand's cock only inches from his tongue.

All of it at once—Brand filling me, Luke licking, and Finn watching like a hunting wolf just in front of us all—took me over the edge. I thought I was done for a moment, but Grigor's wicked laughter filled my mind. I felt invisible hands on my body, tracing lines—runes?

Magic spells? I wasn't sure—that lit up every nerve, and had me coming again and again, my body quivering as Brand held me.

I love you, I thought. Grigor and Glen were stalking out of the water, Glen stripping out of his soggy clothes as fast as he could take them off. Grigor hung back as the others crowded around me, but his mind was so fully enmeshed with mine that in a way, he felt even closer than the others. My shadow, always watching, always protecting.

Always murderous, Brand grumbled as he thrust a little deeper, setting off a new shower of sparks inside me.

"I love you," I said, my voice shaky, though everything else was on solid ground. My heart, my life, our love.

Their love echoed back at me, in waves of joy that were almost as strong as the physical touch of their hands on my skin, the heat of their gazes, and the slide of Brand inside me.

Joy that I'd made it to this place, this time. That all the pain and rejection and evil I'd survived had been to give me this: a life filled with purpose and pleasure, laughter and love. So much love that it would take more than one lifetime to share it.

"I love you," I gasped aloud as Brand filled me. "I need you." I did. But I needed...more.

He held still for a moment. *Who?*

I let myself form a mental image, and choked back a giggle when Grigor's dark eyes widened. Finn, Luke, and even Glen blushed. "All of you."

I'm in, brother mates, Glen thought, a little too loudly. He wiggled his eyebrows at me. *Anywhere, anytime, any combination.*

All at once? Luke whispered, looking at Grigor, and then Finn. *How...?*

Finn winked at me as he moved closer. *If I recall correctly, she's pretty damn good with a staff.*

Absofuckinglutely right. I closed my eyes and let my smile spread as my mates debated how to serve me.

It was good to be queen.

THANK you for reading The Splintered Bond! Download a copy of the extended final chapter by subscribing to Merri's newsletter.

www.merribright.com

Acknowledgments

Finishing this series is bittersweet. I can't wait to follow my muse somewhere new, but I will miss giggling at Flor's made-up curses (possumfucker was a personal favorite), and swooning from my keyboard as her guys showed her how far they would go to earn her love, and lift her up.

Thank you, readers, for supporting her story. For reading and re-reading, sharing with your friends, listening to the audiobooks, and sending love notes as I wrote.

A special thank you goes to a group of the most amazing, loyal readers, some of whom found me on Vella, and some who joined me on Ream: Brandy Stansbury, Elisa Cobb, Jessica Hoppe, Iris Norris, Veronica LaRoche, Tammy S Sanchez, Meeps, Barb C, Eila, Mandy, Mindy, Sarah, Kat Trocha, Jacquie, Danielle, Kathalena, Stevie, Tami Buchan, Kristin Star, Rachel, Susanne, Samantha, Jess, Amy, Starry-Asteria, Vanessa, Nicole, K Schultz, Ellisa C., Tori, Jennifer, Katie, Alice, Taryn, Lyn, Mimi, Liz, Jen, Molly S, SarahRey, Mari, Mareike, and Courtney. Your support and patronage has given me energy, happiness, and money for the covers! I'll write more "Ream Only" spice if you promise to laugh and read along.

Kristin, Tami, Deb, Bek, Courtney, Lorna, Iris, Maria, Sarah, Chloe, and Stephanie, you are the very best readers and partners in crime an author could ever have. Raewyn, my darling friend, my heart is as full of love for you as my early drafts are full of typos.

Flor's story is over, but new stories in the same world are already coming. Subscribe to my newsletter for free bonus content! www.merribright.com

Also by Merri Bright

The Splintered Bond Additional Content

Don't miss the prequel ~

An Ancient Bond, A Pack Reject Story

The Forgotten Angel Series (RH Paranormal)

If you loved Flor, you may also fall for Feather.

Start here ~ Lost Feather

The Billionaire's Betasitter Series (MF Omegaverse)

Start here ~ Sunshine's Grump

The Lost Lines Series (RH Omegaverse Fantasy)

Pick a heroine and read her standalone stories!

Vali:

Prequel The Omega's Mischief

The King's Omega

Epilogue The Queen's Nest

Haven:

The Guards' Haven

Cilla:

The Duchess's Designs

Roya:

The Assassin's Promise

Wren:

Part One The Leviathan's Debt

About the Author

Merri Bright spends her days dreaming up naughty angels, misunderstood demons, sexy shifters, growly Alpha males, and frequently refuses to limit her heroines to just one love interest.

Please join Merri's Mischief Makers on Facebook where you'll discover random giveaways, sneak peeks of new novels, book recommendations, and silly/sexy/funny stuff. You can also email her at merri@merribright.com, or follow/subscribe to reamstories.com/merribright for stories in progress.